Ann McIntosh was born in the tropics, lived in the frozen north for a number of years, and now resides in sunny central Florida with her husband. She's a proud mama to three grown children, loves tea, crafting, animals (except reptiles!), bacon and the ocean. She believes in the power of romance to heal, inspire, and provide hope in our complex world

Cursed with a poor sense of direction and a propensity to read, **Annie Claydon** spent much of her childhood lost in books. A degree in English Literature followed by a career in computing didn't lead directly to her perfect job—writing romance for Mills & Boon—but she has no regrets in taking the scenic route. She lives in London: a city where getting lost can be a joy.

D0256284

Also by Ann McIntosh

Christmas with Her Lost-and-Found Lover
Night Shifts with the Miami Doc
Island Fling with the Surgeon
Christmas Miracle in Jamaica

Also by Annie Claydon

The Best Man and the Bridesmaid
Greek Island Fling to Forever
Falling for the Brooding Doc
The Doctor's Reunion to Remember

Discover more at millsandboon.co.uk.

HOW TO HEAL THE SURGEON'S HEART

ANN McINTOSH

RISKING IT ALL FOR A SECOND CHANCE

ANNIE CLAYDON

MILLS & BOON

All rights reserved including the right of reproduction
in whole or in part in any form. This edition is published
by arrangement with Harlequin Books S.A.

This is a work of fiction. Names, characters, places, locations
and incidents are purely fictional and bear no relationship to
any real life individuals, living or dead, or to any actual places,
business establishments, locations, events or incidents.
Any resemblance is entirely coincidental.

This book is sold subject to the condition that it shall not,
by way of trade or otherwise, be lent, resold, hired out
or otherwise circulated without the prior consent of the publisher
in any form of binding or cover other than that in which it is published
and without a similar condition including this condition
being imposed on the subsequent purchaser.

® and TM are trademarks owned and used by the trademark owner
and/or its licensee. Trademarks marked with ® are registered with the
United Kingdom Patent Office and/or the Office for Harmonisation
in the Internal Market and in other countries.

First Published in Great Britain 2022
by Mills & Boon, an imprint of HarperCollins*Publishers* Ltd,
1 London Bridge Street, London, SE1 9GF

www.harpercollins.co.uk

HarperCollins*Publishers*
1st Floor, Watermarque Building,
Ringsend Road, Dublin 4, Ireland

How to Heal the Surgeon's Heart © 2022 by Ann McIntosh

Risking It All for a Second Chance © 2022 by Annie Claydon

ISBN: 978-0-263-30114-4

01/22

MIX
Paper from
responsible sources
FSC® C007454

This book is produced from independently certified FSC™ paper
to ensure responsible forest management.
For more information visit www.harpercollins.co.uk/green.

Printed and Bound in Spain using 100% Renewable Electricity
at CPI Black Print, Barcelona

HOW TO HEAL THE SURGEON'S HEART

ANN McINTOSH

MILLS & BOON

For Mike, who so patiently explained the finer points of rally driving, and who loves me just the way I am although I don't know a stanchion from a strut!

CHAPTER ONE

DR. DAVID KENNEDY settled into the back of the chauffeur-driven car as it left Liverpool's Lime Street train station and pressed his knuckles against his eyelids for an instant. Then he twisted his head from side to side, trying to ease out the kinks. Beyond the glass, a damp drizzle fell, and the sound of the windshield wipers matched the throbbing in his skull. A tension headache had taken up residence in a band across his forehead, and his eyes were gritty from too little sleep.

Just over three weeks.

That was all the time left before the Rally Round campaign started, and there was so much left to do.

He'd been working nonstop on the logistics—liaising with the rally and classic-car clubs, expanding the events as needed, and drumming up support from news outlets across the UK. Already this morning he'd spoken to his personal assistant three times, answered umpteen emails, and done a radio interview via telephone, all before his eight-fifteen arrival in Liverpool.

That interview had severely tested his patience.

Instead of concentrating on the rally, or even the work of GDK Foundation, the host had wanted to dredge up David's past. Even being adept at deflecting the conversation back to where he wanted it to go hadn't stopped David's temper from rising.

Now, rubbing the back of his neck, he tried to put it behind him, but it stuck in his craw.

Sixteen years was more than enough time for the story to become old news. Yet, nothing he achieved or attempted was enough to divert attention from the past headlines.

Billionaire Financier Dies Leaving Fortune to Son He Never Met

Sir Arthur Knutson's Love Child with Black American Entertainer Inherits

Knutson's Family Sues to Overturn Will

Salacious at the time, with the resulting smear campaigns and court case giving the papers an abundance of trashy headlines, but surely no one was interested anymore?

He was honest enough to admit part of the problem was his initial decision to capitalize on the unwanted publicity he'd received. It was a plan hatched at one of the lowest, most difficult times of his life. A time when he'd felt he'd lost almost everything he treasured and was desperate to make *some* good come of it.

His mother had once told him, "Davie, always remember this: pick your roles carefully, and then commit to them, completely."

At the time he'd thought she meant it literally, in the show-business sense, so he'd dismissed the advice. Even then he'd been fascinated by science and dreamed of a career in medicine or aeronautics. But, as he'd gotten older, he'd realized her words had far wider applications.

They were words he could live by and did. He carefully chose what he was going to do and, once the choice was made, committed to the plan, fully.

He'd wanted to make a positive difference in other people's lives, which led him to become a doctor. Then, spurred on by the mentorship of one of France's top transplant experts, who was one of his mother's friends, he'd specialized in transplant surgery and risen to the top of his field.

When he'd married Georgie, he'd committed to being the best husband he could be. The best father to her young son too, especially since Josh—like David—didn't know his biological father.

And those decisions had led to what David considered a perfect life.

A normal life, far removed from the glamorous, peripatetic, showbiz one David had grown up in, but lovely in its very simplicity. Georgie's brilliant personality, golden as her hair, had been the spontaneous, cheerful heart of their family. Josh—at first wary—had eventually thawed and even allowed David to adopt him legally. Mum—glamorous as always—had flitted in and out of their lives, loving and spoiling them all, while his work kept him busy and satisfied.

Perfection.

Which then began to fall, sickeningly, apart.

Georgie's death from an aneurism, just five short years into their marriage, had almost broken him, the pain and guilt too much to bear.

Josh—who'd needed him more than ever—and his work had been the only things keeping David going during the first year. Those commitments got him out of bed each day and forced him to put one foot in front of the other.

But fate wasn't done with him yet, as he found out all at once a year later.

A diagnosis of palmar fibromatosis put pay to his surgical career, just as he learned who his father had been and about the vast fortune he was to inherit. And when he realized his mother had been in contact with Sir Arthur over the years, David was incandescent with rage.

A rage that carried him through the legal battle and nasty rhetoric but left him cold and hollow inside, emotionally distant from everyone but Josh.

After all, with that much money in hand, who could he trust to be interested or invested in *him* rather than his fortune?

Once the courts had determined Sir Arthur's will was legitimate, David's mother had tried to calm the waters.

"Davie, if you just stay out of the spotlight, it will quiet down. You'll see."

He'd been too grief-stricken and angry—with her, with life—to listen. Instead, he'd taken a lump of his inheritance and created the Georgina Dolores Kennedy Foundation, dedicated to fostering transplant research, education, and networking. Then, as was his way, he committed himself to making the homage to his late wife work and grow, even as he maintained a consultancy practice as well.

Staying firmly in the spotlight allowed him to build the foundation into something truly worthwhile, and he was as committed to its growth as he'd ever been.

Putting his elbow on the door's armrest and leaning his chin on his fist, David stared out the window at the now driving rain and exhaled hard. It was a mark of his exhaustion that he was even thinking about the past this way. Normally, he tried to forget about those horrible, excruciating years and concentrate on the present and the future. And the immediate future was all about the upcoming rally.

Rally Round, originally envisioned as a short classic-car run in the vein of the London to Brighton race, had grown much larger. He'd thought it a good way to publicize the important work transplant teams were doing across the UK, but once his promotional team had begun consulting their contacts to gauge interest, it had ballooned.

And David had let it.

Not everyone was impressed with the widening scope, and a few foundation directors had voiced their concern regarding the amount of money now being spent. David pointing out that they'd already raised public awareness and spurred an important conversation centered around the need for organ and blood donations hadn't satisfied them.

"What you've done is wasted valuable time and resources and turned the foundation into a carnival, with you as the barker," Sir Malcolm, the most vocal of the opponents, had rudely stated.

It was no secret Malcolm's cadre would like nothing better than to oust David from his position as CEO and dismantle many of David's more progressive programs. To them, the foundation was on the verge of collapse because David was determined to take advantage of new technology, particularly social media, to increase visibility.

On top of everything else that was happening, having to deal with their nonsense was exhausting.

This trip to Liverpool had come up unexpectedly but was, in a way, a welcome distraction. As a part of his consultancy practice, he was often called in to evaluate high-risk potential transplant recipients. The young lady he was going to see had both type 1 diabetes and progressive kidney disease, and a decision had to be made as to whether it was suitable to put her on the transplant list.

Being out of his office at the foundation meant he was less accessible and could screen both calls and emails for urgency. He'd always maintained an open-door policy at the London headquarters, allowing people to drop in to his office for a chat or to update him, but he didn't have time for that just now.

For the next few days, his main focus would be on his patient, with the rally taking up whatever spare moments he had. But for these last few minutes, between the train station and the hospital, David tried to get his brain to slow and his shoulders to relax.

When his phone rang, he sighed.

Respite denied.

Then he smiled, as he saw Josh's name on the screen.

"Morning, Dad." Josh's voice made David's smile widen. "Heard you on the radio just now. You sounded like you were a hair's breadth from giving that reporter a frosty tongue-lashing."

David chuckled. "Well, *I* thought I was politely restrained."

Josh chuckled too. "You were, but barely. Did you make it to Liverpool all right?"

"I'm almost to the hospital."

"I'm close to work too but, I've been thinking…"

"Uh-oh. That sounds ominous."

Josh ignored his interruption. "Why don't you slow down a bit, after the rally?"

His son's words made his heart rate kick up and caused a cold ball to form in his chest. Making his tone amused and slightly distant was instinctual.

"Oh? Why? Do you think I'm getting decrepit?"

"No. I think you're overworked. You should get back to some of the things you love but don't do anymore."

There was a slight hesitation before he continued.

"It struck me when I heard you on the radio. I almost didn't recognize your voice. And when I was arranging the delivery of the Daimler, I thought about that Austin we'd been fixing up and never got going because you're always on the move. We should be driving that in the rally, not Mr. Granger's fancy auto."

Josh didn't need to elaborate. There were times when David found himself watching his own actions—hearing his own voice—as though from a distance and wondered who that man was. Yet, the change was effective and suited his purposes. After the way he and his character had been called into question, both in court and the press, a facade of distant arrogance had seemed the best way to react.

"Dad." Josh's voice brought him out of his thoughts, and he grunted in reply. "I know how important the foundation is to you, but you deserve a life of your own. A regular, happy life, instead of all this rushing about and stress."

"I *am* happy." Infusing enthusiasm into his voice was far harder than it should have been. "You know I get intense satisfaction from the work I'm doing."

"Yeah, I do, but think about what I've said anyway, okay?"

"I will." He wouldn't, but the lie tripped easily off his tongue. There was no reason to have Josh worrying unnecessarily.

"I'm just pulling into the hospital parking lot, so I have to go. Have a good day. Talk to you later."

"Love you, son."

And that was no lie. Adopting Josh and raising him after Georgie died were two things in his life David felt he'd done properly.

When he'd met Georgie, she'd been clear about not wanting any more children.

"I've made a hash of raising the one I already have," she'd said, with a glint in her eye that told him arguing wouldn't be a good idea. "If you want a child, you're best off looking elsewhere."

He'd already been too head over heels about her to care and, once they'd married, he'd happily taken on Josh as his own. No one knew that just before her death she'd changed her mind and they'd begun trying to get pregnant. Coming off the pill had thrown her reproductive system into disarray, but on the day she'd collapsed, she'd insisted David attend an all-day seminar, although admitting to a headache.

"Probably just hormones," she'd said, refusing his offer

to stay home with her. "I'll take something and lie down for a little."

The guilt of his decision to do as she said would never leave him, no matter how many years went by. He'd failed to protect her, to be there when she needed him most, and still hadn't forgiven himself for that.

The rain eased slightly, and the traffic, which had slowed, picked up speed again. Pulling himself once more out of the past, he glanced at his watch. He should be on time for his appointment with the transplant-recipient co-ordinator, as the buildings of the St. Agnes Hospital were now visible, and the entrance was just around the next corner.

The car accelerated, and David opened his lips to tell the driver to slow down, but it was too late. With a whoosh, the vehicle hit a puddle, sending an arc of water toward the pedestrians hurrying along the sidewalk.

"Slower, please," he said sharply.

"Just trying to get you to your destination on time, sir."

"I'm sure the people walking to work would prefer I be a bit late so they don't get splashed with dirty water."

"Yes, sir."

Then, as the brief moments of inactivity were almost over, David prepared himself for his meeting and another long day.

Valerie Sterling squelched her way into the ladies' room down the corridor from her office, going as quickly as she could on her aching ankle. The lower part of her coat and legs were soaked, as were her shoes.

If the start of the day was any indication, it might have been better had she stayed in bed.

Yet, there was no time to whinge, which wasn't in her nature anyway. Dr. Kennedy was probably already in her office, and if she didn't hurry, she'd be late.

Between the rain, a bus that broke down long before her stop, and a near fall that had left her with a twisted ankle and a ball of fear in her stomach, she was frazzled.

Being liberally splashed by a passing car had been the final straw.

Getting herself presentable and calmed down before her meeting, all within seven minutes, wouldn't be easy. All she could hope was that Shala, the office assistant she shared with four other managers, wouldn't leave the consultant cooling his heels in the reception area. Sometimes the younger woman could be scatterbrained, and Val could see her doing just that.

Unable to stand comfortably on her right foot, she backed into a cubicle and sat on the closed toilet seat to remove her shoes one at a time and wipe her feet and legs. Thank goodness, once she'd seen the overcast sky, she'd packed her court pumps in her tote rather than wearing them.

Of course, if she'd accepted her neighbor's offer of a drive to work, none of this would have happened. But refusing Tony's offer had been instinctive, and Val had no regrets.

He'd just moved in and had already told anyone who'd listen that he was newly divorced. The few times they'd spoken, he'd gazed at Val with the sort of puppy-dog eyes that had probably initially got his ex to marry him but left Val unmoved.

One thing the long-ago breakup of her marriage had taught her was that being independent and single was smart and putting your happiness in someone else's hands was foolish.

The last thing she needed was to once more risk the type of embarrassment and heartbreak Des had caused.

With a grimace of pain, she got her right shoe on and stood up. The memory of falling, of the woman behind her grabbing her arm to stop her landing on the pavement, tried to intrude and had to be pushed aside.

She didn't know what had caused her to lose her balance, and that was terrifying. If she allowed herself to think about that now, her chances of concentrating in the upcoming meeting would be naught.

Yet the specter of multiple sclerosis was never far from her thoughts these days. And, as she limped out of the ladies' and toward her office, she couldn't help paying intense attention to the sensation of her muscles moving beneath her skin. Checking to make sure they were working the way they should.

Getting to the reception desk, she forced herself to smile at Shala while looking around for the consultant, who was nowhere in sight.

"I put him in your office, Mrs. Sterling," the young woman whispered. "And called down to get you a pot of tea."

Leaning close, Val asked, "Has he been here long?"

Shala shook her head, causing her dangly earrings to dance. They were the kind of jewelry Val always admired but never bothered to buy, not thinking they'd suit her.

"No, he just got here."

Heaving a sigh of relief, Val straightened and replied, "Bring the tea in when it arrives, please."

"I will."

She'd got to her door when Shala said, "Are you okay, Mrs. Sterling?" Val paused and looked back, lifting her eyebrows. "You're limping."

"I'm fine," she replied, opening the door and stepping through before the younger woman could comment further.

"I'm sorry to keep you waiting," she said briskly, nudging the door shut and facing the man rising to his feet from the visitor's seat.

She'd planned to shrug off her coat, but the first sight

of David Kennedy had her freezing in place for an instant, her heart doing a crazy flip-flop.

What a magnificent man.

"Not at all," he replied, his coolly polite words breaking her out of the trance she'd fallen under. "I only just got here myself."

Turning away, she pulled off her wet mackintosh and hung it on the coatrack, her hands ridiculously clumsy and shaky. In her mind's eye, she could still see him, and the image had tingles running up and down her spine.

Oh, she'd seen him in the media and knew he was handsome, but she'd been able to think so in a distant, disinterested way. Up close, though, in person, there was something downright electric about the dark, intent gaze, the way he moved with such fluid grace, and the rich, deep timbre of his voice.

Dressed in a suit that fitted his broad shoulders to perfection, his snowy-white shirt emphasizing the smooth, mocha-toned skin, Dr. Kennedy was just a smidge shy of beautiful. His elegant appearance, however, was perfectly balanced by the strength of his facial features and the cool intelligence in his eyes.

She'd raised a hand to smooth her hair when she realized what she was doing and let it fall. Hadn't she read somewhere that a woman playing with her hair signaled sexual interest?

We'll have none of that, my girl.

Instead, she flattened her expression and, ignoring the warmth rising into her cheeks, made herself walk across the room toward him, her hand outstretched.

"It's a pleasure to meet you, Dr. Kennedy."

His fingers were warm, his handshake firm, but Val had to stop herself from jerking away when her nerves jangled with delight at his touch.

"The pleasure is mine," he replied, and although his

voice was still distant, his gaze seemed anything but, and Val had to turn away before she drowned in it.

Withdrawing her hand from his, she moved behind her desk to her filing cabinet, using the time it took to retrieve the patient's file to gather her shattered composure.

It was going to be a very long three days working with him if she couldn't get herself under control!

Taking a deep, silent inhale, she faced him and said, "Let's get on with it, shall we?"

CHAPTER TWO

DAVID TRIED TO keep his mind on what Valerie Sterling was saying but was constantly sidetracked by the cadence of her voice and the movement of her lips. When their gazes met, his breath caught in his chest, and he was forced to look away lest he get trapped staring into those beautiful aqua-shaded eyes.

Were they bluer or greener? They seemed to change, like the color of the ocean changes during a tempest.

Why did he even care?

But he did, and he tried to figure out why.

Valerie Sterling wasn't beautiful in conventional terms. Some people, noting her nondescript coloring and mousy hair, might even call her plain, yet there was an air about her that David found completely enthralling.

When she'd come in the door—damp blond wisps escaping her low ponytail, a bit of a flush on her cheeks—his heart had seemed to turn over, as though in joyful recognition. And although the handshake they'd exchanged was businesslike and just shy of perfunctory, his fingers still carried the phantom sensation of her skin beneath his.

Her turning away to unlock her filing cabinet left him immersed in a swirl of fresh, womanly scent that went straight to his head.

By the time her assistant pushed open the door and brought in a tea tray, David realized he'd said little to nothing but allowed her to carry the meeting. Even during the pause, while Mrs. Sterling poured, conversation lagged as he fought not to start peppering her with questions about herself.

Where was she from? Was she happily married? What caused her to limp? Did she find her work challenging and satisfying?

It was disquieting and should have had his stress rates through the roof. But strangely, his headache had subsided, even as he wondered at his distracted state and obsession with the no-nonsense woman across the desk.

"Tamika Watkiss's condition has undergone a sharp deterioration over the last month, as you can see from her records." She was completely professional, having already pointed out various test results she found pertinent, yet David was staring at the file in his hand like an imbecile, fighting to concentrate. "At this point, Dr. Laghari believes pancreas and kidney transplants may be her only hope for a normal life. However, there are factors other than her physical and mental condition I think may weigh heavily into the decision of whether to put her on the list or not."

"Oh?"

So stupid to feel almost tongue-tied in her presence, to have his usual eloquence drained away by the merest look in her direction. Self-consciousness made him sound even stuffier—stiffer—than usual, and he could hear her voice changing, becoming sharper with each sentence she spoke.

"Tamika's parents have very different ideas about what's best for her going forward, and those differences have to be taken into consideration. The family unit seems to be, up to this point, a strong one, but there is a distinct chance that if we're not careful, any course of treatment suggested may precipitate a family crisis."

"Which will also disrupt the patient's state of mind."

At least he had the wherewithal to make *one* sensible statement so far, but Valerie Sterling looked less than impressed.

"At the very least. Damage to her family could also potentially have far-reaching health effects for Tamika, whether she's suitable for surgery or not."

Why did it feel as though she were taking him to task? While he was impressed that she clearly didn't think his reputation merited special treatment, it still somehow stung. And when stung, he retreated further into his public persona.

Closing the file in his hand, he smiled the thin, barely there smile he used as a shield, and quietly said, "Well, it's early days to be worrying about that just yet. We still have all the testing to do, which is why I'm here. Have you set up a meeting with the patient and her parents?"

Valerie rocked back in her chair, and her eyes narrowed for an instant, but when she spoke it was in an even, colorless tone. "I informed them you'd be here today and would want to speak to them, yes."

Restless, wanting to be in motion and put some additional air and space between them, David rose and nodded toward the door.

"Shall we, then?"

"As you wish," she replied, getting to her feet and rounding the desk, the skin around her lips tight, her limp more pronounced. "Tamika's mother works nights and usually comes in first thing in the morning to sit with her for a few hours before going home to rest. She should be here by now."

He got to the door ahead of her and opened it, standing aside so she could precede him through, regretting the gentlemanly habit when it left him once more in the wake of her delicious scent.

Perhaps drawing it deep into his lungs wasn't the best option for his peace of mind, but that's what he did anyway.

What an ass!

If her ankle hadn't been so painful, Val would have marched down to the elevator in double time. As it was, all she could do was keep her back as straight as possible and her nose in the air while she limped along, fuming.

Apparently, Dr. David Kennedy had allowed his reputation to go to his head in a big way. He'd hardly spoken, dismissed her concerns regarding the situation between Mr. and Mrs. Watkiss, and, when she'd tried to explain her worries further, had called an abrupt end to the meeting.

If this was how he behaved with everyone, she'd have to be a buffer between him and the Watkiss family or be doing damage control continuously over the next few days.

The nerve of the man!

Oh, she knew he was highly qualified, and his foundation was doing an awful lot of good to educate both medical personnel and the public about the issues surrounding transplants, but come on! It didn't make him a deity. Not by a long shot.

She'd have a heck of a lot more respect for him if he'd continued to operate after inheriting that pile of money rather than all but abandoning his profession. If he had still been operating, she could put his attitude down to that famous surgeon arrogance so many medical practitioners had to put up with. As it was, he was just a consultant, and no matter how highly regarded he was, it was no excuse for bad manners.

She reached out to jab at the elevator button, but Dr. Kennedy beat her to it and their hands brushed, sending another of those tingling waves of sensation along her arm.

And damn him for affecting me this way.

Somewhere, in the midst of all the stress she'd been

going through over the last little while, she must have lost her mind. That was the only explanation for this unwanted—and unwarranted—attraction.

Tense enough to crack, she worked on maintaining a frosty demeanor as they rode down in the elevator. She preceded him out of the lift and then down the corridor toward where Tamika's room was located. Making sure not to indicate which door she was going to until they were right at it, she pushed through without waiting for him to open it for her.

Tamika was sitting at a small table near the window, her laptop in front of her, some textbooks strewn around. When she looked up Val smiled, although she couldn't help noticing how poorly the teenager looked in comparison to when they'd first met. Her skin had lost both color and luster, giving it a grayish hue, and her wide brown eyes were sunken.

"Hi there," Val said, making her way into the room. Mrs. Watkiss was nowhere to be seen. "How're you doing today?"

Tamika scowled, her gaze going from Val to David and back again while she gestured to the books. "All right. But I'm trying to catch up with my schoolwork. I lost almost a whole year, and I really want to take my GCSEs next year, but they won't let me unless I'm up-to-date. Why're you limping?"

Val was suddenly under intense scrutiny not just from Tamika but from the man standing beside her too.

"Just a little mishap this morning, on my way to work. It's nothing. This is Dr. Kennedy," she added quickly before either of them could say a word. "He's the consultant I told you about a couple of days ago."

"Hi."

Tamika looked anything but excited to meet another

doctor, but David went right over and held out his hand, giving her a warm smile.

"Hi," he replied, before pointing to her books. "What are you studying?"

"History," she answered, wrinkling her nose. "I hate it, so I kept putting it off."

David chuckled. "Was never one of my favorites either. I much preferred the sciences."

"I like math best, and I'm not too bad at English, but history…" She shook her head, smiling back at him. "All those dates and so many kings. It's ridiculous."

Pulling out the chair on the opposite side of the table, David sat down, still chuckling. "I agree. So much easier to remember the queens that ruled in their own names because there weren't as many."

"Yeah," she agreed, but with a little pout. "But I usually forget some of them too. If the answer isn't *Elizabeth* or *Victoria*, I probably don't know it."

David laughed outright then, the warm sound wrapping itself around Val in the most disquieting way. How on earth had that standoffish, arrogant ass morphed into this easy-going, comfortable man? A man able to win over an ill teenager, who was often out of sorts and cranky, with little to no effort?

He was asking her about her future plans as though it was a given that the desperately ill teen had a long life ahead of her. Val was surprised to hear the answer.

"Well, it's hard to make plans when you have brittle diabetes and chronic kidney disease, but what I'd really like to do is work out in the open, like on a farm, or a national park. If I can't do that, I think I'll write a book." The look she gave David was level and unafraid. "A person has to have something constructive to do, right?"

Val turned away, so that Tamika wouldn't see the sheen of tears in her eyes. The young woman's courage in the face of life-threatening odds was both moving and inspiring.

"Yes." His voice was suddenly deeper, with a tone that seemed almost sad, although when Val glanced at him, he was still smiling. "Everyone needs a goal. I'll look forward to reading it."

"Your mum's not here yet?" Val asked, after a short silence that seemed too heavy to be allowed to continue for long.

"She went down to the caff to get some tea." Tamika looked down, and her fingers curled into little fists on her lap. "I keep telling her she should go home after work and get some rest, but she still comes every day anyway."

"No doubt because she couldn't rest until she'd seen you and made sure you were all right. I know that's what I'd do, if my son was in hospital and about to go through more testing."

Tamika looked up at him. "You have a son? How old is he?"

David smiled, and Val felt her heart do a crazy flip at the fondness in his expression.

"Josh is thirty-four, and before you say anything, I'd still be at the hospital every day if he was a patient."

Before she could reply, the door opened, and Mrs. Watkiss came bustling in, pausing to say, "Oh, Mrs. Sterling, is this Dr. Kennedy? I hope I didn't keep you waiting."

Val touched her shoulder and smiled, shaking her head. "Not at all. We haven't been here long."

David had risen, and as they shook hands, Val's phone buzzed.

"Excuse me," she said, recognizing her assistant's number. "I have to take this. Will you be okay for now, Dr. Kennedy?"

"Of course." The look he sent her way made heat pool

in her belly, although his voice was cool. "I'll find you when I'm finished here, if necessary."

And, still flustered, although there was no conceivable reason to be, she got out of there as quickly as she could, heaving a sigh of relief once the door had shut behind her.

Dr. David Kennedy was an arrogant, dismissive man, who apparently was exactly the type that attracted her.

How infuriating!

CHAPTER THREE

DAVID SPENT MOST of the rest of the morning with Mrs. Watkiss and Tamika, first just talking generally and then going over some of the tests Tamika would undergo starting the next day.

The Watkiss family, as it turned out, were originally from the Caribbean, although Tamika's parents were both born in England, where they'd met and married.

"My parents were from Grenada," Mrs. Watkiss told David. "And Ricardo's came here from Barbados."

They'd met at church when they were in their teens and had moved to Liverpool from London after Mr. Watkiss had gotten a job with what was then British Rail. He still worked with National Rail and was away from home on assignment periodically.

When David asked if he would be able to meet Tamika's father while he was in Liverpool, Mrs. Watkiss bit her lip and said she'd let her husband know he was wanted.

"He doesn't do so well in hospitals, you know," she said, and in his peripheral vision David noticed Tamika roll her eyes.

When he looked at the teen and raised an eyebrow, she shrugged and shook her head.

"Dad gets soppy whenever he comes to the hospital to see me," she said. "So I told him it was okay and I'd be home soon enough."

"Ricardo looks after Tamika if she's poorly, whenever he's home," Mrs. Watkiss supplied, as though standing up for her absent husband. "He's a good dad, isn't he, sweetie?"

"The best," Tamika said, throwing her mum a little smile. Then, as though very much wanting to get off the topic, she asked David, "Are your parents or grandparents from somewhere else, Dr. Kennedy? Or were they born here?"

Following her lead, David replied, "Actually, my mum was originally from the US."

Mrs. Watkiss's eyes widened, and she snapped her fingers, saying, "That's right! I was wondering where I knew your face from. Your mum is Cerise Kennedy, the singer, right?"

He should be used to it by now, but it took everything he had not to stiffen up and risk losing the rapport he'd been developing with Mrs. Watkiss.

"Yes," he said. "That's my mother."

"Who?" Tamika asked, her brow wrinkling.

David chuckled. "She was popular way before your time."

"Oh, you know who she is, Tam," Mrs. Watkiss said. "Your grandma Olive loved her songs. She'd play them all the time."

And then she started singing. "Some folks are green with envy, others sad and blue, but I'm just tickled pink, to be so loved by you."

Hearing his mother's trademark song brought a pang of sorrow, and although David kept smiling, a weight settled around his heart. It was as though, for an instant, he was transported back to childhood and Mum was leaning over him as he lay in bed, singing that song. To everyone else, "Love in Pink" was his mother's signature song, but to David it was, and always would be, *his* song.

"Oh, yes. I remember that." Tamika turned shining eyes toward David. "I love it. It reminds me of Gran."

"I know my mum would love to know that," he said softly.

"I haven't heard anything of her in a long time," Tamika's mother said. "Is she still with us?"

"Yes, she is," he replied. "Still performing too, but mostly on the Continent—France, Monaco, occasionally in Germany."

Then, before that curious gleam in the other woman's eyes could be given voice, he moved the conversation along to what Tamika and her mother could expect over the next few days.

"We'll be doing extensive testing, including a series of X-rays and ultrasounds, to make sure Tamika is healthy enough to potentially undergo surgery."

As he went over the various tests, outlining what each one was, Mrs. Watkiss listened intently, but he could see Tamika's attention wandering. Eventually, she sighed.

"Mrs. Sterling went over all of this with Mum and me already," she said.

David nodded, ignoring the way his pulse jumped at the mention of Valerie Sterling. "I'm sure she did. But it's my job, ultimately, to make the decision as to whether you'll be placed on the transplant list or not, so I have to be very careful that you and your parents understand exactly what's happening at any given time."

"Hush, Tamika, and let Dr. Kennedy talk."

But as her mother scolded her, David could see a stubborn twist to the young woman's lips, and he smiled, saying, "I'm finished for now, Mrs. Watkiss, and I know you probably need to get home to get some rest. I'll be in tomorrow morning, so I'll see you then."

Tamika nodded, not meeting his eyes as she mumbled goodbye, and her mother rose to walk with David to the door, then out into the corridor. Putting her hand on his arm, she looked up at him with an expression of almost overwhelming gratitude.

"Thank you, Dr. Kennedy. I know my daughter is in the best of hands and you'll do everything you can to make her well."

It was at times like this that David, for all his experience, felt a visceral sense of inadequacy. All he could do was pat Mrs. Watkiss's hand and say, "I'll try to make the best decisions for Tamika's care, Mrs. Watkiss. Please ask your husband to let me know when he's available so I can make sure to keep my schedule open."

That seemingly distracted her from whatever else she was planning to say and, when he opened the door for her, she went back into her daughter's room.

Standing in the corridor for a moment, he considered all he'd learned that morning about his patient and her mother. While, as a part of her assessment, there would be a psychologist examining Tamika and speaking to both her parents, David believed there was much to be learned by simply meeting them himself. That was the real reason he'd come to Liverpool. The doctors at St. Agnes Hospital were perfectly capable of running all the tests needed, and he could have stayed in London and had all the results sent to him for his evaluation.

That had never been—and would never be—the way he worked. He might no longer be capable of operating on patients himself, but both patients and their surgeons deserved every ounce of skill he could muster so as to achieve the best possible outcomes. And that meant being engaged and involved from the start of the assessment process all the way through to whatever the end might be.

Valerie Sterling might not be impressed by him, but he

wasn't there for her approbation, so her questioning, sharp manner shouldn't matter.

Yet it did.

And why on earth was he even thinking about her instead of concentrating on his patient, or even Rally Round? No doubt there were a hundred emails and phone messages waiting for his attention, not to mention his meeting with the team of doctors taking care of Tamika.

All of those matters were a lot more important than the icy woman with changeable, sea-storm eyes, who clearly had no use for him.

A woman who, he'd learned from Tamika's reaction, didn't normally have a limp but had hurt herself on the way to work. The stubborn woman hadn't even stopped to get it looked after before their meeting.

Shaking his head, David strode toward the nurses' station, a crazy, absolutely ill-advised plan forming in his head.

Val looked up as a knock sounded on her door and grinned as her friend, hepatologist Emma Owen, stuck her head into the office.

"Are you busy?"

"Come in," Val replied, closing the file she'd been going over and pushing it to one side. Glancing at her watch she realized how late it was getting. "Heading down to lunch?"

"Already had mine," Emma replied, flopping into the visitor's chair and twitching a stray piece of her red hair behind her ear. "But I have a few minutes before my next meeting and wanted to firm up our plans for the rally."

"What's to firm up?" Val shifted her legs and tried not to wince when her ankle throbbed in protest. "We've got rooms booked through the foundation and time off arranged."

"Yes, but…" Val's antennae vibrated as her younger friend grinned. "What about costumes?"

Val sat up straighter in her chair. "Costumes? What costumes?"

"Well, I was putting together a soundtrack for the rally—sixties music, to go with the Mini—and thought, wouldn't it be cool for us to have some sixties clothes to carry on the theme?"

"No. No, no, no." Val kept talking over Emma's peel of laughter. "Sixties fashions were all miniskirts and go-go boots, weren't they? That's so not my idea of fun."

"Oh, come on, Val. Live a little. I've found a bunch of stuff in thrift stores and online, so you're coming over to my place this evening to try some on. I won't take no for an answer."

Live a little.

As Val looked at her friend, the words echoed in her mind.

She'd been so bogged down with responsibilities over the past years she'd fallen into a seemingly never-ending whirl of motion, none of it fun, a lot of it frightening or saddening. Watching her mother deteriorate, working all hours possible to keep the family's heads above water, then losing Mum, and having both Clayton and Liam move out…

She'd felt wrung out, used up, and rather bitter that her youngest son had decided to go and live with his father—the same man who'd abandoned them years before.

But, most of all, fear of the future had stalked her mind continuously.

Multiple sclerosis was now assumed to be genetic—or at least have a genetic component. Not only had Mum suffered from it, but Val was pretty sure her grandmother had too, although forty-plus years ago the doctors hadn't diagnosed it as such. More and more often, in moments of quietude, Val found her brain circling back to MS, chewing over what she would do should she discover she had it.

At those times, the thought of being a burden, of having one of her children have to take care of her, or going to a nursing home sat like a rock in her stomach.

She couldn't figure out which was worse.

Her GP had told her, "There's no need to worry about it. Just watch for symptoms, and come back to see me if you experience any."

That was, in her opinion, absolutely no help whatsoever.

The symptoms were legion and ranged across the board from physical pain to mental fog, with a host of others in between.

How was she to know whether a sudden fall was due to slippery pavement or MS? Whether her inability to concentrate was due to a long hard day or MS?

Realizing fear of the disease was wearing her down as quickly as the disease itself would, she knew she had to make peace with it somehow. And when Emma had asked her to run the GDK Foundation rally with her and act as navigator, it had sparked something inside. A sense of adventure she'd completely forgotten existed in her soul. Maybe MS was her future, but wasn't that the very best reason to live fully now?

"Oh, all right," she said, earning a fist pump from Emma. "I'm free this evening."

"Brilliant. Text me when you're finished here, and we can leave together. My larder is bare, so we'll pick up something to eat on the way."

Before Val could reply, there was another knock on her door. Emma got up, as Val called out for the person to come in.

When David Kennedy stepped into her office, Val's heart started to race, and it took everything she had inside to keep her expression coolly questioning.

"David, how lovely to see you." Having Emma greet him like a long-lost friend took Val aback. She knew they'd probably have come in contact before, through work, but this seemed a lot more personal. "I thought you'd be in London, getting the rally sorted."

"Emma, good to see you too." The fondness in his expression was unmistakable and left Val wondering if he'd reserved his stiff arrogance just for her. "I got called in for a consult, and I'm sure the foundation staff have all the rally details under control."

Emma chuckled, as they hugged briefly. "As though that would stop you from poking your nose into everything anyway."

David shook his head and gave her a narrow-eyed look, his arm still slung companionly over her shoulders. "Are you saying I'm incapable of delegating?"

"Would I be so rude?" she deadpanned in return.

"Touché, young lady." He gave her shoulders one last squeeze and then let her go, asking, "So how are you? And how's that liver donor faring?"

Emma was on a team supervising a live liver donor, in preparation for the proposed transplant, now about six weeks away.

"Everything is going well with the donor, and I'm getting ready for Rally Round. Val and I are running it together, in Dad's Mini."

David's gaze swung to Val's face for a moment and left her breathless, with sparks firing along her nerve endings from just that fleeting glance.

"Have you run a rally before?" he asked, his attention back on Emma, leaving Val able to collect herself, although she found it more difficult to do than she liked.

"I haven't, but Val has." Emma was quite happy to supply the information, unaware of the strange tension in the room. "She used to navigate for her brother when she was younger."

"Did she, now?" There was something about his voice—slightly mocking, as deep and dark as midnight-blue velvet—that caused a shocking reaction deep in her belly. Val looked down at her desk, hopefully masking her expression. "Mrs. Sterling is a lady of many talents."

"She's wonderful," Emma replied. "She looked after Dad during the last year of his life and treated him as though he were family. Oops, I have to run," she added suddenly and much to Val's relief. "I have a patient in a few minutes. Good to see you, David, and I'll see you later, Val."

Then she was gone, and Val suddenly wasn't as happy about her leaving as she'd been a few moments before. Although Emma wasn't there to spill anything more about Val's life, with her gone Val was suddenly alone with the handsome, disquieting man whose focus was now squarely on her.

Swallowing was more difficult than it should be. Meeting his gaze was even harder.

Taking a deep breath in through her nose, Val gathered her control and lifted her eyebrows.

"Is there something I can help you with, Dr. Kennedy?"

"Actually," he said, the cool, lazy tone once more in his voice, "I came to see if you'd had your ankle looked after."

Completely taken by surprise, Val stammered, "If-if what…?"

"Let me see it."

By his tone you'd think he was asking for a chart or an X-ray rather than one of her extremities. By the way her heart kicked into high gear, you'd have thought he was asking to see something far more personal than her ankle.

Hoping he'd put the rush of color heating her cheeks down to temper rather than anything else, she said, "My ankle is fine, Dr. Kennedy. There's no need to fuss."

"Did you bandage it?"

She'd meant to but, concentrating on work, had forgotten. Then, once she'd sat at her desk, hadn't wanted to get back up and find a bandage.

Not that she'd tell him any of that!

He came around to her side of the desk and went down on one knee. Cupping his hand, he repeated, "Let me see."

The terse way he spoke, the demand in his voice, should have put her back up, but somehow the sight of him kneeling at her feet, those long, dark fingers beckoning, undid her.

He was looking up at her, his eyes dark and unfathomable, his lips firm and somewhat stern, yet eminently kissable. Then he looked down to where her legs were curled to one side beneath her desk, and she realized he had the most ridiculously lush, black lashes.

It was as though time slowed and her brain—usually so unyielding and resolute—went into a state of quiescence unlike any she'd known. Without conscious thought, she swung her chair to the side and, extending her leg, placed the sore ankle into his waiting palm.

"It's swollen," he said, his fingers gently palpating the joint. "But not too bad. I'd suggest rest and elevating it for a while, but something tells me I'd be wasting my breath."

To her shock, he eased off her shoe before placing her foot on his thigh. Val's toes curled at the sensation of hard muscle beneath her plantar fascia, and when he twisted to reach into his jacket, she suppressed a gasp as those muscles shifted.

He brought out a bandage from his pocket and, before she could recover her senses enough to object, began to expertly wrap her ankle.

"I hope you have someone at home to help you so you can stay off your feet tonight."

He was still looking down at what he was doing, and Val was transfixed by the sight of his hands as he worked.

"I live alone," she replied, hearing her own voice as though from afar, experiencing this moment—so simple, really—as though they were involved in a deep intimacy.

Heart racing, toes still curled, heat pooling deep inside, her body reacting in a way she'd begun to think it never would again.

David secured the bandage but kept her foot in his hand, his thumb stroking, just once, along the skin at the base of her calf, causing a hard shiver of reaction along her spine. When he looked up at her, she wondered if any of what she was feeling was written on her face.

God, she hoped not!

"Well, stay off it as best you can."

"I will."

His eyebrows rose. "Will you? I know medical personnel make the worst patients so I have my doubts."

Their words were completely normal. Prosaic. Ordinary. Yet Val couldn't avoid the sensation of falling—into his voice, his gaze.

Wanting to slip off her chair and into his arms.

When he set her foot gently down on the carpet, the sense of loss was unmistakable.

As gracefully as he'd knelt, he rose.

"I'm off to meet Tamika's team and then to lunch with your CEO," he said, pushing back his cuff to glance at his watch. "But if you need me for anything—anything at all—contact me immediately."

And then suddenly, while she sat there undone and breathless, he was gone, leaving her staring at the door, trying to recover.

Hoping contact with him over the next couple of days would be minimal or preferably nonexistent.

CHAPTER FOUR

VAL'S HOPE TO not see David Kennedy again during his time at St. Agnes was scotched a couple of hours later when she got a message saying that Tamika Watkiss wanted to speak to him.

"I'll see if I can contact Dr. Kennedy," she told the nurse.

"I'm sorry, Mrs. Sterling," she was told. "I wasn't clear. Tamika is asking to speak to you both, preferably today."

When she checked, David was still in the hospital, finishing up lunch in the executive dining room. Sighing to herself, still annoyed at her earlier reaction to him, Val asked the CEO's personal assistant to give him the message.

A short time later the PA called back to say Dr. Kennedy would meet Val at Tamika's room in fifteen minutes.

Eschewing her pumps, which wouldn't fit properly with the bandage on her ankle anyway, Val put her still-damp flats back on and made her way down to the third floor. When she got off the elevator and saw David standing there, her silly heart did another of those flips, but by now she'd had time to gather her composure and greeted him with a nod.

"Do you know what's going on?" he asked, as they headed toward the young woman's room.

"I don't," she replied, trying to match his laconic tone. "The nurse didn't say."

Tamika was in bed, sitting up watching TV, and she didn't smile when they came in.

"I don't want to go on the transplant list," she said flatly, her chin jutting in a way that heralded her combative stance. Her gaze went from David to Val and then back again, as though daring them to argue. "So don't bother wasting time and money on all those tests you want to do."

"Okay," David said, pulling the two visitor's chairs closer to the bed, and waiting for Val to sit down before he did. "Would you mind telling me why?"

"What does that matter?" she said, her voice wobbling just a bit at the end. "I don't want it, and you can't make me."

"Of course we can't make you, and we wouldn't dream of forcing you to do anything you don't want to." His tone was easy, gentle, and yet not the tone of an adult speaking to a child but of one adult to another. "But knowing what you're thinking and why you feel this way might help our team understand other patients better."

Val could see the young woman absorbing his words, and her belligerent air seemed to dissipate somewhat.

"I…" She hesitated, as tears glimmered in her ears. "I don't want someone to have to die to help me."

David nodded slowly. "Understandable. But I can't help wondering if you truly know what you're saying."

"What do you mean?" Tamika went once more right into fight mode, making Val want to interject, but before she could. Tamika continued. "Of course I understand. It's been explained over and over, and I looked it up on the internet too. Some people can get transplants from live donors, but I can't. Someone would have to die before I could get a pancreas."

"Very true," David agreed. "But the reality is putting

you on the transplant list doesn't mean someone is going to die to give you a pancreas. In fact, if you're not on the list and a donor that could be a match to you dies, chances are their pancreas and kidneys may go to waste, making a good thing they tried to do not happen."

Tamika's brow creased. "What do you mean?"

"I mean, people who go on the donor lists do it because they're trying to help others. They're being altruistic and hope that even when they die, they can still do some good in the world. Finding matches for our patients is often very hard to do, and since you looked it up online, you must know that just being on the list—if you are placed on it at all—doesn't mean we'll find you a match."

"I know. But if you did…"

She looked down, her hands fisted, a solitary tear trickling down her cheek. David reached over and pulled a tissue out of the box on the bedside table.

"If we did," he said gently, holding the tissue out to Tamika, "it means that someone has died and that there's nothing more we can do for them. But it also means that we're fulfilling a wish they had—that they wanted to give someone else a chance of a better life. Leave a legacy of hope behind. It's a wonderful, noble thing to do, I think. Don't you?"

Tamika took the tissue and scrubbed at her face, not answering for a moment. Then she looked up.

"Are you on the donor list?"

David smiled. "Of course."

"I am too," Val added. "My cousin's little boy needed a bone-marrow transplant years ago, and when I got tested, I signed up for life."

"Did he get one?"

Val wanted to lie but knew it wouldn't help.

"No, he didn't. Back then the match had to be even

better than it can be now, and they couldn't find one close enough."

Tamika bit her lip, considering that, her gaze tracking back and forth between them.

"It's not that I don't appreciate what you're trying to do for me, it's just that I'm not sure I want to go through with a transplant, even if that means…"

Val knew what she'd been about to say, and David did too. What do you say to a sixteen-year-old who was staring her own mortality in the face?

A wave of anger spiked through Val's body, as often was the case in situations like this, but she tempered it so as to say, "It's a big decision, Tamika, and not one you have to make alone. Have you talked to your parents about this?"

Tamika shook her head. "I won't know what to say. Mum is always so cheery, as though everything is really okay, and Dad just looks so sad and tired. He works all the time, probably so he doesn't have to think about it all. I know eventually I need to bring it up with them, but I really don't know how."

"It is difficult, but really it's best if you at least share your fears and worries with them so they can help you. But, in the meantime, may I suggest at least going ahead with the testing, so you can keep your options open?"

"You don't have to make a decision today," David added. "Just think about it, okay? Remember, we still have a way to go before we know whether you'll be a good candidate to even get on the list, so there's no rush to decide."

"All right." Tamika nodded slowly. "I'll think about it, like you said."

"Good. Anything else you'd like to talk about or to know?"

Tamika shook her head. "No. But thank you for coming to talk to me. A lot of the doctors won't talk to me or explain things. They only talk to Mum."

"That's a shame, but in many cases they're aware that you're not old enough to sign on for surgeries or treatments, so they concentrate on your mother because she can give consent. The fact is, though, that you're the one who has to live with the consequences of whatever decisions are made."

"Exactly." Tamika looked fierce for a moment and then shook her head. "Explain that to Mum, though."

"I know how she feels," Val said, a pang of sadness squeezing her heart. "I don't care how old my boys get, they're still my babies. They're nineteen and sixteen and tell me off for treating them like they're still six sometimes, but I don't listen."

That made Tamika smile, just a little, and she said, "Okay, I get it. I don't have to like it, though, do I?"

Neither of the adults were going to encourage rebellion so they just chuckled, and a few minutes later they said their goodbyes and left her room.

Just as they got outside the door David turned to her, and the expression on his face made her heart ache.

"*That's* why I set up the foundation," he said, the passion in his voice, in his eyes, unmistakable. "So that people like Tamika have a chance for a better life. It will only happen right now if we can improve the donor system—make it more diverse and increase the numbers of people who sign up."

He took a couple of steps away and then strode back to snare her gaze with his and hold it, effortlessly, as he spoke again.

"Hopefully one day we won't need transplants, whether of pancreas or islets. Researchers are so close to developing an artificial pancreas, but in the meantime all we're left with is donor transplantation, which too many people eschew. And that's why Rally Round and all educational initiatives surrounding transplant and blood donations are so important."

It was as though she were seeing him, the real Dr. David Kennedy, for the first time. Gone was the air of arrogance, the lazy superiority. Even the easy way he'd spoken to Tamika and Emma had only given a hint of who he really was. Now Val could see the man behind the mask, and he was one of substance and conviction, who she found even more attractive.

And far too magnetic.

She pulled herself together and started walking down the hallway toward the elevator, needing to be in motion and not simply stand there, enraptured, staring at him like a besotted idiot.

Clearing her throat, she replied, "You're preaching to the choir. I'll never understand people's reluctance to signing up to be a donor. It seems such a simple, yet important, thing to me."

"Exactly," he replied, keeping pace with her and then, when they got there, reaching out to push the button for the elevator. "But then, people don't make wills either, even when they have families depending on them to put their lives in good order."

"As though by just thinking about death, they're calling it to them." She shook her head, hoping he was looking at her, but unwilling to make eye contact. The potency of her attraction to him had been rising all day but now threatened to overwhelm her. "And by ignoring it, they can somehow stave it off."

"I suppose we're exposed to death more than most," he replied, as they entered the elevator. "So we're resigned to the fact that it comes for us all, eventually, and often when it's least expected."

She knew his story, or at least what had been written about in the newspapers and gossip columns over the years. His wife had died years before, suddenly and while still young, so he obviously knew what he was talking about. Yet, although there was no bitterness or overt grief in his voice, she had to resist the urge to touch his hand in sympathy.

"*Resigned*?" she countered, making her tone sharply questioning to disguise her softer emotions. "I'm not sure about that. We might be accepting, even recognize the inevitability of it, but we still hold out hope right to the end. At least, that's been my experience." Then, because it felt as though their conversation were getting way too personal, she added, "How did you come up with the rally idea anyway?"

They were back on the floor where her office was, and he matched his far-longer strides to her shorter, limping ones.

"I've always liked cars," he replied. "When I was young, my mother's chauffeur let me hang about and tinker, and he taught me a lot about engines. As soon as I left home, I bought an old banger and fixed it up and continued to do that over the next few years."

He paused, as if the conversation had taken his attention somewhere else for a second, before he continued. "So when I was trying to come up with an idea to attract attention to the work transplant teams were doing, the two things just came together in my mind, and Rally Round was born."

"Are you driving a car of your own, that you fixed up?"

She risked a glance his way, so aware of him that her side tingled at his proximity and saw his lips turn down.

"Unfortunately, the vehicle I had started repairing with Josh isn't finished, so I've had to borrow a classic car for the rally."

"Oh, what kind?"

"I have an Austin Healey, but there's way too much left

to be done on it to run a rally. Makes me wish I'd kept my old Anglia."

She could picture him in a sporty Austin, but the thought of him in an Anglia amused her no end.

"And what will you be driving in the rally?"

It seemed he hesitated for an instant before replying, "A 1930s Daimler, loaned to me by a friend."

That made her snort.

"Fancy, and somehow appropriate, since you're the master of ceremonies for the entire rally."

It was strange, but she immediately felt him withdraw, although she wasn't sure how she knew. Then, when he spoke, she knew her feeling was correct.

"Or, perhaps, the barker at the carnival."

The cool distance was back, and somehow she wasn't able to stomach it the way she had before.

So she stopped where she was to look up at him, eyebrows raised. "A barker, at the carnival? Really, Dr. Kennedy, I can't decide whether you're being snide or sniffing for compliments, so I won't even comment."

Then, even with her bandaged ankle, she set as brisk a pace as she could toward her office.

He caught up to her just outside her door and put his hand on the knob, as though to say something, but thankfully Shala interrupted.

"Mrs. Sterling, Mr. Watkiss just called and is asking to see you. He wonders if five this afternoon will be all right as he can stop by after work."

"I can meet with him then, if that suits," David replied before Val could.

Shala hesitated and then said, "He didn't ask for you, Dr. Kennedy. Only Mrs. Sterling."

"Really? I'd asked his wife to tell him I wanted to see him. I assumed he would be coming so we could meet."

"Call and tell him that will be fine, thank you, Shala. Don't mention anything about Dr. Kennedy, though."

"Yes, Mrs. Sterling."

As she went through the door into her office, Val said, "I'm not surprised he's trying to avoid you. He probably just wants me to tell you what he said. It's a wonder he's actually even coming in rather than just speaking to me on the phone."

It was then she realized he was standing just inside the door, making no attempt to come in any farther.

He shrugged, glancing down at his watch and saying in that annoyingly laconic way he had, "Too bad. I'll be back at five, and Mr. Watkiss can tell me himself what he thinks I should know. In the meantime, I have some work to do."

Then, while she stood there like a ninny, watching, he stepped back out of the office and was gone.

CHAPTER FIVE

DAVID STARED AT his computer screen, realizing he'd read the same sentence three times and still had no idea what it said. Since being set up in an unused office on the executive floor and opening his laptop, his concentration had been severely lacking.

It wasn't as though he didn't have gobs of work to do. At that very moment, he had at least ten documents open on his screen and another dozen or so internet tabs. And that didn't include the thirty or so emails he'd flagged for replies.

This really was the worst possible time to have his attention diverted to a woman.

Even if that woman was enthralling and compelling.

Sighing, David rose and walked over to the window, looking out over the rooftops below, trying to regain some sort of perspective.

Yes, Val Sterling did crazy things to his equilibrium. There was no way to deny that. But what was also undeniable was the fact he had no time for any type of relationship. Not even for a casual fling, should she be interested in one.

Between the foundation and his consultancy work, the rounds of galas and fundraising events, his life and schedule were constantly full. Now, with Rally Round coming up, he hardly had time to breathe. It took everything he had to keep it all straight and moving forward properly.

The best thing to do would be to stop thinking about Valerie Sterling as an attractive woman and think of her only in her official capacity.

Even as the thought entered his mind, his fingers flexed, as he recalled the softness of her skin and the fragrance that teased him whenever they were close together. There was nothing about her he found off-putting—and far too much about her he found enticing. Which, in itself, was strange and disquieting.

It wasn't as though he'd been a monk since Georgie died, but none of the women he'd dated casually had had this effect. Most had been attractive, some were even heralded as beautiful by the press, who seemed overly interested in reporting who he was seen with, but not one of them had disrupted his focus. He'd easily been able to concentrate on work, keeping the state of his private life completely separate and on the back burner.

Surely he could do the same with Val Sterling?

Yet, just thinking about her had his pulse pounding and his body reacting in a most unsuitable way. There was something about her—an undefinable, yet completely overwhelming aura—that wouldn't allow him to simply block her out.

Instead, he wanted to know more about her. Her likes and dislikes, how her mind worked, and what it sounded like when she laughed. Whether she was always so sharp-tongued or if she had a softer side with not just her patients but others too.

He could, he thought, drown in her eyes and not care at all that his breath was being stolen. There was a need to explore her lips, learn their shape and texture and taste with his tongue, until he knew them as intimately as humanly possible.

And it wasn't just her lips he wanted to explore. Her softly rounded body, decorously dressed in a tailored, businesslike suit, made him want to unwrap it, until it lay bare before him and he could touch and savor every inch.

As he'd knelt at her feet bandaging her ankle, he'd wished he had the right to gently stroke his palm up along her leg, discovering the smooth skin of her calf then thigh. He'd actually imagined caressing her, until her legs parted in invitation and his hand could go higher...

Stop that, he said to himself, uncomfortable—both emotionally and physically—and a little appalled at his own turn of thought. *She's a coworker, and thinking like that is completely inappropriate. You'd fire anyone you heard saying something like that.*

Annoyed now, and determined to get as much work done as he could before their five-o'clock meeting, he went back to the desk and randomly pulled up one of the emails needing a reply. Forcing himself to concentrate, he noted it was from the production company that would be filming and putting together a documentary about the rally. They wondered, were there any of the participants he could recommend as interesting interview subjects during the two-week race?

Both Josh and he had agreed to take part, but there were aspects to transplantation that could best be illuminated by medical professionals other than surgeons.

Involving Valerie Sterling would give him a chance to get to know more about her, without displaying his interest. Picking up his phone, he called Emma Owen.

She picked up after just a couple of rings.

"Hi, David. What can I do for you?"

"I've had a request from the production company for suggestions of people they can interview during the rally to get a wide perspective on why people are participating. They're also interested in talking to folks intimately involved in the transplantation process, so I thought of you—and Mrs. Sterling."

"Oh, I'd definitely be willing, and I'm sure Val would be too. Do you want me to tell her about it?"

"If you don't mind," he replied. While he certainly could approach Val with the idea himself, he was sure she'd be more willing to agree if Emma did the asking. "Just let me know when you have a definitive answer."

"I should have one by this evening."

After he rang off, David glanced at his watch. Still another couple of hours to go before his meeting with Mr. Watkiss. Instead of being glad he had additional time to work, he found himself annoyed that the afternoon was going so slowly, and he had to give himself a mental shake.

"Enough." He said it aloud, for emphasis. "Concentrate."

But it took every scintilla of control he could muster to do so, and he couldn't help glancing at his watch periodically.

By four forty-five, his computer was packed and he was on his way down to Val's office, far too eager to get there and see her again.

He'd hardly had a chance to greet her before her assistant announced Tamika's father's arrival.

Ricardo Watkiss was a large, broad-shouldered man, as tall as David and with a crushing handshake. But for all his apparent strength, his gaze was that of an old man, leaving David with an impression of frailty and fear.

"I didn't want to bother you, Dr. Kennedy," he said, after they'd all sat down. "Mrs. Sterling knows how I feel about all of this and could have just told you."

"I'd rather hear it from you," David replied. Yet, it was already clear why Tamika's father hadn't wanted to speak to another doctor about his daughter. Already his eyes were damp, and he knotted his fingers together, as though seeking an anchor in an ever-shifting world. "Just take your time and tell me what you're thinking."

Ricardo took a breath, but it shuddered into his lungs, as though he found it hard to inhale.

"From what all the doctors have told me, my Tamika is dying." He paused and swallowed before continuing. "And what I want—what I think is best for her—is for her to come home so I can take care of her, keep her safe and comfortable, for as long as possible."

His anguish was obvious, his pain undeniable, and David's heart went out to him, even as he considered how best to approach the discussion.

"Mr. Watkiss, Tamika *is* gravely ill, and I know the odds of finding her a donor are slim, but don't you think it's worth exploring that option?"

Ricardo Watkiss shook his head. "Having her poked and prodded more? Do you know what she's gone through since the time she was six years old? Needles every day. Sticking her fingers, injecting herself. In and out of hospital, her blood sugar uncontrollable. We almost lost her a few times."

"But if she finds a donor, her life will be extended."

"But everyone says she probably *won't* find a donor." He held up his hands, fingers fisted, as though prepared to fight. "Why put her through all the tests, the pain, only for it to be false hope?"

Once more a member of the Watkiss family reminded David of his impotence when it came to the most important things in life, and for a moment he was at a loss as to how to proceed. Then Val Sterling spoke.

"Mr. Watkiss, we're all parents here, and I think I can speak for Dr. Kennedy when I say I don't know what you're going through. But what I do know is that you love your daughter and want only the best for her, am I right?"

"Exactly," he said, with an emphatic nod. "And that's

not being subjected to a bunch of tests that won't do her any good."

"But none of us know whether they will do her good or not. Whether she's a fit candidate for the transplant list or not. Why wouldn't you at least want to know that? If she's not a good candidate, well, then you take her home, the way you want to. If she is a good candidate and goes on the list, then…"

"Then we're sitting there, waiting for something that won't happen, living in a fool's paradise."

His passionate interjection roused something deep inside David, and he had to reenter the discussion.

"No, Mr. Watkiss. If Tamika goes on the transplant list, there is hope, and it isn't false as you describe it. Hope never is false as long as it's true. And no matter what the future holds, Tamika needs to know you're as hopeful for her as her mother is. Otherwise, don't you think she'll believe you've given up on her?"

"Tam would never think that. She knows I love her more than anything. But I can't bear to think of her waiting, getting sicker, and being disappointed in the end. Her mother…" His voice cracked, and he had to clear his throat. "Bless her, but Lena is so sure Tamika will get well, I don't know what will happen to her if we have this hope for a miracle hanging over our heads and it doesn't come true."

"What will happen to her if you take away that hope?"

Val's quiet words seemed to shock Ricardo Watkiss. His eyes went wide, and his mouth moved, as though he were repeating what she'd said. When she continued to speak, his gaze never wavered but stayed glued to Val's face.

"Mr. Watkiss, what Tamika needs right now are her parents united. She has to know that, no matter what, you and your wife will be right there with her, and right there with each other. One of the things I worry about most is your family unit staying together and staying strong. No matter how this pans out, whether Tamika gets on the transplant list or not, whether she receives the transplant she needs or not, she needs you—both of you—by her side.

"What she doesn't need is to see her parents' marriage fall apart because you can't agree on her care. She doesn't need to see her siblings suffer more than they already are because of her illness."

"But—"

Val held up her hand, stopping him mid-interruption.

"Mr. Watkiss, I know from speaking to both of you that your and your wife's hopes and expectations about Tamika's health are very different. But there has to be a middle ground, and it is up to you, as Tamika's father, as the one who is determined to look at this situation from every angle, to find it."

"Mrs. Sterling is right." David leaned forward and met the other man's gaze. "I don't agree with your pessimism, but I certainly understand why you feel that way. Seeing your beloved daughter go through all she has must have torn you up inside, but now is not the time to give up or to lose courage. No matter what happens, your daughter needs you, and she always will."

Ricardo Watkiss dropped his chin to his chest and covered his eyes with his hand. His shoulders shook slightly and sounds of his rasping breaths filled the room. When he finally lifted his head, his eyes were red-rimmed, and his lashes were still wet.

"What should I do?" The agonized cry tore at David's heart, and in his peripheral vision he saw Val Sterling shift in her seat. "All I want is what's best for our family—for Tam—and I don't know what that is."

"Mr. Watkiss." David kept his voice quiet and waited until the other man looked at him before he continued. "Neither Mrs. Sterling nor I can tell you what the best course of action is, but my suggestion would be to talk with Tamika and—most importantly—with your wife. Just remember that your wife needs to cling to her hope that Tamika's life might improve, and Tamika, although she can't make the decision herself, needs to be listened to and her wishes taken into account."

Ricardo nodded slowly and took a deep breath.

"I'm frightened for Tamika, and for Lena too."

"It's good that you can admit it," Val said gently. "Some men just shut themselves off from situations like this, and that can only make things worse. Like Dr. Kennedy said, speak to your wife and Tamika, and, just as importantly, *listen* to what they have to say. This decision is one best made among the family and out of love and caring, not fear and hopelessness."

There was a change in the man's demeanor, as though those words had given him renewed strength, helping him sit up a bit straighter, leaching some of the worry from his face.

"I'll do that," he said. "And I guess there can't be too much harm in Tamika getting those tests. At least that way, if you say she's a good candidate and she decides she wants to be on the list, we'll have that information to hand."

David nodded, hiding his relief behind a neutral expression. It wasn't that he was invested in getting Tamika Watkiss on the transplant waiting list. Indeed, as he kept telling her parents, there was much to be done to even determine whether she was eligible to go on it or not. But the bottom line was, in his opinion, her best chance of extending her life expectancy was a transplant, and if she could get on the list she'd have a chance, no matter how slim, of getting one.

Ricardo Watkiss was taking his leave, and David stood up to shake his hand. Then he watched Val Sterling walk him to the door, while his brain shifted gears, focusing once more on the transplant-recipient coordinator.

Val shut the door and limped back to her chair, sinking down into it with a sigh.

"You handled that perfectly," he said, sitting back down too.

She shook her head slightly, as though dismissing his words. "I have personal experience with a similar situation. My cousin and her husband were like Mr. and Mrs. Watkiss. They were on completely different pages about their son's treatment and the potential outcome. No middle ground, at all. And once his father shut down and stopped being involved, things became precarious, including young Colin's medical care at home."

Of course, that was what she'd meant when she'd mentioned Tamika's long-term health earlier. Irrespective of whether the young woman got a transplant or not, she was going to need support to make sure she adhered to her medical regimen. If her parents divorced, the stability of her home life and support system would be eroded. Not to mention the emotional toll it would take.

"Was that the cousin whose son needed bone marrow?"

She nodded and rubbed the back of her neck. "The marriage ended even before Colin died."

There was sadness in her tone, and compassion, and it moved him. There was something so steady about her, so intelligent and caring.

David heard himself say, "Have dinner with me this evening."

Her eyes widened slightly, and in the harsh office lights he could swear the color of her irises changed. Deepened. Then she shook her head and reached to pull a file folder closer on her desk.

"I'm afraid I can't. I have a prior engagement."

She'd said she lived alone, but that didn't preclude a boyfriend. In fact, he'd be surprised if she were single.

Before he could comment further, she lifted her chin and met his gaze, her expression somehow forbidding.

"To be honest, even if I didn't, I still would hesitate to be seen with you outside of the hospital. You have the type of high profile that seems to always make your movements of interest to the press, and since we work together, that might call my reputation into question."

Startled, he was about to argue but realized she was right. Especially now, with his push to make Rally Round a success, he was back once more in the public eye and had been the focus of the paparazzi. Almost every day there were articles in the papers, not just about the rally but with the old, dredged-up stories.

Realistically, he should be relieved by her refusal, but instead it made his nerves tingle and threw him back behind the stiff, curt facade that was now second nature.

"Very well," he said, getting to his feet and nodding her way. "Good afternoon. I'll see you tomorrow morning, when we start the testing on Tamika."

Then, he left before he could make a bigger idiot of himself.

CHAPTER SIX

THE MORNING AFTER the meeting between her, Mr. Watkiss, and David, Val was at work earlier than usual. Considering the debacle of the previous morning, she decided to leave home with plenty of time to deal with any mishaps that might occur on her commute.

Of course, because of that, she got to the hospital in good time, but it was just as well. Having David Kennedy around the day before had completely thrown her off her stride, and there was a backlog of work on her desk.

It would be easier to get through the paperwork if she weren't so tired, she thought, rubbing her eyes. But sleep had been elusive the night before and, when it had come, fractured by dreams. Misty imaginings in which David figured all too prominently and that awoke a long-dormant sensuality in her, leaving her shaken and aroused on waking.

Leaving work the evening before, she'd hoped to forget about David, at least for a little while, but that wasn't to be. It was immediately obvious that Emma was a great fan of his, and she insisted on speaking about him in glowing terms the entire time they were together trying on the clothes she'd amassed.

"He's a really nice man," she said. "And was amazing to work for. It was because of him that I got interested in the entire area of transplantation."

By the end of the night, Val knew far more about David Kennedy than she wanted—at least that was what she told herself—and much of it seemed incompatible with the cool, arrogant man she'd met.

"He adopted his son, Josh, after marrying the boy's mum and, when Georgie died, raised him by himself. David never knew his father, so when Sir Arthur died and left David all his money, it was a circus, but David rode it out with class. I admire him so much," she concluded, seemingly unaware of how quiet Val was.

Val wished she could say she wasn't interested in what Emma had to say about David, but in fact it was the complete opposite. No matter how she told herself she wasn't intrigued by him, there was a real thirst on her part to know more about the infuriating ex-surgeon.

She'd said the first thing that came to mind when he'd invited her out to dinner, but it was only a part of why she'd refused.

Looking back, she couldn't recall ever having the kind of visceral reaction to any other man she'd met, and it frankly scared her half to death. Although she was honest enough to admit a part of her was gratified by his apparent interest, she also couldn't help wondering *why* he'd asked her out to dinner.

Was it just an impulse on his part? Had she misinterpreted, and it was, in reality, a working dinner he'd been after?

Surely the intense attraction she felt wasn't reciprocal?

She shook her head, even while her skin tingled and warmth settled low in her belly, as she remembered the sexy dreams she'd had last night.

There was no way a man as gorgeous as David Kennedy, who could have any woman he crooked a finger at, could be as drawn to her as she was to him.

"Damn it," she grumbled, disheartened and even more

distracted, and annoyed at herself for it. "I don't have time for this."

But, try as she might, she couldn't get her brain to focus on the task at hand so she eventually closed the file in front of her and got up from her desk.

Luckily, she didn't have any reason to interact with Dr. Kennedy that day, as he'd be busy supervising Tamika's tests. Having looked at the schedule the afternoon before, she knew he wasn't due into the hospital until ten so she decided to check on Tamika before he arrived.

Hopefully a walk would help to clear her head and maybe even evict David Kennedy from it.

She should have known that wouldn't be her lot. Before she could even leave her office, her phone rang.

"Val." Emma sounded rushed. "Have you given any more thought to being involved in the documentary? I promised David I'd get back to him today."

To hell with David Kennedy.

The words not only crossed her mind but threatened to come out of her mouth too. Val bit them back just in time.

"I think you'll bring a different and important perspective to the conversation," Emma went on, before Val could answer. "But it's completely up to you, of course."

When Emma had mentioned it the night before, her enthusiasm had been obvious, but Val was more cautious by nature and had asked for time to sleep on it. Having the rally filmed with a variety of people interviewed would definitely amplify the message they were trying to send, but still Val found herself hesitating.

Was that out of annoyance with David, or did she have a deeper reason to want to refuse?

Realizing it was the former, she shook her head at her own foolishness and said, "Yes, I'll do it."

"Wonderful," Emma replied. "Have to run. I'll talk to you soon."

At the elevator, Val pushed the button, as she stuck her phone back into her pocket and contemplated how much bigger Rally Round was turning out to be than she'd expected.

Originally it was billed as a two-week fun run, with stops along the way where participants could talk to locals. A week ago, after hearing increasing buzz about it, she'd gone back to the website and had been shocked at the increased scope. Not only were there hospitals and transplant teams involved, but a wide variety of foundations, research laboratories, and even the blood banks. The number of outreach events had increased too, and the places listed as the venues were large convention centers.

Obviously they were expecting crowds of people.

If they got them, it would be all for the better. The message they were trying to impart—that donors of all ethnicities and types were desperately needed—was important. And the setup of the events, where medical professionals were able to actually talk to the public in a casual, less stressful setting, was brilliant.

No matter how else she felt about David, she had to admit he'd come up with a masterful plan. Whether it would have the hoped-for effect was left to be seen.

When she got to Tamika's room, she found the young woman with her breakfast in front of her but her complete and total concentration focused on the TV rather than her meal.

Then Val heard the voice coming out of the television, and her heart flipped over.

"Rally Round is aimed at informing the public about the work medical teams do to improve quality of life for many patients through transplants, research, and therapies."

Val looked at the screen, and there he was—David Kennedy, dressed in another impeccable suit, speaking in that cool, autocratic way he had, about his pet project.

Tearing her eyes away from the TV, Val said, "Tamika, eat your breakfast."

"Mm-hmm," she mumbled, reaching for her toast, gaze still glued on the morning show. "Dr. David's much nicer in person than he seems on TV, don't you think?"

Maybe to you!

But even as Val thought it, she knew it wasn't fair. She'd seen him with his mask off, and Tamika was right.

Or was the kindly, concerned face he showed his patients and their families the mask, and the cool arrogance his real personality?

The female host smiled, and asked, "So the rally is aimed at transplant awareness? If so, how do blood services come into it?"

David's eyebrows twitched, as though the question was ridiculous, but replied, "Without blood donations, most surgeons can't operate on their patients. There are also a host of diseases that require frequent blood transfusions as part of a course of treatment."

He sat forward slightly, and the camera closed in on him. A shiver ran down Val's spine, as she remembered him kneeling at her feet, his fingers tender on her skin.

When he spoke, it was in the same cool, controlled tone, but she could see the determination in his gaze. "While the rally concept started as a way to highlight the important work transplant teams and researchers are doing, it's morphed into something even more important. It is an opportunity to explain to people just how important they—the public—are in regard to the work we all do. Without donors, much of what we do would be impossible. There are thousands of people on waiting lists who could be helped if their friends, families, neighbors, everyone signed up to be tested or added their names to the donor lists."

The morning show host nodded, as though in agreement, but prompted, "I'm sure that's true, but not everyone is willing to be a donor, are they?"

"No." Val was sure the temperature in the studio must have fallen a few degrees, his voice was so frosty. "And there are some people who can't volunteer to be a donor because of their own health struggles or for religious reasons. But for the thousands who can, even if they don't like the idea of being an organ donor, they may be able to donate blood."

The male host started speaking, but his voice was drowned out by the sound of something crashing to the floor off-screen and the hullabaloo that followed.

"What—?"

Before Tamika could say anything more, a blur of fuzz dashed onto the set and, in a flash, jumped into David Kennedy's lap.

"Oh, Lord," Tamika hooted. "It's one of the dogs from the next segment! They said they were going to show some shelter animals up for adoption."

The consternation the escapee pup had caused continued unabated for a couple seconds, with the morning show hosts laughing and someone off-camera hissing frantically, "Gryphon! Gryphon, come!"

David had a look of such comical surprise on his face that Val couldn't help chuckling. Then, as though he'd heard her, David started laughing too.

Val's amusement dried up as a heated wave rushed over her skin. The deep, melodic sound of his delight seemed to vibrate right into her bones and strike lightning out into every nook and cranny of her body.

She'd heard him express amusement before, but never like this—head thrown back to avoid the dog's kisses, laughing freely, his eyes sparkling.

He was beautiful, and she wanted him at that mo-

ment more than she'd ever wanted anything—anyone—
in her life.

"I'm so sorry." The dog handler sidled into view and
reached for the leash attached to her runaway's collar. "So
sorry. Let me—"

"No. No." David waved her back, settling the dog more
firmly on his lap. "He's fine here. I think he came over to
remind me that dogs and cats sometimes need transfusions
too, so if you have an animal who's healthy and robust,
you can speak to your vet and ask about blood donorship."

"On that note, I'll say thank you to Dr. Kennedy and to
Gryphon," the other host said, just as the camera zoomed
in on man and dog.

Hearing his name, the dog paused in his continued attempt to lick David's face and stared straight at the host,
one ear up and the other down, his expression one of adorable inquiry and unmistakable mischief. The theme music
started playing, and over it, before they went to commer-
cial, Val could hear someone once more apologizing to
David and his responding laughter.

"Aww, so cute," Tamika said.

Unsure of whether she was referring to dog or man, Val
expressed no opinion but reminded the young woman to
finish up her breakfast.

"Did you know Dr. David's mum is a singer?" Tamika
asked, around a mouthful of toast and egg. "Or that he
never knew who his father was until he died and left him
a ton of money?"

"I did," Val replied, silently wondering why she couldn't
seem to escape people speaking about the dratted man.

"And that his wife died young and his son is her son
that he adopted?"

"Did you find all that out during his TV interview?"
she asked rather than replying to the question.

"No. They were mostly only interested in that rally

thing Dr. David is doing now. I looked him up on the internet, after my mum said his mum was the one who sang my Gran's favorite song." She paused with her fork partway to her mouth and asked, "Did you know he's putting on that rally?"

"I did," Val said again. "You hadn't heard about it before?"

Talking about the rally would be a lot easier than having to hear even more about the man she was trying so hard not to think about.

"No. I don't usually watch the news or those morning shows. I only watched today because I heard Dr. David's name as I was changing channels. Are you going to be at some of the information events where people can sign up to be donors?"

"Better than that. I'll be driving in the rally with my friend, Emma."

Tamika's eyes widened. "Ooh, you're so lucky. I wish I could too. He said it was starting in Edinburgh and ending in London. Do you know what the route will be? And what did he mean when he said there would be a gimmick component to it? Isn't a rally just cars racing as fast as they can from one place to another?"

Val shook her head, smiling over Tamika's obvious enthusiasm.

"No, you're thinking of WRC rallies, like you see on TV, where the cars are all going hell-for-leather along the road, jumping over humps and skidding around corners. This rally is what they call a TSD—time, speed, distance—rally. That means the cars have to go a specific distance, within a specific time, while maintaining or even going under the speed limit."

Tamika wrinkled her nose. "That doesn't sound like as much fun as the fast races."

Val chuckled. "Sometimes TSD rallies will have special stages, where the drivers can go as fast as they like, but because the cars in this rally are all older, there won't be any of those."

"Still sounds like fun, even if you're not really racing."

That made Val laugh. "Hey, it's still a race, even if we're not driving fast. If you get lost or don't follow the directions, you'll lose."

"I guess. But what about the gimmick part? What's that?"

"I'm not sure what the gimmick part of it will be. Sometimes you have to look out for special signs along the way and if you see them all you get points, or it could be something completely different. The folks at Rally Round have kept that part of it under their hats, but you could look that up online and see what rally clubs have done before. And, to answer your other question, drivers and navigators never know what the route is until the start of each day, so they can't cheat and check it out beforehand."

"Maybe I can get Dad to take me to see the cars, if you're coming near here."

The longing in her voice was heartbreaking, but Val smiled and kept her voice light as she replied, "And you can watch some of it on TV. They're having daily coverage, taping interviews, and even doing a documentary to air afterwards. I think some of the information is on the Rally Round website."

"Will you be in the documentary?"

Before Val could answer, the door opened, and one of the nurses came in.

"Finished your breakfast yet? It'll soon be time to take you to radiology."

Which meant David Kennedy would soon be putting in an appearance. Val wasn't going to stick around for that!

"I'll see you later, Tamika."

"All right, Mrs. Sterling."

Making her escape, knowing that there was no way David could make it from the TV studio to the hospital in such a short period of time, Val couldn't help glancing around. Although, it was impossible to decide whether she was hoping to see him or avoid him.

That afternoon, as she was doing her rounds of patients she was working with and heard Dr. Kennedy had been called away back to London, she tried to tell herself she was relieved.

Even as she recognized the lie for what it was.

CHAPTER SEVEN

Eight days really wasn't enough to get her equilibrium back, but it was all the time Val got before David Kennedy came back into her life. Returning to her office after a meeting, she opened her calendar to see an appointment with him and the Watkiss family for that afternoon. Heart pounding, her face ablaze from the warmth rushing through her veins, she called through to Shala to ask who had made the arrangements.

"Dr. Kennedy's PA called to say she'd set up the appointment with Mrs. Watkiss, and Dr. Kennedy asked her to find out if you were available to sit in. The PA apologized for the short notice, saying it was the only time Dr. Kennedy could fit them in, but I didn't think you'd mind since you were free anyway."

It was on the tip of Val's tongue to tell Shala the damned man could have simple set up a video conference call rather than have everyone running about after him, but she bit back the words. After all, it wasn't Shala's fault Val's system had instantly gone into a crazy type of hyperdrive just from seeing the doctor's name.

With only about two weeks before the rally, one would think he'd be too busy to be traveling around, but even as she huffed in annoyance, she admired his commitment to Tamika's case. She just wished knowing about his upcoming visit to the hospital didn't make her feel as though she was suddenly on quicksand.

Thank goodness she had a bit of time before they were scheduled to meet, and if she timed it perfectly, they'd spend no time alone beforehand.

Preferably not afterward either.

Leaning back in her chair, she tried to get her breathing and heart rate under control, mystified by her reactions to David Kennedy. She wasn't the type to get all giddy about a man—never had been. Even as a young woman, her approach to the opposite sex had been more prosaic than anything else. And she was far from young now, with harsh experience to tell her not to let hormones take over her brain, so feeling this way was ridiculous, wasn't it? Especially about someone she had to work with, and who was fathoms out of her league.

Then it struck her that, under normal circumstances, she'd be informed what decision a consulting doctor had come to prior to the meeting, so she could be prepared. A quick scan of her email showed no such message, and although there were a few handwritten slips on her desk, none of them were from David.

Now, she was just annoyed, and thankful for that emotion, since it allowed her to focus on his ill manners rather than his other, more attractive, attributes.

Yet, even so, it took a concerted effort—and giving herself a stern talking-to—for her to settle down and actually begin to get work done.

Just as she'd started, Shala rang through from reception.

"Mrs. Sterling, Dr. Kennedy wonders if he could speak to you?"

About time.

Although it was about an hour before the meeting with the Watkiss family, at least he was deigning to clue her in to what was happening!

"Yes," she said, the receiver in a death grip, as she waited for Shala to put him through. When the phone clicked as though the call was cut off, she thought Shala had disconnected it by accident and was totally unprepared to see her door open and David step into her office.

He was clearly on his cellular phone—just not with her.

"Just a moment," he said, touching the earpiece in his right ear. "I'm sorry, Mrs. Sterling, but do you mind if I finish my conversation in here?"

"Not at all," she replied, flustered and feeling silly to be caught with her receiver still in her hand. As she put it back on the base, she added, "Do you need some privacy? I could step out…"

"No, no." Clearly distracted, he shook his head and murmured, "Excuse me," before walking over to the only window in the room and returning to his call.

His preoccupation with what the person on the other end was saying allowed Val to watch him freely, and she took full advantage. He looked different, but it was a few moments before she realized why.

There was a slightly disheveled air about him, in contrast to his usual crisp, sartorial elegance. Instead of a full tailored suit, he was wearing just dress pants and a light blue shirt, the sleeves of which were rolled up, revealing strong forearms. As she watched he reached up and, with a jerk, loosened the knot of his tie, the motion one of terse annoyance.

"I will not be in London on that day, as you well know," he said coldly, the fingers of one hand clenching into a fist on the windowsill. "I will be in Edinburgh for the drivers' meeting prior to the start of the rally."

Whatever the person on the other end of the line said in reply had his eyes narrowing and made his lips tighten into a straight, hard line.

"Perhaps you're unfamiliar with the bylaws governing the matter, but I'm afraid your discomfort isn't one of the few reasons listed for calling an extraordinary board meeting. The only alternative would be a greater-than-two-thirds majority of members agreeing to meet, and you will *not* get that."

While his body language was tense—angry—his voice had been so controlled that the emphasis on that one word cracked like a whip, making Val start. She might have felt sorry for the other person, except she realized that beneath David's so tightly controlled anger lay something else.

Was it fear?

As he silently listened to whatever was being said by the other person, David lightly tapped his fist on the windowsill, which Val interpreted as further evidence of his reined-in fury.

"If you wish to waste time on attempting to sabotage the rally, causing embarrassment, and making the foundation lose more of the very money you say I'm wasting, I wish you luck. I have an appointment with a patient, so good day, Malcolm."

He disconnected the call, taking the earbud out and stuffing it into his pocket, but he didn't turn away from the window. Instead, he stood there for a few moments, staring out, his lips twisting slightly as though his thoughts were less than pleasant.

Then he turned to face Val and said, "So how is *your* day going?"

And, just like that, all she could see was the weariness behind his determinedly smiling demeanor, and something inside her melted.

"Better than yours, I wager, from the sounds of it," she replied, her tone far gentler than any she usually used at work.

Right before her eyes that air of good humor drained

away, leaving him shaking his head as he strode over to the chair on the other side of her desk and dropped into it.

"One of the GDK directors is trying to make trouble and turn the rally into a public-relations fiasco. If he could, he'd have the entire thing canceled."

Surprised both by his statement and his candor, Val leaned back in her chair. "Why would he do something like that? It would ruin or at the very least damage the foundation's reputation."

There was still anger in his expression, but mostly David just looked exhausted.

"He believes that the money we're spending on the rally is being wasted and would be better served elsewhere."

Val couldn't help giving a snort of amusement, although there was nothing amusing about the situation at all. "Doesn't he know that the money used to set up the foundation was yours?"

The look her gave her was searching, as though he was considering what he should say, and then he sighed, one shoulder rising and falling in a shrug.

"I made sure to set up the foundation so that no matter what might happen to me, it would be able to continue on, unaffected, run by the board of directors. I approached Sir Malcolm Hypolite to be a director, knowing he had been closely involved with heart-transplant research in the past. Unfortunately, unbeknownst to me, he'd been a good friend of Sir Arthur Knutson."

He hesitated for an instant, glancing down at his hands before continuing. "My father. Even after fifteen years, Malcolm still seems to think of the foundation's money as belonging to Sir Arthur and feels I'm some type of interloper who had little to no right to the funds to begin with."

He said it casually, but somehow now she was able to see beyond the mask he usually wore around her to the man who'd gone through more than most people could even imagine. She found herself wanting to ease the strain she could see in his gaze and lighten the atmosphere.

"Fifteen years, you say? Apparently, Sir Malcolm is a slow learner, hmm?"

And his burst of laughter made her almost ridiculously happy.

The last thing David thought he'd be doing that day was having a moment of levity with Val Sterling. He'd been in turns angry with her and with himself, since under normal circumstances this trip to Liverpool would have been nothing more strenuous than a conference call. Yet, here he was, all because he couldn't get the woman seated across the desk from him out of his head.

In the midst of all he had going on, constantly thinking about Val had caused his already sky-high stress levels to become stratospheric. Even though she'd already told him she wouldn't go out with him, and knowing he really didn't have time to do anything about the attraction, he'd known he had to see her again.

Trying to convince himself to wait until the rally didn't fly.

Neither did the long days of work, which should have left him too tired to even consider driving the almost three hours from his home in Oxfordshire back to St. Agnes Hospital. And even the myriad tasks he could achieve in the time he was wasting making the trip somehow didn't seem important.

All he wanted was to see Val again—a need that left him feeling ridiculously juvenile.

So, instead of concentrating on Rally Round and all of the other million issues on his agenda, he was seated in her office, basking in the smile she was sending his way.

And speaking to her about things he would normally never discuss with anyone.

There was something so honest and straightforward about her that he instinctively trusted her.

In response to what she'd said about Malcolm, he replied, "A slow learner or, at the very least, tenacious."

"Ahh," she said, still smiling and nodding slowly. "So *tenacious* is the latest synonym for *bloody-minded*, is it? Fifteen years is definitely too long even for tenacity. You'd think he'd have moved on by now."

David leaned back, feeling much of the stress he was carrying in his shoulders ease. "You would think so, wouldn't you? To her credit, right after I was informed about the inheritance, my mother did try to warn me it might happen, in her euphemistic way."

"Oh?" Val's eyebrows rose. "What did she say?"

"'Dahling, there may be some people who'll be a teensy bit upset when this gets out.'"

Val snorted, and he wasn't sure if it was because of his mother's words or his drawling impersonation.

"Your mum is a master of understatement, I see."

"My mum doesn't like to discuss anything that she deems *unpleasant* and, rather than speak the truth, would prefer to hide behind smiles and laughter."

The old bitterness was still there, tempered by life and the passage of time, yet by no means gone or forgotten.

Val seemed to hear it and tilted her head slightly, those remarkable eyes searching his face as though looking for passage to his soul.

"You don't get on with your mother?"

Normally he would have withdrawn from the conversation long before this point, ducking behind the barriers he used for protection, both of his privacy and his pride. But somehow, with Val, he was comfortable enough to say, "We're cordial, but it's never been the same since the truth about my father came out."

Now her brow wrinkled. "Why?"

This was new territory. He'd never spoken to anyone about the time right after being informed by the attorneys that he'd inherited Sir Arthur's considerable fortune. Shellshocked, still grieving Georgie's death, he'd gone to his mother for clarity and comfort and received even more shocking news.

"I was angry when I discovered she'd been in touch with Sir Arthur over all the intervening years but never told me, even when I'd become an adult."

The coolness was creeping back into his tone, but a dam had broken inside, and he couldn't seem to stop talking.

"When I was a child, I'd ask her about my father, and she'd say things like 'Don't worry about him' or 'He doesn't matter' or 'Aren't I enough?' effectively guilting me into not asking anymore."

Restless energy made him want to get up and pace, but he forced himself to stay where he was, although he couldn't stop himself from shifting in his seat.

"Did you ever wonder why?"

If she'd sounded as if she were sorry for him, or even too avidly interested, David might have found the impetus to stop, but her voice was as calm as ever.

"I thought maybe he was some kind of gangster, and she was afraid. Or, when I got older and realized she never stuck to one man for long, I wondered if it were a case that she didn't know who my father was or if I were the product of an assault. To find out that she was in constant contact with the man who'd fathered me but she didn't even allow me to meet him…"

He didn't want to talk about how painful that had been, or how, even now, just saying it out loud opened a cold void in his belly.

"Did she tell you why?"

"As I said, she's not one to talk about anything unpleasant."

"Is that what you really think was stopping her?"

"No. I think she was protecting Sir Arthur—his reputation and standing in society."

Val leaned forward, placing her elbows on her desk and rubbing the fisted fingers of one hand slowly under her nose, her deeply contemplative gaze affixcd to his.

"What?" he asked, self-conscious under that silent perusal. "If you're hesitating to say what's on your mind, just spit it out."

"I just wondered if you mightn't have it backward," she said slowly, "and that the person your mother was trying to protect was you."

CHAPTER EIGHT

DAVID WAS STARING at her as though she'd slapped him, and Val felt a searing wave wash over her face. Yet, having come this far, why turn back?

"Think about what you went through after news got out that Sir Arthur was your father and that he'd left you all his money and property. His family set out to vilify you and your mother. Do you think it would have been any different if you were a child?"

"I don't know," he said, in that cold, lazy way he had of speaking, but she wasn't fooled by it anymore. Not now, when she recognized it for the defense mechanism it obviously was. "But she could have told me at any time between childhood and when he died."

Val shook her head, her heart aching. "We're both parents, David, and know how tough a job it is. Worse when you're a single parent, facing myriad decisions that will affect your children and having to make them alone. It's a juggling act."

His face softened slightly, and he slowly nodded. "That I do understand. After my wife died, I second-guessed everything, wondering constantly if I was doing the right thing for Josh."

"Exactly, but raising my boys after their father walked out on us, I faced a heartbreaking dilemma: What do I tell them about their father when he's done something hurtful? How do I react when they're upset because he said he was going to do something and didn't? Or explain why he left in the first place, without making him out to be a horrid person?"

David opened his mouth as though to respond, but she raised her hand, letting him know she wasn't finished.

"Think how much more tolerant people are now about mixed-race relationships and babies born out of wedlock in comparison to fifty years ago, when you were born. Imagine your mum wondering what making your paternity known might do to her career and how it might affect you both in the short and long term. And maybe back then your father had to wonder about his career too. Yes, he came from a wealthy family, but from what I've heard, he forged his own path in life also. Perhaps he figured you'd be better off without his acknowledgment while he was still alive, but at least he remembered you—acknowledged paternity—when he died."

"That's all well and good, but I would have preferred to at least get to know him, even a little, while he was alive." The sound he made was undecipherable, but it made the ache around Val's heart deepen. "I was going to refuse the inheritance, let his nieces and nephews have it, but I was too angry to, especially when they started slandering my mother and me. How could any of that be better or worse than if my parents had been honest from the beginning?"

Val lifted her hands, signaling her understanding of how helpless he must have felt. "I can't hazard a guess as to what was going through your parents' minds at any point in time. And, realistically, if your mum doesn't want to talk about it, you may never know the truth either. But don't you think it's time you put that part of your life to rest rather than let it color your relationship with her? Having just lost my mother not too long ago, my advice to you is to treasure the time you have left, so you and Josh fully enjoy her while you can."

"Josh has a great relationship with her," he replied, but the words sounded automatic, and his voice was quiet, almost introspective. "And it's not as though we're always fighting."

He fell silent, and Val left him to his thoughts, hoping he would at least consider what she'd said. Having lost her father at a young age and nursed her mother through her long illness, Val was well aware of the value of family. Even though she'd been hurt when Liam had moved out to live with Des, she'd maintained contact as best she could with her son. No matter how fraught the relationship was, it was no reason to lose the connection she had with her youngest.

"Why did he leave?"

Startled, Val looked up to find David's gaze intent on her face.

"I'm sorry, what?"

"Your husband. Why did he leave?"

It was on the tip of her tongue to tell him to mind his own business, but what actually came out was, "My mother had MS and couldn't manage on her own anymore. I told Des I wanted her to come and live with us, and he told me it was her or him." She lifted her chin, to show she had no regrets. "It should have been a far harder decision than it was, but although my ex-husband pretended to be the consummate family man, once he showed his true colors, it was easy. Instead of Mum coming to Newcastle to live with us, I packed up the boys and moved in with her in Scotland, and we lived there until she died, eight months ago."

"I'm sorry for your loss," he said, and somehow, she knew he really meant it and wasn't just mouthing platitudes. There was a wealth of understanding about grief in those simple words. "Emma had mentioned you looked after her father before he died, and I assumed it was in a hospital or long-term facility. Now you have me wondering how you managed with your sons and mother and full-time work too."

Easier now, to move to something a bit less personal— and painful.

"I left my hospital job when Mum needed additional care and was lucky enough to be able to do some home-care work, so I could be nearby and have a more flexible schedule. Mr. Owen was one of my patients, and he was a lovely man. We used to talk about all kinds of things. He was an archeologist and had traveled extensively and loved cars. My brother was into anything with an engine so we had that in common too."

"Which is how Emma knew to invite you to navigate for her in the rally." It was a statement rather than a question, so she just nodded. "Are you looking forward to it?"

Casual conversation, but there was an undercurrent that had Val's skin prickling with awareness and made the complex attraction she felt for him come sharply back into focus.

"I am." Strange how her brain, which moments before had been completely clear and focused, seemed to get foggy, so that she wasn't paying attention to what she was saying. "I've been wanting a bit of an adventure, and I think the rally will do nicely."

His eyelids dipped, not as though he were looking down but as if shielding the expression in his eyes. Her heart rate accelerated, and her body reacted as though touched, as she shivered with the knowledge that this was a man who could tie her in knots without even trying.

If she allowed him to.

Before either of them could say another word, the phone on her desk rang, and Val hastened to answer it.

"Yes, Shala?"

"Dr. Laghari is wondering if you have a minute."

Remembering the previous misunderstanding, she asked, "Is he out there?"

"No," came the reply, in a surprised tone. "On the phone, of course."

"Put him through, please." Covering the mouthpiece, she said to David, "It's Dr. Laghari, no doubt wondering if I've heard anything about your decision regarding Tamika."

"If her parents agree, I think she's a good candidate for the transplant list."

She tried to rein in her instinctive joy and remain professional but knew she'd done a poor job of it when David nodded and smiled back at her.

David watched Val as she spoke to Dr. Laghari on the phone, his thoughts not on the patient who'd ostensibly brought him to Liverpool but on the conversation they'd just shared.

What was it about this woman that led him to open up to her in such a way?

And how was she able to cut through years of anger and pain and resentment with a kind of common sense he was kicking himself for not having from the start?

His only excuse was that he'd been in the thick of it all those years ago and had been functioning solely on the need to survive—and to care for Josh too. Rage and grief had helped him get through it and, somewhere along the line, he'd forgotten to let them go.

Now, it felt as though a burden he hadn't even realized he was carrying had lifted, and he owed that to Val.

She hung up the phone, and he could see she'd pulled her businesslike cloak around herself once more by the way she pulled the file on her desk closer and laid her hands on it. But he wasn't ready to let go of the intimacy they'd shared quite yet.

Before she could speak, he said, "Thank you."

Surprise had her eyebrows going up. "For?"

"Being so sensible and showing me that I was being as bad as Malcolm—holding on to a grudge I should have abandoned a long time ago."

She shrugged and looked down but couldn't hide the pink blush that touched her cheeks.

"You're welcome, but I think you'd have figured it out yourself, eventually."

"You're too kind." He couldn't help chuckling, although the moment felt too heavy for levity. "After saying Malcolm was a slow learner, I'd have expected the same criticism."

When she looked up, he was surprised to see what appeared to be a sheen of tears in her eyes.

"It's harder to see these things when you're in the middle of them and they bring you genuine pain." Then she shook her head and smiled slightly. "The situation with your father's estate is none of Sir Malcolm's business. He's just *being* a pain."

He couldn't help laughing and watched in delight as she laughed too. Then, wanting to test the limits of this new phase of their relationship, he said, "I know you don't want to be seen with me, but I'd like to see you, outside of the hospital."

Expecting her to immediately turn him down, he was surprised when she didn't answer and another wave of pink tinged her face.

"I don't think that would be a good idea."

But there was no conviction in her voice, and he couldn't suppress the wave of triumph that sliced through his system.

"Think about it," he said. "And let me know if you're

interested in a different type of adventure. No pressure," he added, as it looked as though she were going to refuse outright. "I have to drive back to Oxfordshire after our meeting anyway."

"You do know you could have just set up a conference call instead of coming all this way, right?"

In for a penny, in for a pound.

"Yes, but I wanted to see you again."

Her eyes widened and darkened, and he wanted to kiss her in that moment more than he wanted his next breath.

Then she looked away, glancing at her watch, but she licked her lips before saying in a voice that probably wasn't as brisk as she would have liked it to be, "The Watkisses will be here soon."

With a sigh and a nod, he reached up to straighten his tie, lifting his collar to make sure it was properly centered, as Val got up to go to her filing cabinet.

While she was walking back to her seat, she said, "Your collar is sticking up a bit at the side."

"This one?" he asked, fumbling a little.

"No," she replied. "Here, let me…"

Then she was beside him, her fingers brushing his neck as she got his collar settled and, not one to pass up an opportunity, he caught her fingers in his and pulled them gently to his lips.

He'd meant to kiss the back of her hand only but couldn't help touching his lips to her fingers too. Her hand trembled in his, and her indrawn gasp was unmistakably one of pleasure rather than censure, and she didn't pull away. So he turned her hand over and kissed her fingertips and then her palm.

And letting her go was the hardest thing he could remember doing in forever, but he forced himself to do it anyway.

"Think about it," he said again, looking up into her rapt face, his voice raspy with longing. "Please."

And then had to leave it at that as her phone rang and she hurried back to the other side of the desk, leaving him to try and steady his racing heart and put on his doctor hat before the patient and her family arrived.

CHAPTER NINE

VAL FELT AS though she could hardly catch her breath as she tried to compose herself before the Watkiss family got to her office.

David Kennedy had turned her inside out with just the lightest of touches—his lips on her hand—and she wasn't sure how she hadn't spontaneously combusted.

Think about it.

His words echoed in her head until she could hardly bear it, since she knew she'd be thinking about little else for a very long time.

The simmering tension between them was both sexual and something deeper, and all of it was scary.

Her every reaction to him said David could easily wrap her up emotionally as well as physically, and that was a road she didn't want to go down.

Whatever this was brewing and simmering between them couldn't last. She wouldn't let it. After meeting him and becoming insatiably curious, she'd read everything she could find on the internet about his life. It had been illuminating, and a little overawing, but certain things stuck out to her, when looking at the articles.

First was the pain and heartache he'd gone through—something he'd confirmed during their conversation. No amount of money in the world could make up for not knowing his father, losing his wife at such a young age, or being alienated from his mother.

With the threat of MS hanging over her, she had no intention of inflicting that kind of uncertainty on anyone else, so a relationship with David or any other man was out of the question.

She also had a difficult time comprehending the media bubble he'd existed in since his inheritance. One he seemed quite happy to inhabit. Just the thought of constantly being under prying eyes filled Val with horror.

She had learned the hard way what could happen when a relationship fell apart and outsiders got involved. Where she'd lived during her marriage in Newcastle was like a village within the city. It seemed like almost before she and Des had decided to part ways, everyone was talking about it and taking sides. Pride dictated Val not talk to anyone about what was going on, but Des had no such qualms and had made her out to be the villain. It had been a relief to leave, just to get away from the wagging tongues.

The ordeal—having the father of her children spread lies about her, just to make sure no one thought him the bad guy—had left her scarred and mistrustful. How much worse would it be if she'd been involved with a high-profile individual, like David Kennedy?

No, that was an additional complication she neither wanted nor needed.

But with the way her body came alive around him, reminding her she was once a sensual woman with robust needs and desires, if he offered a no-strings affair? That, she thought, suppressing a little shiver of longing, was something she would certainly consider.

If, just a week ago, anyone had suggested she indulge in a hot, sexy encounter, she'd have scoffed. Not that she didn't like sex. She'd liked it a lot when she was younger, before the pressures of life had made it seem unimportant and not worth the bother.

But now she was thinking she'd happily bother for David Kennedy.

Just the thought made her want to squirm and had her forcing her brain to abandon such thoughts so she could focus on the meeting about to start.

The consultation with the Watkiss family went better than Val expected. It quickly became apparent that Tamika, Ricardo, and Lena Watkiss had finally had a heart-to-heart and now were on the same page.

When David advised them that he was recommending Tamika go on the list, all three of them nodded, and it was her father who replied.

"All right. Put her on the list, please." The trepidation was still in his eyes, but he was holding his wife's hand. Mrs. Watkiss dabbed at her damp cheeks, even though she was also beaming. "And we'll take it a day at a time."

"Dr. David, I want to help with Rally Round." Tamika's tone was serious and far too mature for her age. "I think you should have them interview me, so people can see the real diversity of people needing transplants. That's part of what your rally is all about, isn't it?"

"It is. But are you sure that's something you want to do? Believe me, being in the spotlight isn't always a good thing."

She shrugged, her expression solemn. "I don't care who knows what's happening to me, but you're the one who said on the TV that there's a real need for minority communities to realize how many of their own are in need. Do you already have someone of Caribbean descent in your documentary?"

"I don't think so. I'd have to check with the producers."

"Well, if you don't, I'll do it."

David looked at her parents and asked if they would

be willing to sign off on her participation, and both of them agreed.

"I'll get back to you about it, but please, remember being a part of the documentary won't necessarily improve your chances of finding a donor."

Tamika nodded. "You've told us my chances are small already, but I couldn't help thinking that there are a lot more people like me out there, in the same boat, you know? Whose families came here from somewhere else, and they need their community to get involved." Then she gave that cheeky grin that never failed to make Val smile, even as its bravado broke her heart just a little too. "Besides, I'm cute and still a child. People go gaga over cute kids, don't they?"

David laughed and agreed. "Yes, they definitely do."

Then, far sooner than Val was prepared for, the meeting was over, the Watkisses were taking their leave, and she was walking them out. She reiterated that she would be sending them paperwork to sign, but her mind was already cycling back to David, who had made no move to leave her office.

After she closed the door behind the departing family, she hesitated for a moment, taking a deep breath before turning to face him.

And promptly lost the air from her lungs all over again.

There it was again. That hooded gaze that made her knees wobbly and had all kinds of erotic, chaotic thoughts running through her head.

"This is crazy."

She hadn't meant to say it aloud, but heard the words as though from a distance.

"I agree," he replied, his voice so low and deep she could swear she felt it in her bones. "There's no denying there's something between us, but I'm not sure what to do about it."

There was desire there but also confusion and what she

could only interpret as frustration too, and it had her cross-ing the room before she'd thought it through.

Then it was too late, because he took her in his arms, and that gorgeous, stern mouth was on hers, and there was no space for contemplation—only sensation.

She expected ferocity. After all, the attraction between them felt explosive, and in her experience that should give a frantic edge to this first encounter as the barriers came down. But David didn't take. Instead he seemed on a quest to entice her full, unwavering complicity.

Sipping, tempting, exploring her lips until her entire focus—her being—was centered on where their mouths met. Oh, she was fully aware of the lean, hard length of his body, the strength of his arms, and the luscious scent of him filling her head, but it was his kiss that stole her breath completely. Cracked her inhibitions, then shattered them into tiny pieces, so that she was the one who deepened their kiss and pulled him closer in ever-growing desire.

When her phone rang, it took a long moment to even realize what it was and all her strength to not just ignore it.

David pulled back, and they exchanged a long look. Val was glad to see he was as breathless as she, and the blaze of need in his eyes made her shiver.

He let his arms slide slowly from around her, and she gathered enough strength to walk away, when all she wanted was to stay exactly where she'd been.

By the time she'd dealt with her call, he was standing behind the guest chair, and from his somber expression she knew the interlude was over.

"I have to go."

"Yes." She nodded as though it didn't matter, although inside she was straining toward him, wanting him to stay.

"Val, with the rally and everything else that's going on right now, I don't have the time you deserve me to give you."

"Yes," she said again, although she was thinking *I'll take whatever you want to give* and was despising herself for the impulse.

"Don't do that."

"What?" To salvage her pride, she raised her eyebrows, feigning mildly questioning interest.

He strode around the desk. Swinging her chair around so she faced him, he bent so they were nose to nose.

"Don't pretend you weren't just in my arms, making the most delicious little sounds in the back of your throat as we kissed, seducing me with that sweet, sexy mouth."

She gasped at the rush of renewed arousal his words brought, and he nodded, that erotic, heavy-lidded gaze doing crazy things to her determination not to give in to her own lust.

"We're not kids, Val, and I won't pretend or make believe as though we were. I want you, in my arms, in my bed, but I'm trying to make sure I can treat you with the care and respect you deserve. And if that means waiting until my life slows down, then I'm willing—reluctant, but willing—to do it."

He was melting her, from the inside out, and Val knew she couldn't allow him to do that, yet couldn't seem to stop it from happening. Right then she wanted to resent him. To tell him it wasn't what she wanted and he should just leave—forget it all—but neither the emotion nor the words would come.

Instead, as she sat trapped by his gaze, her body humming as though filled with a million volts of electricity, all she could do was nod silently. That way she wouldn't tell him his high-minded, gentlemanly intentions could go hang, because if he wanted her, she was ready and willing.

"Damn it," he growled. "When you look at me like that—"

Bending, he took her lips. Not gently now but with a

driving need that showed her, despite his words, they were actually of the same mind.

But before she could get her arms around his neck, he was pulling away—walking away, with a stiff-backed stride of sheer determination.

Pausing at the door, he looked back to ask, "May I call you later?"

"Yes." As though she could refuse him anything, with her brain still consumed by arousal and her body clamoring for satisfaction.

And when he'd left, closing the door behind him, all Val could do was drop her head down onto her desk, not sure whether to laugh or cry.

David dragged himself back to his car, bogged down not by weariness anymore but by the urge to turn around and go back to Val. To stay in Liverpool and convince her to spend the night with him. But he'd told her the truth when he said he didn't have the time to do right by her. In truth, he barely had time to get the important things in his life done, much less to be contemplating striking up a new relationship.

One that cried out for him to commit to it, the way he did to everything important in his life.

But the commitments he had already shouldered were almost too much, and if he tried to stretch himself any thinner, he might just snap.

If he had any sense at all, he'd walk away altogether and forget about Valerie Sterling.

He considered that idea as he got into his vehicle and put on his seat belt.

Yes, that would be the best course of action. Keep his concentration on the foundation and his work, since those were the most important. Channeling energy into any kind of distraction could cost him everything, and he wasn't willing to pay that price.

And it wasn't as though he were a stranger to having to exert willpower to get what he wanted—which was to ensure what he'd built continued to help as many people as possible.

Navigating through Liverpool, he determinedly turned his thoughts away from Val and back to Rally Round. Using the car's hands-free capability, he put in a call to his PA, Mrs. Rowland.

"Rolly," he said, when she answered the phone. "Do you have any updates for me?"

"Yes, David. Mrs. Duhaney emailed to say there will not be an extraordinary meeting of the board."

She said it in her usual calm manner, but he'd worked with her long enough to hear the vague question in her voice.

"Sir Malcolm," he replied succinctly and heard her sigh in understanding.

"Well, you can put that aside for now." Then she continued briskly. "All but three of the classic-car and rally clubs have submitted their routes and gimmick clues, and I've called the others, requesting they send them by the end of the week, no later. The last thing is…"

She went on talking, but the mention of Sir Malcolm diverted David's thoughts to the conversation he'd had with Val earlier. It was strange how easily she'd put things into perspective with just a few words and a gentle joke. Somehow, now, the older man seemed far less of a threat than David had previously thought, although nothing had really changed.

Except for those intimate moments when he'd opened up to Val.

Intimate moments.

Immediately his mind jumped to holding Val in his

arms, her plump, soft breasts brushing his chest, her lips opening to his tongue, the sucking motion of her mouth, which caused his brain to short-circuit. He couldn't remember a time when he'd been so aroused, so quickly. Like her mouth held a quick-acting aphrodisiac that rushed through his veins, creating devastating heat and making him hard.

He'd wanted to pull her even closer, so close that only if they were naked could they get any nearer. Thought what it would be like to cup her buttocks and lift her, so she'd imagine how it would be if she were to open her legs to him, take him deep into her body.

Had she been as wet as he was hard? If he'd lifted her skirt and been able to get into her knickers, would she be hot and slick—ready for him, the way he'd been for her?

"So, which would you prefer, David?"

Rolly's voice broke him out of his erotic dream, finding him disoriented and indescribably turned on, which is the last thing he wanted his PA to know. He also hadn't heard a word she'd said, so in an effort to disguise that fact he replied, "You do what you think is best."

Shocked silence met that response. Then she said, "I'm sorry? What?"

Best to carry it forward with some kind of authority.

"Rolly, you make a decision, and let me know. You and I have worked together for more than five years, and there's no one I'd trust more than you to do the right thing."

She stuttered, and in her confusion he heard his own overwhelming need to constantly be in control of every little thing. Just the realization of how tightly he always held the reins was food for thought.

"If there's nothing else?" he asked, and he hung up when she hesitantly said no and goodbye.

When had he gotten that hidebound?

Oh, he'd always had the tendency to make sure everyone working with him knew he'd never ask them to do anything he wouldn't do himself, but that was different. Over the last decade he'd taken on more and more and delegated less and less.

Was that what Josh had been trying to point out to him when he'd asked if David planned to slow down?

And, even more importantly, why was he suddenly thinking about these things rather than concentrating on Rally Round and all his other responsibilities?

Even as the question crossed his mind, he knew.

"Damn, Valerie Sterling. I don't have time for you right now, and maybe I never will."

Yet, even as he said the words aloud, he heard the untruth in them and wondered what to do next. Because not doing anything probably wouldn't fly.

CHAPTER TEN

HAVING NO FURTHER appointments for the day, Val told Shala she was leaving early and went home, too confused and frazzled to give her best to her job just then.

On the bus ride home, she tried not to think about what had happened in her office, and the way she'd felt as she and David kissed. It had thrown her into erotic confusion, and now she wondered where the prosaic, no-nonsense woman she knew herself to be had disappeared to.

Once upon a time sex had been fun and something she craved. By the time her marriage ended, their love life had faded into drab routine, which Val rarely if ever initiated. She really hadn't missed Des when they broke up.

Thereafter, she'd been too exhausted by work, looking after the kids, checking on her mother, and doing house-work to want anything more than to fall into bed and sleep. Over time, desire had waned into nothingness, and she'd stopped even wondering whether that was healthy or not.

It made no sense to stir a pot she had no interest in dipping into.

Yet, now there was no way to avoid the knowledge that with one kiss David had shattered the illusion of her being disinterested in the sensual side of life.

Val shivered, her body heating all the way through, as she chided herself for letting the memory rise again into her consciousness. But there was no way to stop it, really.

It was indelibly ingrained into her mind, and there was no way to suppress it.

And how she'd behaved in response to that kiss!

He must have thought her a love-starved beast from the way she'd sucked his tongue into her mouth and pressed so close, as if to disappear into his body. Every atom inside had strained toward him, and if he'd taken her clothes off right there and then, she'd have done nothing to stop him.

In fact, she would have been an eager assistant, desperate to feel his hands—and anything else he wished to share—on her body.

That realization should be shocking, but Val couldn't bring herself to care. After all, what had happened that day probably wouldn't be repeated. Hadn't David said he didn't have time for her?

At least, in that respect, he was being completely honest, although that didn't stop his words from hurting.

And while he said it as though that were a temporary situation, she didn't believe it. Even before he'd conceived of Rally Round, Val had been aware of his presence in the transplant world and how his name seemed to crop up everywhere. If he wasn't guest-speaking at some conference or hospital, he was making the rounds of fundraisers. And that didn't include any of his consultancy work, which wouldn't receive the publicity the rest of his life did.

As she walked the short distance to her front door, she rather sourly considered how much easier it would be if David Kennedy were just a handsome, sexy man. If he'd continued to present himself in that initially cold, arrogant way, she could discount his appeal as not worth thinking about.

Instead, each encounter they'd had revealed different facets of his personality, each more intriguing and attractive than the last.

Letting herself into the house, she locked the door behind her before going down the narrow passage and into the sitting room. Out of habit, she turned on the TV, the low volume of sound giving the house some background noise, breaking the lonely silence.

Going into the kitchen, she put her handbag and tote on the counter before opening the fridge, trying to decide what to eat later but not really seeing anything she wanted. The transition from cooking for four, then three, then far too swiftly one, hadn't been easy. There were days when just the thought of fixing something for tea made her feel exhausted and she had to force herself to have a meal anyway.

On an afternoon like this, it was impossible not to wish there was someone else to share the rest of the day with, before retiring to bed. Funny to realize that until David had pulled her into his arms, she'd not missed having a warm, hard body beside her during the night, but now she was afraid she would.

"Okay, Valerie Denise Sterling," she said aloud, slamming the fridge door shut. She was channeling her mother by using her full name, just as Mum had when Val was in trouble. "That's more than enough of mooning over a man you hardly know when nothing will ever come of it."

Thoroughly annoyed with herself, she grabbed her bags and marched upstairs to her bedroom.

"A shower first, and then I'll think about food."

Stripping off her work clothes, she had a brisk shower. After toweling off, she realized she'd forgotten to bring her robe with her and padded, barefoot and naked, into her bedroom to get it. Passing the full-length mirror affixed to the wall, she paused and took stock of her body for the first time in years.

It wasn't too bad, she thought, turning first one way and then the other. She'd never been slender. Her breasts were ample, her hips wide, and her bum full, all a bit more than they had been when she was young. But while gravity was proving to be no friend, nothing was sagging horribly, and her active lifestyle kept her flexible and pretty well toned.

Yet, of course, she couldn't help noticing the imperfections—the silvery shadows of stretch marks, the wrinkles here and there, and...was that a gray hair in her pubes?

That warranted turning on a brighter light, so as to investigate.

Yes, damn it, it was a gray hair.

Who got a gray hair down there at forty-five?

Yet, why was she even worrying about that? She'd never been a looker. In fact, more than once in her younger days, compliments had been of the backhanded variety. She wasn't flashy at all. In fact, she'd been called *mousy* more than once, usually followed by placating comments about how nice her personality or character was.

But she was sure personality wouldn't be enough to make a man like David really interested. She'd seen lots of pictures of him with one gorgeous woman or another on his arm.

Not to say she didn't know her own worth as a woman. Her parents had raised her to be independent, to strive for the career she wanted, and to be the best she possibly could. If anyone asked, she'd admit to being proud of all she'd achieved in life, but she was also honest with herself about her shortcomings.

There was no way she could compete with those tall, model-thin, and mostly classically beautiful women David apparently favored.

And no number of kisses would ever change that.

Besides, who knew what the future held? The brief interlude earlier in the day might have temporarily taken her mind off the most pressing worries in her life, but there really was no escaping them.

Lifting her chin, she stared herself down in the mirror for a long moment, standing on first one leg then the other, flexing and clenching her fingers, before raising her arms above her head. Now her concentration wasn't on the extra girth around her waist or whether her breasts jiggled or swayed but on the sensation of her muscles—the still-fluid movement of her limbs.

Erotic excitement was all well and good but totally unnecessary. What was important was that her body hadn't begun to betray her—yet.

Deliberately turning away from the mirror, she walked over to her closet and, pulling out her terry-cloth robe, shrugged into it. Where before she'd been teetering between euphoria and shock, she was now back to normal, the sensible side of her nature reasserting itself, much to her relief.

Although there was also a twinge of sadness.

Forty-five wasn't old, as her sons seemed to think, but it certainly was middle-aged. She'd signed up to run in the rally because she wanted adventure, and she'd make sure to enjoy it because it might be all the fun she'd have for a long time.

She was about to grab her phone and head back down to the kitchen to find something to eat, when it rang.

Dr. David Kennedy

She froze, staring at the name on the screen, her heart immediately going into overdrive, her palms dampening and her knees getting shaky.

Answer or not?

But she was already reaching for it, even as the question entered her head.

"Hello?"

At least she was adult enough to keep her voice level,

with just the right amount of question in it, to let him know she was surprised he was calling. That, despite the fact she had to sink down on the bed so she wouldn't end up in a puddle on the floor.

"I wanted to thank you again."

His words caught her by surprise.

"For what?"

"What you said earlier, about my mother. It has me thinking I've been sulking like a child when I should have let it go a long time ago."

He was using that laconic tone, but it didn't fool Val. Just the fact that he was speaking about his relationship with his mother told her all she needed to know.

"What do you plan to do about this new revelation?" she asked, glad he'd had a change of heart, but curious about whether he'd act on it or not.

He chuckled slightly before responding. "You're very task-oriented, aren't you? You see a problem and imme-diately set about making it right."

"I like to think I have a logical turn of mind, if that's what you mean." She knew she sounded defensive but couldn't stop herself. "What's the use of seeing something that's gone wrong and not at least making a plan to get it back on track?"

"I'm not complaining," he said quickly. "Believe me. Maybe if I'd had someone like you around before, things wouldn't have gotten this bad between Mum and me. I plan to call her this evening when I get home."

"Glad to hear it."

And she really was. Hearing David speak about the rift between himself and his mother had made her mostly sad, but there'd been a kernel of anger in her as well. When Mum died, the loss had been almost too much to bear. The sensation of abandonment, of becoming an orphan still lingered, even months later. While she could understand his anger at having never known his father, couldn't he see what a gift it was to still have his mother, alive and healthy?

Suddenly he said, "I should have asked before, but I hope I'm not calling at a bad time?"

"Not at all." All her concentration was fixed on their prior conversation, which was why she came out with "I just got out of the shower."

The silence on the other end of the line was telling, and Val closed her eyes in embarrassment, a blush firing up from her chest into her face.

"You do know that telling me you're naked while I'm driving down the M40 is a rather good way to get rid of me once and for all, right?"

"I didn't... I never..." Hearing herself blustering in the most ridiculous way, Val got the best grip on herself as she could and, after a deep breath, replied, "I never said I was naked."

"Are you?"

"No. I have on a robe!"

The sound he made had the hair all over her body rising, and her nipples peaked beneath the onslaught of goose-flesh peppering her chest, back, and arms.

"With nothing underneath?"

It was a low, feral growl, and Val bit back the moan rising in her throat.

She should put a stop to the conversation right there and then. Demand he ring off if he'd said all he needed, but she didn't want to. What she wanted, instead, was to see how far it would go, irrespective of the fact that she would probably be left wanting more than she could have.

"Nothing," she confirmed, trying to sound matter-of-fact, although tremors were shivering over her skin.

There was that sound again—the one that turned the tremors into a shudder of desire run amok.

"Now I want to turn around and head back to Liverpool."

There was no amusement in his voice, just need so raw her own arousal grew in response.

"Why?" she asked, not to be coy but because she wanted to know whether he was feeling even a fraction of what she was. And to try to understand what it was about her that could possibly be causing him to want her so.

"Because I can still taste you on my lips, feel your body against mine. The scent of you is rising off my shirt to fill my head, and all I can think is that I want more. So much more."

"I don't understand why this is happening." It was little more than a whisper, but she knew he'd heard by his sharp intake of breath. "But I feel the same way."

"Does *why* matter?" he asked, still in that low tone, which vibrated through her bones and then out into her blood in a hot wave. "Can't we just enjoy the fact that it is happening and make the most of this unexpected gift?"

"Make the most of it?"

"Yes." There was a decisive note in his voice. "I don't know about you, but I couldn't tell you when last I've felt this way about anyone, and I want to explore it further. This kind of attraction doesn't come along every day, and I don't want to take the chance of walking away and then regretting it."

She knew what he meant. Didn't they have more life behind them than they could realistically expect to have ahead?

Yet, her main reason for turning down his dinner invitation before was still completely valid.

"I'm not prepared to have a relationship, with anyone," she told him. "And, as I said before, even if we have a fling,

being seen with you will place me squarely in a spotlight
I have no interest in."

The silence that followed had her holding her breath,
although she wasn't sure why.

Then David said, "Come and stay with me this weekend—no strings attached. It'll give us a chance to figure
out what we want to do in a private setting."

Tomorrow was Friday. Not much time to think. Should
she go?

"But you must be run off your feet just now, with the
rally a couple of weeks away."

It was an attempt to give herself more time to consider
the possible ramifications, when inside she just wanted to
agree without any further thought.

"Everything is pretty well in hand," he said. "And I'm
confident the foundation staff can handle anything that
comes up unexpectedly. If you don't want to drive to Oxfordshire, I'll come and pick you up in the afternoon, if
you'd like."

"I'll drive," she said, surprising herself at how quickly
the decision had been made. "Just text me the address."

"Wonderful." There was no mistaking the triumph in
his tone, but Val couldn't bring herself to mind. "I'll send
you the address and look forward to spending some time
with you."

Then, before they could get into any more conversations
about her state of undress, she ended the call. Sitting on
the edge of her bed, Val tried to figure out whether she'd
done the right thing or not.

"I guess I'll know after this weekend," she muttered as
her racing pulse finally began to slow.

How could twenty-four hours suddenly seem like a life-
time away?

CHAPTER ELEVEN

WHEN DAVID SAID he lived in Oxfordshire, Val had assumed he was near the city of Oxford, renowned for its medical-research facilities. That would have made perfect sense, in light of his occupation and interests. But a look at the directions on her phone showed his home was further north and closer to Liverpool than she'd expected.

Afire with anticipation and a healthy dose of fear, she'd spent the afternoon after their call alternatively rifling through her wardrobe and trying to talk herself out of going.

She had, in her opinion, absolutely nothing worth wearing.

Even her nicest clothes and underwear were outdated and a little tatty.

When she realized she was contemplating the state of her unmentionables, she blushed and couldn't help giggling. Oh, David may have said it was a no-strings arrangement, but if the timing were right and they both wanted it, Val wouldn't object to getting intimate.

The urge to grab ahold of life with both hands, while those hands still worked the way they should, was driving her forward. This was, in the truest sense, living for and in the present: refusing to let the past stop her or fears of the future deter her from this unexpected journey.

Since it was still early evening, she ran out to a department store and bought a couple of new outfits, a nice pair of casual shoes, and some pretty underwear. Then, on the way home, she stopped at the neighborhood launderette and sanitized the new panties, suppressing chuckles the entire time.

She was, she knew, acting like a teenager planning her first sexual encounter but couldn't seem to control her excitement.

And why should she squelch it? Life really was too short to get caught up in the worry of what might happen. She'd go into this with her eyes open and no expectations other than a good time with a man who could set her blood ablaze with one heavy-lidded glance.

With her bag already packed, she was on her way right after work on Friday. Just before she got going, she texted David to let him know she was on her way then, putting on her favorite radio station, she started the three-hour drive.

Spring was in the air, and she was thankful the rain they'd been having over the last few weeks had seemed to clear up. While it was hard not to think about what lay ahead, she forced herself not to try to figure out exactly what would happen when she arrived but, instead, concentrate on her driving.

Following the directions on her phone, she passed through a lovely village and then turned onto a narrow lane. David had given her more specific instructions, and she slowed slightly as she passed a signpost, on the lookout for the entrance to his driveway.

Stone gateposts loomed ahead on her left, and she turned in hoping she was in the right place, since she didn't see a house or any other signs of civilization.

Up a long, well-maintained drive, set between paddocks and the occasional stand of trees, and then, just as she was wondering if she should turn around or stop and call David, a house came into view.

More than a house. A jewel box of a Georgian mansion, complete with columns on either side of the sweeping front steps, that had Val whispering to herself, "Oh, crikey!"

As she slowly drove along the driveway, which curved around a fountain in front of the house, the door opened, and David stepped out. Where just moments before she'd seriously considered not stopping—overawed by her surroundings—now her heart leaped, and she brought the car to a halt.

He looked completely different. Although surrounded by the splendor of house and gardens, he was casually dressed, his smile was welcoming, and he appeared more approachable somehow.

He came around and opened her door.

"You didn't have any problems finding the place, I hope?" he said as she got out of the car.

"No," she said, feeling suddenly almost shy, wondering how to best greet him, which made her voice take on a brisk, no-nonsense tone. "Your instructions were spot-on."

Then he bent and kissed her cheek, his lips lingering softly against her skin for a moment longer than strictly necessary, but not as long as she'd have liked.

"Thank you for coming."

He'd straightened slightly, but just enough that the contact between them was broken and the sensation of his breath across her cheek was sublime.

"Thank you for inviting me."

Such polite words, which Val knew had nothing to do with what either of them was feeling or really wanted to say. The temptation arose to turn her head enough to meet his mouth with hers, but she held back.

If she started kissing him now, outside of his house, she might not want to stop.

David apparently felt the same, as he pulled back far

enough to meet her gaze with his own, and his expression had heat firing out from her chest to all her extremities.

"Come inside," he said. "Let me get your bag."

"Thank you."

But neither of them moved for a long moment, and Val's heart seemed destined to hammer its way right through her chest and fall at his feet.

David moved first, gently touching her cheek, where his lips had rested.

"When you look at me like that, all I want to do is toss you over my shoulder and run off with you. But I promised myself I'd take things slowly, so I'll let you walk inside under your own steam."

A huff of laughter escaped her tight throat, and she stepped back, putting enough distance between them so as not to drag him close.

"I appreciate your forbearance," she replied, although she really didn't. Being carried off, having not to think or make choices, sounded rather lovely just then.

He nodded, his lips tilting up into a little smile that melted her even more. Then he stepped around her to open the back door of her car and take out her bag.

"You look gorgeous," he said, as they walked toward the front door. "That color makes your skin glow."

"Thank you," she replied, smoothing the collar of her brilliantly pink blouse, the silky fabric a tactile treat. "I love it too. It's so bright and cheerful."

"That's my mother's signature color, so it's a favorite of mine," he replied, as he turned the massive ironwork handle and pushed open the thick oak front door.

"Is it?" Suddenly self-conscious, she could only hope he didn't think she'd worn it on purpose because of that fact. "I didn't know."

He slanted her an amused glance, his smile both teasing and reassuring.

"Cerise is her name, and she's certainly taken that to heart over the years, but unless you're a fan, you wouldn't have known. She was popular way before you were born."

They were in a massive, double-height vestibule, with tasteful black-and-white marble tiles and, at the other end, a sweeping central staircase leading to a landing on the floor above. High above them was a brilliant chandelier, and there were doors both to her right and left, all of them closed. Val couldn't help gaping at the splendor of it all.

"How beautiful." She turned to him, found his gaze fixed on her face, so that it took an effort to ask, "But it's so huge. How do you manage?"

"By closing off most of the rooms, and having a company come in twice a year to air everything out and give it a good clean. I only use a small part, or I'd be rattling around like a pea in a basin."

"That makes perfect sense."

"I'll show you around tomorrow, if you'd like. The rooms themselves are worth a look, although most of the furniture is under covers."

Before she could reply, a sharp yap came from the other end of the house, and David chuckled. Placing his hand gently on the small of her back, he led her toward a small door, recessed into the wall, to the left of the staircase.

"We've been summoned. Apparently His Highness has decided he's been ignored long enough."

"Oh, you have a dog?"

"A recent acquisition." The humor in his voice was evident. "I don't know what I was thinking at the time, but I've become attached anyway."

They were going along a narrow corridor, most likely once used by the servants. Almost at the end was another door, and David opened that to reveal a large room, obviously used as both living and dining rooms. And there, prancing about as though he hadn't seen his master in eons, was the dog that had jumped into David's lap during his TV interview.

"You adopted him," she cried, ridiculously wanting to cry but grinning instead.

His lips twitched into a rueful smile as he scratched behind Gryphon's ear. "You saw Griff maul me, live on television?"

"I did." It was impossible not to laugh at his words and the ecstatic expression on the dog's face. "He's adorable."

As though realizing he was the topic of her conversation, Griff turned his attention to Val and came toward her, his tail going so hard it was a blur, and his bum wagged with it.

"Oh, you sweet thing," she crooned, enamored by his tongue-lolling smile and one-up-one-down ears. "Come and get some love."

Was it ridiculous to be envious of a dog? If it was, then David knew himself to be the height of absurdity, because he wanted to be the recipient of Val's every attention.

And yes, he'd even take it in the form of the belly rubs Griff was getting, if those were all that was on offer.

He'd been loitering in the vestibule for ages, waiting to hear her car approach, even though he had no idea when she'd actually arrive. Feeling like a randy teenager. Tempted to revert to childhood and start biting his nails again, although he'd stopped when he was about six.

Then, when he'd opened her door and she'd looked up at him with those gleaming, gemstone eyes, his heart had done a crazy flip. Gripping the door tight so as not to drag her straight into his arms, he'd been shocked at the visceral nature of his reaction.

There was something about this woman that called to him in a way no one else did. And not just physically, although his hands itched to touch and explore every inch of her body. Since meeting her, he'd mentally gone over every conversation they'd had, wanting to understand her and know her more intimately than he'd ever known any other.

With her, he felt he could be himself. Just plain David. Not Dr. Kennedy, or Cerise Kennedy's son, or even the inheritor of Sir Arthur Knutson's wealth.

Just a man, with thoughts and feelings he longed to share and felt he could confide to her.

She looked up just then, beaming with pleasure from her interaction with Griff, but whatever she saw in his expression had her smile faltering and her eyes darkening.

And, just like that, he knew once more—was reassured—that she felt it too. The electricity that flowed between them.

The desire.

Need.

He forced himself to smile and be casual as he said, "I prepared some supper. Would you like to rest a bit or eat now?"

"Whatever suits you," she replied, still stooping down to pet Griff.

"Now, then, I think," he said, in need of something to do with his hands. "It stays light late enough that I can show you the gardens afterward."

"Sounds wonderful."

"I'll just be in the kitchen," he told her and reluctantly tore himself away to put dinner together.

He'd set the table, and most of the food was ready. The lamb roast and potatoes were still hot, and all he needed to do was steam the fresh asparagus for a few minutes. While they were cooking, he took the garden salad to the table.

"There's a bathroom just through that door," he told Val, pointing her in the right direction as he went back for the rest of the food. "If you want to wash up."

Dinner was a success, with Val appreciative of his culinary skills.

"I taught my sons how to cook," she told him with a laugh. "But I have no idea whether they're any good or not. Clayton had no interest, and Liam did everything he could to get out of his turn, although I never let him get away with it. Each Sunday one or the other had to cook the evening meal, and no matter how bad it was, we all had to eat whatever they'd cooked."

"Are they both still at home with you?"

He thought he saw a flash of pain in her eyes, although she was still smiling.

"No. Clayton originally left to go to uni in London but decided it wasn't for him and started working as an apprentice with a bricklayer instead. He's doing well and still living in London, so I only get to see him every now and then. Liam..." She hesitated and then lifted her chin, as though to deny the words the chance to hurt. "Liam decided he wanted to go and live with his father about six months ago. Des—my ex—is in Newcastle, where we all used to live before the boys and I moved in with Mum, so it's a bit of a haul."

Although she was being deliberately casual, he could hear the hurt in her tone. He'd assumed that when she advised him to let the past go and rebuild his relationship with his mother, she was thinking about the pain of losing her mother. Now he realized, as a mother distanced from one of her sons, she was probably also sympathizing with Cerise.

"I'm not speaking out of school when I say the rally will be going through Newcastle, so maybe you can arrange to meet up with him while you're there."

Her eyes lit up, and then her lips turned down slightly as she said, "I'll mention it to him and see what he says."

The way her excitement peaked and then faded left

him wondering what had happened between them, and he wanted her to know if she wanted to talk, he was more than willing to listen.

"Did you have a falling-out?"

"Not really," she said, then was quiet for so long that he thought that was all she was willing to say. Then she shrugged and continued. "After Mum died, and I got hired to work at St. Agnes, he decided he didn't want to move to Liverpool. Although he hadn't spent that much time with Des over the years, I guess he thought going somewhere familiar was better than a whole new city."

Still sensing there was more to the story, he was about to probe further, but she changed the subject to the provenance of the asparagus. Then they were talking about the farming activity taking place on his land.

"Sir Arthur bought this estate back in the sixties, when the original owners couldn't afford to keep it anymore. Luckily for me, in the long run, he was a financial and taxation genius. When he died, the death duties were minimized, and I was able to pay them and still retain the house without worrying about maintenance costs because the farmland is so productive."

Her eyes were wide, questioning, but then she looked down at her plate without saying whatever it was that was on her mind.

"I thought about giving it over to the National Trust," he continued when she remained silent. "And even considered signing it over to his nieces and nephews, who claimed it was a part of their family legacy. But once they started making my life miserable, I decided to keep it, more out of spite than anything else. And here I am, fifteen years later, and I still haven't figured out what I ultimately want to do with it."

"You could leave it to your son."

He chuckled and shook his head. "Josh has already

made it completely clear he isn't interested in inheriting it. Realistically, even though my mother moved in entertainment circles when I was growing up, the type of wealth I fell into is alien to both me and Josh. I never wanted or expected it, and it holds no great interest to him either, and I'm glad of that."

She chewed thoughtfully for a moment, and then, having swallowed, said, "It must have been so strange for you when it all happened."

Funny to realize her words brought him neither anger nor pain nor embarrassment. Since the entire debacle all those years ago, that had been his instinctive response when thinking about his father and the inheritance. Now, suddenly, those emotions were gone, and he searched to figure out why but could find no answers.

So instead, he just smiled at her and said, "It was a crazy time, but I've been able to move past it."

And the relief he experienced at the truth of his statement created a sense of euphoria, which must have shown on his face, as Val's eyes widened slightly, and she smiled in return.

"If you're finished," he said, wanting to kiss her so badly his skin felt overheated and too tight, "we could go for a walk in the gardens."

"I'd like that," she replied, then chuckled as, at the same time, Griff jumped up from his bed and gave a low woof. "I guess he knows what W-A-L-K spells."

"He does, indeed. It's one of his favorite words. Although I think he's now learned T-R-E-A-T too, and that's his absolute favorite."

She laughed, her face alight with amusement, and David's breath caught in his chest at the sight.

Gathering his control, he said, "Come on, then. Let's get some fresh air."

Hopefully that would cool his ardor, at least a little bit.

CHAPTER TWELVE

AT THE REAR of the mansion, which David told her was called Guildcrest House, was an elegant marble terrace with wide steps leading down to a manicured lawn surrounded by flower beds.

"I can just imagine the parties they must have had here," she said. "All the ladies in beautiful dresses, the men resplendent in their evening clothes, standing around sipping cocktails."

She was trying to make small talk, to fend off the ever-quickening surges of attraction and desire urging her to move closer to him and touch him.

He'd said he wanted to take things slowly, but Val realized that wasn't what she wanted at all. If she'd been honest with herself, she'd have known that from the moment she'd run out and bought new knickers, but she hadn't wanted to admit it.

Now, strolling beside him in the evening glow of sunset, she couldn't help being fully, totally aware of his every movement, every breath. The sound of his voice was a caress to her senses. The anticipation of getting close to him was an invitation to sin.

And she could hardly wait.

They strolled across the lawn toward a hedge, and Val's temperature rose as David took her hand in his. The conversation was still general—light and meandering from one inconsequential subject to the next—but the majority of her attention was on the feel of his fingers on hers.

There was a cleverly placed path between the tall shrubs of the hedge, offset so it was invisible until you were right beside it, and David led her through, into a secluded garden space.

"This is, I understand, called a knot garden," he said as he paused so she could appreciate the intricate design of the shrubs and flowers. "And my gardener informed me it was one of the finest in England, so it had to be preserved."

"It's gorgeous. I can see why he's adamant about it."

On they walked, Griff snuffling about and then running ahead, as though knowing where his master was going. On the far side of the garden, there was another opening in the surrounding hedge and, on going through, Val came to a halt with a gasp.

The house itself commanded far-reaching views, but from where they were standing the land sloped gently away to a lake with an island in the middle, creating a fairy-tale vista. The illusion was compounded by the hump-back bridge crossing the water and the delicate gazebo at the center of the island, all gleaming in the setting sun.

"Oh, David. How lovely."

"I thought you'd like it," he said quietly. "Would you like to walk down to it?"

"Yes, please."

There was a terraced path and, as they sauntered down it, the light breeze picked up, making Val glad of her long sleeves. Griff had partially circled the lake and sniffed his way into the trees bordering the water, disappearing from view.

"Will he be okay, loose like that?" Val asked, worried, knowing David had only had the pup for a little while.

"Yes. There's actually a fence on the other side of the woods, to keep the farm animals out, so he can't go too far. Besides, I've brought him down here almost every evening, and he seems to realize I only spend about thirty minutes, so he always comes back before I'm ready to leave. If there's one thing Griff likes, it's his creature comforts. There's no way he's sleeping rough rather than in his comfy bed."

That made her chuckle, and she was still smiling as they crossed the bridge and she got her first real look at the gazebo. It was built like a very fancy summerhouse, with creamy stone floors and glass on all sides, some of the panes having sheer, flowing drapes. When David opened the door, Val saw there were upholstered couches and chairs, along with metal occasional tables and a selection of indoor plants completing the dreamy look.

David closed the door while Val walked across to look out over the water and the wooded landscape beyond. The moon was rising on the horizon, and they stood side by side watching the silvery disk slide into view, as evening faded to the first softness of night.

It was the most romantic setting Val had ever been in, and it would be perfect if David would stop being so damn noble and kiss her.

Or perhaps she should just take the bull by the horns instead?

Without giving herself time to develop cold feet, Val turned and found his gaze fixed on her face, and the temperature at her core rose, so she was assailed by the sensation of melting.

"I should like to make love here," she said, refusing to be shocked at her own boldness, although she could feel a blush heating her cheeks. "It's so beautiful, it's almost surreal."

"As are you," he said, in that low, rasping tone that never failed to excite.

She wanted to argue, to tell him she didn't need his

pretty lies, but the way he was looking at her seemed to say that, to him, it was the truth.

Something bloomed inside her—a sense of rightness, of being perfect, and in the perfect place, with the perfect man, at the perfect moment. It gave her the confidence she needed to make the first, desperately wanted move.

"Would you object if I kissed you?" she asked.

He didn't reply in words but in actions, opening his arms, stepping forward to meet her, as she aligned her body with his and raised her lips.

Once again David surprised her with his gentleness, although there was no mistaking the passion behind his kisses. He teased and tasted, luring her into a sweet erotic stupor with his mouth, until she was gasping, wanting more and more.

When she captured his tongue between her lips, she held onto a modicum of control, enough to take a lesson from his book. Slowly, softly she sucked, hearing him growl with pleasure as she teased him in return.

He raised his head fractionally. "Val…"

She heard the question in his voice and burrowed her hands beneath his shirt to touch his heated skin. "No. Don't stop," she said, rejoicing as goose bumps rose beneath her fingertips and his muscles rippled against her palms. "Don't you *dare* stop."

Then he was kissing her again but harder now, the command in his lips unmistakable. Slowly he eased her backward, holding her hostage with his plundering mouth, until her legs bumped one of the soft, upholstered seats. Then he eased her down to sit. Only then did his mouth ease away from hers to trail heated kisses to her ear.

"I want to see all of you. Touch all of you. Kiss every inch of your skin. Will you let me do that, Val? Will you let me make love with you in the moonlight?"

ANN McINTOSH

"Yes," she whispered, without an iota of hesitation. "Yes, *please.*"

He knelt at her feet, as he had that day in her office, and she watched him slip first one of her shoes off, then the other. His fingers caressed her arches, then ankles, and she pressed her legs together, imagining those hands traveling up to her thighs and beyond.

But she was wearing trousers and cursed herself for it.

He rose and held out his hands to her. When she placed hers across his palms, he tugged her gently to her feet and turned them both so he could sit, keeping her standing in front of him. Then he unbuttoned her cuffs, before setting to work on the placket of her shirt. By the time he'd pulled the tails out of her waistband and undone all the pearly buttons down her front, she was shivering with reaction.

"Are you cold, sweetheart?" He held the two sides of her blouse closed across her chest, as though to keep her warm. "Would you prefer we go back to the house?"

"I'm burning up, David. Please, don't stop."

He groaned, the sound tipping another tremor along her spine, and slid the satiny fabric along and off her arms.

Holding her waist, he looked at her in the gloom, and his fingers tightened slightly on her skin.

"I feel as though I've waited for this moment forever," he growled. "And now that it's here, I'm almost afraid to move forward."

Oh, she understood that impulse all too well, but she had no intention of giving in to her fear.

"Do you want to stop?" she asked, her voice a rasp. "I don't."

"No." The word cracked, making her knees tremble. "I don't think I can stop, now. I want you too much."

"Do you want me to finish undressing myself?"

"No." Another emphatic denial, and it made her smile. "Turn around."

She did as he demanded, so she faced away from him, and the moonlit night lay in front of her, almost too glorious to be real. His fingers brushed her, finding and unhooking her bra, but rather than pushing the straps off her shoulders, he held her waist and laid his mouth against her back.

A gasp caught in her throat as his tongue swirled circles down her spine and then up again, until she was panting, fighting to draw sufficient breath into her body.

When his hands cupped her breasts, Val wobbled on her feet, knees even weaker, her thighs trembling with want. The dual sensations had her arching and flexing, soft sounds of rising desire issuing from her lips with each breath, the moon wavering before her passion-struck gaze.

Then he pulled her back a little more, so her thighs were fully between his, and she realized he was undoing her pants, and shudder after shudder started firing through her flesh. She helped him as best she could to get them and her undies over her hips, lifting her feet at his command, and stepping out of them both.

She was naked, and his hands skimmed over her body slowly, almost reverently, pushing her need so high she was a quaking mass of desire, almost unable to stand anymore.

As though realizing she was on the verge of collapse, David eased her down onto his lap. Spreading her thighs over his, he opened them so the cool air touched her in the most intimate way, making her groan again with longing.

"Watch the moonlight, sweetheart," he whispered, his lips against her shoulder, even hotter than her skin. His erection pressed against her lower back, thrillingly hard. "Let me make you come in the moonlight."

"Please." Her throat was dry from the desperate gulps of air she was drawing into her lungs. "Yes, please."

His hands skimmed up her inner thighs, and she tensed

in anticipation. Yet, he refused to be rushed, even as she mewled and lifted her bottom in invitation.

"Hush, darling. Relax," he said against her neck as his fingers found her core, and he groaned in turn. "God, you're so wet and hot. I want to be inside you so badly right now."

"Then, do it," she said, goading him, wanting him the same way. "Don't make me wait."

"Not yet." He bit down gently on her neck, heightening the sensations bombarding her. "Let me…"

His voice faded into a growl as his fingers explored her further, one dipping deep into her body, sliding in, then almost back out before reversing course again. She arched to meet it, spreading her legs even wider, wantonly demanding more. David complied, adding a second finger, stretching her deliciously.

The pressure inside her built. Her hips rocked in time with his hand, as they found the perfect rhythm, but it wasn't enough.

Panting, desperate for the orgasm she could sense teasing just beyond her reach, Val strained toward it, but David growled into her ear once more, "Relax, darling. Relax."

She tried. Took a deep breath, willed her muscles to go as lax as she could.

He thumbed her clitoris, the unexpected stimulation catapulting her into the hardest orgasm of her life.

She cried out, the waves so sharp, so hard, she no longer saw moonlight but stars dancing behind her tightly clenched eyelids.

As the sensations waned, David murmured, gentling her, although his hands were still on her trembling flesh, keeping her arousal simmering. They stayed that way for a few long, drugged moments, as Val's breathing slowed, and her heart rate got back into within normal parameters.

David sighed and kissed her neck, his breath washing over her and raising fresh goose bumps in its wake.

"The only way this could be more perfect is if I could have watched you come." His fingers moved, and Val gasped, arousal immediately washing her anew. "Later, I will."

"I like the way you think," she said, caught between need and amusement.

"Mmm," he replied, his teeth scraping a line of sweet pain across her shoulder. "But now…"

Before she knew what he was going to do, his hands moved to her waist, and he was getting to his feet, lifting her at the same time. When he set her down on the couch, she thought he'd undress but, instead, he knelt in front of her, and ran his fingers lightly up her calves, to the inside of her thighs.

"I want to taste you." He said it simply—a straightforward request—yet the erotic kick it gave her had her nipples peaking, and her belly quivered. "Will you let me?"

Unsure if her voice would even work just then, she simply let her thighs fall open, and in the dim light she saw his lips curve, and the tip of his tongue touch the lower one. She groaned, unable to stop the sound, and his teeth flashed as his smile widened.

"Watch the moonlight, sweetheart," he said again, as his head dipped.

She sagged against the back of the couch in anticipation, knowing, without a doubt, he was about to take her to even higher heights of pleasure.

And he didn't disappoint.

CHAPTER THIRTEEN

THEY WOULD HAVE made love there, in the gazebo, if Griff hadn't come scratching at the door just as David was starting to disrobe. His curse of annoyance would have made her laugh if she hadn't felt the same way about the situation.

"Damn dog," he groused, pulling his shirt back on over his head, while Val started getting dressed. "If I didn't like him so much…"

Val laughed, knowing it was at best an idle threat.

"Griff has you wrapped around his furry paw, and it would be his little finger if he had one," she teased, having seen the way David had fussed over Griff's evening meal. "If you could, you'd have fed him the lamb and potatoes instead of that fancy doggy kibble."

He chuckled, turning her around to button her blouse.

"The ladies at the shelter made me promise not to feed him human food, no matter how hard he begged. Otherwise, I'd have just set a place for him."

They were still chuckling together as they went back over the bridge, but Val couldn't help looking back at the gazebo and the moon hanging higher now in the sky.

She'd never feel quite the same about moonlight from now on.

They meandered back toward the house, hand in hand, and Val marveled at David's control. He'd lavished her body with attention, brought her to orgasm thrice without any relief of his own, but you'd never know it from the way he strolled along, as though in no hurry at all.

Val wanted to start running but quelled the impulse.

"I can't wait to get you into my bed," he said quietly, his thumb brushing over her fingers. "Right now I'm savoring the anticipation, but I was hanging on to control by a thread back there. I'm glad Griff interrupted when he did, or I'd have probably embarrassed myself."

And then she understood.

Back inside, he locked up the house and settled Griff into his crate. Picking up her bag from where he'd left it earlier, he led her down another corridor and up a steep flight of stairs. When he opened a door in the passageway above, he entered ahead of her to turn on the light and then stood back so she could walk past him.

The bedroom was huge, with intricate plaster molding on the ceiling and huge windows that no doubt would bathe it in light during the day. There was a large sleigh bed, a couple of dressers, a dressing table, and a large bookshelf in the room, but it still looked sparsely furnished.

Setting her bag down on the rack at the end of the bed, David turned to look at Val, and suddenly she had no more interest in the room.

All she could see was him.

"Where were we?" she asked, already toeing off her shoes and unbuttoning her blouse.

He didn't move, his gaze fixed on her, as she methodically removed each piece of clothing until she stood unselfconsciously naked in front of him. When he didn't move, she lifted her eyebrows at him and shook her head.

"So am I the only one to be without clothes right now?"

Then she held her breath as he began to disrobe, going much faster than she had, and by the time he was naked too, she was struck mute with awed desire.

He was perfect.

Delicious, with his dark flesh stretched over toned abs, broad shoulders, and thick thighs. Formally dressed in his bespoke suits, the absolute strength of him was somehow hidden, while naked it was on full, glorious display.

"If you look at me like that, you might end up in a hostage situation, because I'll not want to let you leave."

She licked her lips, wanting to tell him she might not want to leave on Sunday anyway, but she kept the words to herself.

David moved toward her, and she stepped forward to meet him halfway. As his arms went around her and his mouth sought hers, she distantly wondered why being in his embrace felt like coming home, but the thought was lost under the onslaught of sensation.

They moved to the bed, still kissing, hands all over each other, learning contours and parameters, seeking out special places that elicited gasps and growls and sighs of pleasure. David touched her as though she were precious, looked at her as though she were the most gorgeous woman in the world, and Val drank it all in.

No matter how this ended, she would always consider this one of the best nights of her life.

Moonlight and laughter, desire and pleasure, all wrapped together to create something both erotically charged and infinitely precious.

Watching him pull a condom out of a drawer in the bedside table, knowing he was oh-so ready, she tried to get him to hurry, but David ignored her attempts. Instead, he brought her to orgasm once more with his mouth, and she couldn't argue once she saw the intensity of his pleasure doing so.

As she came down off the high, he confirmed her thought by saying, "I could do that all night. Just hearing the sounds you make, feeling you come apart, makes me happy."

"I can't complain," she said, between gulps of much-needed air. "But now—"

She rolled him onto his back and straddled his thighs. When she palmed his erection, his hips jerked, and his face tightened.

"Val, I'm on the edge."

It was a warning. Stark, with a feral edge that tempted her to tease him some more. Would that tender man disappear then? And who, or what, would replace him?

She swiped her thumb softly over the tip of his penis, found it slick, and felt a pulse at the base. His lips drew back, his nipples tightened, and his hands gripped the sheet on either side of his hips.

No, she'd resist the temptation to test his control—this time—because, in truth, she wanted him inside her right now.

Releasing him, she grabbed the condom and tore it open.

David held out his hand, fingers beckoning.

"Give it to me. If you put it on me, I won't last a minute more."

Silently she handed it over, watched as he slid it on almost roughly. When he'd finished the task, she slid up his thighs and leaned forward, placing her hands on his stomach.

"Shall I drive?"

"Yes, please," he said, sounding as though his teeth were clenched.

Then she hesitated, unsure for the first time that evening. He must have seen something in her expression, because he immediately touched her thigh softly.

"What is it?" She shook her head, feeling silly, but he

persisted. "Tell me. If you've changed your mind, just say it. We don't have to—"

"No. Of course I haven't changed my mind, David. It's just…"

"What?"

"I haven't had sex in so long, I'm worried it won't be any good for you."

He sat up in one fluid motion and pulled her into a hard embrace.

"Don't think that way." He murmured into her ear, his voice comforting, totally without judgment or amusement. "To hell with me. I just want it to be good for you."

She leaned back so as to see his face, and the warmth in his eyes gave her courage. She nodded, but he didn't let her go.

"How about I drive this time?" he said, using her own words, so there was no mistaking his meaning.

When she nodded again, he gently tipped her off his lap, supporting her weight until she was lying on the bed with him leaning over her.

"You tell me when you're ready, Val. We don't have to rush."

She touched his face, moved by his tenderness. "I am ready, just a little afraid. It's been years…"

"If you change your mind, no matter how far we've gone, promise me you'll tell me so I can stop."

"I will," she replied, although she wasn't sure she would.

Using one knee, he parted her thighs to kneel between them. She tensed, and he stroked a hand along her thigh, the other over her stomach.

"Relax, sweetheart."

She expected him to position himself for penetration, but instead he stroked through her folds with a gentle finger, finding her clitoris and circling it. Val squirmed and spread her legs a little wider, lifting her bottom up off the bed as he slipped two fingers into her and began to stroke.

"Yes," he murmured, as she felt the now, once again familiar pressure building inside. "That's it, sweetheart. Is that good?"

"David, please. I'm ready. Now."

And she was. What he was doing felt so good, but it wasn't enough anymore. She wanted to feel him inside her, filling her to the brim.

She reached for him, to urge him near.

His fingers retreated, and she lifted her head to watch as, still on his knees, he positioned himself and then pushed forward, stretching her little by little.

How could she have worried? It was sublime, an amazing sensation that fired out from her core to fill her entire body.

Now, to her, he was going too slowly. Taking too much care.

So she wrapped her legs around his hips and pulled him close. As close as possible, so he was buried in her as far as he could be.

Caught by surprise, David shuddered, his back arching.

Then he was moving, trying to go slowly, his teeth gritted and his lips drawn back, visual evidence of his fight for control. Catching his rhythm, she added her own beat—a counterpoint that changed the intensity of sensation, increasing her pleasure.

"I can't—" He growled it, the speed and power of his thrusts increasing.

Suddenly, without warning, he thrust once more then held absolutely still. Val thought it was over, and she didn't begrudge him the orgasm, although it was hard not to beg him to go on, since she was so close herself.

When his thumb found her clitoris, she cried out, lifting her hips, already barreling toward the cliff edge once more, going over in an instant.

And taking him with her.

David drifted up from sleep the following morning, then was rudely jolted wide awake when he realized the bed beside him was empty.

Had he dreamed the entire night with Val?

No. It had been real and one of the best of his life. They'd made love until early in the morning, their desire unquenchable, the passion between them unmistakable.

Only when, obviously exhausted, Val had fallen asleep in his arms, did David reach over and turn off the light. Lying beside her, savoring the sweet weight of her in his arms, he'd relived the evening in his head, committing each moment to memory all over again.

It felt right to have her here. Very few people got invited to Guildcrest House, and he'd never brought a lover back to his country retreat. If he was taking a woman home, it was to his London flat, at the top of the town house where the foundation was headquartered. He didn't consider that home. Not like Guildcrest, although it had taken him years to admit he actually liked the house.

Seeing it through Val's reactions had made it even more special, and he'd never look at the gazebo in quite the same way again. Just thinking about it now was making him hard all over again.

Which brought him back to the question: Where was Val?

Sitting up, he was relieved to see her bag was still on the rack at the foot of the bed. At least he could be assured she hadn't taken off back to Liverpool. Just the thought made his teeth clench.

Getting out of bed, he went to the window and pulled back the curtains, and there she was, walking through the walled garden at the side of the house, Griff jauntily trotting beside her.

And, just like that, David felt the stress he didn't even realize had tightened his shoulders and neck dissipate.

Hurriedly washing and dressing, he made his way downstairs and into the kitchen, where he found a pot of tea, still hot, on the hob. Pouring himself a cup, he followed her outside.

It was quite early, the grass wet with dew that the weak morning sun hadn't had a chance to burn off yet. Going around the corner of the house to the garden gate, he watched Val go from flower bed to flower bed, touching a bloom here, bending to sniff another there.

Griff noticed him first and let out a happy bark as he ran over to David. Val looked up, and David couldn't help smiling at the little wave of pink that touched her cheeks, as he opened the gate and went through.

"Good morning," he called, still watching her even as he bent to pat Griff, who was capering around his legs. "Sleep well?"

"Like a log," she replied, with a sly twist of her lips. "You?"

"Never better."

The pink deepened on her cheeks, and she looked away, waving her hand at the open space left in the center of the garden.

"This would be a great place for a vegetable patch. How come you haven't put one in?"

He shrugged. "I'm not much of a gardener, and the tenants are happy to sell me produce. Besides, I'm not here consistently enough to make it worthwhile."

She frowned slightly and looked around once more. "That's a shame. It's south-facing, so it would be perfect for it."

Then she seemed to shrug the thought off, as she moved

toward him, and he stepped forward to meet her halfway, bending to place a firm, lingering kiss on her delectable mouth. Her lips were a little puffy, and he felt no guilt knowing it was his attentions that had given them that bee-stung pout.

In fact, it gave him great pleasure.

"Thank you for the tea," he said, wondering if it would be overdoing it to suggest she come back to bed. "Would you like some breakfast?"

"Thank you. That would be lovely."

How polite they sounded. It was so British, he had to chuckle.

"What's so amusing?" she asked, slanting him a questioning glance, as they walked back to the house.

"We are," he replied. "And it reminds me of my mother saying you could run over an Englishman with your car and, while he was being taken to the ambulance, he'd apologize for having gotten in your way."

He opened the door for her to precede him into the house, and she paused on the threshold to look up at him.

"So which of us got run over last night?"

"I'd say me," he admitted. "And if you give me a moment, I'll find your car keys so you can do it again."

She laughed and walked farther into the room to stand beside the kitchen table, putting her mug down on it.

"I'll be happy to be of service," she said, her eyes darkening, and the corners of her lips twitching into a sultry smile. "In fact, there was something I wanted to do last night but never got around to. I'm out of practice, but hopefully it'll come back to me with time."

That look in her eyes, the way she bit her lower lip, had his pulse pounding in an instant.

"Oh?" He was almost afraid to ask what she meant but didn't have to, as she took his hand and led him into the living room, firmly closing the kitchen door so Griff couldn't follow them.

And it was a long time later before they had breakfast, but their appetites were extremely good, whetted by vigorous and satiating lovemaking.

CHAPTER FOURTEEN

For Val, the weekend was revelatory and went by all too quickly. Having been convinced there was little in life left to look forward to, she now had to admit her bleak outlook may have been a bit pessimistic.

Make hay while the sun shines was an expression her mother had been very fond of, and Val was beginning to appreciate the advice.

They'd made love—a lot—and talked about their lives, which had made her even more aware of how boring her existence had been in comparison to his.

David had grown up moving from one grand location to another with his mother and been surrounded by her fabulous and famous friends. The list of singers, costume designers, entertainers, and actors he'd met as a child, some of whom he referred to as *Uncle* or *Aunt* was impressive. But one of the important things she'd learned during their time together was the origin of the stiff, cool persona he used as a shield.

"My mother's way of dealing with celebrity hounds was to constantly smile and seem full of joy and friendliness while never actually allowing anyone she wasn't sure of to get close. I found it easier to assume a standoffish persona, and the practice I got into in childhood served me well later on."

He didn't need to elaborate. That more recent part of his past was one she already knew.

Instead, she asked, "Speaking of your mother, did you call her, the way you said you wanted to?"

He gave a rueful smile. "I tried, only to find out she was cruising the Mediterranean on someone or other's yacht and won't be back to shore until next week. Trust Mum to be out of contact exactly when I want to speak to her."

Val smiled with him, glad to hear only gentle amusement in his voice.

By the time Sunday came, Val had to give herself a stern talking-to so as not to feel depressed about leaving. It was, after all, just a brief interlude—for them both.

"I forgot to tell you," David said, as he was walking her to her car before her departure. "The producer wants to interview Tamika for the documentary and suggested using a clip from it as part of the prerally promotion, which will be airing through a variety of news outlets."

Val smiled, as he put her bag on the back seat and closed the door.

"Tamika will like that. Let me know what the plan is, when you know."

"I will. They were suggesting they do the interview at the hospital, but that's up to your CEO and her parents."

Standing by her door, she nodded, wondering if they were talking about Tamika and the rally so as to avoid other subjects, like whether this was the last time they'd be together this way.

As though reading her thoughts, David said, "I'd like to see you again. Will you come and visit again next weekend?"

She wanted to say yes right away but hesitated, eventually saying, "I'm not sure I'll be able to. I'll let you know."

"Okay," he said, with a little smile. "Drive safely, and please let me know when you get home?"

"I will," she replied, stupidly warmed by his concern.

Then he moved in close and kissed her until her head swam and she clung to him for dear life. And they might have stayed that way until Monday morning if Griff, apparently feeling he was missing out on something important, hadn't jumped up on them.

"Not fair," she gasped as they broke apart and David got Griff settled down.

He just gave her a cheeky look from beneath those long, dark lashes and grinned.

But although he was smiling, his voice was serious when he said, "I can't get enough of you."

Before she could do something silly, like drag him back inside, she got into her car and started it. Then, with one last wave, she was on her way.

Every day that week at work dragged, with Val eager to get home in the evening, knowing David would call. She could hear his tension building, as Rally Round's start date came ever closer, and found herself encouraging him to talk about it, hoping to alleviate some of his stress.

Then, on Wednesday night, he told her he'd be in Liverpool that Friday, to participate in the taping of Tamika's interview.

"It's not scheduled until midafternoon," he said. "So I'm planning to take the train from London about midday and stay over that night, leaving Saturday morning."

"You could come and stay with me," she found herself blurting, having not given it even an instant of thought.

"I would love to." His voice dropped low, striking sparks in her belly and raising goose bumps on her back and arms. "I was hoping you would offer."

Not as good as spending the entire weekend together, but she craved his company and his touch too much not to grab what she could get.

Especially knowing whatever there was between them couldn't last.

Not that she'd want it to, anyway, she reminded herself stoutly. Although she'd be the first to admit she was totally smitten by him and completely overwhelmed by his lovemaking, they were chalk and cheese. With her being a stick of schoolroom chalk and David some kind of exotic, expensive cheese, like that one she'd read about made from Balkan donkey milk.

Just the night before, he'd told her about an upcoming gala event at the Theatre Royal, where even royalty would be present. He'd spoken about it as a nuisance that he had to attend on behalf of the foundation, while she'd been wondering who he'd take with him, both jealous and glad it wouldn't be her.

There was no way she'd fit into that type of lifestyle, even if she wanted to—which she didn't!

Besides, she reiterated to herself, at this stage of her life she had to be realistic. Giving her all to or becoming dependent on someone else wasn't what she planned to do ever again. If she'd learned anything over the years, it was to take care of herself and not expect anything of substance from others.

That way when they let you down or abandoned you, it didn't hurt that much, if at all!

David knew full well he was using the interview with Tamika Watkiss as an excuse to see Val again, and even though this wasn't the time to be rushing off out of London, he didn't care.

The memories of their time together had haunted him, and although he tried to give his all to his work, just as he always did, Val never truly left his mind. Often it felt as though he was living for their nightly calls, and although he realized their relationship couldn't develop the way he suspected he'd eventually want it to, he couldn't stay away. Or stop wanting her.

His life was devoted to GDK and always would be, and that devotion included a lifestyle Val had no interest in but David felt he needed to maintain, for the good of the foundation. Being absent most of the time, traveling about to keep things ticking over and to fulfill his roles as both CEO and consultant meant he was away from home more than he was in residence. No woman would stand for that.

He'd even been questioning his decision to adopt Griff, although God knew having that mischievous pup around had certainly lifted his spirits. But the way his ears drooped each time David left him behind—either with his housekeeper or Rolly, both of whom doted on him and treated him like a prince—was a wrench.

Griff was a master at canine manipulation and guilt-tripping. David didn't need a woman getting in on the act and making him feel even worse.

He texted Val when he got to Lime Street Station, letting her know he had arrived. The interview was going to be at the Watkiss house rather than the hospital, and he was going straight there. As important as the interview was, David couldn't help just wanting it to be over, so he could see Val.

Tamika looked wan, and her eyes were sunken, but her spirits were high.

"I got my hair done," she told David proudly, showing off her braids. "And Mum got me a new outfit too." She lowered her voice and gave him one of her mischievous grins. "Mum had an awful row with Dad when she told him he had to wear a suit and tie, and he put his foot down. 'Let Dr. Kennedy wear a damn suit. I ain't wearing one.'" She giggled. "So don't be surprised if Mum tells you how nice you look, just to get a dig in at Dad."

It took everything he had to keep a straight face when,

after greeting him, the very next thing Mrs. Watkiss said was, "My, don't you look smart in your suit!" and he heard Tamika's muffled laughter.

The interview went well. David had made sure the interviewer knew Tamika wasn't to be tired, and they were to keep her part of the taping short. The teenager was wonderful—natural in front of the camera, forthright about her condition and her prospects too.

"I know I probably won't get the donations I need," she said, looking straight into the camera. "As Dr. David said, I'm in a minority and can't get a pancreas from a living donor. Not that many people sign up to be organ donors when they die, so that narrows my chances even more. But there are lots of patients who need organs they can get from live donors, and they might have a much better chance if donors sign up and get tested to see if they're a match."

After they'd filmed Tamika's part, they taped extra footage with her parents and older brother, as well as David, although he thought people were probably tired of seeing his face on TV.

Finally, it was over, and he texted Val, who texted him back a few minutes later to say she was on her way home and he could come over whenever he liked.

Instead of using a car service, he'd opted to rent a vehicle, so it was only a matter of putting her address into the navigation system and he was on his way. Ridiculous to feel his stomach twist and dip, as he drew closer to her house, and for his heart to be racing by the time he found a parking spot on the street.

Walking up the short driveway, it struck him how much her house reminded him of the one he and Georgie had bought when they'd first been married. Then the door opened, and all thoughts fled at the sight of Val's smiling face.

He made it inside before he dropped his bag on the

floor and, as soon as she'd closed and locked the door, dragged her into his arms for a series of long passionate kisses. When they finally came up for air, he tried to convince himself to behave, but having her resting so pliantly against him didn't help.

"Hello," he said, his throat tight. "I guess I should have said that first, before mauling you."

She giggled and kissed the corner of his mouth so quickly he didn't have a chance to capture her lips again.

"I don't mind. And I'd say *Carry on*, except I have a pot on the stove, and I'd hate to burn dinner."

He followed her into the neat living room and then stood in the archway leading to the galley kitchen to watch her bustle around.

"That smells delicious."

"It's chicken paprikash. My mum's quick and easy version. It was our family's favorite meal when we were late getting home."

"We could have ordered in, to save you the effort."

She slanted him a look he didn't know how to interpret.

"I don't mind. Cooking is one of the few household chores I actually like. How did the interview go?"

"Perfectly, I thought. Tamika was a star."

He told her all about it, including about Mrs. Watkiss and the suit, which sent her into peals of laughter, which set him off too.

"And, because of that little wretch Tamika, I had to stand there, biting the inside of my cheek not to laugh out loud, while she's giggling away in the background. I couldn't look at either Tamika or her father in case they got me going."

"I'm glad I wasn't there." Val was doubled over, holding her side, still laughing, her eyes filled with tears. "Oh, I wouldn't have been able to restrain myself."

Just seeing her that way made his heart sing, although he tried to ignore the sensation.

Over dinner she asked about another patient he'd talked about, who needed a bone-marrow transplant but was proving impossible to match.

"Still nothing," he said, frowning, that horrid and all too well-known feeling of impotence flooding him. "We're running out of time for him, I'm afraid, although I'm hoping maybe with the help of the Rally Round campaign, there might be a miracle."

Then, because he hated that sense of having his hands tied, he changed the subject to something less depressing.

After they'd finished eating, he helped her wash up, and as she dried her hands on a kitchen towel, she gave him a level look and said, "May I take you upstairs and have my wicked way with you now? I feel I've exerted as much restraint as should be reasonably expected of me."

"I thought you'd never ask."

They showered together, and David found it almost unbearably erotic. Val naked, wet and slick, was a complete turn-on. By the time they'd washed each other off, they were both panting, and he was tempted to pick her up and make love to her right there.

"Don't even think about it, David," she said, her voice firm, if tremulous. "Neither of us is as young as we used to be, and we know better."

So he laughed and stepped out of the shower, pulling her along with him.

"You're the boss," he told her, grabbing the towels off the hooks and leading her into her bedroom. "I don't mind either way, as long as you pay the toll for putting me off."

And he set about exacting sweet, passionate revenge, with nary a complaint from Val.

CHAPTER FIFTEEN

DAVID'S FAR TOO brief overnight stay was both extreme pleasure and, after he'd left to go back to London, way too much pain for Val's peace of mind. Physically she was sated, but emotionally she felt raw, while confusion clouded her thoughts. The quagmire of conflicting feelings left her restless, and she decided to take advantage of the sunny day to wash her car, just to get out of the house.

As she changed into suitable clothes, collected all the paraphernalia she needed, and went outside, her brain was still trying to process all that had happened the evening before.

Strangely enough, the things that stood out, causing her disquiet, had nothing to do with David's lovemaking, although she had to admit it could easily become addictive. No, the things that were stuck in her mind were actually simpler.

The first was the laughter they shared whenever they were together or even spoke on the phone. Not that Val thought of herself as taciturn or particularly ill-humored, but she hadn't laughed as much in years as she had over the last week. That shouldn't be a bad thing, but it did leave her questioning the path her life was on. When she eventually stopped seeing David, would she regress to that woman who barely smiled, who had no one to laugh wholeheartedly with?

Just the thought of it made her sad.

The second incident that kept circling her brain had occurred after they'd made love and were tangled up together under the sheets.

She didn't know where the impulse came from, but she'd come right out and asked him a question that had been on her mind since they'd first met.

"Why did you give up surgery? From all accounts, you were brilliant at it."

There'd been a part of her that wished he'd say it was because he'd inherited his father's billions and didn't have to work as hard anymore. It was what all the media outlets assumed to be the case, and if it were true, she knew he'd drop in her estimation, even with the foundation and whatever else he did.

He was silent for so long she wondered if he would even answer, and then he said, "Guildcrest House and his money weren't all I inherited from Arthur Knutson. I have palmar fibromatosis. Dupuytren's contracture."

Lifting up onto her elbow, she'd searched his face. Nothing about his expression indicated any undue distress about it, but his eyelids were lowered, hiding whatever might be revealed in his eyes.

She knew what it was, of course—a thickening of tissue under the skin of the hand that, if untreated, could cause the fingers to bend permanently in toward the palm.

"But it usually happens to men over fifty and comes on gradually. You couldn't have been more than—"

"Thirty-four when I realized something was wrong."

He hadn't retreated behind his cool wall, but somehow this easy disclosure was worse, and she wasn't sure why.

"Once I found out, I stopped operating and sought treatment. Luckily, I was able to get into an experimental blind study, and it worked, although I was warned it might not be a cure, since at the time there was no way to be sure. I couldn't take the chance on it being a temporary fix. Not when peoples' lives would be at stake."

"And then you inherited the money."

"Actually, the two things—finding out about the Dupuytren's and about my father—happened almost simultaneously. And I later found out Arthur Knutson had the disease too, with early and severe onset, and obviously passed the gene for it on to me. Do you know what they used to call Arthur in financial circles? The Nordic Raider, in honor of his Scandinavian heritage."

"Viking disease," she'd murmured under her breath, suddenly remembering one of Dupuytren's other names.

"Mm-hmm."

Here was another secret David had shared with her. One that hadn't come out in the suit against him filed by his cousins or in any of the tabloids since. Many of the reports she'd read stated the *brilliant* surgeon, Dr. Kennedy, had abandoned his fast-rising career once he hadn't had to work for a living.

There'd been a sneering tone, as though high-minded people should condemn him for making that choice, the reports casting him into a greedy, grasping light.

As if anyone else, no matter what their profession, might not be tempted to give it all up if they were handed billions of pounds!

She couldn't help wondering, though, if there had been an inciting incident that caused him to seek treatment. After all, Dupuytren's really didn't come on swiftly, although, as he'd explained, his father had suffered from it too.

And, most importantly, why had he shared all of this with her?

Was it an indication of how much he trusted her or that he needed someone to confide in and she was handy? Or perhaps an amalgamation of both scenarios? Perhaps he thought she should feel honored to be entrusted with his secrets, but she truly didn't feel that way at all.

Instead, it felt like a burden.

By telling her information not in the public sphere, he was putting her in a position to do him harm, even inadvertently. So now it was even more imperative they keep their affair secret so she wouldn't accidentally let something injurious to him slip.

Another worry to add to her growing list.

This morning, before he left, she'd said, "This time next week, Rally Round will be underway. Are you ready for it?"

"As ready as I'll ever be," he'd replied, looking dapper in his suit and totally out of place at her small dining table. "Are you and Emma?"

"I think so. All except for making a final decision about the costumes."

He'd leaned back, eyebrows raised in question. "Costumes?"

She'd chuckled, saying, "Emma decided we're to wear 1960s outfits to go with her car, so she's been scouring secondhand stores for some. She didn't realize that most of the vintage styles—the ones that have stood the test of time, anyway—weren't made for a figure like mine. We're to meet up again later, so I can try on some of the new ones she's found."

His eyelids had drooped in that sexy way, and he'd said, "Your figure is perfection, so the designers were the crazy ones. I can't wait to see what you come up with. And I have to say I'm jealous. I wonder if Josh would be willing to do something similar?"

"Top hats and canes, to go with the Daimler?"

"Something like that. And we can provide contrast for each other—the thirties and the sixties, side-by-side."

It was then she knew she had to make it clear that they

couldn't be seen together during the rally. But when she'd said it, as though reminding him of a fact they both already knew, he'd retreated behind that laconic drawl as he'd agreed. And it felt as though their parting kiss was a cool, perhaps even final, farewell.

If that were the case, perhaps it was for the best.

She knew what she felt for him went beyond liking or physical attraction, and she couldn't afford to allow those emotions to grow.

Realizing she'd been standing in one place staring into space, she pulled herself together and went to fetch the bucket she'd filled with soapy water.

Enough woolgathering for one day. Yet, even as she started on her chore, thoughts of David kept intruding.

He was so focused, so completely dedicated to the foundation and its work. Turning what must have been a horrible time of his life into something worthwhile was inspiring. No matter how things ended with them—and they must end, if they hadn't already—Val knew she'd always treasure the memories of their time together.

She just had to make sure she didn't get used to having him in her life, since there really was no place for her in his, irrespective of how casual they kept their relationship.

That thought made her frown as she stretched to get at the very middle of her car's roof. But, as painful as the reality was, she wasn't taking the chance of losing sight of it either.

Val turned to rinse off her sponge, and the next thing she knew, she was falling and then hitting the wet pavement, hard.

Winded, she lay there, trying not to let the fear overcome her, and heard someone shout her name.

Damn it.

It was Tony, her new neighbor with the puppy-dog eyes, and he dropped to his knees beside her.

"Are you all right? Do you need an ambulance?"

"No," she said, batting away his hands, as he seemed set to try and pull her to her feet. "I'm okay. I just need a moment."

"You fell hard." He sounded as though he were about to panic, and Val's annoyance level rose with his words. "Are you sure you don't need an ambulance?"

"Tony," she said firmly, just two shades away from rudely. "Just stop, please. I need to self-assess, but I'm sure I don't need an ambulance."

He rocked back, giving her a hurt, hangdog look. "I'm just trying to help."

Ignoring him, she checked each extremity and joint, one by one, finding them all okay, although she was sure she'd have some bruises. She really had gone down hard, smacking her shoulder and hip on the cement.

Sitting up, she made one more check of her various parts, then rolled to her knees and got up without assistance.

"See?" she said to her neighbor. "I'm perfectly fine."

He looked slightly annoyed at being dismissed, his pleading gaze turning cold.

"Shame that fancy friend of yours didn't stay to help you, isn't it?"

She wanted to snap at him, held the impulse at bay by the skin of her teeth.

"I'm perfectly capable of washing my own car. So, excuse me while I get on with it."

And as he skulked off back to his side of the fence, she wasn't sure what scared her more—the thought of him having seen David leaving her house and possibly recognizing him or not knowing, again, what had made her fall.

He should be pleased. Happy, even.

Rally Round was on track to be a great success.

The board of directors—especially Malcolm—had been quiet, and there'd been no further interference with his plans so far.

His work commitments were under control.

He even had what was, for him, a somewhat regular sex life—something that had been sorely lacking for years—with a beautiful woman who made no demands on his time.

A woman with whom he could be completely and simply himself, without barriers or even secrets.

Someone he'd grown to trust implicitly but didn't have to commit to in any way.

Yet, there was a feeling of discontent gnawing at David's insides, and he couldn't put his finger on what it was.

On the train ride back to London from Liverpool, while he tried to concentrate on work, his brain kept drawing him to whatever that sore spot in his psyche was.

Poking at it, the way you sometimes can't help picking at a scab, even though it hurts and you know it won't do you any good.

Might, indeed, do harm.

David stared out the window at the scenery flashing past and tried to pinpoint the source of his dissatisfaction, but to no avail. Letting his mind roam, there were flashes of thoughts, none of which seemed connected.

Josh asking him when he would slow down.

The sensation of homecoming as he walked up to Val's front door, which reminded him of a simpler time, long past, as well as seeming to offer him something valuable in the present.

Rolly's surprise when he'd said she could deal with a problem herself rather than wait for his direction, and then again, when he'd told her he'd be taking last weekend off.

His mother's voice, Southern US accent now firmly overlaid with an upper-crust English one, as she'd followed his lead and told him about her Mediterranean cruise.

Mum had never been one to express too much surprise over anything, but he'd heard the questioning note in her voice, as he'd engaged her in the kind of chitchat that had been lost between them for years.

Just catching up, rather than a call about a specific topic or with an aim in mind.

At the end, she'd said, "You sound well, Davie. And it's been lovely hearing from you."

"It's been lovely talking to you too, Mum." And it had been. He'd never acknowledged it before, but missing her had left a huge hole in his life. "When will you be back in England? I'd love to see you."

"I didn't have any plans to go back, but... I could make some?"

Strange to hear Mum even slightly hesitant, but once he'd expressed the wish that she would, she became once more her bubbly, outrageous self, and he'd been grinning when he hung up.

Healing the rift between them had been long overdue. He'd decided not to ask any more questions about her relationship with his father or why she'd kept it all secret all those years. Realistically, it was of no importance. Knowing wouldn't give him back anything of what he'd lost or repair the parts of his heart that had been damaged, but forgiveness and understanding toward his mother definitely could.

Besides, as a parent himself, especially one who'd had a sometimes-rocky relationship with his son, shouldn't he have been more understanding all these years?

So he had work he loved and that kept him busy. He was mending the relationship with his mother and doing his best to nurture the one with his son. He had a... What could he call Val, really? She seemed to defy description. Lover, yes. But also a friend, he thought, and a confidante who both simplified and complicated his life.

Talking to her about the Dupuytren's contracture had been easier than he'd expected. The only people who knew about it before had been Josh, Mum, and David's doctors. It was something he'd never even wanted to speak about to anyone else. The urge had been there to even tell her about the worst bit—the episode that had kept him awake night after night for years, but he couldn't bring himself to do it. If he'd seen the same contempt in her eyes that he'd felt for himself, he wasn't sure how he'd react, but that would definitely have been the death knell of their relationship.

And although she'd made it clear that their relationship was only transient due to her need to stay out of the limelight and, realistically, his life generally, he didn't want it to end that way.

She'd reiterated the fleeting nature of their friendship again this morning, when she'd said they wouldn't be able to spend time together during the rally since they'd all be under scrutiny. What if they were caught together on the documentary crews' cameras?

He wouldn't care, but it was obvious she would, and that meant abiding by her decisions, which should be fine with him, shouldn't it?

Without having to think about Val or try to coordinate how they could meet up, he could put his full focus where it really needed to be, which was on Rally Round. After all, its success or failure could be make-or-break for the foundation and particularly his place in it.

And without GDK, he'd have next to nothing.

Why did that thought, which wasn't at all new, make him even more ill-tempered than before?

It was the way things had been for the last fifteen years and hopefully would be for another fifteen. He had Josh, the foundation, his renewed relationship with his mother, and he didn't need anything more.

Did he?

CHAPTER SIXTEEN

THE ATMOSPHERE AT the convention center in Edinburgh on the morning of the first day of the rally was electric. Crowds of drivers, navigators, onlookers, and well-wishers milled around, waiting for the start of the event.

Val tugged at the back of the A-line color-blocked mini she was wearing.

"Stop," Emma laughed, swatting at her hand. "It's not coming down any farther, no matter how you pull at it. Besides, you look fab. Your legs are terrific."

"Thank you for that. However, I feel ridiculous. How did I let you talk me into this, again?"

Emma just laughed and leaned against the fender of her bright red Mini.

"Thank goodness we're not too far back," she said. "Number fifteen puts us right about in the middle of the pack, and George and Tess are just ahead," she continued, referring to the friendly older couple they'd met the night before.

"Yes," Val agreed. "The middle of the group is a good spot to be."

She'd been surprised at the number of cars that had signed up for the rally, and the foundation had had to put a cap on it of forty. However, a lot of classic-car owners who hadn't been able to sign on had been encouraged to bring their cars out anyway and display them for the pub-

lic. David had told her he hoped it would encourage even
more people to come out and see the vehicles and hopefully sign up as donors or give blood at the same time.

Val looked around, realized she was searching the
crowd for David, and couldn't get herself to stop. To one
side the celebrity drivers, news anchor Ryan Winterhauer
and comedian and documentary presenter Kaitlin Proctor, were holding court beside their Rover P4, signing au-
tographs and posing for pictures.

Val and Emma had been briefly introduced to them the
night before at the drivers' meeting, since the producers
were running around, trying to line up times for interviews. It had been decided that on the leg out of Newcastle
upon Tyne, Val would navigate for Kaitlin and be interviewed, while Ryan would navigate for Emma.

"Lovely to meet you," Kaitlin had said, her sharp blue
eyes darting about the room, giving the impression she was
looking for something or someone, her dangly earrings
twinkling in the lights. "I'm sure we'll have a grand time."

When she'd strolled away, long, thin legs eating up the
ground, her bum swinging like a church bell, and headed
straight for David, Val had her answer. And when his dark
head had dipped to hers and Kaitlin ran one of her earrings through her fingers, the rush of jealousy had taken
Val by surprise.

And she'd despised herself for it.

David had been in full-on Dr. Kennedy mode: cool,
calm, and collected man-about-town. Looking at him, it
had been hard to reconcile that image with the intensely
passionate man who'd knelt between her thighs in the
moonlit gazebo and made her cry out in pleasure.

As though hearing her thoughts, he'd looked right at
her, and Val had had to turn away so he wouldn't see the
blush staining her cheeks.

Despite her thinking she wouldn't hear from him again,

he'd called almost every night since the Saturday before. And although each time she hung up she told herself it was time to call a halt to their relationship, she'd somehow never got around to telling David.

Which was entirely unlike her usual straightforward approach to life.

Somehow she'd convinced herself they could carry on a little bit longer—that the twin specters of someone finding out about them and her having MS weren't yet urgent.

"Are you all right?" Emma asked, startling Val out of her musings.

"Of course. Why do you ask?"

"You were rubbing your arm and clenching and unclenching your fingers. Did you hurt yourself?"

She hadn't even been aware of doing it, and a cold stab of fear went through her stomach. But somehow, she was able to smile in the face of Emma's probing look and her own fear to say, "Oh, I took a fall last weekend, and I've been a little sore."

Thankfully, just then, there was a stir, and the crowd nearest to the building started to clap and then laugh. Val saw why, when David and a blond, younger man she recognized as his son Josh stepped up onto the stage. They were both dressed in full eveningwear, but from a bygone era, complete with top hats, satin capes, and canes. They were even carrying champagne glasses in their hands.

Then she saw Griff and sputtered with laughter. He too was wearing a cape and white tie. The only thing missing was the hat, which probably wouldn't have stayed on anyway.

"Ooh, those sneaks," Emma muttered. "I'd begun to think we were the only ones dressing up, but they've definitely stolen our thunder. Even the dog looks like a swell from one of those black-and-white musicals."

"I wonder if he'll be lounging in the back of their Daimler, drinking champagne?"

Emma laughed. "Well, since he's the only one who doesn't have any work to do, I don't see why not."

David made a quick, pithy speech, welcoming everyone, reiterating the importance of the message, and thanking the volunteers, then started his wrap-up.

"The organizers already have all our cars nicely lined up and in about ten minutes will start to distribute the rally sheets. Navs, remember to check the gimmick list of things to look for and photograph, and submit them at the end of each day to the email address at the top of the sheet. The contestants who find the most will be entered into a special prize-draw at the end of the rally. Good luck, remember the rules, and stay safe.

"I now declare Rally Round officially started!"

There were cheers, and a piper started playing what was, for the bagpipes, a jolly tune, as the contestants closest to the front of the line of cars began to move toward their vehicles. David and Josh got down from the stage and, to Val's surprise, started coming their way, hindered by people wanting to shake hands or take a quick snap.

"I'm going to run to the ladies'," Emma said, to Val's surprise, since they'd both gone not that long before.

"We have at least twenty-five minutes before we start," she said. "Don't you want to wait?"

But Emma was already on the move and just waved.

Val braced herself, as David and Josh came closer, putting on as bland a face as she could, even though just watching David walk was enough to make her heart race. He had a kind of smooth grace to his movements that reminded her very much of how he performed in bed, and the memories were enough to make her melt.

They were close enough that Griff recognized her and

started prancing, tugging Josh along after him as he rushed to greet Val.

"Hello," she said, stooping down to hug him and having to avoid getting her face washed. "Aren't you dapper today?"

"Valerie." There was that laconic tone, but when she looked up his gaze was anything but lazy or cool. "How are you?"

"Very well, thank you," she said, trying for a similar intonation, as she straightened, feeling at a disadvantage stooped down in front of him. "And you?"

"The same. I don't think you've met my son. Josh, this is Mrs. Sterling. She's transplant-recipient coordinator at St. Agnes, in Liverpool. Val, my son, Dr. Josh Kennedy."

Josh grinned as he shook her hand. "Just Josh, Mrs. Sterling. There's only room for one Dr. Kennedy in this race, don't you think?"

She couldn't help smiling as she agreed. "Besides, you wouldn't want the responsibility that comes with the name here, would you?"

"No, I wouldn't," he replied with great emphasis, then said, "Dad, I'm going to take Griff for one last potty run before we head out."

"Thank you, son."

And before she was ready to be alone with David, even in such a crowd, it was just the two of them. He moved fractionally closer, and Val had to stop herself from reaching out to touch him, the craving making her knees weak.

"I've missed you," he said, his voice a low growl, all coolness disappearing, as though it had never been there. "Come to my room tonight."

"David…"

He held up his hand, stopping her refusal before it could even be properly formed.

"I've had to make alternate arrangements for my accommodation, because of Griff. I'm nowhere near the hotels where the rest of the competitors will be. No one—"

It was her turn to stop him, and she had to look away too, because she knew anyone with any sense would probably see the way she looked at him and realize she was crazy for him.

"Send me the address, and I'll see what happens. But Emma and I have adjoining rooms, so there's no guarantee I'll be able to slip away."

The five-minute warning horn blew, and she risked a glance at his face in time to see him nod and the mask come down over his expression again.

"See you later," was all he said, before he was striding off toward the start line, where the Daimler waited.

And thankfully she had enough time to get her breathing under control before Emma came back.

"All ready," Emma said, sounding a little breathless.

"Me too," Val replied, absently, watching Kaitlin Proctor walk back toward her car. She'd passed Val, trailing a camera operator, not long after David walked away, following in his path. "Did you bring those beads and jewelry findings you said you were going to?"

"I did," Emma said. "Why?"

"I want to make a pair of dangly earrings," Val replied. "Will you help me?"

Emma's eyebrows went up, but all she said was, "Sure. We'll do it during lunch, since I promised to have dinner with George and Tess tonight."

"Perfect," Val said as her heart gave a little leap.

Maybe she could get away to meet David after all.

The first day of the rally took them out of Edinburgh by a slightly circuitous route, then west for a short run, and south to Carlisle through Gretna Green.

David had been pleased with Josh's navigational skills

and the fact his son had deciphered all of the gimmick clues on this leg: Arthur's Seat, dyed sheep at Bathgate, the Famous Blacksmiths Shop at Gretna Green, and a fragment of Hadrian's Wall being the most memorable. Each time they'd stopped to take the picture, they'd taken turns posing in the shot, many of which had a blurry Griff cutting a caper in them as well.

The members of the car club that had put them together had done a great job, but David had to remind himself not to say anything to Josh about the clues he remembered. His conscientious nature made him want Josh to figure them all out on his own.

Since they were the first car out, they were also the first into Carlisle, but David was pleased to see the turnout of other classic vehicles and people at the venue.

Carlisle was one of the smaller overnight stops, but even in those less populated urban areas, local hospitals, charities, and blood-collection services had set up all-day awareness events. The GDK Foundation support of those smaller events had been one of the many complaints Malcolm and his fellow malcontents had put forward, but David was proud of the wide support for the venture.

If it meant spending money to make them all a success, in his mind it was worth it.

Parking the Daimler, he took Griff for a potty walk in a convenient spot, doffing his hat to anyone who gave him funny looks.

He rolled his shoulders and stifled a yawn. The last week had been crazy, and he hadn't been sleeping well. In fact, he hadn't had a proper night's sleep since last Saturday, when he'd spent the night in Val's bed.

There was something going on with her, and he didn't know what exactly. There had been times, as they spoke on the phone, when he'd heard a strange note in her voice, but when he asked her if anything was wrong, she denied it.

If she weren't such a straightforward woman, he'd think she was lying.

Georgie had been like that too. No whining or complaining about every little thing, but a workmanlike ability to just get on with things, no matter what.

His stomach roiled at the thought, and he froze for a moment.

It was that trait that had led him to feel comfortable leaving Georgie at home alone the day she died, when she'd told him it was 'just a headache' and he should go to his all-day meeting.

Yet, it would be silly to compare the situations. Whatever was bothering Val could be anything and nothing to do with him at all. That didn't preclude him from wanting to know and trying to help her, if he could.

He'd asked if she'd be meeting her son in Newcastle, but up until then she still hadn't been sure, and he got the impression she didn't want to talk about it so let it drop. She was, he realized, very private, as well as having an exceptionally independent spirit. Not the type of person one pressed for information.

He knew that well, since he'd learned to keep his business to himself too. Or, as his mum used to say, "A closed mouth catches no flies."

Griff had finished doing his business and was nosing about in the grass. While David cleaned up after him, he chuckled, thinking how silly he must look, dressed in old-fashioned evening wear, picking up doggy poop. Once that chore was done, he checked his watch.

If they'd followed the directions and hadn't got lost or turned around, Val and Emma should be coming into the final checkpoint of the day any minute now.

As a few drops of rain pattered around him, he started back toward the hall where the booths had been set up, steeling himself for the meet and greet ahead. Josh came out the door just as David tossed the baggie in the garbage receptacle outside the main door, and the rain started coming down harder.

"There you are, Dad. I was beginning to think you and Griff had taken off in a swirl of your capes." Instead of holding the door open, Josh stepped out to stand under the small portico.

David chuckled, calling Griff to him, so as to get the pup out of the rain. He wasn't looking forward to sleeping in the room imbued with the scent of wet dog.

"You know Griff. He had to sniff the entire patch of grass before finding the perfect spot." He hovered by the door, glancing back into the parking lot. A fair number of cars had already come in, but there was no sign of the red Mini. "I was lucky he got done before the rain came down."

Just as he was thinking it was ridiculous to be lingering outside, he heard the unmistakable sound of a Mini's engine and glanced over his shoulder, relaxing as he recognized the car.

"I'm going in," Josh said abruptly. "Are you coming?"

"In a minute." Moved to honesty, he said, "I'm exhausted and dreading the meet and greet. I just want a few more minutes to decompress."

Josh gave him a sympathetic look but didn't offer to stay. Instead, he said, "Give Griff to me, and I'll get the schmoozing started for you."

David smiled. "Thanks."

Then Josh pushed through the doors, Griff in tow, and David turned to see Val and Emma dashing through the rain toward him.

Emma stopped for a moment but then went in, and he was overjoyed when Val lingered outside with him.

"Tell me something," she said abruptly. "Is there a problem between your son and Emma?"

"Why?" he asked, not to be difficult but curious as to how she'd figured it out.

"Emma seems to be avoiding him at all costs. Just now, she sat in the car, fussing over something silly, but as soon as he turned to go inside, she got out."

There was no reason for her not to know. "They were an item, a few years ago. I'm not privy to why they broke up, but I guess it wasn't particularly amicable."

Pursing her lips, Val sent a glance toward the door.

"Well, for what it's worth, I don't think she's completely over it. If she were, she wouldn't care whether she saw him or not and wouldn't avoid him."

"Hmm," he said, thinking that might make life difficult for Emma in the near future, but keeping that thought to himself. As much as he liked the young woman in question, he had more important things on his mind. "Will I see you tonight?"

Heat stained her cheeks a rosy hue, but her sea-storm eyes never wavered, as she replied, "I suspect you will."

And, suddenly, he was ready to face the rest of the afternoon.

CHAPTER SEVENTEEN

THE FOLLOWING MORNING, Val dodged questions from Emma about her looking so tired by saying she never slept really well in a strange bed, which was patently untrue but satisfied her friend.

There was no way she was going to admit she'd been in David's private suite, having wild sex until after midnight! Nor would she admit that if she had the chance, she'd be going back for more.

David's lovemaking was definitely addictive, and knowing time was probably running out on their affair, she wanted to take full advantage while she could.

Leaving Carlisle, although Newcastle upon Tyne was almost directly east, the route took them south, dipping into the Lake District before sending them northeast again.

It took all of Val's concentration to keep them on track and figure out the gimmick clues, because the closer they got to Newcastle, the more antsy she got.

She'd called Liam several times over the last couple of weeks, but he hadn't picked up the phone, finally forcing her to leave him a message, telling him she'd be in the city and would love to see him.

He hadn't responded.

If it hadn't been for seeing him posting on social media, she'd have been a lot more worried. As it was, she just had to accept he needed more time before he'd be willing to patch up their relationship.

His brother leaving home and then his grandmother's death had been hard on him. He'd never really settled in the village outside of Glasgow where they'd moved to take care of his grandmother. Originally, Val had thought to move her mum into the house in Newcastle where she and Des had lived. But once Des had put his foot down and issued his ultimatum, it had been easier to take the boys and move into Mum's cottage.

It had turned out to be a great choice for Val but far more difficult for her boys. When, after his gran died, Liam declared his intention to move back to Newcastle, Val had been devastated and left feeling like a failure.

With a bit of time and distance, she was inclined to think it might have been the best thing for her son. They'd both been grieving, in very different ways. He'd withdrawn, while she'd thrown herself into tying up her mum's affairs, preparing the cottage for sale, and searching for a new job. Surrounding herself with lists and tasks and motion when, now she thought, all Liam probably wanted was some peace and quiet and the ability not to have to be in her whirlwind.

He wasn't to know that storm had calmed. Hopefully, she thought, one day she'd be able to show him it had, and they could start to repair the holes in their relationship.

Until he was ready, though, she wouldn't force it.

As they drove into Newcastle, Emma said, "I'm starving. Those sandwiches and crisps they handed out at the lunch stop just barely kept me going, and I need something more filling before manning the booth."

Val nodded as she wrote up the last of her notes, before getting out at the designated spot and going to the marshal's tent to sign them in and submit their time sheet. As the marshal commended them on their almost flawless run, Val made a mental note to congratulate Emma on her driving. For someone who'd never run a rally before, she was doing marvelously.

As she was walking back to where Emma had parked, she could see a crowd standing near the door to the convention center and hear a band playing just outside the entrance. Unfortunately, she couldn't see what was going on, but as Emma came to join her and they moved that way, she suddenly heard a familiar voice calling, "Mum!"

Spinning around, she was already smiling with tears in her eyes, as her son picked her up and gave her a huge bear hug.

"Liam!"

When David and Josh had reached Newcastle, they'd been greeted by the mayor and a band, neither of which was expected. And while Josh took Griff off to do his business, making sure the pup didn't pee on the mayor's leg, David had found himself—as Josh called it—schmoozing.

David was quite sure he'd gotten that expression from his grandmother, since it sounded like a word Cerise would use.

It was while he was taking a turn around the conference center with His Worship the Mayor that he saw Val with a young man who could only be her son and had to stare.

He'd never seen her so radiantly happy.

She was glowing, her smile so wide as they walked along, arm in arm, that David was dazzled and had to look away so as to be able to concentrate on what was being said around him. Then the mayor insisted on David joining him for lunch, which, as these things often did, stretched far into the afternoon, so that he missed the entire first day of the Newcastle event.

Later, when he was about to sit down to supper with

Josh, he'd gotten a call from a GDK director, warning him Malcolm was up to his old tricks.

"The numbers have started coming in regarding new donor sign-ups, and he's already saying turnout is below the expected rate and the foundation will suffer irreparable harm."

"We've run two days," David replied. "And had three sign-up events. What kind of miracles would satisfy him?"

And while the director had sympathized, she'd also cautioned that David should tread carefully.

"He might not be popular or well-liked, but Malcolm is well-respected."

The call, on top of everything else the day had brought, had raised his stress levels exponentially.

The one bright spot in his evening had been a talk with his mother, who said she was planning a trip to England and would let him know as soon as the dates were finalized.

He might be fifty years old, but age hadn't dimmed the bond. Only misunderstanding and intolerance had, and he was determined to make it right.

After loading the pictures submitted by competitors and bystanders via email to the foundation webpage set up to chronicle the race, he sat back and rubbed his eyes. Earlier in the day he'd sent Val the address of the house where he was staying. Now, he really wanted to call, just to see how she was doing, but hesitated to disturb her, in case she was with her son.

Was it ridiculous to be disappointed that she hadn't invited him to meet Liam? Her imposed secrecy about their relationship was really beginning to chafe. Not being able to be with her in public, having to hide their relationship, was no longer as acceptable to him as it had been at the beginning. Surely she realized they were past that stage now?

But whenever he suggested going out together, to eat

or anything else, she refused. It made him wonder where their relationship was going—if anywhere.

Shaking that thought off and refusing to dwell on it, he called to Griff and, clipping on his lead, took him out for a walk in a small, nearby green. As he was coming back, still thinking about the events of the day, his mother came back to mind, and he started singing her signature song, in a low voice so as not to disturb the neighbors.

As he turned into the path leading to the cottage, Griff gave a delighted woof and took off toward the door. Taken by surprise, David had the leash jerked from his hand and made a grab for it, but it was too late. Griff was already capering around Val, jumping, trying to lick her face, as she laughed and fended him off.

"Down, Griff," she said, still laughing. "Down, sir." She sent David a slanting, upward glance. "You know, if the medical career doesn't work out for you, you could always take up singing. You have a nice voice."

Bending, David snagged the leash, saying, "I didn't expect you."

Her laughter faded, and she gave him a long, searching look. "Is my being here inconvenient?"

"Not at all." God, he sounded stiff, even to his own ears. Opening the door, he waved her through. "Please, come in."

"Are you sure this is a good time?" she asked, as she preceded him inside.

"I am. And I'm sorry I sound surly. This hasn't been the best of days. Although I think it's safe to say it was a truly excellent one for you."

Her face lit up again, and she laughed. "You saw?"

"I did," he replied, unable to resist touching her, even if it was just to take her by the wrist and lead her over to the couch so they could sit side by side. "Just for a brief moment, before the mayor dragged me away for an overly long and hardly digestible lunch."

"I was hoping to introduce you to each other, but I didn't see you. He'll be back tomorrow, though, and he's promised to help at one of the tables. I was surprised at how much he knew about what we were doing. I guess when he heard I was driving in the rally, he took an interest."

Before he could answer, his phone rang, and he sighed. "Excuse me for a moment?"

She nodded, but some of the light in her eyes dimmed.

When he identified himself, a male voice said, "Dr. Kennedy, this is Dr. Hiroshi, from Synthe Laboratories."

"Yes, Dr. Hiroshi. What can I do for you?"

"I wanted to tell you that there is a potential match for one of your patients, Mr. Swelo Mdele. Of course, further testing will have to be done to confirm if they are truly compatible, but I saw the notice of urgency on the file and wanted to inform you right away."

David's heart rate had picked up at the name of his most ill patient, and he felt his stomach twist. "That's excellent news. Can you tell me where in the country the sample came from?"

"Edinburgh."

That was surprising. "Please send the information to the doctor of record as soon as possible, so the additional testing can begin immediately."

"I will, as soon as we hang up, but as you were listed as the consultant on the case, I wanted to contact you first."

"Thank you," he replied, keeping his voice level and professional, while inside he was yelling like a twelve-year-old boy at a drag race. "I appreciate it."

As soon as he hung up, he punched the air. "Yes!"

"What happened?" Val was watching him, amused.

"That desperately ill patient I told you about? There may be a match, out of Edinburgh, of all places."

"Oh, David, that's marvelous."

"It is. But even better, I can use this to show the board Rally Round is already showing signs of success."

She hesitated, then said, "Be careful that you're not placing too much store in this. You still have the HLA testing to do, as well as—"

"I know, but this will, at the very least, get Malcolm off my back and make it harder for him to have me voted out as CEO."

The look she gave him was long and level and made him frown.

"I know you're happy about it, and I don't blame you," she said slowly, one hand closing and opening rhythmically. "I'm just worried that if the match isn't viable after all, you'll be in a worse position than you are now."

He felt it then—that soul-deep fear of things potentially slipping from his fingers—although, in the moment, he wasn't sure what it was he feared losing. He needed her to see. To understand what it meant to him.

"I made a promise when I created GDK, to make it the best it could be and help as many people as it could. When I make a commitment, I see it through to the end, and no matter what Malcolm or anyone else wants, that's what I plan to do."

She nodded, but there was something in her eyes that made a cold ball form in his stomach.

"Yes. I can see you doing just that, whether it's good for you or not."

He tried to parse out her words, could make no sense of them.

"What do you mean by that?"

She shook her head, a smile tipping the corners of her mouth, but it looked almost sad.

"I just mean that you're a fine, decent man. And that's one of the things I admire about you the most."

Then she leaned close and kissed him, as though to stop whatever he was planning to say from leaving his lips.

He let her have her way for a few moments and then broke away, knowing there was more to her words than she'd actually said.

"Tell me," he demanded.

But she just shook her head and reached for the side zipper of her dress, pulling it down to bare the smooth skin beneath.

"No more words, tonight," she replied, and her smile seemed to wobble, just a bit. "I don't want to talk anymore."

And when she slipped off her dress, then straddled his lap, David agreed whatever still had to be said could wait.

Making love with Val couldn't.

CHAPTER EIGHTEEN

VAL AWOKE THE morning of the second day in Newcastle heavy-eyed and inclined to stay in bed. Only the knowledge that Liam was coming back to spend the day with her at the convention center had her getting up.

She couldn't stomach breakfast, though, her insides roiling with the knowledge of what she had to do.

It had come to her the night before, when she heard David talk about commitment and his drive to fulfill promises made.

That was exactly the type of man he was—dedicated and focused on doing the right thing—and his being that way was exactly why she couldn't keep seeing him after the rally.

She'd woken up during the night, her hand numb and tingling, her arm aching. It had happened before, and she'd put it down to sleeping on it the wrong way, but last night she'd faced the truth.

There was no point in putting it off any longer. As soon as the rally was over, she had to go to the doctor, and that could mean she was about to find out she had MS.

And she had to put a stop to their affair before that happened because David was just the sort of man who would feel as though he had to stick with her, even if he really didn't want to.

Even if he didn't love her the way she was forced to admit to herself she loved him.

Putting on a happy face had never felt more difficult, but somehow she achieved it and got through the day, talking to people as they came to the transplant-info table she'd been assigned to.

Before lunchtime, she was pleased to see Liam interacting with the visitors too. He answered basic questions or referred people either to her or the doctor working with them if he didn't know the answer.

When David came over, she introduced them, but the excitement she'd felt at the thought of it happening the day before was gone, and she was glad when David was called away. She needed to distance herself from him, as best she could.

Emma had lunch with Val and Liam and struck up conversation with him, showing him pictures of the answers to the gimmick clues, while Val sat back and watched them chat and laugh together.

Later that evening, after Liam had gone home, as the two of them walked to a pub to get some supper, Emma said, "He's smart and a really nice lad. Do you think he'll go into medicine?"

If anyone had asked her that question a year ago, or even two, she'd have said no way, but now she just shrugged and said, "I don't know. He might, and I rather wish he would. He has the brains for it."

David had texted to say he had to meet with local dignitaries that evening and wasn't sure how late he'd be getting back to his room. Sad to miss even one night with him, with their time together so short, she'd also been somewhat relieved. It gave her a bit more time to gather her composure—and figure out what to say—before seeing him again.

The next morning, one of the documentary producers

came to get Val for her stint navigating for Kaitlyn Proctor, who turned out to be the type who complained most of the time. A strange way for a comedian to behave, Val thought, but she suspected no one could spend their entire time smiling and joking.

"Who the hell came up with this route? Are you sure we're going the right way?" she groused as Val called out the turns.

"Yes," Val replied, trying to keep her growing annoyance out of her voice.

"This will have us ending up in the Pennines, which is just stupid. Probably some more of that gimmick nonsense," Kaitlyn grumbled. "Make sure you get the pictures when they come up."

"You'll have to slow down for that," she said mildly. "As it is, you're going too fast for the route instructions."

"Once we start filming, I'll slow down," Kaitlyn said, her lips tightening, as if even though Val was the navigator, she really didn't want any instruction from the passenger seat.

Then, when the camera came on, she was suddenly a completely different person.

Warm. Charming. Funny.

Val couldn't help comparing it to the two main facets of David's personality, except, of course, his was the opposite. To the world at large he was cool and distant, while to those he knew well, he was caring, lovable, passionate.

Val's interview seemed to go well, as she explained what she did at the hospital, spoke generally about the importance of transplantation, and gave some insight into how things had improved over the years.

Although having a hard time concentrating on the instructions, gimmick list, and interview questions all at once, somehow she got it done. Perry, the cameraman in the back seat, stopped filming.

"So what's your relationship with David Kennedy?"

Caught off guard by Kaitlyn's question, Val's brain seized for an instant, before she could gather her composure.

"The left turn is coming up quickly, and then there's a right turn immediately afterwards," she said, glad to have those additional seconds to shore up her defenses. "And to answer your question, Dr. Kennedy and I have worked together."

From the corner of her eye, she saw Kaitlyn send her a sideways glance.

"That's it, eh? I thought maybe you knew each other better than that. There seems to be a certain…electricity when you're together."

The knot that formed in her stomach actually steadied her since it short-circuited her horrible habit of blushing when startled.

"No." She gave the word no emphasis but made her voice cool, happy with how composed she sounded, although her heart was pounding.

Kaitlyn lifted her hand off the gear lever and waved it in a careless gesture.

"I just wondered, having seen you two together quite a bit. And don't get me wrong, I wouldn't blame you if you made a play for him. Not only is he gorgeous, but think of all that lovely money he inherited just waiting to be spent on things that are far more fun than transplant research."

Val bit back the words rising to her lips and checked the paperwork, not wanting to encourage the odious woman.

Kaitlyn seemed completely unconcerned and continued. "I just got rid of my fourth husband, but if I were going to make that mistake again, I'd be happy to make it with David Kennedy."

"You'd love to get your mitts on all that cash, wouldn't you, Kay?"

Perry's comment had Kaitlyn sending him a poisonous glance in the rearview mirror.

"Why not?" she asked. "His wife's been dead for twenty-plus years. If anyone's going to share in his fortune, why shouldn't it be me?" Val glanced over and intercepted another sideways glance. "Unless Mrs. Sterling wants to set the record straight and tell me he's off the market."

Val shrugged, feigning cool unconcern although she was seething inside. "I wouldn't know anything about Dr. Kennedy's status. Perhaps it's best to ask him?"

Kaitlyn laughed, the sound grating and unpleasant. "Maybe I will...later."

And thankfully they came to a gimmick clue, which meant filming for a few minutes and taking the requisite pictures, and by the time they got back into the car the subject was changed.

But Val was left with a sick feeling, deep inside.

She'd come to the decision to stop seeing him by the end of the rally, but apparently, she and David didn't have that time left. If someone like Kaitlyn Proctor had noticed the connection between them, it was time to end it, completely, before anyone else did.

Thankfully, they were to switch back to their original driving partners at the lunch stop, and it was a relief to bid farewell to Kaitlyn and Perry and go off to find Emma.

It took all her strength to pretend everything was fine for the rest of the day, when inside a maelstrom of emotions was battering her. By the time they got to Leeds, Val had a headache brewing but refused to give in to either the pain in her head or her heart.

There was no sign of David at the venue, and when she overheard someone saying the Lord Mayor of Leeds had taken him off somewhere, she was relieved.

Part of her just wanted to get the upcoming discussion over with, but mostly she never wanted it to happen at all.

When his text inviting her over that evening popped up while they were packing up the booth, her heart turned over, and ice trickled down her spine. Taking a deep breath, she replied she'd be by in about an hour, but her hands were shaking, making it hard to thumb in the letters on her phone. And it felt like the longest, most difficult hour of her life, as her feelings ran amok and tension wound her tighter and tighter.

By the time she found her way to his rental apartment, her brain had shut down her emotional center, so it felt as if she were underwater.

He noticed as soon as she walked in, and she could feel his gaze on her as she bent to pet Griff, who whined gently and nudged her thigh, as if sensing that something was amiss.

"What is it?" he asked, in his forthright way. "What's happened?"

Her knees were shaking, so she eased past Griff to perch on the edge of a handy chair. The pup followed and placed his head in her lap.

"Kaitlyn Proctor knows there's something going on between us."

David relaxed, his shoulders dropped slightly, and he smiled, although his gaze remained watchful.

"Well, someone was bound to realize at some point. I think it means we should preempt any rumors and go public ourselves."

Val shook her head. "I don't. I think we should stop seeing each other."

David froze, just for an instant, then said, "That's a little drastic for the situation, don't you think?"

"No." She'd thought it through carefully—knew what she planned to say, so he wouldn't glean the truth. "Perhaps it seems that way to *you*, but for me it's the only solution. You're used to being a public figure, but I'm not. I have no interest in having my life put under a microscope, being dissected for other people's entertainment."

He took a step closer, then looked around, as though disoriented, before sinking down onto the couch. "Val, it's not as bad as all that. And everything I do is to help the foundation. To move it forward. I've worked too hard to make it a success and can't give it up, not even for you."

"I'm not asking you to." It was his Achilles' heel—this wonderful organization he'd built out of his pain and grief—and she felt guilty for using it this way. But she had to keep his attention focused there so he wouldn't ask questions she didn't want to answer. "I'm just saying that, while you wouldn't suffer from us being seen together, my life would be turned upside down."

"I don't see how."

He'd retreated into the cool, lazy tone she'd come to recognize—and despise—but this time she was glad of it, hoping it meant he accepted her words at face value.

"No one will be casting aspersions on you, but I'll be the gold digger, the mantrap. I'll be the subject of speculation and nasty rhetoric, both at work and in my private life."

"I don't think you're a gold digger. Doesn't my opinion outweigh everyone else's?"

"In a perfect world, of course it would, but this world is far from perfect, isn't it?" She held up her hand to stop him interrupting. "Not even a perfect world, but just the ordinary world, like the one I'm used to rather than the rarified one you live in. In that world, no one would give a damn who I was seeing, but in *this* world, I'll be stalked and talked about, especially after we inevitably break up."

He leaned back, and something hot and angry gleamed in his eyes.

"So you'll run away rather than give us a chance, just because of what people will say? Just because the work I do means I have to be in the spotlight and you don't like the glare? I thought maybe we'd gone beyond that—that we had further to go, together. I—"

He hesitated, then fell silent, his gaze hooded, not in desire now but as a shield. Val felt the barrier she'd built around her emotions cracking, and she knew she'd have to finish this and get away, before it broke completely.

"David." She made her voice firm and brisk, although it was one of the most difficult things she'd ever done. "We both know this wasn't meant to last. Why put myself through hell for a passing fancy? You have your life and your devotion to the foundation, and I have my own quiet, happy existence. Let's just agree to keep them separate, completely."

He could never know that she'd go through all of it, every ring of hell, to stay with him, but the pain once again radiating down her arm reminded her of just why she couldn't dare.

So she gave Griff one last scratch behind his pricked ear and stood up.

"Good-bye, David. I wish you well."

And although she told herself not to be surprised or hurt, she still was when all he said in return was, "Good-bye," as though it meant nothing at all to him that she was walking out of his life.

CHAPTER NINETEEN

DAVID SPENT THE rest of the evening and long into the night trying to come to terms with the implosion of his relationship with Val but could make little sense of it. Angry—hurt beyond belief—he tried to rationalize what she'd said, but everything was a jumble in his head.

She'd been completely clear, and although it hurt to admit it, he knew what she'd said was the truth.

There could be no reconciliation between his life and the one she wanted. Not when he'd invested everything he had and was into the foundation. When GDK stood as a tangible monument to what good he'd been able to do in his life, as well as offering him redemption for the things he'd messed up. Giving it up—any of it—was unthinkable.

And her privacy, so highly valued, would disappear in his world.

Even just a month ago, had a woman he'd seen a handful of times said she didn't want to continue with their relationship, he wouldn't have cared. Yet, when Val told him her decision, he'd wanted to beg for another chance, tell her anything she wanted to hear, just to get her to stay.

He'd almost told her he loved her but had bitten the words back.

Why make himself even more ridiculous in the face of her surety?

In the deepest recesses of his heart, he knew he'd do

anything in his power to protect her from harm and to make right whatever wrongs she encountered through association with him. Just how he'd do so, he had no idea, but still it hurt that she didn't see that.

After a restless night, he put on a smiling face for Josh, and they made the run into Manchester, surprisingly without incident. For the first time he was glad to be in the first car, since once he'd taken care of Griff, he could plunge right in to being Dr. David Kennedy, CEO of GDK.

Somehow, for the first time in fifteen years, the mask didn't quite fit the way it usually did but felt askew.

Making his way around the room, he saw Emma but not Val and wondered if asking for her would be too obvious. He was still feeling too raw and hurt so he didn't, and he spent another restless night wondering how she was, and if she'd contact him or speak to him if he called.

It was juvenile, but there was nothing he could do to stop.

The following day she was at the information event in the morning, looking as wan and brittle as David felt, but she disappeared after lunch. Unable to take it anymore, he circled the room as casually as he could, until he was at the table Emma was manning. When she looked up and smiled, he tried to smile back but obviously didn't achieved a natural expression, as Emma sent him a sympathetic look.

His stomach clenched, but he relaxed as she said, "Poor David. You look absolutely exhausted, but it must be satisfying to see how well things are going."

"It is," he replied, trying to sound enthusiastic. "Your nav's skived off, has she?"

Emma shook her head, the corners of her lips turning down. "I sent her to rest. I've been worried about her for the last few days. She hasn't been herself."

"Oh?" He tried not to sound too interested, but his pulse rate kicked up. "What's been happening?"

Emma's frown deepened, as her brows contracted, causing lines above her nose. "I'm not sure. She's so private and independent she won't say, but I've caught her rubbing her arm periodically and clenching and relaxing her fingers as though they're numb. Then the last couple of days she's just seemed... I don't know...off."

Before he could ask anything more, he felt a touch on his shoulder and turned to find the journalist, Ryan Winterhauer, standing beside him.

"Can I have a word?" he asked after they'd exchanged greetings and he'd apologized for interrupting.

He led David off to one side, away from the crowd, where they wouldn't be easily overheard.

"Listen, I don't know if you've already been told, but there's a rumor going around about impropriety regarding the reports being issued by the foundation. Something about falsifying of numbers of attendees, sign-ups, and matches being made."

Stunned, David stared for a moment, an icy chasm opening up in his belly.

"What?"

Ryan nodded, pulling David farther back from the crowd.

"My producer just called to tell me and to ask my opinion on the report. I told her I thought it was hogwash. Attendance has been phenomenal, and while I've been working the kidney-disease info booth, we've had so many people sign up and give blood samples the lab's been hard-pressed to keep up. But is there anything you can tell me about a patient who was told there was a match, but it turned out not to be viable?"

Anger—red-hot and explosive—chased the chill from David's skin, and it took everything he had inside not to curse out loud. He had no doubt this was Malcolm, up to his old tricks, trying to put an end to the rally and wrest control of the foundation from David's hands.

But he'd gone too far this time, and he might very well end up destroying GDK entirely.

"I can't comment on the last point, but I can say no doctor, in my experience, tells a patient about a match until absolutely sure it's viable, so if that occurred, it must have been from an outside source." He reached for his phone, as he continued. "Excuse me, will you? I need to figure out what's going on before this gets out of hand."

"Of course. Let me know if you figure it out, will you?"

"If I can. But thank you for giving me the heads-up."

He was already outside the door talking to Rolly when what Emma had said about Val floated from the back of his mind to the forefront, and the pieces of the puzzle fell into place.

"I'll need to call you back," he said, cutting his PA off midsentence. "If you find out anything, let me know, but there's something I have to do."

Then he was heading back inside to find Emma.

Val heard the knock on her door and pulled herself off the bed to go see who it was. Seeing David standing in the corridor had her stepping back, as though perhaps he'd burst through the door.

Impossible to catch her breath or to subdue the wild rush of color to her face, and she considered not answering. But then he knocked again, harder this time, and she instinctively knew he didn't intend to stop until she let him in.

Inhaling as best she could, she held the air in her lungs for a moment before opening the door. He strode past her, then turned, and the stern expression on his face, the almost-feral glint in his eyes, made her legs weak.

"What are you doing here, David?" She wished she

didn't feel so off-kilter—heart pounding, her palms sweating, untamable emotions rampaging through her system. It made her voice quaver, just when she needed it to be firm and decisive.

"You think you have MS, don't you?" It wasn't really a question but a statement, fierce and forthright. "And you didn't want me to know."

The air left her lungs, and the blood rushed from her head, making her dizzy. "What?" she finally gasped, still trying to maintain the lie, not wanting to have this conversation. "What?"

"The way you've been rubbing your arm, bending and flexing your fingers." He held up his hand, making a fist then opening it again, twice. "You're worried that what you're feeling are symptoms of MS."

She somehow made it to the bed, just before her legs gave out on her. "You don't know what you're talking about."

But her voice was weak—shaky—and she despised herself for it.

"I'm a doctor, Val, and although neurology isn't my specialty, I know MS can be genetic, and you told me your mother died from it. It's not hard to put two and two together."

He'd retreated into that cold, lazy way of talking, trying to mask his anger, and it sparked an answering ire in her.

"What difference does it make?" There. Now she sounded more like herself, and the heat firing out from her chest gave her much-needed strength. "You can think what you want, but it's still over between us, David."

He stepped back, as though her words physically struck him.

"Why? Because you don't want me to be around if you have MS? Or you think I wouldn't love you—take care of you—no matter what?"

You love me?

The words almost came out, but she pushed them back, not wanting to acknowledge them. In fact, after the first rush of pleasure, they made her angrier.

"No! Because I know you would, even if you didn't really want to. Because I refuse to become another project you take up and see through to the end."

She tried to keep her voice cool, controlled, but she couldn't. Not with every nerve in her body on fire with rage, and anguish, and the kind of love she'd never thought she'd find.

"Do you know what my mother said to me, when she was dying? She said, 'I'm so sorry you have to tend to me this way, Val, but I'm glad your dad isn't here to be burdened with me—to have to take care of me.' And I knew what she meant, David. I'm a nurse, and looking after her, seeing her like that, was the hardest thing I've ever done in my life. I'm *not* putting anyone I care about through that."

"Even if they want to be there for you? Even if *not* being there would be worse than taking care of you?"

"I don't want you." The rage built inside her, overtaking her, pouring out through the hateful, hurtful words. "I don't need you to take care of me. I don't need anyone. Just go away, David, and stop playing the noble knight intent on saving the helpless maiden who is actually neither helpless nor in need of saving."

For a long moment the only sound in the room was the rasp of her breath sawing in and out of her throat, but the sound of her heart pounding in her ears almost drowned it out.

Why won't he leave?

She wanted him to go because the anger that had sustained her was fading, fast, and if he stayed much longer she'd break down. Just dissolve into a crying mess, which was the last thing she wanted him to see.

Taking matters into her own hands, she heaved up off the bed and marched to the door. Flinging it open she stood there, silent, her chin up, daring him to say another word.

He didn't. Instead, he shook his head, his expression morphing from anger through pain to disbelief.

Then he left, and Val could let loose the tears of pain and loss she'd refused to shed in front of him.

Next morning, Val made sure to get to the venue just before the start of the day to avoid seeing David. Emma gave her a long, searching look, but Val didn't have the kind of personality that allowed self-indulgence for long. So thankfully, although she hadn't slept much, there was no evidence of her crying the afternoon before.

"Feeling a bit better?" Emma asked, as they prepared for the next leg of the race.

"I am," Val lied. "I think I'm getting too old to be running rallies. It's completely messed up my sleep habits."

Emma snorted. "Sure, you are. You run rings around half of the younger volunteers, so try that line on someone else. Did David stop by to see you yesterday?"

Luckily, as she asked the question, the marshal waved them forward, and Emma had to concentrate on her driving, so she didn't see Val's instinctive reaction. So that's how he'd known where to find her.

"He did," she said mildly, having got herself under control. "Nice of him to check on me."

"I thought so too. By the way, I think there's some problems back in London, although I don't know exactly what kind. I heard a rumor that David's heading back to headquarters as soon as he gets to Birmingham."

Not wanting to hear anything more about David just then, Val changed the subject to the list of clues, and that discussion lasted until it was their time to start out.

Being mentally distracted, Val missed a clue, and they

circled back quickly to take the requisite picture since, as Emma pointed out, they were on track to a perfect record. As they started off again, the Mini gave a cough and a buck, and Emma cursed under her breath.

"It's probably the gas line," she said. "Hopefully it'll get us to Birmingham."

Val half hoped it would break down, allowing her to go home rather than face seeing David every day for the next eight days, but knowing how keen Emma was to finish the race, she kept quiet.

But although it sputtered a few more times, they made it into the city before it decided to give up the ghost.

"I'm going to stop here, rather than try for the official parking area," Emma said, once they got to a likely spot, pulling the Mini over and out of the way of the other vehicles.

They both got out, and Emma was releasing the catch on the bonnet when a local news crew ran over to them, the reporter asking questions before he was even alongside them. Clearly annoyed, Emma waved him and his cameraman away, and Val stepped back, trying to get out of their path.

And then there was the sickening sensation of falling, and everything went dark.

CHAPTER TWENTY

DAVID MADE IT to the station in Birmingham just in time to catch the train that would get him into London in time for the emergency board meeting and dropped into his seat with a sigh.

Malcolm had finally had his way, and the night before David had got the notice for the meeting, giving him enough time to do some investigating as well as put out as many fires as he could. He'd had to call in favors from participating groups, asking them to forward all possible data, then get staff to work overtime, collating all they'd received, to prove there was no falsifying of numbers.

Someone had also leaked information anonymously about the Edinburgh match for Mr. Mdele, although thankfully not mentioning his name. They'd made it sound as though it had been touted to the patient as a certainty when it actually wasn't a good match at all. Just finding out the match was no longer considered viable was a blow. Having that fact plastered all over the newspapers and in the electronic media was almost as bad.

His main focus should have been on ensuring the survival of GDK, even if it meant sacrificing Rally Round, but his last encounter with Val insisted on intruding. Even now, while he knew he should be concentrating fully on the upcoming meeting, it was Val who invaded his thoughts and wouldn't leave.

He'd told her he loved her, and she hadn't even acknowl-edged it—perhaps didn't even believe it—but it was true, and he refused to believe there was nothing to be done to get her back.

She was the first—the only—woman who'd made him truly feel since Georgie died.

Brave, proud, independent Val, who'd rather face the specter of a degenerative disease on her own than lean on anyone else.

Rather than lean on him.

I'm not putting anyone I care about through that.

It was only those words that gave him any hope what-soever. By admitting she cared about him, she'd left the door open, in his mind, even if it were just a sliver. It was up to him to try and figure out how to make it swing wide.

There'd also been a ring of truth to what she'd said to him the night in Leeds, about her not wanting to live in the glare of publicity that surrounded him almost daily.

At the time he'd thought she'd meant it generally, but with new insight he thought even then she'd been thinking about the MS. To be under constant scrutiny while fight-ing a disease that could cause a myriad of symptoms at any given time would be untenable.

He wouldn't want that. Not for her, and not for him-self either.

It was time to face the truth: in Val he'd found a return to normalcy that had been missing from his life for over fifteen years.

Funny now to be able to see that he'd been constantly running, constantly busy, constantly striving so as to avoid the realities of his past. That while the foundation was definitely worthwhile, he'd used it not just to do good but as a smoke screen to hide behind and a barrier to keep ev-eryone but Josh out.

Although he still believed in the foundation's mission,

meeting Val had forced him, for the first time, to examine his true role in it. No, he wasn't the barker in the carnival Malcolm accused him of being, but neither was the older man completely wrong in his assessment. His father's death had put David in the middle of a circus, and he'd picked up his top hat, tails, and whip and had fashioned himself into the ringmaster.

Now, he could finally admit it wasn't healthy. Wasn't right. No longer made him happy or fulfilled.

If it ever had.

Yes, GDK was worth saving, but wasn't his life worth saving too? And, most importantly, wasn't his relationship with Val worth everything else? Even if she ultimately rejected him, she deserved to know the truth: that what they'd found together in the moonlight was more important to him than anything.

At peace in a way he hadn't felt for more than seventeen years, he sat for a while, formulating a plan. The he took out his phone and called Val. When she didn't answer, he wasn't really surprised so he left her a message, hoping she'd call him back.

Then he made one more call, resolved to come clean so as to start anew, whether with or without Val.

Although, he hoped to God it would be with, since he didn't think he'd be whole, ever again, without her.

On the morning after the run to Birmingham, Val woke up disoriented, wondering where on earth she was—why the sounds she was hearing were so familiar and yet completely out of context.

Then she remembered.

She was in the hospital, after tripping over a cable, falling, and hitting her head. She'd been kept overnight for observation, making sure she didn't have a concussion.

As it turned out she did have a mild one, but the doctor

had reassured her she'd be released today. He'd also said she was cleared to go back to the rally if she wanted to. Luckily for her, her attending physician was a rally buff, so he knew what a TSD rally was about and that it didn't involve high speeds and crazy antics. It also helped that the next leg didn't start until the following day, so she could rest.

Sitting up in the bed, she glanced over at her phone, tempted to pick it up and listen to the recording of David saying "Please call me" again.

Yet, she didn't.

Nor did she call, as he'd asked.

She'd said all she'd meant to, and even though she loved him, she couldn't give in to the urge to backtrack and tell him she'd changed her mind.

If things were different, she'd gladly deal with the whirlwind, high-flying life he lived, although it was so far outside of her experience she'd be terrified. The cool, drawling society figure most people saw wasn't attractive to her. Instead, she yearned for the solid, gentle, passionate man she'd come to know and love.

Her moonlight lover.

Accepting that none of it was to be broke her heart and made her feel emotions she hadn't known existed inside her. He'd shattered her self-image, showing her she wasn't only the prosaic, practical, mousy woman she'd thought she was, revealing the joyful, sensual side she'd forgotten she had.

She couldn't regret knowing him, though. He'd come into her life when she was unable to see her way ahead and taken her on a lovely, fairy-tale journey at a time when she'd thought romance of any type behind her.

If nothing else, meeting David had shown her there were still adventures to be sought and had given her the strength to seek them.

"Good morning." A nurse's aide bustled in and set down a tray on the lap table.

"Good morning."

"I brought you some breakfast, and Nurse Sawyer says the doctor will be by to see you about the results of your scan first thing this morning."

"Thank you," she said, as her heart gave a kick in reaction to her words.

"Oh, you're one of the rally people, aren't you?"

"I am."

"Well, that hunky Dr. Kennedy is on TV, giving an interview about it."

Before the young woman left the room, Val had the remote in hand and the set turned on. Flipping through the channels, she found the right one, just in time to hear a journalist asking David a question.

"...out who was behind the story that cast aspersions on the validity of the rally?"

"We have, and the matter has been dealt with, which is all I can say, legally."

"So where do you go from here? Will the rally continue?"

"Of course. Everyone involved has put in too much work for us to stop. Besides, I've received statistics showing on average a twenty-five-percent increase in donor sign-ups, testing, and blood donations after only the first week. I think that makes all the work worthwhile, don't you?"

"And what about your future with the foundation, Dr. Kennedy? One of the rumors was that you would be stepping down, not just as chairman and CEO but from the board completely."

David smiled, and Val realized there was something very different about him. He looked more relaxed. More comfortable in his skin.

"I'm afraid that was wishful thinking on some people's part. I'll be remaining on the board, but in a lesser capacity."

"Can you tell us why? Are you being forced out of the leadership position?"

"No. It's a decision based on the fact I'd like to go back to a more normal life. Recently I've been reminded of what's important to me, personally—things like moonlight, and vegetable gardens, and especially the people I love. Even when things are difficult or painful, I know those people mean more to me than anything, but I can't be the man they need me to be if I put the foundation rather than my personal life first."

Val's breath stuck in her chest, as his words struck home, knowing—believing without a doubt—he was telling her he wanted to be with her, no matter what.

She watched the rest of the interview in a daze, shocked to hear him talk about those horrible years, starting with his wife dying and ending with the court case. He even talked about the pain of never knowing his father and the Dupuytren's contracture and how it had put an end to his surgical career.

It was like watching someone fling wide the doors of a previously locked closet and take everything out and then repack it one item at a time, so all the contents were visible.

By the time the interviewer thanked him and the theme music was playing, Val was crying, and she knew it was combination of fear and hope and happiness for David.

Because he'd made a fresh start, and she knew he'd be happier for it.

But listening to him talk about Georgie, and how her death had affected him, could she really take the chance of putting him through a similar situation again?

She really wasn't sure she wanted to, because she loved him.

CHAPTER TWENTY-ONE

WHEN DAVID LEFT the studio and turned his phone back on, there must have been a hundred or more messages, but none from the one person he wanted to hear from.

Val.

Maybe she hadn't seen the interview, although he'd suggested to Josh that they inform all the participants in the rally that it would be on. Or perhaps she didn't care the way he'd hoped.

He was being driven back to the station when his phone rang. His heart turned over but then settled down again when he saw it was Josh.

"Dad…" Josh's voice cracked, and David heard him clear his throat before he continued. "Dad, that was one of the bravest things I think I've ever seen anyone do."

"Thank you, son," he replied, his heart full. "I'm heading back to the train station now, so I should be in Birmingham in two and a half hours."

They chatted for a few more minutes and then rang off.

He obsessively checked his phone every two minutes all the way to the station and then on the train. Less than an hour away from Birmingham, he got a call from a number he recognized. It was St. Agnes Hospital to inform him a donor had been found for Tamika Watkiss.

"We called Mrs. Sterling, and she said she'll be on her way back as soon as she can get a train from Birmingham."

"I will be too," he said, going on to explain where he was.

As soon as he hung up with them, finally Val called.

"David?" She sounded tentative. "Did you hear from St. Agnes?"

"I did. I'm heading toward Birmingham now. Where are you?"

"I'm going online and buying my ticket to Liverpool. Should I get one for you on the same train?"

He noticed she hadn't answered his question about her location. If she wanted to play it cool, he would too, although his heart was hammering, and his palms were damp.

"Yes, as long as it doesn't leave for at least fifty minutes."

"All right. I'll see you at the station then."

He wanted to tell her he loved her, but he bit his tongue. If she didn't want to hear it, he wouldn't force the issue, even though it would break his heart all over again.

The rest of the trip into Birmingham, he was on pins and needles. Val emailed his ticket to him and told him she was on her way to the station, and he called Josh to let him know what was happening.

"I'll take care of everything, Dad. Don't worry."

And bearing in mind his new resolution to delegate more, he simply said, "Okay, son. Thanks, and let me know if you need any help with anything."

As the train drew into Birmingham, David's heart was beating so hard he felt slightly ill, and when he stepped onto the platform and saw Val waiting, he froze in fear for an instant.

Then he got closer and realized the tip of her nose was pink, and her eyelids were puffy, and he didn't know what that meant, but knew he couldn't go another step without finding out.

Stopping a foot away from her, he said, "You've been crying. Why?"

"I saw your interview. What did you mean, about moonlight and veggie patches?"

Hardly able to get his lungs to work properly, he replied, "That I love you, and I want to be with you. I needed to make sure you know you already have my heart, whether you want it or not, and that I'm yours, no matter what the future may hold, for either of us."

She didn't reply. Not with words, anyway. But since she was in his arms and kissing him as though she never wanted to stop, he didn't mind.

Not one little bit.

Then they had to make a dash for their train, but there were still things David needed to say, and once they were in their seats and had caught their breath, he took her hand.

"I don't care if you have MS. We'll deal with whatever comes, together, if you're willing. Even though I didn't realize my heart was still broken, even after all these years, you've healed it, and I love you more than I thought I could ever love again."

Her gaze was intent on his face, her eyes more blue than green just then, and so beautiful he felt their impact straight through to his soul.

"Meeting you has made me realize life, no matter how tenuous or frightening, is worth living to the fullest," she said softly. "Thankfully, I don't have MS right now, although that doesn't mean I mightn't get it later. I found out there were no lesions on my brain when they scanned it in the hospital yesterday to make sure my concussion wasn't too bad."

He leaned back to look at her, his heart suddenly faltering. "What concussion?"

She explained about tripping and getting knocked out at the finish in Birmingham, ending with, "At the hospital I explained to the doctor what had been happening, and he suggested that, since they'd be scanning my brain anyway, they'd check for lesions at the same time. He also said he thought the arm pain and tingling in my hands may be a pinched nerve, so I'll get it looked at by my GP."

He was so thankful that for a moment he couldn't even speak, just hold her close and absorb the sensation of her body against his.

When he finally found his voice again, he said, "I'll never desert you, love. Not in this life, or the next. No matter what comes. Will you marry me, Val? I want to live with you for the rest of our lives and share every moment we can together, from now until forever."

"By sun and by moonlight," she said. "Yes, darling. Yes."

* * * * *

RISKING IT ALL FOR A SECOND CHANCE

ANNIE CLAYDON

MILLS & BOON

To Ann and Charlotte,
with grateful thanks for nudges to the steering wheel
when I needed them!

CHAPTER ONE

EVERYTHING HAD BEEN going so well.

Dr Emma Owen and her driving partner, Nurse Val Sterling, had reached the halfway point of the GDK Foundation's classic car rally. Emma's shiny nineteen-sixties Mini had taken them south from Edinburgh in a snaking route that went through countryside and cities. The foundation's events, held along the way to promote awareness and encourage people to donate blood and consider signing up to the various organ donor registers, had been far more successful than anyone could have dreamed. Just one more week to go, and Val and Emma could collect the sponsorship money that had been promised for the foundation. Val had taken a few minutes out from navigating the route this morning to work out how much they'd be raising per mile, and Emma had let out of whoop of achievement, as if the money was already safely in the bank...

Planning ahead like that was always a recipe for disaster. Because from there on in, everything had slowly gone pear-shaped.

The Mini's engine had cut out a couple of times during the drive, and as they crossed the finishing line in Birmingham it had started to sputter again. Emma had pulled to one side and stopped, releasing the catch to open the bonnet. A local TV news crew who were covering the rally had zoned in on her and she'd waved them away crossly. Then all of Emma's attention had been diverted to Val, who had tripped over a trailing cable and hit the ground with a sickening thump, knocking herself out cold for a few seconds.

An ambulance had been called and the crew had agreed with Emma's assessment of the situation. Val expressed the expected outrage at being mollycoddled, but still, she sank back onto the ambulance gurney with an expression of relief. Emma left her car keys with one of the stewards, so they could move the Mini out of the way, and climbed into the back of the ambulance, ignoring Val's protests and taking her hand.

She left the hospital three hours later. Val was being kept in overnight for tests, and had already decided that she'd be fine after a little rest and promised to be back before the rally set off again from Birmingham. Emma had kept her doubts to herself, telling her friend that everything would be okay and she could find another navigator easily if Val needed a few more days' rest.

Things didn't improve from there. She found the Mini in a service bay, away from the other cars that stood beneath the fluttering banners that announced the foundation's rally and awareness event. Emma got in and tried to start it and the engine choked into life and then died again.

'Hi, Emma. You've just got back?' George Evans was standing by the car, his hands in the pockets of his overalls. He had the grace not to ask how things were going—the noise from the engine made that pretty obvious.

'Yes. Val's staying in hospital overnight but she should be back tomorrow.'

George nodded, scratching his head. He and his wife, Tess, had been retired for five years and had spent that time doing all the things they'd wanted to do but never got the chance. George was a car enthusiast, and his putting his aqua-blue 1946 Alpha Romeo through its paces was his main reason for joining the rally, although Tess's appetite for any good cause had added to their enthusiasm. They'd quickly become the rally's go-to couple if anyone wanted advice on mechanics or anything else.

'You think she'll be okay to continue?'

Emma shrugged. 'I'll be giving her the once-over when she gets back whether she likes it or not. I'm not going to allow Val to spend all day in the car navigating, if she's already got aches and pains.'

'What'll you do for a navigator?'

Emma could think about that when the time came. 'I might not need one. I have to see if I can get the car repaired first. It might be a blocked fuel line; I'll see if I can get it fixed tonight.'

George pursed his lips. He knew as well as Emma did that how easy the fix was going to be rather depended on where the blockage was.

'Why don't you go back to the hotel and check in? Get yourself something to eat and a good night's sleep. I'll be here first thing and give you a hand, eh?'

Emma swallowed down the impulse to shake her head and say that she could fix the car herself, tonight. George was far too good a mechanic to believe that and he didn't treat Emma as if she didn't know one end of a spanner from the other, like many of the men here did.

'Thanks, George. You're right, as always.'

'Off with you, then. Everything will look better in the morning.'

Everything *did* look a little better. The Birmingham awareness event would be starting at nine o'clock and there was a bustle of activity around the cars, which were lined up and newly polished, and in the booths where GDK staff were getting the information packs and donor cards ready. The blood donor mobile unit stood at the far end of the open space, along with a couple of smaller vans where green-uniformed NHS staff were setting up their information stand.

George and Tess were sitting on camping chairs, next to the Mini. Two grey heads, tilted towards each other because they still had something to say, even after forty years.

'Emma…!' Tess waved, bending to pick up the thermos at her feet. 'I've got some tea.'

'Can we save that for later, love?' George gave her a smile. 'We'll be needing to get started…'

The call came at lunchtime. Val was back at their hotel and feeling fine. But she'd just heard from the hospital where she and Emma worked and been told that a donor had been found for a seriously ill patient. As transplant co-ordinator, Val really should be there, but how was Emma going to manage without her?'

'Don't worry about things here. You go; the transplant is far more important. You're sure that you're all right?'

Val assured her that she was, and that the tests had given her a clean bill of health. She apologised a couple of times more and Emma told her that she had someone lined up already who would be able to navigate for her tomorrow, injecting an optimism into her tone that she didn't feel. She told Val she'd catch up with her when she got back to Liverpool, and they'd drink to the success of the rally, and the good health of Val's transplant patient.

'You've found someone?' Tess had returned with sandwiches and more tea, and was staring at her as she ended the call.

'No, but Val's needed in Liverpool. She and David are working with a patient who's been waiting for a kidney and pancreas transplant and now that a donor's been found Val has to go. I don't want her to feel guilty about leaving.'

'What about you?' Tess asked.

'I'm not involved with this particular case. I specialise in managing diseases of the liver. I'll be staying to finish the rally.'

Tess frowned. 'Well, you should have a cup of tea and something to eat. George can repair the car while you go and find a navigator—' She fell silent as George shook his head.

He knew. As they'd worked, Emma had told George that this was her dad's car. That she'd been 'helping' him service the engine since she was so small that she had to climb up on the bumper to see what he was doing, and that when she was sixteen she'd sketched out the design for the gold sunburst pattern around the back wheel arches. After Emma had left home for medical school, Dad had waited for her to visit before he took the engine apart, and they'd worked together on the Mini until he became too ill to go out into the garage. A year after his death, this rally was just as much about her dad, and how he'd have cheered the Mini across the finishing line, as it was about the cause she felt so strongly about.

'It's Emma's car, love. We've cleaned out the fuel transmission lines and it's just a matter of putting everything back together now. We'll let Emma do that while we ask round for a navigator.'

'Do you mind?' Emma shot George a grateful smile.

'"Course not.' George started to unbutton his overalls. 'We'll have a cup of tea and then Tess and I will go and see what we can do.'

Emma had refitted the fuel line that ran under the car, which was the hardest part, and now she just had to connect the flexible hose that ran into the carburettor. George and Tess weren't back yet, and she knew they were probably having less success in their endeavour. The thought of having to give the rally up now was crushing.

One thing at a time. Emma bent over the engine, reaching over to position the hose, and felt something brush against the back of her knee. She jumped, looking down into a pair of brown eyes, which were accompanied by one ear up and one ear down, along with a mottled black and brown coat and a wagging tail.

'Griff…!' Emma's voice splintered into an embarrassing squeak, as her throat dried and she noticed the feet planted next to him.

Griff wasn't the problem and nor was his usual companion, David Kennedy, the CEO of the GDK Foundation. But she'd heard that David had been called away to London last night, and clearly his son was filling in for him. Josh Kennedy, temporary dog-minder, transplant surgeon and, in David's absence, rally organiser. None of those job titles were particularly confronting; it was the ex-lover part that was making Emma's heart thump wildly.

She'd met Josh three years ago, through David. Emma had gone to the GDK Foundation to ask for help with a patient, and in addition to giving her some very solid advice, David had introduced Emma to his son. There had been a thrilling, world-turning affair that had lasted three months, and then it had all ended badly. So badly that Emma had thought twice about participating in the rally, but she'd wanted to come and reckoned that it would be easy enough to avoid Josh.

That had worked for the last week. It hadn't been so difficult because he'd obviously been avoiding her as well, and on the occasions when Emma hadn't seen him coming he'd been the one to swerve suddenly away. That unspoken agreement was clearly off the table and right now it felt that fate had saved its most uncomfortable blow, for last.

But there was nothing she could do about it. Emma

dragged her gaze from his green and white sneakers and looked up at him.

'Hi, Emma. I heard that Val's out of the hospital. Is she okay?'

Okay. At least his first question wasn't an indignant enquiry about where the blazes she'd disappeared off to, three years ago...

'Yes. I spoke to her a little while ago and she's fine.'

Just as Emma was beginning to think that things couldn't get any worse, he smiled. That blue-eyed grin was all warmth and mischief, wrapped up in one gorgeous bundle.

'I'm glad to hear it. Fuel line problems?'

Since she was holding part of the Mini's fuel line in her hand, it wasn't exactly a stroke of diagnostic genius. 'Um... yes. I think so. Dad and I have had to unblock it before.'

Josh nodded. 'I was sorry to hear about your father's death. How's your mum doing?'

Her parents had liked Josh. Dad had involved him in a two-hour conversation which ranged from medicine to archaeology to the difficulty in getting spare parts for a classic car, and then nudged Emma and whispered to her not to let this one get away. Then she'd been the one to do the running...

'As well as can be expected, I guess. It was the first anniversary of Dad's death last month and that was hard for her, but she's keeping busy as usual.' Emma turned away from him quickly. The warmth in Josh's tone made her want to cry.

Fiddling with the fuel line was a good way of not looking at Josh. Maybe he'd just come to ask about Val and when he saw she was busy he'd leave her alone. But he didn't move, even though Griff was capering around in circles at the end of the lead.

'I...um...wanted to ask you something.'

His tone indicated that whatever it was, Emma wasn't going to like it. In David's absence for the day, Josh was clearly taking his second-in-command duties seriously and he had an annoying habit of wanting to plan everything down to the last excruciating detail. Emma straightened up.

'You heard that my father was in London last night, at an emergency board meeting?'

Curiosity got the better of Emma and she couldn't help asking even if it did threaten to prolong the conversation. 'I knew he wasn't here. There's been a problem?'

'There were some allegations about irregularities in the way the rally's been organised. He's succeeded in putting them to bed.' Josh shrugged. Clearly that was all sorted now, and wasn't his point. 'I've just heard from him; he was on his way back here, but he's been diverted to Liverpool.'

'Yes, Val's...' Emma bit her tongue. If Josh was in the same position she was, then it was better not to mention that she was in need of a navigator. 'I heard that they've found a donor for the kidney and pancreas transplant that David was supervising. That's good news.'

'Yes. Although it means I'm on the lookout for a driver so I can finish the rally. And I gather that Val's gone back to Liverpool as well.'

Emma froze, as the unthinkable presented itself as the obvious solution.

'Yes, that's right. George and Tess are finding me a replacement right now.'

At least she hoped they were. A whole week, in a Mini, with your ex. It didn't bear thinking about. And she was sure that Josh would be able to find a partner for the Daimler. Who wouldn't want to ride round in luxury with him as the perfect travelling companion?

'I just spoke with George and Tess. They're not having any luck. I was wondering if you'd like to join me and we can both finish the rally in the Daimler. It's comfortable and you could take your choice of either driving or navigating. I can have your name put on the car's insurance policy.'

'No!' At least she had the words she needed to reject *that* proposal. 'This car's started the rally and it's going to finish.'

'For your dad?' Josh instantly put his finger on the reason.

'Yes. For my dad. I'm sure you'll find someone else.'

He nodded quietly, pushing his corn-blond hair back from his brow, in the way he always did when thinking around a problem. 'Or we could do things the easy way. I can navigate for you in the Mini. That way we'll both be able to finish and collect all the sponsorship money we have promised.'

'There's not much room.' It was all she could think of to say, other than, *Have you considered the possibility that we'll be at each other's throats before lunchtime?*

'We could try it out.' Josh shrugged. 'For the sake of the sponsorships…'

It went against the grain to be the inflexible one, because that was Josh's speciality. She waved him towards the car and he pulled the front seat forward, letting Griff sprawl across the back seat. Then he got into the passenger seat.

His long legs were bent uncomfortably and Emma gave in to the obvious. 'You could push the seat back a bit. The lever's—'

Josh was already reaching for the lever under the seat. He pushed it back as far as it would go and Griff shifted a bit, then lunged forward, resting his head on Josh's shoulder. Josh chuckled, his long fingers caressing the dog's ears.

'Not so bad. We'll manage.'

His knees were no longer rammed up against the dashboard and if he kept his elbows to himself, then he wouldn't be getting in the way. Emma sighed.

'Do you have a restraint for Griff?'

'Yeah, and there's an attachment to his car harness that fits into a seat belt clip.'

Emma nodded. The seat belts in the car were the only thing that wasn't completely authentic. The Mini had been their family car and Dad had never compromised on safety.

'I've got a blanket for him as well, so he doesn't get dog hairs all over your seats. Dad seemed to think that it would be a familiar scent for him and calm him down.' Josh's fingers strayed to the dog's muzzle. It appeared that the one thing that calmed Griff was human contact, and he'd get plenty of that in the cramped confines of the Mini.

'I suppose... All right, then. We'll try it out for the run to Hay-on-Wye tomorrow and see how it goes. If I can get the engine running, that is.' Josh loved the security of a definite plan. The uncertainty would at least concentrate his mind a bit in looking for viable alternatives.

Josh got out of the car, and Griff bounded up to her wagging his tail, as if he knew that they were going to be teammates and he was determined to play his part.

'Thank you.' His lips twitched. 'I won't be bringing any elephants with me. There isn't the space.'

That was Josh all over. The smile, the charm. The acknowledgement that they did have a history, but that he could ignore the elephants in the room if she could.

'Yes, it would make things a bit cramped.' Emma turned, trying to keep her face straight. At this rate, the biggest hazard of driving with Josh wasn't that they might be at each other's throats. The temptation to connect with him on a far more intimate level was making her heart thump.

She could deal with that tomorrow. When she'd got the Mini running.

'I'd better get on.'

'Would you like a hand? Griff and I are both pretty enthusiastic assistants…'

Yeah, right. Blame the dog. Josh knew as much about cars as she did.

'Thanks, I'm fine. George has been helping me and this bit's a one-person job. I'll text you and let you know whether this works and I get the car running.'

Admitting that she still had his number stored in her phone wasn't so terrible, but it was embarrassing that she *knew* that it was still there without looking. It was doubtful that Josh's quick perceptiveness had missed the faux pas, but he didn't comment on it. That was a start, at least.

'Great, thanks. If I don't hear from you I'll give you a call.'

He led Griff away, leaving Emma to turn back towards the car. Trying to ignore the thought that was throbbing in her head, now.

Josh still had *her* number too.

Emma still had her fire. Of course she did, it was something that wouldn't—couldn't—ever be contained. Her red hair was neatly tied back, the plait tucked down the back of her overalls, but Josh knew how it shimmered when spread loose across a pillow. He was just trying very hard not to think about it.

She would have had every right to tell him no, and to maintain the radio silence they'd been keeping for the first week of the rally. If he'd been asked his opinion, he would have said that was the thing to do and damn the consequences. But he'd had no choice but to ask, both for the sake of the sponsorships and because the rally needed as many cars as possible taking part. And it seemed that Emma had felt she had no choice but to say yes.

'We'd better be on our best behaviour, eh, Griff?' At the

sound of his name, Griff looked up at Josh, his one-ear-up-one-ear-down making it look as if he was querying him.

'Yeah, okay. *I'll* be on my best behaviour. You'll be fine.' Griff's tendency to do just as he pleased, whenever he pleased, would match Emma's view on life perfectly. It was Josh who had to show her that he could go with the flow.

As David Kennedy's adopted son, Josh had been given all the benefits of that—a good education and plenty of opportunities. David was his father in every possible sense of the word except one, and that was the one that mattered least to Josh. His biological father was just someone that his mother had known before David, and who Josh hadn't known at all.

He'd felt the consequences of his actions though. His biological father had kicked his mother and Josh out when Josh was just a baby. They'd had nothing, and his mother had been afraid to ask for help, in case Josh was taken away from her. For ten years the two of them had scraped to make ends meet, moving between squats and temporary housing until Josh hardly knew which way was home. David had fallen in love with Josh's mother's bright and unquenchable habit of making the best of things, and Josh had added his own surly disobedience to the mix. Why bother to fit in with David when they'd be moving on soon?

But they hadn't moved on. David and Georgie had got married and they'd formed a small, blended family of three. Josh had never had anyone he could call 'Gran' before, and David's mother didn't fit any of his expectations. A Black American woman with the cut-glass English accent of her adopted home, who brought with her a waft of expensive perfume, a shower of affection for her new daughter-in-law and grandson and fascinating stories about her travels whenever she arrived on their doorstep. He'd never had anyone he could call 'Dad' before either and having a father who actually knew who he was, let alone took any interest in him, was a novelty that Josh didn't always appreciate as much as his glamorous grandmother. But it didn't escape his notice that his mother was happy, and Georgie's imaginative charm had blossomed to fill every corner of their lives.

David had been the quiet, unassuming glue who held it all together. He'd adopted Josh, and patiently set about giving him a stable, secure home. And despite his unspoken rule of never really trusting anyone other than his mother, Josh had started to love him. When his mother had died suddenly when he was a teen, Josh had run away, reckoning that it would save David the trouble of handing him over to social services. But David had come for him and taken him home, telling him there was no place Josh could go that he wouldn't find him. It was tough love. Josh had been grounded for a month and told that he was expected to help out with David's latest project in the garden. David had been there, working with him and talking to him the whole time.

Emma had seen the man that David Kennedy had helped make, which was fair enough because Josh never talked about the frightened boy. When things had started to get serious with Emma, Josh knew he had come on too strong. Her carefree love of life had reminded him so much of his mother's, and Josh had reacted without thinking and changed his whole approach to the relationship. He'd always reckoned that he would give his own children the stable upbringing that he hadn't had for the first ten years of his life, and he'd responded badly to anything that Emma said or did which felt like a threat to the secure home he wanted to build with her.

So she'd done the only thing possible. The only sensible thing to do in the circumstances. She'd run. Josh had been heartbroken, and known he'd been at fault. But he'd never called to explain, or tried to make things right. He'd coped the way he always had with loss, turning his back on it and pretending it had never happened.

But now, it looked as if Emma was agreeing to putting the past behind them. Forgetting was out of the question— Josh would be the first to caution her against that—but forgiving... No, that was probably out of the question too. But one man and his dog were a sufficient number of passengers in a Mini, and from the involuntary twitch of Emma's lips when he'd mentioned the elephants, it appeared that she too felt that it was best to leave them behind.

CHAPTER TWO

EMMA WAS BUSY counting her blessings. She'd been up early, fidgeting nervously as the race mechanic checked the repairs on her car. He'd passed the Mini as roadworthy, and the pre-dawn chill was beginning to give way to what promised to be a fine, clear morning... Those two would have to do.

Getting dressed for the rally wasn't as much fun as it had been last week. Not all of the rally teams were matching their costumes to the date of their cars, but she and Val had thrown themselves into the idea with enthusiasm, and they'd swapped accessories, done each other's hair and egged each other on to try out different make-up styles. But now her green minidress felt agonisingly short, instead of just a bit of fun, and the purple sparkly star on her cheek too frivolous. Her hair had refused to curl and the 'peace' sign on the pendant around her neck seemed like an impossible ambition for a day that would be spent with Josh.

She packed her luggage into the boot of the car and arrived late to the briefing for the day's driving. Josh was sitting in one of the front seats, already leafing through the information pack for the day. The route that the cars would take was carefully mapped out, and checkpoints along the way had to be noted in the navigator's log. There were some fun tasks to complete, and the cars had to conform to a strict speed limit—anyone who drove too fast over any part of the route would lose points.

Emma stood with a couple of the other drivers, at the back of the room. It was up to Josh to make sure they completed the course correctly; her job was to drive. The thought didn't fill her with as much excited anticipation as it had last week when Val had been her travel companion. Josh would undoubtedly stick to the plan, because making plans was what he excelled at. That wasn't such a bad thing in this context, but it brought with it the taste of sadness and anger, because it was what had broken them apart.

He was the same man that she'd fallen in love with, and it would be so easy to do it again. But from the moment they'd foolishly whispered those words to each other, wrapped up in the moment, Josh had changed. He'd started to talk about security and stability, mapping their lives out as if what they'd be doing in twenty years' time was an urgent decision that had to be made today. His easy-going nature had disappeared and life had become one big flow chart, with every possibility mapped out and recorded. It had become difficult to breathe, and Emma had known that if she didn't leave now, she never would.

It had taken a long time before she'd wanted to be anywhere other than in Josh's arms. Slowly she'd started to look forward, and then her world had stopped again when her father had been diagnosed with terminal cancer. She'd taken a job close to her parents' home so that she could be there for both of them.

It had been a long and painful year. Her plans for the future, which she'd always shared with her father with such joy, suddenly seemed hollow and meaningless, and when he'd died Emma had felt immobilised with grief.

But her mother no longer needed Emma's daily companionship. And Dad had always told her to keep her wheels turning. That was why she was here on the rally—in the hopes that something that would have given him joy would give her back her sense of moving forward in the world. And the one person who could shatter that fragile sense of new momentum was Josh.

As soon as the briefing was finished, Emma slipped away, ignoring the pairs of drivers and navigators who were looking through the information packs together. Josh would already be forming a clear idea of what came next and Emma had very little to add to that. Driving with Val had been teamwork, but this would be more a matter of listening to Josh's instructions and getting through the day.

She walked back to the Mini, then drove it to its place in the queue of nearly forty cars that would be checked out by the stewards at one-minute intervals when the rally got under way. Right on cue, not too early and not too late, she saw Josh walking towards her.

'You look great.' He was smiling and she saw Griff was dressed for the occasion, with a flowery patterned kerchief wound around his collar. Josh looked...

Gorgeous, as always. Almost golden in the morning sun, with his long corn-blond hair and tanned skin. He was wearing a collarless shirt, with the sleeves rolled up, and a pair of battered jeans, with his green sneakers. Simple, and as much of a nod to the nineteen-sixties as could be expected on such short notice.

'You too.' Emma hoped her words sounded like a polite response rather than a compliment. 'That's *all* of your luggage?' She pointed to the small holdall he was carrying, a rolled-up dog blanket stuffed between the handles.

Josh nodded. 'I reckoned there wouldn't be too much space, and the only part of the nineteen-thirties costume I could use was the shirts. So I packed the rest up and it's going back to Dad's place in Oxfordshire today, with the Daimler. Do you have room for this?'

Plenty of room. Emma had squashed her luggage into

precisely half of the space available and Josh was clearly travelling much lighter than she was. He opened the boot, dropping the holdall inside, and then ducked into the Mini, spreading the blanket on the back seat, while Griff pulled on the extending lead, nuzzling at Emma's legs.

'What do you think, then, Griff? Not quite as much luxury as you're used to.' Emma bent down to stroke his head, and the dog started to lick her hand.

'He'll be fine. Won't you, mate?' It seemed that addressing Griff as a go-between suited them both. Josh held the passenger door open, pointing at the back seat. 'In you go, then, Griff.'

Griff looked at him amiably and then ignored him, in favour of sitting down at Emma's feet and raising one of his paws to her. Griff loved being with people and he'd already learned a couple of tricks that were bound to get him attention. Emma clasped her hands behind her back, trying not to encourage him too much.

'Griff!' Josh's voice was a little firmer, his gesture towards the back seat a little more emphasised. 'Come along, it's time to get in the car.'

Nothing. Griff was looking up at her, his eyes pleading for attention, but if Emma gave it she was going to disrupt Josh's agenda. Then she heard Josh sigh.

'Okay. Whatever...'

That wasn't fair. It was the Josh she'd first met, comfortable in his skin, laid-back and able to go with the flow. The one she'd fallen in love with.

Then he gave her the smile that had once made a prisoner out of her heart.

Emma bent down, stroking Griff's odd ears, trying to keep her thoughts away from how good it felt to be in Josh's arms. She'd been there, done that...all of it...and it hadn't worked out. That should be enough to keep her mind focused on the rally and not on Josh.

Griff nuzzled against her, uncomplicated and undemanding, and when she stood up and walked around to the driver's door, he followed her. Emma got into the car, and Griff clambered over her, scrambling onto the back seat. Josh leaned in, grinning, to fix his harness into the seat belt clip. The cars ahead of them in the queue were moving forward, and he got into the passenger seat, moving his arm quickly when the back of Emma's hand grazed it as she reached for the gear stick.

They were close. Intimate, even, in the confined space. The Mini was a great car, but it didn't have Tardis technology installed, and it could get a little crowded. It was feeling extremely crowded at the moment, but perhaps when they started driving she wouldn't feel so bad. Emma cranked the handle to wind the window down, so she could at least rest her elbow on the open frame.

'Which way are we heading?' She really should have taken a bit more interest in the briefing session this morning.

Josh consulted the map that was perched on his knees. 'First left past the starting line, and then straight on for about…half a mile, until you get to a roundabout.'

That would do for starters. 'And what's our first clue?'

Josh chuckled. '*Swings and Roundabouts.* I think that one's easy enough, we'll be going past a park.'

He had everything under control. Of course he did. Today would probably go without a hitch and be easy driving. Just as long as she kept her eye on the road and not her navigator.

The morning had gone smoothly. Josh had given her exact instructions in good time, and Griff had piled out of the car with them to have his photograph taken, posing next to Emma on a swing. Then on, through the outer suburbs of Birmingham, the route twisting through back roads until they reached the country roads that snaked southwest into Wales and towards Hay-on-Wye.

The clue for their lunch stop was easy and they drew up outside the Unicorn Pub, taking turns to pose under the sign for pictures. There was an enormous sign announcing their arrival, which had obviously attracted some attention because the car park was full of people who'd come to see the cars, and the stewards had to clear a path so that Emma could manoeuvre into a parking space.

Everything was ready for them, and a large, open-sided marquee had been set up in the garden, serving drinks and food. Almost as soon as Josh had got out of the car, stretching his legs and back, the production assistant from the film crew that was accompanying the rally's celebrity team beckoned him.

'No rest for the wicked.' Josh grinned and Emma tried not to blush. She knew exactly how wicked he could be. 'Do you mind looking after Griff? We have an interview organised, but I think he could do with some water—his bowl's in my bag.'

'That's fine, I'll sort it out.' Emma wasn't going to go into Josh's bag though; that felt a little too much as if they were friends. Griff accompanied her over to the marquee, obviously delighted to be surrounded by people, and wagging his tail furiously. A bowl of water was found for him and as he lapped it up enthusiastically Emma glanced across towards Josh.

He was looking relaxed and cheerful, sitting down in front of the camera with a woman in a GDK Foundation sweatshirt and an older man. Ryan Winterhauer, the news presenter, joined the group, and the buzz of conversation around Emma subsided as the production assistant called for quiet. Griff tugged at the lead, seeming to realise where everyone's attention was now centred, and Emma followed him to the circle of people who had gathered to watch.

Emma had spent a day with Ryan during the first week of the rally. He was a nice guy, and fiercely committed to the foundation's work, being a transplant recipient himself. She wondered how Ryan's nose for a human interest story might track with Josh's predilection for facts and figures.

'This is Ryan Winterhauer, on the eighth day of the GDK Foundation classic car rally. We had a great day in Birmingham yesterday, and...' Ryan turned to Josh. 'I hear we had a record number of people sign up for donor cards?'

Josh nodded. 'We did, and we'd like to thank everyone who did so.'

'Absolutely. Today, we're on our way to Hay-on-Wye and we've stopped for lunch at the Unicorn Pub. We have the landlord here to thank for a very warm welcome.' Ryan turned to the older man. 'Jim, I gather you've been collecting pledges all week from potential blood donors.'

'Yes, when David Kennedy approached me on behalf of the GDK Foundation, this seemed like a really good cause for us to support. We have a wall of hearts inside, where people can sign their names, and anyone who can show me their blood donor card gets a free drink.'

Ryan nodded. 'That's great. I've had a sneak preview of the wall of hearts and you've obviously been working hard to get all those names. This kind of support means a lot to you, doesn't it, Josh?'

Josh nodded. 'Absolutely. As a surgeon, I see every day why the generosity of blood donors is so crucially important. Jim's not just collecting names, he's saving lives.'

Nice. Jim was clearly pleased with the thought as well, because he nodded, beaming at Josh.

'And we have someone here with us who can tell us a bit more about why it's so important.' Ryan turned to the young woman sitting beside Josh. 'Maya, you have a very rare blood group, I believe.'

Maya smiled nervously. 'Yes, that's right. My parents

come from India...' She looked up at Josh, obviously a bit lost for words.

'Maya's blood group occurs in about one in every ten thousand people of Indian ancestry, and in only one in a million people of European ancestry. This is why we're trying to reach as many people as we can from many different ethnic groups, so that appropriate medical care is available to everyone on an equal basis.' Josh had the numbers at his fingertips and Maya nodded gratefully.

'You give blood, don't you, Maya?' Josh prompted.

'Yes, I do. And I'd like to appeal to everyone in the Asian community to consider donating blood as well. And everyone else, of course.'

Josh nodded. 'Absolutely. Maya's made an important point. Every donation is vitally important, whatever your background or blood type. But at the moment, in addition to people of Asian heritage, we're also particularly appealing for donors of African and Caribbean heritage to come forward.'

'And why's that?' Ryan asked Josh.

'Certain blood disorders such as sickle cell disease, which are treated by giving blood transfusions, are more often found in people of Black African and Caribbean heritage. That means that there's an increasing demand for subtypes such as Ro, which are also more commonly found within that group.'

Ryan nodded. 'And as we've already heard that this doesn't just apply to blood donations, it's true for organ and bone marrow transplants as well. Patients from minority ethnic backgrounds currently face a longer wait for a donor match, don't they, Josh?'

'On average, yes, and that's why we're looking to diversify the register and support alternative treatments to keep patients well while they're waiting for a match. As I'm sure you understand, Ryan, each case is unique.'

'I do indeed. Which brings me on to another question. I know that many people have the same experience as I had when I needed a new kidney, which was that my brother offered me the gift of one of his.'

Josh nodded. 'Yes, it's not uncommon for family members to donate kidneys to their loved ones, and it's also possible to donate a section of your liver. The liver possesses the capacity to regenerate; both the transplanted section and the remaining section will regrow to normal size.'

'Fascinating. And I think you have a personal understanding of some of the issues involved in finding a suitable donor, because you're adopted, aren't you, Josh?'

It was no secret. But the slight flicker at the side of Josh's jaw showed that this question had come as a surprise.

'Yes, that's right. But I have no need for a suitable donor. I'm more interested in my patients' needs.'

'Absolutely.' Ryan had found his human interest angle to the story and Josh's reticence was like a red rag to a bull. 'But I think that your situation is relevant to many people who *are* waiting for donations.'

'That's true. People like me, who are adopted, may also face difficulties in finding an organ match.'

'Is that because they aren't in touch with their real parents? You aren't, are you?'

Josh's lip curled slightly. So imperceptibly that you'd have to know him well to see it, and maybe Ryan didn't realise that he'd just touched on what seemed to be a very sore point for Josh.

'My mother died when I was sixteen. And my real father is David Kennedy.'

'Yes, of course.' Ryan had the grace to look a little chastened, but not so much that he was going to give up his line of questioning. 'But you're not in touch with your biological father?'

'No.'

Ryan nodded. 'That must feel…' He left the question open, clearly wanting Josh to fill in the gap.

This was too much. It wasn't relevant to the GDK Foundation's core message, which was to work to provide treatment for every patient. And it was perfectly clear to Emma that Josh didn't want to talk about this. Emma knew that Josh was adopted, and that he saw David as his true father, but Josh had never said a word about the circumstances of his adoption.

Griff had been pulling on the lead, and it was obvious what was on his mind. Emma let go of the lead and he galloped over to Ryan, putting his paws up onto his knees and making a lunge for the microphone. When Ryan jerked it out of his reach, Griff flung himself at Josh, in a frenzy of canine love. Josh laughed suddenly, and Maya leaned over to stroke Griff, who responded by nuzzling against her hand.

The moment of awkwardness was broken, and Ryan bowed to the inevitable. He made a joke about Griff being the rally's most enthusiastic competitor and then turned to Jim.

'I think now's the time to go and see your donor wall, if that's okay, Jim?'

'Of course.' Jim got to his feet quickly, clearly pleased to be able to show off his efforts, and Ryan beckoned to the camera and followed him inside the pub.

Josh was on his feet too, talking to Maya and shaking her hand. A man approached them, carrying a toddler, and it looked as if an introduction was being made, because Josh shook his hand as well. He stopped to talk for a few minutes and then bade them a cheery goodbye, walking back over to Emma.

He knew what she'd done. The look on his face was unmistakeable, and it was making her heart thump. An understanding that went beyond words and touched at the intimacy they'd once shared.

'Griff to the rescue.'

'Difficult to keep him under control, sometimes.'

Josh nodded, the warmth in his eyes reminding her of how he'd once looked at her. 'Yeah. You know the story of how Dad got to meet him?'

'No.' Whatever it was, it was obviously nothing to do with her relationship with Josh, which was a relief.

'He was appearing on a chat show, and the next guests were involved with an animal shelter and had brought some of the dogs along with them. Griff was one of them, and he managed to slip his leash and bounded out onto the set, wanting to make friends with Dad.' Josh laughed. 'My father doesn't like to make this known, but he's a really soft touch. He fell in love with Griff on the spot, and ended up taking him home with him.'

'So Griff's our press liaison officer, then?' Emma ventured jokingly.

'Yep. Seems he's a very good one.' Josh stroked Griff's head approvingly. 'Buy you lunch?'

He didn't need to. Emma would have done exactly the same thing for anyone who'd been put into the position that Josh had been in.

'That's okay. Jim's making no charge for the competitors' lunches.'

'That's generous. Can I *collect* your lunch, then? You go and find a seat, and—' Josh handed her Griff's lead '—keep a good hold on his lead this time.'

The mischief in Josh's grin was too hot to handle. Emma nodded, turning away to scan the pub garden for a couple of empty seats.

CHAPTER THREE

THIS WAS…EXCRUCIATING. Excruciatingly awkward at times, and Josh was having to keep on his toes to avoid the elephants that insisted on appearing around them. He'd reckoned that he could be an adult and keep his longing for Emma under control, but that was excruciatingly difficult at times too.

Her ebullient love of life was firmly subdued while she was in the car with him. But it popped to the surface like a cork when she got out, posing under signs and next to waypoints that were listed out in the day's route plan. Josh had taken photographs—because the rules demanded that photographic evidence should be submitted—but there were a lot more than strictly necessary on his phone. He hadn't been able to resist capturing just a little bit of everything he'd lost.

He hadn't been able to resist dwelling on their parting either. The way he'd changed, trying to reconcile his love for her with the fear that her free spirit would cause just as much havoc as his mother's had. Their last bitter argument had driven Emma away, but it wasn't that which had convinced him that there was no going back. It was his fear of loss, which had led him to obliterate her from his life, as if she'd never existed.

But the sight of Emma in a green minidress, her red hair backcombed and tucked into a ponytail, was pushing buttons that Josh didn't even know he had, and really didn't bear thinking about. He'd kept his eyes on the map and on the road ahead, and when they crossed the finishing line in Hay-on-Wye, he'd grabbed Griff's lead and taken himself off to present the stewards with the evidence that they'd completed the route correctly, while Emma took the car to find a parking spot. The awareness events for smaller towns were low-key and organised by local GDK Foundation representatives, and so Josh was able to escape to yet another hotel room, sitting down with Griff sprawled awkwardly across his legs, to check his email.

There were a few that had nothing to do with the rally, and a quick glance through them was enough to ignore them until later. One was from David, and was surprisingly jocular in tone, given the fact that he'd just had to abandon a rally that he'd worked hard to organise for over a year now. Josh replied to him quickly, telling him that everything was going swimmingly and not mentioning that he felt he might drown at any minute. That left the mass of emails from the other rally participants.

Social media really wasn't Josh's thing. Neither were blogs. But since the rally was all about awareness, the GDK Foundation had been making as much use as it could of both, and David had been uploading photographs from each day on the blog that the foundation's IT guru, Evie, had integrated into their website. Now that was Josh's job, and he decided that it needed yet another call to Evie.

'Hey, Evie, I'm really sorry about this…'

'No problem. IT questions are what I live for, and yours are always remarkably easy to answer.' Evie's voice floated across the ether. The idea that there was even such a thing as an easy-to-answer question right now lifted his mood.

'Have I mentioned that you're a star?'

'You did. A couple of times yesterday, actually.'

It had been well deserved. Evie had given up part of

her evening to talk Josh through putting the photographs from the awareness event up onto the blog. At least he'd managed to phone during working hours this time, and if he kept it short he wouldn't be keeping her late at work.

'I'll think of some other flattering epithet for tonight, then. You couldn't just run through how to set up a new blog post again, could you?'

'Of course. Are you sitting comfortably? Laptop at the ready?'

'Yep.'

Evie chuckled. 'Then I'll begin…'

Josh had cut his conversation with Evie short at precisely five thirty, so that she could go home on time, and then carefully consulted the notes he'd made, repeating the instructions until all of the photographs were up on the blog. When he previewed the post, it didn't have quite the effortless design style of David's posts, but then Josh hadn't had the advantage of regular lessons with Evie before the rally started.

It was good enough though, even if it didn't quite satisfy his surgeon's appreciation of precision. And it would have to do, because Griff was getting restive. This was a dog-friendly hotel, but they might object if Griff was howling all night, and if Josh didn't take him out to work off some of that excess energy, that might well be what happened.

He jogged with Griff down to the centre of the town. The book festival in Hay-on-Wye had finished a couple of weeks ago, but there were still lengths of bunting, fluttering in the breeze, and the bookshops, although closed, were good for a little window gazing. He had his hand cupped against a glass shop front, so he could see some of the titles at the back of the display, when Emma's voice behind him made him jump.

'It doesn't look as if Griff shares your interest in books.'

Josh turned, and in the split second that he allowed himself to look at Emma, he was rewarded with the sight of her in blue jeans and a cosy jacket, her red hair loose around her shoulders and glinting in the evening sun. Then he looked down at Griff, who was busy gnawing at a Victorian boot-scraper beside the entrance of the shop.

'Griff! Stop that!' He rolled his eyes. 'I swear, the first thing I do when I get back to London is to sign my dad and Griff up for some obedience classes.'

Emma grinned suddenly. 'Obedience classes for David, you mean? Griff's a bit wayward but that's what everyone seems to love about him.'

She'd caught him with his hang-ups showing again. There was nothing wrong with Griff's free spirit, although it might be nice if he actually came when you called him.

'Since the relationship between my dad and his dog *is* largely Dad doing what Griff tells him, then that's probably going to be the way forward. I can think of worse solutions.'

Emma nodded. 'Yes, me too.'

This was nice. Together in the cool of the evening, with enough room to give each other a little space and maybe talk a bit. 'Which way are you walking?'

'That way.' Emma pointed along the high street. 'I thought I might stroll past a few bookshops and look in the windows.'

Just as he'd been doing. 'May I join you?'

'Yes, of course.' Emma started to walk, keeping Griff in between them. But she hadn't hesitated in agreeing, so in the absence of evidence to the contrary, Josh was going to take that as an indication that they might learn to be a bit less stiff in each other's company.

They walked slowly along the high street, their breath misting the glass as they peered through the windows of second-hand bookshops. Griff began to join in, standing on his hind legs to see the irregular rows of books, their spines faded with age. Emma looked down at him, smiling and ruffling his ears.

'Your father always seems so reserved and businesslike at work. Griff shows him in an entirely different light...' Emma tilted her head slightly, in an indication that this might be a question. Josh imagined that she meant it to be whatever he wanted it to be. She had clearly seen his discomfiture about the questions that Ryan had asked, because she'd enlisted Griff's help in doing something about it.

And he wanted to explain. If she knew that his behaviour during their short-lived love affair had been provoked by fear, then maybe they could be friends. Or at least slightly more comfortable as driver and navigator.

'Dad's got his soft side, even if he doesn't show it much. He has a way with waifs and strays...as I found out when I was a kid.'

'I'd always assumed that you were adopted as a baby. Not that you ever said.' Emma was interested now. He could see it in the way that she suddenly looked up at him. But she quickly looked away again, still refusing to ask an explicit question.

'No, Dad adopted me when I was eleven, when he married my mum. She was only sixteen when she had me, and her parents put a lot of pressure on her to marry my biological father. That fell apart pretty quickly and I never knew him.'

'So she brought you up on her own? Until she met David...' Finally Emma had asked an actual question. She obviously wanted to know, and maybe she needed to draw a line under the past as much as Josh did.

'Yeah. Although it seemed sometimes as if I was her travelling companion rather than her child. Mum was great. She loved me, and she had a knack of making the best of things.'

Emma thought for a moment, pursing her lips. And when she asked, warmth flooded through Josh. 'It sounds as if *things* needed to be made the best of?'

'She had nothing when my biological father kicked her out. We moved around, from squats to temporary accommodation, and I was at a whole succession of different schools.' He shrugged. 'I never had the right uniform.'

That had been one of the preoccupations of his young life. Not where the next meal was coming from, because somehow his mother always kept his stomach full, even if she didn't eat herself. Not toys or games, or whether he had his own bedroom, because they were transient things anyway and he'd been used to not getting too attached. But having the right school uniform had meant that he could at least pretend to fit in with the other kids.

And Emma seemed to understand, nodding gravely. 'We moved around a lot for my dad's job when I was little. As he was an archaeologist we went where the digs were. But it was different for me. Mum and Dad always gave me a sense of security and belonging. It was just the things around me that were changing.'

'The first person I really felt I belonged with was Dad. I'd been used to running wild before we went to live with him, and it was a bit of a shock to find that he had a set of rules.'

'I'll bet he did.' Emma chuckled. 'I wouldn't like to be the one that broke David's rules.'

Josh laughed, the warm feeling of understanding and acceptance making him feel slightly light-headed. 'No, I found that out very quickly. It was hard, but he turned my life around. Mum loved him to bits, and I learned to.'

'And then you lost your mother.' Emma was grave again.

'Yeah. I didn't believe that David would want me after

that, and I couldn't bear to face another loss, so I took matters into my own hands and ran away. I didn't get very far,
and he managed to catch up with me.'

'And he was furious?'

'Incandescent, more like. He told me that there was nowhere I could possibly go where he wouldn't find me and
bring me back. He grounded me for a month and took time
off work and made me help him with the garden shed he'd
been meaning to build. I pretended to mind, but I knew he
was angry because he loved me. We made a great job of
the shed together as well. Brick built, with a bow window
that Dad had hauled out of a skip.'

'David built a shed! With bricks...?'

'Yeah, he can do that kind of thing. He doesn't do it
much now; the inheritance from his father, that he set the
GDK Foundation up with, changed all that. But if you ever
need any advice on shed-building he's your man.'

'Always good to know, I'll bear it in mind.' Emma
grinned impishly. 'Does he do garages?'

'Dad's multi-talented, a garage is a piece of cake. Why,
you're thinking of having one?' Josh couldn't quite see
Emma wanting to build a garage. That implied ownership
of property and the idea that she might settle down in one
place at some point.

'No, not really. Just so I know who to ask if I ever do
want one. It's best to keep an older car off the road.'

Maybe it was his imagination, but Emma seemed to be
walking a little closer. Maybe she understood why he'd
acted the way he had, and didn't blame him so much for
it, now. But it seemed that would remain unsaid, as she
turned to look into the next shop window.

They walked the length of the high street and then
turned and strolled back to the hotel. Emma stopped just
outside the entrance, saying she wanted to go and check

on the Mini, before turning in for the night, making a fuss of Griff before they parted.

It hurt. More even than when they'd rowed and Emma had stormed away from him, because then there had been no understanding, just hurt. It felt as if things had changed a lot in the last hour. But they probably hadn't changed so much for Emma, and Josh swallowed his feelings and bade her a goodnight.

'Josh…' They'd both turned to walk away, but Emma called him back. There was evidently one last thing she had to say, probably something about the rally.

'Yep?' His gaze met hers and suddenly the rally was the last thing in his thoughts.

'We're alike in a lot of ways but… I never realised just how different we are as well.'

He could almost hear the thunder of elephants stamping over the horizon. And that was okay, because maybe they did need to talk about the one thing that had been on his mind almost constantly, and which seemed to have been on Emma's as well.

'Alike enough to be friends and different enough to make a real mess of a relationship?' Josh ventured the observation.

'Yes. That…' Emma shrugged, and Josh wondered if she regretted it as much as he did.

'It was my fault, Emma. I was a very insecure kid, and…' It was hard to admit even now. 'I don't talk about it and I've tried to put it all behind me. Sometimes I can't.'

Emma shrugged again. 'None of us can put those formative years completely behind us.'

It was time to apologise. It couldn't make things right, but it was the right thing to do. 'I'm sorry for what I said. About you being irresponsible…' And unable to settle. Childish, reckless, thoughtless…

'Consider it unsaid. I'm sorry for what I called you too.'

Stick-in-the-mud, joyless, unimaginative... That had really stung, even though Emma had added the caveat *outside the bedroom*. She'd always been fair-minded, even when she was ferociously angry.

'Consider that unsaid too. Although I think you may have been right. If we'd known then what we know now...'

They would have known they were incompatible and never would have considered a relationship. But despite all of the pain, it was something that Josh couldn't bring himself to wish away.

Emma nodded. 'We know it now. I guess I'll say goodnight, then.'

He didn't want her to go. He wanted to take her in his arms and tell her never to change because she was perfect just as she was. But they'd come to a fragile understanding, one that was very overdue, and Josh wouldn't risk damaging that.

'Yeah. Goodnight.'

CHAPTER FOUR

EMMA HAD BEEN up early, after a night spent thinking about things that hadn't been said and the differences between her and Josh. She'd come to no conclusion, apart from the fact that it was impossible to traverse a space which seemed to have no footholds.

She spent a little more time on her outfit, choosing a slim-fitting cheesecloth shirt and flared hipster jeans with a rainbow-coloured belt. Flat leather sandals and strings of beads around her neck completed the look, along with a small bell that jangled annoyingly every time she moved. Bells and beads were okay in theory, and definitely a sixties look, but how on earth did they put up with the constant noise?

Josh was already in the hotel lounge, which had been commandeered for the morning briefing. This time he sat alone, his copy of the day's information pack placed on the chair next to him. Saving her a seat was one thing, and a nice friendly thing to do, but did he *really* have to look at her with those come-to-bed eyes?

Emma reminded herself that he couldn't help it. She'd always liked Josh's eyes, and from the first moment they'd met they'd seemed to be beckoning to her. It was *her* appreciation of them that gave them the come-to-bed quality, and nothing that Josh did. She gave him a wave, squeezing past the people already seated in that row, and plumped herself down next to him.

'You're sitting on our information pack.' Josh gave her a simmering smile.

'Oh. Sorry.' Emma shifted, handing him the typed pages. Josh was clearly enlarging on the hippy theme he'd adopted yesterday, and had added a strip of fabric and a leather thong tied around his wrist. The splash of colour drew attention to his arms, which in general was a good look, but only made Emma think of the way he might be holding her while he gave her the come-to-bed look.

Enough! Today was all about the rally. If it also promised the possibility that they might be a little more friendly with each other, that should have nothing to do with Josh's allure. In fact, thinking about anything other than friendship was going to make said friendship out of the question.

'I've got something for you. To add to the look.' Emma took one of the bead bracelets from her own wrist and handed it to him, hoping he wouldn't take the gift the wrong way.

He looked at the black and grey beads, and the tiny 'peace' sign next to the clasp. The curve of his lips told her that he was taking this the right way.

'This is yours?'

Emma shook her head quickly. 'Val and I brought along a jar of beads and some bead wire, so we could make our own jewellery along the way. I made this for you. If you like it, that is…'

'Yes, I do. Thank you.' He fiddled with the clip, trying to fasten it, and Emma leaned forward, securing the beads around his wrist, next to the leather thong.

'Everybody…!' The race co-ordinator's voice sounded above the chatter and the room fell quiet. Emma breathed a sigh of relief. Now perhaps she could concentrate on what came next.

* * *

Everything about Emma was perfect. The way she looked and the things she did. Even the tiny 'peace' sign that was now hanging from his wrist. The beads had been a nice thought, but Emma never did anything without understanding its connotations. If she'd given him a 'peace' sign, then that was what she'd meant to say to him.

Today they'd be making the run into Cardiff, the second of the British capital cities that the rally was visiting. They squeezed into the Mini with just as much care as they'd done yesterday, but this morning felt a little different. The anger and resentment was gone—or at least well under wraps. When Emma reached for the gearstick and Josh moved his leg slightly so that the back of her hand wouldn't brush his thigh, it was more a matter of knowing that her touch had the power to spoil the fragile peace between them.

As they drove out of Hay-on-Wye, Emma wound down the car window, waving a joyful goodbye to the town. Josh smiled to himself, concentrating on giving her plain instructions in good time, and today they weren't met by silent compliance, but with a nod of the head and sometimes a few words. They were getting there, in more ways than one.

The distinctive, flat-topped outline of Crug Hywel rose on the horizon, and there was the obligatory picture of Emma, her arms above her head so it looked as if she was supporting the vast bulk of the mountain. Then back into the car again to follow the road, which alternated between the soft dappled sunlight of woodlands, and the wonderful views of the Brecon Beacons. Suddenly Emma pulled over to the side of the road.

'Straight on, here...' Straight on wasn't the best description of the twists and turns in the road, but since it was the only route available, Josh reckoned it was obvious. He turned to Emma questioningly.

'Yes, I know.' She grabbed at the beads around her neck, disentangling a small bell that hung amongst them. 'This bell's driving me nuts. I'm going to put it in the glove compartment.'

Josh chuckled. He'd been thinking that the bell was rather charming, and that Emma had hit on a sixties icon that everyone understood with her bells and beads. He supposed that if you were actually wearing the bell it might be a little less adorable.

'It's going to drive you nuts in the glove compartment; you'll be thinking that it's the engine rattling. Here, give it to me.' Josh peeled a piece of sticky tape from the vinyl cover of today's information pack, and Emma leaned forward, dropping the bell into his hand without taking the long chain from her neck. His hand shook a little at the unexpected intimacy of the move, but he managed to secure the sticky tape around the tiny striker of the bell.

'Better?'

Emma leaned back, rattling the beads together, and Josh heard no accompanying jingle from the bell. 'Ah, nice job. Thanks. Having a surgeon in the car does come in handy, after all.'

They seemed to be moving from silence, through careful pleasantries and on to cheerful teasing. That had been the most delicate operation, and Josh was pleased it was going well.

'Let's get moving, then. We don't want to fall behind schedule.'

Emma shot him a grin and started the car. Climbing through woodlands, the road opened up again into a spectacular view of the mountains, and suddenly she turned off the road.

'Wait… This isn't right…' Josh looked up from the map as the car accelerated, bumping along an uneven track.

Then he saw it. It was nothing short of a miracle that Emma had noticed the flash of aqua blue from the road, as the Alpha Romeo was tucked into a fold in the landscape. But Josh could see it now, the driver's side of the bonnet crumpled against a large tree.

Emma slammed on the brakes and Griff complained momentarily from the back seat, before his head sank back down to rest sleepily on his paws. Emma was already out of the car, tucking the mass of beads into her shirt and buttoning it up as she went.

'Is that George and Tess?' Josh followed her.

'Yes.' Emma pulled the boot open, moving her own luggage out of the way so that she could reach a surprisingly bulky first aid kit. She handed it to Josh and they jogged together across the uneven ground.

As they got closer, Josh could see two grey heads, still in the car, and that the driver's side of the windscreen was smashed and buckled. George and Tess had been talking just the other day about how retirement seemed like one long holiday. It looked as if the holiday had just come to an abrupt end, and Josh hoped against hope that neither of them were too badly hurt.

'Tess… Tess…' Emma had run round to the passenger seat of the car, and Josh saw her lean in, and heard the sound of Tess crying. George seemed to be motionless in the driver's seat, and Josh made for him.

'He's bleeding, Emma… I can't stop the bleeding.'

Emma glanced up at Josh, who was carefully prising the driver's door open as far as it would go. George seemed to be unconscious and pinned to the front seat by a strut that had come loose from the side of the windscreen. There was blood everywhere.

'I've got George. Will you call for an ambulance?'

Emma pulled out her phone and dialled, tucking the phone between her chin and her shoulder as she opened the passenger door. Before she could stop her, Tess got out of the car, seemingly not badly injured, and Emma led her away, talking quickly on the phone. Josh turned his attention to George.

She'd clearly made the same assessment of the situation that he had, because Josh had barely located the source of the bleeding, tearing George's shirt to expose the wound, when Emma appeared again at the open passenger door.

'Airways are clear and he's unconscious.' Josh automatically reeled off his observations. 'One of the support struts for the windscreen has been driven right through his shoulder and is pinning him to the seat. I don't see any other bleeding.'

Emma nodded. Josh was about to ask her if she'd come around this side of the car and monitor George's wound, while he got inside to check on him, but she was already in the car, squeezing past the buckled dashboard to reach George.

'There's some gauze in the first aid kit. And gloves...'

This was probably the best use of their resources, but Josh didn't like it that Emma had crawled into the car, while he was safely outside. She'd done it now though, and he bent to open the box at his feet, keeping one hand on the wound to stem the bleeding and hooking out a packet of gauze with the other.

'How's his pulse?' Josh quickly packed the gauze around the wound.

'Steady. His breathing's okay.'

'Then let's keep him in situ for a moment while I take a look at the back of the seat to see if I can get the strut out if I need to.'

'All right.' Josh felt her hand on top of his, keeping the pressure up on the wound as he craned around. He could see the slender tip of the metal protruding from the back of the seat and it looked as if there was nothing that would prevent him from withdrawing the strut from the other side.

If he did that, then he could well damage an artery and George might bleed to death. He'd almost certainly do more damage to his shoulder than if the strut were removed in an operating theatre. But if George stopped breathing or his heart failed, they'd have to take those risks in order to get him out of the car and resuscitate him. Emma was closest to George and she could monitor him more thoroughly, which meant that the decision about whether it was safe to keep him in the car until the ambulance arrived was hers alone.

It was a huge weight of responsibility, and Josh had wanted to take that burden himself. But now there was no option, and he knew exactly what she needed. It was what he needed in the operating theatre: support and communication from the people around him.

'I can get him free and out of the car. It's on your word, Em. I need you to tell me if it looks as if he's in difficulties.'

She puffed out a breath, and then nodded. 'Okay. I'm going to get closer.'

Emma wriggled round, in a manoeuvre that Josh couldn't have managed in the confined space, carefully swinging so that she could directly face him. Josh used his free hand to steady her.

'Thanks. There's a stethoscope in my bag.'

Josh hooked the stethoscope out of her bag with one hand, putting it around her neck and positioning the diaphragm against George's chest. Emma clipped the earpieces into her ears, listening for a moment.

'Sounds good. Let me listen to his chest.'

Josh moved the diaphragm again, and Emma nodded. 'Good. Surprisingly so. We'll stay here.'

'Okay. The bleeding is stopping…' Now all they needed to do was to keep things that way, until help arrived. 'Did they say how long the ambulance would be?'

'About ten minutes. They're sending a fire and rescue truck as well. Should be here any time, now.'

'Good. Hang in there.'

She glanced up at him for one moment, but that was enough. Josh saw the motion of her lips, framing the words *Thank you*, and knew that Emma was relying on him.

They kept working. Checking and then checking again that George's vital signs were stable and that there was no internal bleeding. He saw Emma's smile when the sounds of sirens reached their ears, and popped his head out of the car for one moment, calling to Tess, who had jumped to her feet.

'Tess, please stay there. We're doing all we can for George and he's stable at the moment.'

That was all he could say in the way of reassurance right now, but in the few minutes she'd spent with her, Emma must have managed to impress on Tess that she could best help by staying out of the way. Tess sat back down, hugging her arms around her chest and rocking silently.

They kept working, and when the ambulance crew arrived, Josh ducked quickly out of the car to speak to them, telling them he was a doctor and showing them the ID in his wallet, then quickly relaying George's condition. He broke off, as he heard Emma call out to him.

'Josh… Help me, he's waking up.'

Josh returned to the car and dropped to one knee again. George was showing every sign of beginning to regain consciousness, and at any moment he would be in a lot of pain. The paramedic saw immediately what was needed and confirmed that he was carrying analgesic, and Josh agreed to the intended dose.

'I'm going to try to hold him still, but you need to talk to him, Em.' If anything could calm George it would be the sound of her voice.

It was a lot to ask, but Emma nodded. She leaned down, tapping the side of George's face with her finger as Josh braced his arms around his shoulder to keep it still. 'George. It's Emma. Listen to me, George...'

George was moaning now, and starting to move. 'George. It's Emma. Try to stay still for me.'

'Tess...' The one word sounded like a howl of pain.

'Tess is all right. She's fine, she's waiting for you, George. Stay still for me.'

Emma kept talking to him, as the paramedic squeezed alongside Josh, administering the shot. George was whimpering with pain, but he was listening to her and doing his best to keep still, which made it easier for Josh to hold his shoulder steady.

Emma had done it. Josh had been dreading what might happen when George woke up but she'd got them over that hurdle and the fast-acting analgesics would be kicking in soon. They still had a lot left to do, but they were a team now, thinking and acting as one. If anything could get George out in one piece, it was their teamwork.

Josh had been her strength. He'd been calm and supportive, helping her to monitor George and make the decisions that she needed to make. The analgesics were taking effect, and Emma was able to gauge George's condition better now using the ambulance equipment that Josh was handing in for her.

'Tess...' George's speech was beginning to slur.

'Tess is fine, George. She's got one of the ambulance crew with her, and they're looking after her.' Josh had been keeping her informed about what was going on out-side the car as well.

'I have to see her.'

'I know, and you'll see her soon. There's a team working right now to get you out of the car. You've been so brave. I just need you to hold on a little bit longer.'

'I'll…try…' George's eyelids were beginning to droop and Emma gently tapped the side of his face to keep his attention. It was a delicate balance; George wouldn't feel any pain if he slipped back into unconsciousness, but it was important to keep him awake so that he was able to register any distress.

'Don't you wanna shout, *Stay with me*?' George's dry sense of humour surfaced suddenly, probably encouraged by the level of opioids in his bloodstream.

'I could do. Best not to shout though, or Tess will hear me.'

'Uh.' George winced as another wave of pain gripped him. 'Yeah. Good girl.'

'The fire and rescue guys are ready. Want me to take over?' Josh's voice caught her attention.

Yes. Emma was scared and she wanted to stretch her cramped and aching limbs. But Josh couldn't get into this confined space and George was trusting her to stay with him.

'I'm fine. Tell them to get on with it.'

One moment. It was more than enough time to feel the warmth of his blue eyes washing over her. Comforting her and giving her strength. She'd seen the trace of concern in his face when she'd got into the car, and if Josh reck-oned that her actions were irresponsible or reckless, he was keeping it to himself.

'Okay. The protective shield's on its way.'

She felt his fingers brush her arm as the firefight-ers moved in to tuck the flexible shields around her and

George. Feeling Josh there made it easier to be strong for George, and she could tell him what he needed to hear quietly and confidently.

She heard the order to stand back, but knew Josh was still there. She could hear his voice, and focusing on that made it easier to comfort George effectively.

The car vibrated as the fire and rescue team peeled its roof back, like the skin of an orange. George swore quietly, at the thought of his beloved Alpha being cut to bits, but Emma had already prepared him for it, and he knew it had to be done. More noise and vibration as the seat was freed from its housing, and then the protective shields were removed, and Emma blinked in the afternoon sun.

'Time to move, Em.' Josh was back again.

'Uh... Give me a moment.' She'd been crouched in the same position for so long now that it felt as if her arms and legs had locked into position.

'Relax. Let go.' Josh wrapped his arms around her, lifting her away from George. As he set her on her feet she felt his lips brush her cheek. Probably by accident.

No. Not by accident. There had been no room for error this afternoon and the look in Josh's eyes told her that this was no accident either. But he had to go now, and he turned away, helping the ambulance paramedic carefully support the strut that pinned George's shoulder, as the fire and rescue team lifted the seat, with George in it, out of the car.

In a triumph of good timing, which was consistent with the rest of the operation, a dull beat announced the sound of the arrival of the air ambulance, which would reduce George's travelling time into the main hospital in Cardiff from over an hour to minutes. Emma stretched her aching limbs, stumbling over to the Mini. She pulled an oversized T-shirt from the boot over her head, which was enough to shield her as she wriggled out of her bloodstained shirt and then opened a bottle of water, using it to wash her hands before walking over to Tess. The ambulance driver who was sitting with her got to his feet, saying he had some calls to make and leaving the two women alone.

Tess was cradling one hand in her lap, and Emma could see that, above the wrist support she'd been given, her fingers were swollen. She sat down next to her.

'He'll be all right, Tess. It all looks really scary, but that's because everyone's doing their best to keep the injury to George's shoulder stable. Josh is making a decision now about whether they can lift George out of the seat without doing any damage to his shoulder.'

'Thank you.' Tess shrugged tearfully. 'Will he be able to use his arm?'

'I don't know the full extent of his injury, Tess, none of us will until he's in surgery. What I can tell you is that Josh has done everything he can to minimise the damage, and that the surgeons will do all they can to restore the use of that arm. The techniques they use…' Emma shrugged, grinning at Tess. 'You don't really need chapter and verse about the techniques, do you? Just that some of them look a lot like miracles.'

'I've had my miracle for the day. You and Josh found us, and… I care about George's arm, of course, but all I really need him to do is to stay alive.'

Emma put her arm around Tess's shoulders wishing that she knew how it felt, to have someone whose name was the first thing on your lips when you were hurt and frightened. She'd seen it time and time again, in the course of her work, but she'd never worked with Josh before. Today had made her feel that calling *his* name might not be a completely outrageous thing for her to do.

Although he wouldn't hear… Josh would be staying in London after the rally, and she'd be going back to Liverpool. She might want him around in an emergency, but their differences were too great to withstand the everyday.

That was the test that George and Tess had taken on, and they seemed to have passed with flying colours if their easy camaraderie over the last week was anything to go by.

Tess was hugging her tight, and right now nothing else mattered. The air ambulance flew over their heads, and Emma looked across at the team working with George. Josh must have decided it was safe to take him out of the car seat, and was supervising his transfer onto a carrycot from the ambulance.

The air ambulance was coming in to land now, and it looked as if they'd be on the move soon. Emma waited for the roar of the rotor blades to subside, so that they could talk again.

'Has the ambulance driver said where they'll be taking you, Tess? If he gives me directions I'll follow you.' It looked as if Josh would be going with George, and Emma hoped that Griff wouldn't get distressed when he saw Josh leave. He'd been sitting in the back of the Mini, quietly watching through the open window, and even when the helicopter had landed he hadn't started to bark. That was yet another miracle to add to the total for today.

'Don't you worry about that, Emma, you've done more than enough already. They're sending someone from the GDK Foundation to meet me at the hospital. I'll be fine.' Tess smiled up at the ambulance driver, who was walking back towards them. 'Has everything been sorted out, Henry?'

Henry squatted down in front of her. 'Yes, your husband's going straight to the main hospital in Cardiff. Apparently the man you were with is a surgeon, so he's going to accompany him in the air ambulance.'

'Josh?' Tess turned to Emma.

'Yes, that's right. Josh will take really good care of George and he'll be able to speak to the surgeon in Cardiff and tell him exactly what's happened. That'll help with the decisions he has to make about how best to repair the damage to George's shoulder.'

Henry nodded. 'And as for you, Tess, I've called your rally people back and they said that Erica from the GDK Foundation is at the local hospital waiting for you. You know her?'

Tess smiled at him. 'Yes, I know Erica. Thank you.'

'Right. I'll make sure that Erica has the number for the Cardiff hospital, where they're taking your husband, and as soon as we've finished with you at the local hospital, she'll take you there.'

'Thank you, Henry.'

It seemed that Emma would be making the journey to Cardiff on her own. Josh was needed elsewhere, and she'd have to make do with giving Griff a few extra-large hugs instead. Emma helped Tess to her feet, and she and Henry walked slowly with her to the back of the ambulance.

'I wish I was going with him.' Tess looked back at the air ambulance, tears in her eyes.

'I know. The best thing you can do for George right now is to let Josh take care of him.' Emma put her arm around Tess's shoulders. 'I promise he will take really good care of him.'

'I know. Thank you. Will you... Can you tell him that I love him?' Tess seemed a little bashful in sharing the message with Emma, but it was obviously important to her.

'I'll go and speak to Josh now. I dare say you know what his answer's going to be.'

Tess blushed slightly. 'Yes, I know.'

Emma left Henry to settle Tess in the ambulance and jogged back towards the group who were clustered around George. Josh saw her coming and turned to her. There was time enough for a few words...

'Tess has a message for George. Tell him that she loves him.'

Josh smiled. 'I'll make sure to tell him.'

'Okay. I'll…um…see you later on? At the hotel?'

'I may be a while, but if you want to wait here, I'll head back and we'll finish the drive to Cardiff.'

'It doesn't matter how long you are. I'll wait.' Josh knew how much this meant to her. She'd wait all day and all night for him if he said he was coming back.

He shot her that melting blue-eyed look of his. The one that said she could trust him. 'Sit tight, then. I'll see you later.'

Emma had called the rally supervisor, and he'd said that there would be someone there to check them in, whatever time they arrived. He would also arrange for the local car club, who were helping with this leg of the rally, to come out and salvage whatever was left of Tess and George's car.

It didn't seem that there was a great deal to salvage, but Emma had been around car enthusiasts all her life, and seen gleaming cars carefully reconstructed from husks that were much more damaged than this. If George and Tess wanted to spend the next phase of their retirement recreating the Alpha, then at least they'd have the chance to do so, and she guessed she wouldn't be alone in showing up and offering to help. Emma let Griff out of the Mini, fastening his lead to his collar, and took him on a long walk to find and retrieve the various car parts that were scattered along the Alpha's trajectory from the road to the tree trunk.

A taxi brought Josh back, almost three hours later, as she was finishing what was left of the sandwiches that had been stowed away in the boot of the Mini, out of Griff's reach. By yet another miracle, he was holding a paper carrier bag and two large cardboard cups.

'Coffee?'

He sat down beside her on the grass. 'No. What do you

want with coffee, when I have a nutritionally balanced, high-roughage health drink for you.'

Emma grabbed one of the containers. 'It's coffee. I can smell it.'

'I've got sandwiches as well.' Josh snatched the carrier away, as Griff ambled over to investigate it.

'You can share them with Griff. I've just eaten all the emergency sandwiches I had in the boot.'

'You had emergency sandwiches?' Josh turned the corners of his mouth down. 'I wish you'd told *me*.'

'And when were you going to eat them? You were busy. How's George?'

'In surgery. It looks as if they'll be able to get the strut out without damaging the primary nerves, but we'll have to wait and see. I left before Tess arrived—I didn't want her to see me with George's blood all over my shirt—but I called her from the taxi and gave her an update.' He took a long swig of his coffee, throwing Griff's ball, and the dog ran after it barking joyfully.

He left the bag of sandwiches on the grass beside her and got to his feet, opening the boot of the Mini and pulling a clean shirt out of his bag. Then Josh glanced back in her direction.

'Turn around.'

He'd caught her staring and stopped unbuttoning his shirt.

'What do you mean turn around? You're happy to take your shirt off in full view of any passing motorists, but I have to turn around?'

'Yeah, you do.' Josh grinned suddenly. 'That's our deal.'

Shame. He was right though, they needed rules that they could stick to. Particularly now, when she felt so close to him. Emma turned around, picking up her coffee cup. 'Remind me, Josh. What did *you* do after you helped me out of the car this afternoon?'

'That was a friendly kiss. On the cheek.'

So it *was* a kiss. Emma heard his footsteps behind her and wiped the smile off her face before he sat down next to her, rolling the sleeves of his shirt up.

'I'm reckoning that honesty's a part of the deal too. You were so brave, and I couldn't help it.'

'Not reckless?' She'd been hoping that the word hadn't occurred to Josh.

He shook his head. 'You were able to squeeze in there a lot better than I could. And maybe you just went ahead and did it because you thought I'd object...'

'That crossed my mind. I thought you'd understand though; you had everything pretty well planned out.'

'Not...down to the last excruciating and needless detail?'

He remembered what Emma had said to him, just as clearly as she remembered what he'd said to her. 'No. None of the details were excruciating or needless.'

'Right. Glad we spoke, then.' Griff returned with the ball, dropping it at his feet, and Josh threw it again.

'I see you've organised for the Alpha to be salvaged.' He gestured towards the now empty piece of grass where George's car had come to rest. 'Should we go and check that nothing's been left behind?'

'No, the local car club came and did it. About twenty of them turned up, and they were really organised and got everything loaded up in the back of a truck in less than an hour. *And* they swept with metal detectors to make sure they hadn't missed anything. We can get back onto the road as soon as you've eaten and I've drunk my coffee.'

Josh nodded, obviously turning something over in his mind. Then he turned to her. 'It was nice working with you, Emma.'

That meant a great deal, and Emma needed to tell him. This was the first and last time they'd find themselves working together like this, and she wouldn't have the chance to say it again. They'd already left far too much unsaid.

'We did more than just working together, didn't we? You were the friend who gave me the strength to do what needed to be done. And you're the friend who came back for me, to finish today's leg of the rally.'

He smiled suddenly. 'This friendship thing. I'm starting to really like it.'

CHAPTER FIVE

JOSH WAS TIRED. Not just I-could-go-to-sleep tired, but the kind of tired he remembered from his first year of surgical training. The last few days had been non-stop, trying to fill in for David, take part in the rally and get his head around his relationship with Emma. Then the intense concentration involved in getting George out of the car and keeping his mind on the road as they drove into Cardiff, stopping to complete all of the challenges as they went.

'You're out of time for any bonus points on today's leg.' The steward who was waiting for them at the finishing point in Cardiff shook both his and Emma's hands. 'But congratulations, both of you.'

Emma had smiled up at him, and Josh had felt suddenly awake. The sensation didn't last long though, and by the time they'd parked and made their way across to the hotel, he was beginning to doze on his feet.

'I spy a coffee lounge.' Emma tugged at his sleeve. 'I wonder if they do cocoa?'

'I expect they do, but I'm going to have to take a rain check. I need to take Griff for a walk and then do the blog post for tonight.' Josh looked down at Griff, who wasn't displaying his usual excitement at hearing the word *walk*. Emma looked almost as tired as he felt, and perhaps Griff's team instinct was kicking in and he'd decided to curl up and fall asleep too.

'I took him for a walk *and* spent an hour throwing his ball for him—that's got to be enough for today surely. And how long is the blog post going to take, fifteen minutes? You could do it over cocoa...'

Emma seemed determined to divert him and it *was* tempting. Very tempting, particularly as the coffee lounge had deep armchairs to sink into and the thought of relaxing with her at the end of a long day when so much had happened seemed like perfect bliss at the moment.

'Fifteen minutes for you, maybe. It took me three hours and a call to GDK's head of IT to get it right last night. I'm not the founder of the organ recipients blog, remember?' That had just slipped out. Something from their past together; in fact, pretty much the first good thing from their past that either he or Emma had spoken about.

'Well, that's just outrageous. Three hours and a phone call, and you couldn't even get the photographs lined up?' Emma had clearly been checking yesterday's blog out.

'Like I say.' Josh grinned down at her, the familiar forthright humour sending tingles down his spine. 'I don't have your natural ability.'

'Clearly not. Give me your laptop.' She held out her hand. 'We'll have some cocoa, you can show me where everything is and then you can go out with Griff if you think he wants a walk. I'll have it done by the time you get back.'

'You don't need...' Actually, he wanted her to. Very much.

'I'm not taking any arguments, Josh. We're in this together.'

It really felt as if they were. Josh gave in to the inevitable, opening his bag and handing his laptop over. They found a sofa where Emma could look over his shoulder at the screen, and Griff needed no encouragement to curl up in the space under the coffee table for a snooze. A waiter brought two cups of cocoa, and Josh opened his email, downloading all of the attachments and logging on to the GDK Foundation's blog.

'All right. I can take it from here.' She tugged at the corner of the laptop and Josh handed it over.

Emma set to work, cropping photographs and adding captions, seeming to know exactly how much to cut to make the images seem as vibrant and full of life as she was. She was absorbed in her task, but she turned suddenly as if a thought had occurred to her.

'You've decided against taking Griff for a walk?'

Josh nodded down towards Griff, whose paws were twitching, clearly in the grip of some doggy dream. 'I might have to carry him, and that rather defeats the object. I'm watching and learning.'

She grinned at him. 'Right, then. You want me to go a bit slower?'

Nope. The regular, repetitive actions on the screen, along with the quiet rattle of the beads around Emma's wrist, were strangely soothing. Josh stretched his legs out in front of him, leaning back on the soft cushions…

'Ow!'

Waking a guy up with a soft kiss… Josh knew full well that Emma knew how to do that. Clearly she also knew exactly how to wake someone up with an elbow to the ribs. He hoped that his reaction had satisfied all of her expectations.

She was smirking. Clearly it had.

He wiped his hand across his face, trying to gather his thoughts. 'Am I supposed to say *sorry* for falling asleep on you?'

Her smile broadened. 'Didn't I just relieve you of the necessity?'

'Probably. You've finished?' Josh leant over and saw that the screen displayed the new blog. 'It looks good. I really appreciate it.'

She nodded, brushing his thanks away. 'I might take the job over. Since I'm better at it than you.'

She did that a lot. Cloaked her kindness with a brisk smile and a smart answer. Josh was just wondering whether he ought to point that out, when a tone sounded from his laptop and a box popped up on the screen announcing a video call. He felt Emma jump, and move suddenly away from him, out of range of the camera, and realised their shoulders had been almost touching.

'What does David want?' Emma's tone held the implication she'd been caught doing something she shouldn't.

'I have no idea. I expect it's about what happened today.' Josh reached forward and answered his father's call.

'Dad. How are things?'

David smiled. 'Fine. Very good. I heard about George and Tess.'

'I guessed you must have. Erica called you?'

'Yes. What's your assessment, Josh?'

'I had a word with the surgeon who was going to operate on George's shoulder, and stayed while they took X-rays and did some tests. First indications are that the strut from the car hasn't caused major damage, and that in time and with some intensive physiotherapy he may well recover full use of his arm.'

David nodded. 'Good. And Tess?'

'Fractured wrist along with some cuts and bruises. Erica found a nice hotel close to the hospital and is staying with her tonight.'

'That's great. I've told Erica that I'll personally cover anything that they need, including physiotherapy and ongoing medical consultation for George.'

That was exactly as Josh would have expected. 'Thanks, Dad.'

'It made a lot of difference that you and Emma were

there. I hear you both played a big part in getting George out of the car without making his injuries any worse.'

Suddenly, Josh wanted his father to know. That Emma was here, and that after all the pain and uncertainty of the past they'd finally managed to do something good together. Maybe Emma did too, because suddenly she leaned over, smiling into the camera.

'Hi, David. I'm right here, so don't say anything too nice about me.' She grinned brightly and David's fleeting look of surprise turned into a smile.

'Sorry, Emma. I think I'm going to have to embarrass you. You and Josh did a fine job. The fact that you then went on to finish the course and secure your sponsorships for the day is an added bonus.'

'I waited with the car and Josh came back for me.' The small catch in her voice told Josh that it had meant something to her. He'd hoped it had.

David nodded, taking a sip of his drink. Emma was staring fixedly at the screen now, as if something wasn't quite right. 'How are things going in Liverpool?'

'Well. Very well. In fact, I have some good news... Although I wanted to tell you in person, Josh.'

David always reckoned that good news was better in person, and Josh was inclined to agree with him. 'We'll be in London in a few days. You're coming down for the wrap party, aren't you?'

'I wouldn't miss it for the world. I'll catch you then and we can talk. How's Griff?'

'Asleep at the moment. Hold on...' Emma ducked down, rubbing behind Griff's ears to wake him, in a much gentler fashion than she had Josh. The sound of David's voice prompted a frenzy of tail-wagging, and when they said their goodbyes David was all smiles. It was good to see him so relaxed and happy.

'I wonder what the news is...' Josh closed his laptop,

glancing at Emma, who was pressing her lips together thoughtfully. 'You know, don't you?'

She jumped like a startled gazelle. 'No! Um... David should tell you.'

She knew. Josh leaned back on the sofa. 'Five days. It's a long time for you to hold out.'

Emma reddened.

'Especially when I'll be catching you unawares, asking you when you least expect it. Watching every move, putting two and two together...'

'Don't! Josh, it's their news, not mine.' She clapped her hand over her mouth, reddening even more.

'See. Two minutes and it's *their* news, not just Dad's.' Josh was brimming with curiosity now. 'You can't hold out, Em, you'll tell me sooner or later.'

Emma puffed out a breath. 'Stop looking at me like that, Josh.'

Josh was quite aware he'd been looking at her—who wouldn't look at Emma whenever they got the chance—but *like that*? Maybe his gaze still did have some effect on her, and if it was a fraction of the seductive warmth that hers had on him, she'd tell him everything. When he smiled, Emma rolled her eyes and puffed out a breath.

'Don't make things easy on me, will you? I suppose...it wouldn't do any harm to get used to the idea before David breaks the news. I'd like to put it on record that you forced this out of me though.'

'I applied intolerable pressure.' He could put a little more pressure on her and kiss her. Right now. Anytime, in fact. Sadly, it looked as if that wasn't going to be necessary.

'David was sitting on Val's sofa. And did you see that purple mug with the hedgehogs on it that he was drinking out of? That's Val's favourite mug. She never gives it to anyone else.'

Josh stared at her. 'Dad and Val?'

'It would explain where Val kept disappearing off to during the first week of the rally. *And* the dangly earrings.'

'Dangly earrings? Is that code for something?'

'No, but Val made them from the jar of beads we brought along. She never wears dangly earrings.'

Josh thought back. 'I remember them now. They suited her.'

'And your father clearly agreed.'

Josh thought for a moment. 'Do you think I should call him back?'

Emma looked at him pleadingly. 'And say what? That I just told you his big secret? He obviously wants to tell you face to face.'

'Yeah, I expect he does. I'd like it better too. You can't really shake someone's hand and slap them on the back via the internet. It's about time he turned his mind to something other than work.'

'It's about time Val let someone into her life too.' Emma was fiddling nervously with the beads at her wrist. 'It's really not weird at all, is it…?'

It might have been…slightly…if his and Emma's relationship had survived. 'Nah. Maybe we can just say that we played our part in bringing them together. Since we were both so understanding about their sneaking off in the evenings.'

Emma puffed out a relieved breath. 'Yes, that's nice. You don't mind?'

Josh shook his head. 'It's been twenty years since my mum died. Dad's been alone for a long time, and Val's perfect for him. We'll give them a bit of space and let them tell us in their own time.'

Emma puffed out a breath of relief. 'Thank you.'

'Now I know how Dad felt when I first brought a girl home.' Josh couldn't help smiling at the sudden reversal of roles.

'How's that?'

'Well… I really hope he doesn't do anything stupid and mess this up.'

'I was just thinking that about Val. I reckon they'll manage just fine without us.'

They were both laughing now, and Josh realised that his arm was around Emma's shoulders. He wasn't entirely sure how it had got there, just that it felt right. Josh had never realised just how good they could be together as friends, and he was still coming to terms with that.

Coming to terms with it didn't mean taking things any further. They'd tried that already and it hadn't worked so maybe Josh should be concentrating on not messing up with Emma. He let her go, and leant forward, picking up his laptop and hugging that instead.

'I really *have* to sleep.'

Emma nodded. 'Me too. I'll see you in the morning.'

The next morning Josh woke late, to find Griff sprawled across his chest and licking his cheek. He'd dreamed that it was Emma, only she'd been kissing him and her breath smelled sweet. Josh groaned, pushing Griff's nose out of his face, and stomped downstairs to enquire as to why the hotel staff hadn't given him his early morning wake-up call.

It turned out that Emma had cancelled it. The Mini was gone from the hotel car park and Josh combined Griff's morning walk with a jog over to where they'd be lined up for the awareness event. Cardiff was one of the three most important capital city stops and he couldn't help feeling annoyed. That evaporated slightly when he saw that the event was in full swing, and glimpsed Emma right in the thick of things, giving out leaflets and talking to people who were crowding around her car.

'All right, you made your point. You didn't need me, after all.' The thought hurt more than it should because Emma looked particularly radiant today, dressed in a blue miniskirt with a matching longline jacket, her hair caught up in curls and shining in the sun.

'Oh, Josh! Of course we need you. What about all the calls you've been making from the car to organise things, while you're trying to navigate?'

'*Trying* to navigate? We haven't missed anything, have we?' He was still feeling a little grumpy.

'No, we haven't, which only goes to show that you can do two things at once. All the work you've done to hold the rally together means that it isn't going to collapse in a heap if you get a bit of sleep.' Her attention was caught suddenly by a little boy who was tugging at her skirt. 'Hi, sweetie. Where's your mum and dad?'

The boy pointed over to a couple who were standing a few yards away and Emma nodded to them, then bent down to hear what he was saying. 'You want a car like this when you grow up? With sunshine around the wheels?'

She leaned forward, again nodding as the boy whispered something else. 'Is he? What's your brother's name?' The boy whispered again and Emma smiled. 'Well, thank you for coming here today to tell me about him.'

Emma beckoned the parents over and turned to Josh. 'Matthew's brother has just been put on the list for a kidney transplant. And he'd like to go for a ride in the Mini so... I think I've just found a new navigator. You're out of a job there too.'

The mischief in her smile when she said it made Josh laugh. 'Okay. Message received and understood.' He turned to Matthew's parents, holding out his hand. 'Hi. I'm Josh Kennedy. I'm a transplant surgeon and I'm here

with the GDK Foundation today. I gather your son is
waiting for a new kidney...?'

The last few days had been unbroken sunshine. They'd
driven across the Severn Bridge, and into England, stopping in Bath. Emma had accompanied Josh and Griff on
a long walk, which took in the outside of some of Bath's
more famous tourist attractions which were all closed for
the day.

'It would be nice to come back and sample the Roman
baths, sometime.' She wasn't sure whether Josh's comment
was just a comment or an invitation.

'Yes, it would.' Emma wasn't sure either whether her
reply was an acceptance or not.

The next morning she woke to an almost night-time
darkness in the sky. Heavy thunderclouds covered the sun,
and she added a black plastic mac and sou'wester that she'd
found in a vintage shop to her outfit. As they drove out of
Bath the skies opened and it began to rain heavily.

'Had to happen, I suppose.' The windows in the Mini
were misting up, already. One of the disadvantages of a
classic car was that they were considerably more comfortable to drive in good weather.

'Yeah, we've been lucky with the weather so far.' Josh
leaned forward, wiping the windscreen so that she could
see out as thunder rolled in the sky over their heads.

They made it out of Bath, the route winding through
minor roads until there was a short stretch on the busy
road that passed Stonehenge. Of course there were pictures to be taken, and Emma found a spot where she could
pull off safely.

'Here we go, then. Time to get our feet wet.' She reached
for her mac and sou'wester that were rolled up under the
seat. They had to take turns, Josh getting into his waterproof jacket first, while Emma squashed herself against

the driver's door, and then giving Emma room to pull on her mac.

Stonehenge stood in the distance, surrounded by mist, the dark clouds blending with the grey stones. This seemed like the best way to see it, travellers arriving after a long journey as they had for thousands of years. Griff was more than happy to stay in the car, while Emma shivered and posed for a photograph, water trickling down her neck.

As Josh was wiping the lens on his phone camera, a flash rent the sky, followed by the deep growl of thunder. Then another...

'Josh! Did you get it?'

'Think so...' He turned, running for the cover of the car.

Griff protested a bit, shaking himself as scattered drops of water landed on him when they got back out of their coats. Then Josh handed her the phone, and Emma flipped through the pictures.

There were a couple of her standing in the rain, then one blur as he'd raised the phone quickly and then the perfect shot. Thunder and lightning over Stonehenge. Despite the busy road on one side of them, the one-angled view of the camera made it seem that she was standing alone, in a wild and mysterious landscape.

'Ah! I love it, Josh!' She stared at the photograph.

'Worth getting wet for?'

'Yes, absolutely. Don't you think it's wonderful?'

He laughed, nodding. Josh might be ever practical, but he always appreciated a bit of outrageous fun when it presented itself. 'Yeah. It's wonderful.'

They kept driving, back on the country roads now. They were easier because there wasn't so much traffic, but Josh had to keep a close watch for hazards. The skies cleared, and then closed over again, a sudden, heavy downpour bouncing water from the surface of the road. Emma stopped the car, peering ahead of them.

'What do you think?' A stream of water was crossing the road, moving fast down the hill. A tractor was negotiating its way slowly through it, but the Mini was a lighter, lower vehicle.

'We can't get through that, Em.' He noted the time and the hazard ahead of them on his navigation notes. 'Hold on, I'll ask this guy if there's a different way round.'

He donned his jacket again, running to the side of the tractor that had stopped right in front of them. Their conversation seemed to involve a fair bit of pointing and then Josh ran back to the car, raising his hand in thanks to the tractor driver as he started his vehicle and drove away. He took his jacket off before he got back into the car this time, letting it shield him from the worst of the downpour as Emma leaned over, pushing the door open.

'He says we'd have to go all the way back to where we turned onto this road, and around...' Josh traced his finger on the map, along the route they'd have to take. 'But this road always floods in heavy rain and it'll drain off down the hill pretty quickly. He reckons if we wait half an hour there'll be no problem getting through.'

'I say we wait, then. It'll take us more than half an hour to get round and we'll miss some of the clues for stops. We won't lose points for stopping as long as we note the hazard.'

'Yeah, agreed.' Josh put the map down, stretching his legs as far as he could. The windows of the car began to mist again, and Emma pulled off the road while she could still see well enough to manoeuvre. There was a long lay-by at the side of the road, suggesting cars regularly waited here in the rain.

'Where is everyone?' She scanned the empty road. Any delays usually precipitated a small tailback of rally cars, as the gaps between them closed up.

'Maybe they've stopped further back. I dare say they'll be catching up with us when this downpour eases.'

Josh looked around as Griff began to register his dis-approval of the situation. The back window was leaking, drips of water getting in through the rubber window seals, landing on his nose and ears. Emma stretched back, but couldn't reach the seat belt clip.

'Josh, let him come in the front with us.'

He reached back, and Griff scrambled forward, onto her lap. Emma hugged him and he quietened down a bit.

'You okay?'

There was no escaping Josh's perceptive gaze. Maybe she didn't want to.

'That seal's always leaked a bit. My dad did everything he could with it, but when it rained really heavily like this I still used to get wet in the back of the car. Mum kept a little waterproof jacket to cover me up with.' Those old memories seemed so much more precious now.

'If this is the only leak, your dad did a good job.'

Josh always remembered to acknowledge the things that Dad had done with the car over the years. Emma liked that he did, but the moment seemed even more bittersweet for it. She stroked Griff's ears, too wary of reaching out for Josh, which was what she really wanted to do.

'I miss him.'

Josh nodded. 'Yeah. It's only been a year.'

'I thought things were supposed to get better after a year.' That's what all the articles she'd read said.

He reached over, his fingers stroking Griff's head. It seemed that Griff was getting all the human contact that Emma really wanted with Josh. 'I suppose if you want to draw up a timetable, then a year might be a ballpark figure to play with. You said you stayed with your mum for six months afterwards, before moving down to Liverpool?'

Emma nodded. 'Yeah, she needed me around for a while. Then she told me that she was fine and that she wanted me to go and live my own life.'

'Has it ever occurred to you that those six months were mainly taken up considering her needs? And that she made you go so that you could start feeling the things you needed to feel?' Josh's voice was tender.

'No, it hasn't. I guess Mum's a bit smarter than me.'

Josh shook his head. 'She's just seen a little more, that's all.'

'You still miss your mum, don't you?' Emma knew that Josh did, although he never spoke about it.

'Yeah. It does stop tearing at you though. Dad helped me a lot with that, even though he was grieving for her as well.'

That was a good way to describe it. Emma could operate perfectly normally, but there always seemed to be something tearing at her.

'I just feel…you know, that we always moved around a lot, for Dad's job. I loved it, a new place every summer when he went to join a different archaeological dig. When he was ill, he would tell me not to bother about him, and that I should be living my life. Keeping my wheels turning…' A tear rolled down Emma's cheek.

Josh leaned over, brushing it away. The contact meant everything, because it *was* so fleeting, and even though it was inevitable that they touch in this confined space, they'd always done so before by mistake.

'That's a hundred percent right and a hundred percent wrong, all at the same time, isn't it?' Josh was thoughtful.

'And how do you calculate the maths of that?'

'Something Dad said to me when my mum died.' He grinned suddenly. 'Imagine us carting bricks…'

'Difficult…' Emma closed her eyes and the picture in her head made her smile. 'I'm imagining.'

'He said he wasn't sticking with me out of duty, and there were times when it wasn't much of a pleasure. He was doing it because it was his *right*. It was your right to stick by your dad when he was ill, and I'm guessing that both your parents understood that, and that you have no regrets about exercising it.'

'No, I don't. What's the other side of the equation?'

'That, right now, you can remember the part about living your life. Keeping your wheels turning.'

Emma opened her eyes. 'I came on the rally thinking that driving all this way would be a way of doing that. At the moment though it just seems that I'm on the move but still stuck in the same place.'

'Give it time. You'll find that feeling of moving forward again. You're at your best with your wheels turning.'

It was nice of him to say that, considering it was what had broken them up in the first place. A car drew up in the lay-by behind them, and they both looked round.

'That's Ryan and Kaitlin.' The celebrity duo seemed to have decided to wait in the car, which was wise because even though the downpour had eased off a bit it was still raining.

Josh nodded. 'I should go and have a word with them.' He hesitated, obviously wondering whether there was anything else that Emma wanted to say.

'Go. I'm going to do the really hard job and keep Griff dry.' She grinned at him and Josh nodded.

'Okay. Well, good luck with that.' He reached for her again, brushing his fingers across the back of her hand. One tiny gesture, limited by all of the things that they were most afraid of, but it meant everything. And then he was out of the car, pulling his jacket around him as he jogged back to the other vehicle.

'How does that happen, eh, Griff?' Emma hugged him and he wriggled with joy, resting his head on her shoulder. 'That we're so alike and yet so different.'

Griff didn't know, and neither did Emma. Maybe Dad and Josh were both right, and if she just kept the appearance of moving forward, one day she really would.

CHAPTER SIX

JOSH HAD CALLED David from the car that morning, when it had become apparent that the Salisbury event was going to be washed out. His father had told him to leave it with him, and as they crossed the finishing line, and were directed over to a large standing area for the cars, it became apparent that David had anticipated the possibility of rain and his contingency plans had swung into action. Emma caught her breath.

'David called out the army?' There were a couple of squaddies in waterproofs, directing cars into a line, at the edge of a long awning that protected the information tables and people who'd come to watch from the rain.

'Do you know how many contacts Dad has?' Josh chuckled.

'Well...yes, but...' Emma waved brightly to the squaddie who was indicating the Mini's place in the line. 'Thank you!'

Josh found the senior officer present, and shook his hand, thanking him. Emma pressed a leaflet into his hand, her impish smile suggesting that since he was here he may as well take one, and the officer smiled, beckoning to one of his men and telling him to make himself useful and give some leaflets out. He then turned back to Josh, asking how his father was these days. Clearly the foundation had been of assistance to him at some point, and he'd welcomed the chance to volunteer for this.

The event was smaller than planned, but everyone being squashed together to keep out of the rain had injected a camaraderie into the proceedings. He took some photos, emailing them to David, who replied with a smile emoji. He and Emma got back to their hotel late, after having helped with the clearing up, and he left Emma at the door of her room, expressing a craving for a very long, very hot shower. Josh went to his room, trying not to envision that.

The following day was bright and clear again, one of those days after heavy rain when everything seemed greener, even in the town. The trip from Salisbury to Brighton was a relatively long one and everyone was tired. The knowledge that London was only two days away now had become the driving force behind the smiles and camaraderie of the rally teams. When they crossed the county boundary from Wiltshire into Hampshire, Emma peeled out of the car, racing to pose for the camera next to the sign by the road. And Hampshire to Sussex elicited a whoop of joy that woke Griff up as he dozed in the back seat.

'Catch a falling star…' Emma frowned at the final clue that would gain them extra points. 'It'll be dark by the time we get to Brighton, so I suppose… Look for stars? Maybe there are some on the Brighton Pavilion; I've never noticed them.'

'We'll wait and see.' This was the one clue that Josh knew the answer to ahead of time. David had let it slip when he'd been talking about the arrangements for the rally.

'You *know*, don't you? Are you playing hard to get?'

'Yep. But I can't tell you. Dad swore me to secrecy.'

Emma frowned. 'So…how did you manage the fact

that David knew the answers to all the clues? Were you two cheating?'

'No. He didn't tell me any of the others. When we were driving I had to get all of the clues for extra points.'

'Hmm. Very honourable of you both. And it's too late for me to try and wrestle the answer from you.' Emma shot him a mischievous look that, yet again, made Josh's insides go to jelly.

Just outside Brighton, the stewards stopped them, closing up the gaps between the cars so that they could drive through the town almost in procession. It was getting dark, and Emma was tapping her finger excitedly on the steering wheel and craning to look up for any stars that might be shooting across the heavens.

'It can't be *real* falling stars. It's a bit cloudy and David would have thought of that. He thinks of everything.'

'Yep.'

She turned to him. 'You mean, *Yes, it's real falling stars* or *Yes, David thinks of everything*?'

'Yep,' Josh teased her, and Emma puffed out an exasperated breath.

'Josh, so help me, I'm going to threaten you with something you won't like…'

There was nothing that Emma could do to him that he wouldn't like. Josh let the idea simmer in his mind for a moment, and the car jolted as she put her foot on the accelerator to move forward another hundred yards.

When they reached the town centre the streets were alive with people, just as you'd expect from an early summer's Friday evening in Brighton. Many had stopped to see the procession of cars, working its way down to the promenade, and the GDK Foundation's local supporters were out in force, giving out flyers along with card signs that were being waved enthusiastically.

Emma sounded the horn, in response to the cheering and waving, and a few other cars followed suit. Josh reached back to lay his hand on Griff's head, but he was clearly loving the commotion going on around him.

'Is he all right?'

'He's fine. You know how Griff loves a crowd.'

'But where are the stars…?'

They inched down the hill towards the seafront, and as the first cars began to turn left, three beams of light shot up into the air from somewhere out at sea, dipping and wheeling together. And then lasers from the buildings around them showered the street with light, falling stars playing around the rooftops.

'Ooh! Look, Josh!' Emma was practically dancing in her seat, pointing ahead of them. 'Look at the pier!'

The small boats that David had arranged were invisible in the gathering gloom, as were the careful calculations that were behind the laser show. The magic of stars, falling from the top of the Palm Court, and drifting down into the sea was all that Emma saw, and it was suddenly all that mattered.

'You like it?' Silly question. It was clear that Emma *loved* this.

'No. It's horrible. I want to go home.' She turned to glance at Griff, who was standing on the back seat, wagging his tail furiously. 'Griff hates it as well.'

'Okay. We'll go home, then.'

At the bottom of the hill, stewards were directing cars into the lane to turn left. Emma stopped the car and wound the window down.

'I want to go right.'

'No, love. If you go half a mile to the left, there's a section of the seafront that's been closed off…'

'Okay, I'll go left in a minute. I want to go right first.'

The steward frowned, and Josh leaned over. 'We'll go right first and then left.' He flashed the ID card clipped to the back of today's information pack that gave his name and bore the word *Organiser* in red at the top. The steward stepped back and waved them left.

'I didn't know you had that.' Emma grinned at him.

Josh shrugged. 'I haven't had to use it before now. Why are we going right?'

'The clue says *catch* a falling star. There's a place just a bit further down this way…'

'Right. I guessed it was something important.' Clearly most of the competitors were happy with just getting a photograph of the falling stars, but Emma had set her heart on catching one.

She drove a little way along the promenade, and then turned right into a narrow side street, driving around the block to put the sea ahead of them again before she parked.

'What do you think?' Her hand grazed his sleeve and Josh shivered. Then she leaned towards him, as if trying to see exactly what he saw.

'Perfect.' It *was* perfect. A clear view of the pier smothered in stars. If they crossed the road and took the steps down onto the deserted beach, then Emma could reach up and the flattened perspective of the camera lens would see her catching stars. If that was what Emma wanted, then it was what *he* wanted too. Just to share in a little bit of her magic, before the opportunity was lost.

She was looking up at him, her eyes wide in the darkness. The street was deserted and the constant activity of the rally seemed a very long way away.

He reached for her and she didn't move back. In the warm welcome of her gaze, he summoned the courage to touch her, brushing his fingertips against the back of her hand. She curled her fingers around his, raising them to her lips.

Too much, and yet not nearly enough. It was what Emma had always been to him. She overwhelmed his senses, and he'd always wanted more, but was afraid to take it. But the possibility of catching stars meant that tonight was no time for fear.

'Em…?'

She lay one finger across his lips. 'I don't want you to think about it, Josh. You'll never do it if you do.'

Maybe she was right. He *couldn't* think at the moment. Josh folded his arms around her, and kissed her, feeling the warm sweetness of her lips…

A click sounded from the back seat, as the seat belt released. Griff was clearly feeling a bit left out, and he'd clambered forward and was doing his best to lick the side of Emma's face.

'Ew! Stop slobbering.'

'You mean Griff, I trust?' Josh caught Griff's collar, pulling him back. 'I haven't had much practice lately but…'

'Of course I mean Griff.' The light was still dancing in Emma's eyes. 'And *out of practice* really suits you.'

Good to know. He'd felt her hunger too, and Josh couldn't let this go. He wound his free hand around her waist, and Emma wrapped her arms around his neck, pulling him towards her. She kissed him with all the sweetness and magic that he remembered her for, the feeling even more intoxicating for having missed this so much.

It was even more amazing for being so awkward—trying to hold Griff back, while also finding a way to hold her in the tight space. He was a prey to Emma's hands, caressing his neck and sliding down to his chest. He shivered. There was no holding back, just a desperate craving for her.

She drew back just in time, before he lost all control.

'Hmm. Shooting stars.' Her eyes were still clouded with desire.

Shooting stars, streaking across the sky and then exploding, igniting an inferno. One that could so easily lead them into places that they really shouldn't go. Josh smiled at her.

'You want to go and catch one?'

She hesitated, her fleeting mask of disappointment matching his own feelings. 'Yes, I guess so. Even if ours were better.'

It was good to get out of the car, and into the cool evening air. When Josh examined the seat-belt clip, he could find no reason for its sudden failure, until Griff stood up on the seat, pulling the webbing tight and nonchalantly hitting the release with his paw. The restraint flew free and he heard Emma's snort of laughter behind him.

'Smart pooch. You've got to admit he has timing.'

Emma had the same capacity to laugh whenever things went wrong that his mother had had, and at the moment that thought didn't carry with it all the usual reservations. He grinned, clipping Griff's lead to his collar. Hopefully he hadn't found a way to get out of that yet, or they'd be spending the evening chasing after him on the beach.

She linked her arm in his as they crossed the road, walking down the steps to the sand. It took a while to find the exact place for the photograph, but that didn't matter, because the wind blowing in from the sea seemed to be bringing a new start with it.

After a few tries, Josh adjusted his camera phone to capture both Emma and the stars projected onto the pier. Some photos of Emma jumping and flailing wildly, and then doubled over with laughter and then everything came together, and he got the perfect shot. Emma, in mid-air, her fingers appearing to be almost in reach of the stars.

Then it was Griff's turn. She grabbed the extending lead from Josh, making a throwing movement with her arm. Griff took the bait and jumped for the invisible treat, and Josh managed to catch him, his nose extended up towards the stars. Unaware of this triumph, Griff started to nose miserably on the sand for his lost treasure and Emma turned her mouth down.

'What have I done? Poor Griff!'

Josh chuckled, spinning a treat from his pocket in Griff's direction, which he caught adroitly. Emma ran towards him, straight into his arms.

'Josh to the rescue...' Suddenly she was still, staring up into his eyes. 'I missed you so much.'

'I missed you too.' He felt a lump form in his throat at the thought of the tearing longing that had never properly subsided. Wondering how she was, and what she was doing the whole time they had been apart.

'I...' She seemed to think better of what she was about to say, pressing her lips together.

Thinking twice didn't much suit her. 'You what?'

'I spoke to David. Asked after you...'

Maybe she was thinking that he'd like the idea that she hadn't just forgotten about him. He did, but...

'Dad never said.'

'No.' Emma laid her hands on his chest. 'I asked him not to.'

That was Dad all over. His honourable streak wouldn't allow him to betray a confidence, however much it cost.

'That's how he knew your father had died?' Josh had always wondered, but had pushed the question out of his mind, glad that he had the opportunity to at least write some words of condolence to Emma and her mother.

'Yes. He'd agreed to keep quiet about our conversations, but he told me he wouldn't keep that from you. I was glad he didn't, your note meant such a lot to both Mum and me.'

'You spoke with him more than once?'

She was suddenly still, all the excitement draining out of her. The tinderbox that had ignited passion between them also had the capacity to ignite all the feelings of anger that had burned in their hearts. Maybe that was inevitable. Josh couldn't hold her any longer, and he turned away, walking towards the steps that led back up from the beach.

'What, Josh?' Emma couldn't let it go any more than he could, and she was following him, tugging at his arm. Rage floated over him, like a mist from the sea, seeping into his bones.

'So you were talking to my father, on a regular basis. But you didn't let him tell me how you were?'

'It's not his fault, Josh!' She frowned at him and, for once, Emma didn't seem to be able to divine what he was thinking. 'You know David...'

'I blame *you*, not him.'

Blame was an ugly word. But all the promise of their kiss, and then this sudden realisation... That was ugly too.

'I didn't want you to think that I was coming back, Josh. I wasn't.'

'But you still phoned Dad?'

It was unfair. But Josh wasn't in a mood to be fair, because he'd just been reminded of how unfair life could be.

'Don't be ridiculous.' Emma was angry now too. 'David and I weren't exactly pen pals. I made four or five calls in the space of three years, and all of them were about patients that I was treating at the time. I just...asked him how you were when we'd finished the business talk—it's not exactly stalking.'

'But you didn't let *me* know how you were. Did you for one minute think I didn't want to know?'

The aghast look on her face told him she hadn't. That didn't help, because what use was Emma's broad and vivid imagination if the one vital fact—that he'd loved her—hadn't occurred to her?

'I thought...' She gave a miserable shrug.

'You *thought*? You'd planned it all out, had you? And you accuse *me* of being controlling.' That was the most hurtful thing about it.

'All right, so I made a mistake. Since when have you been perfect? I was hurting, Josh.'

'And I was hurting too.' Could Emma not see that now? Could she not understand that when she'd left, all the complicated feelings over his mother's death had surfaced? That Emma had crossed herself off the list of people he could rely on, the same way that Josh had felt his mother had?

They stared at each other. Both seeing only the hurt, only the differences between them. Maybe that was all they really had in common.

There was nothing more to say. If he'd hoped that Emma might find something to make it all seem less hopeless, now was the moment for more disappointment. Josh couldn't even look at her any more, and turned, walking back up the steps to the promenade.

Griff trotted quietly beside him, as if he knew that something had just happened. Josh bent, giving him a reassuring stroke.

'Not your fault, mate. Don't worry about it.' It wasn't even Emma's fault. There was an abyss between them that they'd dared to try and cross.

All the same, he turned. In the shelter of the gloom around him, he watched her walk up the stairs, seeing that her shoulders were drooping and the spring in her step was gone. Then Emma straightened, waiting for a gap in the traffic before she crossed the road, her whole body stiff with anger now. As soon as she was safely in the car, Josh turned again, and strode away.

It was too much to expect that Josh would have stopped off, on the other side of the pier, to join in with the almost carnival atmosphere around the parked rally cars. It was a lot to expect of herself, but Emma did it anyway.

Anger was one of those convenient emotions that

blocked everything else out. As hers started to fade, others started to crowd in. Hurt, that he couldn't see her point of view. Guilt, that she hadn't seen his. Confusion and despair. She'd had to call David about one of her patients, and asking about Josh had been an impulse that she'd regretted. One of those reckless things that Josh had accused her of. So she'd made David promise that he wouldn't tell Josh that she'd been asking after him.

And David, being David, had kept the promise. He'd called her back, to see how her patient was doing, and asked her to keep him updated. When her father had died, David had called her again, having heard from the hospital that Emma had taken a leave of absence.

None of that mattered, now. Maybe it was fate that they'd kissed and then argued. A reminder that they couldn't do all the same things a second time and expect the end result to be any different.

Josh must know that too, and when she managed to escape the festivities on the promenade, and drove back to her hotel for the night, he wasn't waiting for her. He was at a different, dog-friendly hotel tonight and that was probably for the best.

She borrowed a laptop from one of the other competitors, accessing her email online. Nothing from Josh—she didn't expect that—but the emails with the day's photographs had been automatically forwarded on to her account. The rally must go on, and she accessed the blog to post the photographs. She couldn't imagine how she and Josh would be able to get themselves to London tomorrow without a lot of shouting, but tomorrow was going to have to take care of itself.

CHAPTER SEVEN

JOSH MUST HAVE been up very early. Emma hadn't been able to sleep much, but when she went to check on the Mini the next morning he was already there, sitting on the low wall that surrounded the hotel car park, with Griff leaning against his legs. Even now, seeing him still made a lump rise into her throat.

Griff made a lunge for her, yelping excitedly and trailing the extending lead out to greet her. Emma bent down, wondering whether speaking only to Griff, the way they had at first, might work for them today as well.

'Hi...'

His one word was clearly for her and not Griff. Josh had obviously come to the same conclusion that she had and decided to put his own feelings on hold in favour of finishing the rally.

Emma swallowed hard. 'Hi. All set for today?'

He shook his head. 'Not even remotely. There's something I have to do first.'

He seemed calm and she should stay that way too. Whatever he threw at her, she wouldn't cry, and she wouldn't hit back at him.

'Okay...?'

'I want to apologise. For the things I said and the way I said them.'

Emma shrugged miserably. 'It doesn't matter.'

'I called Dad last night.' He must have seen her alarm, because he shook his head. 'I didn't tell him anything about what happened, that's between you and me. I knew I'd been unfair, and wanted to know exactly what I need to apologise for.'

'You don't have to apologise for anything.' Although it meant something that he had.

'Dad told me that he'd been calling you as well, and that he'd asked you to keep him updated about your patient. And I do have something to apologise for, because I didn't listen when you tried to explain.'

Joy was beginning to seep through her. Right to her fingertips, which were tingling with the possibility that today might bring some kind of reconciliation. Emma walked over to him, sitting down next to Josh on the wall.

'I wasn't really *trying* to explain. I was too angry.'

'Yeah. I wasn't really trying to listen. I was too angry.'

Emma puffed out a sigh. 'We hurt each other, didn't we?'

Josh shook his head slowly, as if trying to make sense of it all. 'I was busy pretending to be one kind of person, but…when I was a kid I only had my mum. I used to make lists of people who might be there for me if something happened to her and…generally they were quite short.'

Josh and his lists. His flow charts. Emma was seeing all that in a different light, now.

'And I was on your list, and then disappeared. I'm sorry for that.'

He smiled suddenly. 'Sorry in an it's-all-my-fault kind of way? Or sorry that things happened the way they did?'

'The all-my-fault kind of sorry is tempting.' She smiled back at him. 'But since you mention it, I guess that I'm just sorry it happened and that you were so hurt by it. We should have talked more.'

Josh nodded. 'We're talking now…'

'Yes.' That felt good. As if there was some way to heal the past, even if they couldn't change it.

'You did the blog post.'

It was nice that he'd noticed. 'Of course I did the blog post. What, you were thinking that I'd be that petty?'

'Never. And it looks great, but I didn't send you the best photographs. I emailed them this morning.'

Emma hadn't looked at her email yet. She pulled her phone out of her pocket and saw that she had mail from Josh, with two photographs attached. Her and Griff, reaching for stars.

'Have you had breakfast?'

Josh shrugged. 'Coffee.'

Now that she could bear to look him in the eye, Josh was clearly as tired as she felt. More coffee and a good breakfast would set them both up for the day.

'They've an outside dining area where we can sit with Griff, and if you bring your laptop I'll add the photos now.'

He reached down, opening the holdall at his feet. 'I've got something else for you.' Josh drew out his MP3 player and speaker.

'Mixtape?' Josh knew she liked a good music mix, and his were generally really good.

'Mixtape. I downloaded some sixties stuff last night.'

She could kiss him. Though maybe they weren't ready for that just yet, even if it would have been just a friendly kiss on the cheek.

'Thank you, Josh.'

He grinned broadly. 'My pleasure.'

Emma had outdone herself for this final leg of the rally. A suede miniskirt, with a matching fringed shoulder bag, and a bright swirly patterned blouse. Her hair was tucked up into a baker boy cap, and a pair of low-heeled boots finished off the outfit. Josh was beginning to really like sixties fashions.

She'd spent some time with a screwdriver, removing the seat-belt clip in the back of the car so they could secure the dual clip of Griff's harness to the housing behind the seat. Josh strapped him in securely, and Griff curled up on his blanket. The GDK volunteers were out again in force this morning, leafleting and waving to each car as it passed, and their progress through Brighton was slow. But soon enough they were on the open road, the sun rolling lazily across the chalk hills of the Sussex Downs.

'Oh... Turn that up, I love this one.' Emma's finger had been tapping on the steering wheel, in time with the mixtape.

'"Love in Pink"?' Josh grinned. 'You know that's my gran, don't you?'

'What? Cerise Kennedy is your grandmother? And you didn't tell me?' Emma took one hand off the steering wheel to give Josh a reproachful nudge. 'That's it, Josh Kennedy, I'm never speaking to you again.'

They'd been so bound up in each other during their short affair that nothing else seemed to exist. Josh could rectify that now.

'Shame. I won't be able to introduce her to you at the wrap party for the rally, if you're not speaking to me...'

'She's going to be at the wrap party? Cerise Kennedy?'

'Yep. Dad mentioned she'd be there last night. You are coming, aren't you?'

'Well, I am *now*.'

Clearly Emma had been reckoning on giving it a miss. Much as Josh had, last night. But now there was no question that they'd both be there. Emma was singing along with the chorus, and Gran would have appreciated her enthusiasm and the fact that she knew all the words, even if her hit and miss approach to the tune left something to be desired.

'Cerise Kennedy is David's mother. I can't believe it.'

'The clue's in the name.'

Emma shot him a pained look. 'Yes, but… She's so fabulous. And David's so sensible. Don't they argue?'

'They did have a falling out, some years ago. Gran was a single mum, and she never told Dad who his father was. He only found out when his father died and left him a fortune.'

Emma winced. 'Tricky…'

'Yeah, very. They weren't speaking for a couple of years. Even now, things aren't quite the same between them. They talk but they don't ever really say anything.'

'But if she's coming to the party…?'

'It surprised me when Dad said he'd invited her. I'm wondering if Val's influence has had some part in this, and keeping my fingers crossed that it's a sign that Dad and Gran have finally dug up the hatchet and burned it. Although, knowing Gran, there would have been a bit of drama involved along the way. They never let their differences affect me though. Even when he wasn't speaking to her, Dad still let Gran take me off on holidays and for weekends.'

'Because it was important for you to know that she was still there. You'd lost enough of your family already.' Emma was suddenly thoughtful.

'Yeah. Gran never let me go. She could have just disappeared from my life, or Dad could have shut her out of it, but they didn't. About the only thing they agreed on was that I needed to know they were both there for me, whatever their differences. She used to send me postcards from all the places she went on tour. I had hundreds of them.' Each one sent with love and adorned with Gran's ostentatious kisses at the bottom.

'She sounds wonderful. And I'm going to meet her…

or at least maybe see her across the room…? Will she be singing?'

'You'll be meeting her. And Gran will definitely be singing, just try and stop her.'

'Fantastic. Go back…go back.'

Josh picked up the MP3 player, flipping the back button until 'Love in Pink' started to play again and Emma began to sing along, playing havoc with the tune all over again.

Maybe he should take a moment to revisit the idea that the complications of the situation between David and Cerise took any of the joy out of their reconciliation. Josh wasn't sure that he'd ever be entirely comfortable with Emma's wait-and-see attitude to the future, but maybe he could learn to live with it. Love it, even, the way he loved the optimism that went with it.

He glanced down at the map that had been lying forgotten on his knees. 'Wait… Stop!'

Emma came to an abrupt halt on the empty road. 'What?'

'That left turn we passed about half a mile ago. That's where we should be going.'

Still humming 'Love in Pink,' Emma turned the car in the road, heading back the way they'd come.

All of David's work, negotiating red tape and writing letters, had borne fruit. The cars travelled across Tower Bridge on a bright summer's day and snaked through London towards The Mall, parking up on the borders of St James's Park, where preparations were already taking place for the Awareness Day tomorrow. When they'd crossed the last finishing line of the rally, Emma had let out a whoop of triumph, and Josh had added a round of applause. Even Griff had woken up from his sulk at no longer being able to free himself from his car harness and started to bark joyously. Josh knew that this was a personal triumph for her, and that she was sharing it with her father.

Emma got out of the car, chatting excitedly with the other drivers and the GDK Foundation volunteers, some of whom Josh recognised from Brighton, and who must have caught the train up to London so they could be there for both the start and the finish of today's run.

This was the end. The end of squeezing himself into a confined space. The end of laughing at Emma's terrible jokes and listening to her tone-deaf renditions of whatever song was playing in the car. The end of having to stop himself from taking her in his arms and kissing her.

It was for the best, because even if this was an ending, it might not be final. They'd both found some closure on the bitterness of their first parting, and this one carried with it some hope that in the future they might be able to greet each other as friends, rather than avoiding every mention of the other's name. It was time for him to take what he had, and leave.

But he didn't get away so easily. He felt a tug on his arm and turned around to find Emma there, holding two plastic cups.

'I got you some champagne. Just a taste, to celebrate.' She pushed one of the cups into his hand, tipping hers against it. 'We made it.'

'Yes, we did. Cheers, Em.' It sent a shiver of gratification through him that she wanted to share this toast with him. That she'd run after him, to do it.

'You're not going, are you?' She took a sip from her cup, looking up at him.

'I've got a long list of things to do for the wrap party that Dad emailed through, so I need to pop into the office.' That was largely true. He did have a long list, but it generally consisted of checking that everything had being done, and it would probably take Josh about half an hour to do that.

Emma turned the corners of her mouth down. 'But you'll be here tomorrow, won't you?'

'Yes, I'll be here. And there's still the party on Monday.'

That made her smile. 'Yes, I'm looking forward to that. I'll see you tomorrow, then.'

Walking away from her was hard. But Josh was going to have to get used to that.

CHAPTER EIGHT

THE LONDON AWARENESS event had been a massive success, and he and Emma hadn't had a chance to exchange more than a few words, there were so many people there. He'd caught her just as the day was winding down, asking what she'd be doing tomorrow, and Emma had blurted out something about dresses, highly secret missions and looking forward to seeing him at the party in the evening.

That was enough for Josh. The look on her face told him that he could anticipate a spectacular evening, and if it took all day to prepare for it, then that was good too. David would be driving down to London this evening, and Josh had said he'd call in on him first thing in the morning.

The next day went as planned. It was a pleasure to see David so happy and they'd talked all morning and gone for a long lunch together. Josh had popped into the hospital afterwards, finding that everyone was managing perfectly well without him, and then gone home to dress for the evening, a feeling of anticipation already livening his pace.

The GDK Foundation's office was a tall, white painted Georgian town house, in a quiet Notting Hill square. The steps up to the front door were flanked with torches, to add a little drama when darkness fell, and inside the reception area and the conference room had been cleared, and the partition between them folded back, to make one enormous space.

David always kept it simple for parties. The high ceiling, decorated with moulded plasterwork, and the shining parquet floor was enough to add grandeur. And Gran was more than enough to add sparkle.

Gran was obviously keeping an eye on each new guest as they entered, and she made a beeline for him. Pink, sequins and fabulous were Cerise Kennedy's trademark, and tonight she'd outdone herself.

'Gran.' Josh bent to receive an air kiss. 'You look particularly wonderful tonight.'

'Thank you, darling. Let me look at you.' Gran stood back, smoothing her fingers across the lapel of his evening jacket. She gave a nod of approval, and then took his arm, leading him slowly across to the drinks table.

'I want a word with you, darling.'

Josh chuckled. Gran's cut-glass English accent had slipped momentarily into the Southern American drawl of her childhood. That usually happened when Gran expressed tenderness towards her family, and he suspected that he was in for one of her 'talks.'

Gran signalled to the waiter, who immediately poured two glasses of champagne, handing them both to Josh. Clearly Gran had everything under control already.

Which was no particular surprise. Gran liked to pretend that she hit the right note every time by serendipity, and that everything around her simply fell into place of its own accord, but she had a ferocious work ethic, and Josh knew that nothing around her happened by chance.

The light pressure of her fingers on his arm steered him over to the piano, which stood in one corner. There was a high stool next to it, under an arch of pink and silver balloons, which no doubt Gran had insisted on. She sat down on the piano stool, making room for Josh to sit with her, and accepting her glass from him with a little nod of thanks.

'Now, Josh. This whirlwind romance of your father's. You knew about it?'

'He didn't say anything, but Emma and I had worked out there was something going on. I didn't know he and Val were getting married until he told me this morning.'

'Emma?' Gran was always on the lookout for any romantic interest in Josh's life and she fixed him with a tell-me-more look.

'Emma was my driving partner for the second week of the rally after Dad and Val left for Liverpool. She's a good friend of Val's.'

'Oh.' Gran looked suitably disappointed, but rallied quickly. 'Well, this is very important. I'm sure that Val is perfectly nice, and your father seems blissfully happy, but I don't want you to think that she can ever replace your mother. Your father really loved Georgie...' Gran took his hand, squeezing it hard to emphasise the point.

'And it's obvious that he's head over heels in love with Val as well, Gran. I couldn't be more pleased for them both.'

'Ah!' Gran fanned her face with her gloved hand, as if she'd just averted a crisis. 'Well, I'm glad you feel that way, Josh. David will always be your father.'

'I know. Thanks, Gran.' Josh tipped his glass towards hers. 'We'll drink a little toast to them, shall we?'

'Indeed.' Gran was all smiles, now. 'I haven't met her yet. You'll have to point her out to me when she arrives...'

No need for that. There was a commotion in the doorway, and David and Val entered arm in arm. Josh hardly recognised Val. Her hair was swept sideways, curls cascading down one side of her face. She wore a dark green dress, the shimmering pattern of the black beads that covered it marking it as distinctly nineteen-twenties in style. At the hem, a glittering fringe of beads sparkled as she walked.

'Josh!' Gran grabbed his hand. 'Is that her?'

Josh wasn't sure how David could have made it any more obvious. He was looking down at Val with an expression on his face that was akin to worship. 'Yes, that's her.'

'She looks wonderful. And look at your father... Doesn't he look happy.' Gran let go of his hand, fanning her face again.

All those wasted years. His father and grandmother had both borne them stoically, but it was clear that they'd both been hurting. Maybe you never quite got over losing someone that you loved, and he would always miss Emma.

Josh leaned over towards his grandmother. 'Are we going over to say hello?' Gran always preferred to meet new people with someone on her arm to make the introductions.

'Thank you, dear.' Gran was dabbing at her nose with a filmy handkerchief that must have been in a concealed pocket in her dress. She may be glamorous, but she was also intensely practical. Josh stood, offering his arm to his grandmother.

Val looked a little nervous, but just as Gran was able to make people shake in their shoes with just one look, she also had the ability to make them feel at ease, and she'd clearly chosen the latter approach. She kissed David and then turned to Val, complimenting her on her dress and talking excitedly. David was beaming from ear to ear, clearly happy to have the chance to share this with Gran, and Val was smiling now too. Josh melted away quietly to watch.

'That's nice. Val was *terrified*.'

Josh turned to see Emma standing next to him. His heart began to thump.

Her hair was in a shining pleat at the back of her head, and she wore a high-necked halter dress, the pale blue fabric falling just above her knees and encrusted with swirls of beads and sequins. A nod to the sixties that was squeezing at his heart remorselessly.

'Emma.' It was the one and only word that summed up how gorgeous she looked.

'What? Are you all right?'

'No, I'm a long way from all right. Were you planning on having to resuscitate me when you dressed for the evening?'

Emma laughed. 'You scrub up pretty well yourself. And don't make me resuscitate you. I had to get Val to do deep breathing in the taxi on the way back from our shopping trip.'

'So *that* was what you were up to today?'

'Yes. Val wanted something that might allow her to subtly fade into the background.'

'She did? I'm afraid your secret mission failed, then.'

'I took her to a vintage clothes shop on the Kings Road and made her try on a few things. I think we've both blown a bit of a hole in next month's pay cheques, but you can't get away with incognito when you've got a rock like that on your finger. Have you seen it?'

'Not yet. Dad did Val proud?'

'Oh, yes. Diamonds and a beautiful green-blue aquamarine. Aquamarine's her birthstone and it matches her eyes.' Emma tucked her hand into his arm, murmuring quietly, 'Are you okay with this whirlwind proposal?'

'I'm really happy for them both. Care for some champagne, to celebrate?'

'Just water for me, please. I want to be stone-cold sober when I meet your grandmother so that I'm not tongue-tied with adoration.'

'I wouldn't worry too much on that score. Gran loves tongue-tied with adoration.'

Emma was officially bowled over. Josh's grandmother had insisted that she call her Cerise and whispered to her that she would be singing 'Love in Pink' especially for her.

Josh had laughingly reminded her that Cerise might have promised just the same to a few other people, when they danced together to the song, but that didn't matter. Emma was happy to share.

The night was full of laughter and music. As people started to leave, she wanted to bar the doors and keep them here, in this bubble. Tonight should last, because tomorrow she'd be going back to Liverpool.

To her friends, her job, the small cottage in the suburbs that was her home for the time being. Keeping her wheels turning. But the only thing that seemed to mean anything at all was that she'd be leaving Josh behind in London.

Josh had sent David off home, taking the keys to the office from him so that he could lock up. Perfect timing, as always, because Val's bright excitement had begun to give way to fatigue.

'We're leaving… Going now…' David had smilingly called out the words, as he and Val twirled in a half-embrace, half-dance right to the front door. Then he escorted her down the steep steps, and into the nineteen-thirties Daimler that David had driven during the first week of the rally, which was waiting for them outside.

David was so good for Val. Somewhere out there, a guy who would be that good for Emma was waiting. Or maybe he was standing right next to her…

Liverpool. Tomorrow. Since the evening really *was* ending now, and people were leaving, everything she did had to be in that context.

'Darling…' Cerise looked as fresh as she had when Emma had first laid eyes on her, taking her hands between hers and dispensing air kisses. 'It was enchanting to meet you. The next time I'm in Liverpool, I'll have to show you a few of the places that have special memories for me.'

Cerise leaned in, whispering in her ear, and Emma's hand flew to her mouth.

'You didn't...'

'He wasn't a household name then. Very talented young musician though, and *very* handsome.' Cerise put her gloved finger to her lips and Emma smiled. Josh's gran had suddenly taken yet another step up in her estimation.

'Care to share that with me?' Josh gave Cerise hug goodbye.

'Of course not. It's a grandmother's prerogative to hint at youthful indiscretions without going into the details.'

'That's true. Particularly when the details might take a while.'

That was obviously Cerise's intended meaning, and she smiled, planting a kiss on Josh's cheek. He rubbed at the lipstick mark, and Cerise took the arm of the chauffeur who was waiting to escort her to her car.

Cerise had avoided smudging her lipstick all evening, but she was clearly willing to make an exception for her grandson. The way that Josh was grinning at her, as she turned for one final wave, told Emma that he was well aware of the privilege.

He walked next to her, back into the building, sorting through a bunch of keys as he went. 'Dad said that there was something you wanted to find from the library. You want the key?'

'Yes. Thanks.' They were getting closer and closer to their goodbye and Emma didn't really want to waste any of the precious time they had left together, but the GDK Foundation's library had material that was difficult to get elsewhere.

'I'll leave you to it, then.' Josh snapped the key from the ring and put it into her hand. 'I'll say goodbye to the last of the guests and take a walk round to check that no one's been locked in the bathroom.'

The caterers were busy clearing up, and they too would be gone soon. Emma walked through the glass-ceilinged conservatory at the back of the house, and opened the door at the far end, which led to the library. She found the paper she needed and switched on the scanner to take a copy.

Josh appeared in the doorway, just as she was finishing. 'All done?'

'One minute...' She found the space on the shelf that she'd taken the publication from and replaced it. If she fussed over turning the scanner off for a moment, then maybe he'd turn away and stop looking at her like that. This parting was difficult enough already.

But he didn't. Emma switched off the light, and locked the library door, and he was still there. She dropped the key back into his hand and went to walk past him to get her coat, but the brush of his fingertips on her arm stopped her in her tracks.

They'd acknowledged a lot in the last week, and maybe saying this wasn't such a bad thing.

'It's been a wonderful evening, Josh. I didn't want it to end.'

'Does it have to?'

'Sometime. Unless you happen to have a time machine.' Not just for tonight. It would have to go back and change their whole lives, who they both were. All the things that were set in stone, now.

'Sometime isn't quite yet though.'

'It's soon. I have to go back up to Liverpool tomorrow afternoon.' And Josh would have to cross her off his list of people who wouldn't leave him behind.

He must see it. She could see it in him—he wanted to throw caution to the wind and make the most of the night. Take all the things they couldn't have, just one more time. Emma wanted that too.

But Josh was far too much of a gentleman, too nice a

guy, to press her. He nodded, putting the library key into his pocket, and started to walk back through the conservatory.

'Josh!'

He turned. 'You're right, Em. It's been a great week, and I really hope that it's laid the foundations for us to meet up again sometime. But right now, we have to get on with our lives.'

'Tomorrow. We have to get on with our lives tomorrow. And we both know that, so it's not as if we'd be making any promises that can be broken.'

Josh was staring at her. Emma knew exactly what she wanted, and she knew what he wanted too. Maybe they could both learn to deal with parting a little better.

'Our last goodbye...' She shrugged uncomfortably. 'It was bitter. I left and I was determined on never seeing you again. We could do much, much better than that, this time.'

He still hesitated. 'It's not the traditional way of saying goodbye to someone.'

'Who cares? All that matters is whether it works for us, and we want it to happen.'

His eyes softened. In the presence of those eyes it was impossible that tonight could end now.

'Never be in any doubt that it's what I want, Em.'

No more words. He went to fetch their coats and closed the front door behind them in silence. It was ten minutes' walk to Josh's mews apartment, but hardly a word passed between them. His arm around her waist, and way his body moved in perfect harmony with hers when he shortened his long stride, was enough.

The quiet cobbled mews was just the same, and so was Josh's apartment. Emma took his hand, leading him up the staircase that ran from the ground-floor garage up to the open-plan living area. And then the second flight, which led to his bedroom.

'You're sure, Em?' His fingers caressed the side of her cheek. 'I could make you cocoa, and show you to the spare room...'

'You want that?' Emma stood on her toes, kissing his mouth.

'No.'

'Me neither.'

He backed her against the wall. Lifted her up, so that she could wind her arms around his shoulders, her legs around his hips. Josh specialised in long delicious nights, and he was clearly in no mood to miss a moment of this one. He kissed her and the long, slow dance began. Rediscovering each fine curve of his body. Feeling the ever-increasing wash of desire as he reacquainted himself with all the things that made her sigh with pleasure.

The bedroom was in darkness, their bodies silhouetted in the light from the streetlamps outside.

'I have to see you, Josh.' Not just an outline. Emma wanted to see the light in his eyes as he made love to her.

He chuckled, putting her down and reaching out to punch the switch that closed the curtains. A whirr sounded as the room was plunged into darkness, and then Emma blinked as he switched the light on.

'Better?'

'Much. You still have the seduction cave curtains, then?' The automatic curtains had been in the apartment when Josh had bought it, and they'd laughed over opening and closing the curtains with the control at the bedside.

'I do. Not that they've been getting any use for the purposes of seduction.' He bent to kiss her. 'In case you were wondering.'

She had been. It was beyond belief that Josh wouldn't have had anyone in the last three years, but she couldn't quite forget the *out of practice* comment he'd made when they'd kissed in Brighton.

'So the last time for both of us was right here, then.' Forget the usual platitudes about wanting to move on and be happy. There had been no one else for either of them, and Josh clearly wanted to hear that as much as Emma did.

'Which makes me all the more hungry for you.' Their pace became more urgent as they both undressed and then Josh picked her up, laying her gently down onto the bed. 'All the more keen to make this last.'

That wasn't going to happen. Emma had had three years to think about all the things she missed about Josh, and to regret all of the things they'd never had a chance to do. She rolled him over onto his back, feeling in the drawer of the bedside cabinet.

The condoms were in exactly the same place. It might even be the same packet for all she knew; it looked like the ones they used to use. Josh propped himself up on his elbows, watching as she rolled the condom down and then straddled him.

'All for you, Josh. Just enjoy.'

He reached for her and she batted his hands away. When she sank down, taking him inside, he let out a sharp sigh.

'Emma... Wait, I can't...'

'You can't hold on? That's exactly what I want.' She moved her hips and he groaned. 'You like that?'

'What do you think?'

He liked it a lot. Josh liked it even better when she took the pins from her hair, shaking it free as she moved her hips in an ever-increasing rhythm.

'Em...' His body was shaking now. 'Please, Em, I need to feel you...'

She knew what that meant. He needed to feel her come, before he could let go. Usually he would make sure that she came more than once, in a long and delicious climb that robbed her of all control. It was Josh's turn to find out just how amazing that loss of everything felt.

And he was close. She leaned forward, finding just the right angle to please them both. Josh reached for her, and she caught his wrists, pressing them down against the mattress. She leaned forward to kiss him, and then straightened a little, cupping her breast in her hand.

'Emma... Em, please...'

Josh choked out the words and she came, hard, and without any warning at all. He must be able to see it and feel it, because suddenly he lost control, calling out for her again as his body jolted with a release that seemed to go far beyond pleasure. Far beyond anything they'd ever done together.

Josh had wanted tonight to be all for her, but Emma had purposely turned everything onto its head. This wasn't just a fond goodbye. It had the power to change everything.

She drew the covers of the bed over them and curled up in his arms. Maybe she was unaware of the fact that he'd lost control, but he very much doubted it. This one act had taken all of the hurt, all the hope and all the pleasure of the last week, and in a moment of world-rocking pleasure it had set him free.

'Are you done with me?' He kissed the top of her head.

'I don't think so.' Josh felt her fingers tracing small circles on his chest.

'Good. I'm not done with you yet either.'

Emma laughed lazily. 'You are for the time being, sweetheart.'

Yes and...no. He rolled her over, pulling her back against his stomach. When he wound his arm around her, one hand cupping her breast, the other sliding between her legs, Emma's sharp gasp told him that she still wanted him. She was going to want him even more in a minute...

'Maybe you'll beg,' he whispered in her ear, and she shivered against him.

'Like you did?'

'Yep. Just like that...'

CHAPTER NINE

IT HAD BEEN a long, delicious night. It was ironic that this one, last goodbye seemed to have freed them both to reach out for things that had eluded them before. But Emma was under no illusions. As soon as they tumbled out of bed, sleepy-headed and a little achy, the things that kept them apart would still be there. Josh would always want one kind of life, and Emma would always want another. And they'd always be limited by the things they feared.

It was past noon, and Josh had brought her coffee and toast, when her phone rang. Emma picked it up, pressing her fingers across her lips before answering it.

'Hi, David. I was going to call later and say thank you for last night. It was a lovely party.' Emma sat up in bed, automatically wrapping a sheet around her, despite the fact that Josh's father couldn't actually *see* what she was doing.

'Thank you for being there, Emma. Your presence made our evening.'

Always the charmer. Like father, like son. But David seemed to be a little more inclined to talk business this morning…or afternoon. Emma took another mouthful of coffee, trying to push herself out of the sleepy languor that was probably sounding in her voice.

'I've been speaking to a few colleagues about Iain War- ner, the live liver transplant donor that you've been taking care of up in Liverpool. It should be going ahead any day now.'

'Yes? That's good. Val has everything sorted?' Iain had been attending St Agnes's Hospital in Liverpool for counselling before the transplant of a section of his liver went ahead, and Emma had carried out the medical checks that were needed, to make sure he was in good health.

'It's all arranged. As you know, Val's been working with Iain in Liverpool, and I've been working with the recipient and her family in London. The transplant co-ordinator at the London Metropolitan Hospital has been off sick, and it was envisaged that Val and I would be liaising over the donor and recipient's respective needs. But now that Val's handed in her notice at St Agnes, they'd prefer she spends as much time as possible with her replacement. I'm also hoping to make my involvement rather less hands-on...'

David was keeping the promise he'd made to Val. Of course he was. 'What can I do to help, David?'

'I was wondering if you might spend some time at the London Metropolitan Hospital, overseeing the medical and pastoral needs of both donor and recipient and liaising between the two teams. Val and I will both be available if you have any questions or concerns, and if you're agreeable I can square things with St Agnes. As Josh will be the surgeon for the recipient's team, you'll be working closely with him as well.'

Emma swallowed hard. This was a senior position, one which she hadn't expected to be offered for a few years. It was only for two weeks, but it would be really valuable experience.

And she'd be working closely with the guy she'd just been saying *goodbye* to. All night. In the most incredible way possible.

'Have you spoken with Josh about this?'

'I wanted to speak with you first. It'll be a challenging

two weeks for you, but I wouldn't give you this opportunity if I didn't think you could do it. And in case you think that I'm pulling strings, I'll mention that Dr Khan spoke to me the other day. I know you haven't been at St Agnes's Hospital for very long, but he's very impressed with your work already and he asked me if I might suggest some opportunities that would broaden your experience.'

Dr Khan had said *that*? The head of the Transplant Unit at St Agnes's rationed out his praise sparingly, but everyone knew that a *well done* from him was worth a great deal. And since Josh was sitting right next to her, then he couldn't possibly think that this was something she'd sought out, just to postpone the moment of parting.

'What's your answer, Emma?' David prompted her gently.

'I... Thank you. I'd love to be involved with this case and... I'll do my very best to make everything go smoothly. As long as Josh is happy with it.'

'Why wouldn't he be? And your best is always good enough, Emma. Don't forget that I'm only a phone call away, and I'll expect regular updates from you.' A voice sounded in the background. 'And Val sends her love.'

Despite herself, Emma smiled. It was nice to hear David's softer side reflected in his voice when he spoke Val's name.

'Give her my love, David. And thank you. This is a really exciting opportunity.'

'I'm glad you think so. Val and I will be driving up to Liverpool this afternoon, and so we'll see you tomorrow. In the meantime, I'll speak with Josh.'

A sudden moment of panic swept over Emma. Did David somehow know where she was? But then David ended the call, and Emma laid the phone down in front of her, on the bed.

'What did Dad want? And why do I need to be happy

with it?' She felt Josh's hand on her spine, and shivered. How was she going to tell him?

'I…um… He…'

The sound of Josh's phone saved her the trouble. He looked at the display, and grinned. 'Looks as if he can tell me himself.'

Josh didn't spend a great deal of time in his office. It was quiet and comfortable, and being on the fourteenth floor it had a great view, right across the centre of London. But on the whole, he preferred to be either in the operating theatre or on the wards. Shutting himself away in here seemed like time wasted to him.

But today, it was where he needed to be. His conversation with David had convinced him that this was a great opportunity for Emma, and that she should grab it with both hands. It was awkward that it should come so soon after what was supposed to be a fond goodbye—*very* awkward, actually, since that night had felt a lot like the start of something and not the end—but Josh was just going to have to deal with it.

Emma's first reaction had been much the same as his. She'd jumped out of bed as soon as he'd ended his call with David, and he'd shouted his own approval of the arrangement through the door of the shower. She'd come out pink-faced and a little jittery, grabbing a towel to wrap around her before she kissed him. One moment of stillness, in warm remembrance of their night together, and then they were both on the move again. Josh had thrown on a pair of jeans and a sweatshirt, and Emma had twisted her hair into a tight plait without even bothering to dry it. He'd driven her back to her hotel and remembered to mention that he was looking forward to seeing her again and working with her. One last kiss and she was gone, saying that she would email him and let him know when she'd be arriving back in London.

When her email came, it gave her ETA as nine a.m. on Thursday. Clearly she wasn't planning on popping in for cocktails, or anything else, as soon as she got to London the night before. She was setting the tone for the next two weeks, and Josh was grateful for that.

She arrived at two minutes to nine, carrying a briefcase and two cups of coffee. He pushed the wastepaper bin, where he'd just thrown his empty coffee cup, under the desk with his foot.

'Coffee. You're a lifesaver.'

Emma smiled. She was dressed for business, in dark trousers and a white shirt, her hair tied back in a fishtail plait. Not quite as much fun as her sixties minidresses, but Josh wasn't sure that he'd be able to concentrate on anything else if she turned up in one of them.

She put the coffee down on his desk and sat down in one of the visitors' chairs, bending to open her briefcase and drawing out a thick file. Josh could sense that beneath her air of calm, she was nervous. He was nervous too...

'Good trip down?'

'Yes, thanks. I decided to get the train.'

No red Mini in the hospital car park, then. 'Where are you staying?'

Her cheeks reddened slightly. 'A hotel in Battersea.'

'Comfortable?'

'It's fine. I'm not planning on being there all that much.'

Uncomfortable, then, but presumably cheap. Josh would have offered her his spare room, but that would be a step too far for both of them.

'This is...'

Emma nodded. 'Awkward.'

'Yes.' The room seemed suddenly very quiet as well. 'What do you say we run through some preliminary details, if you have time?' Emma smiled suddenly. 'It's somewhere to start.'

Josh peeled the plastic lid from his coffee cup. 'Yeah. That sounds good.'

'Okay. The donor has been attending St Agnes's Hospital for counselling and tests. He's twenty-eight years old and teaches at the university. His family are all in London so he'll have good support after the operation. He's also in very good health—try as we might, we can't find anything wrong with him.'

'Good.' The procedure was actually more risky for the donor than for the recipient in these kinds of transplant, and there was a whole barrage of tests to be done before the transplant could go ahead. 'And he's not related to our recipient.'

'No. He joined the organ donation register about a year ago, and our counsellor is satisfied that he knows the risks and that this is what he wants to do.' Emma paused to take a sip of her coffee.

Josh knew that this was all Emma would be telling him about the donor, because donor and recipient each had separate medical teams, so that they could make decisions about the welfare of each patient without any conflict of interest. Donor and recipient were also kept apart, as a matter of course, and Emma was one of the few people who would have access to both of them and all their medical notes. She could also call on the resources of the GDK Foundation if they were needed.

It was the difficult job his father did, involving discretion, balance and medical knowledge. Emma would have access to David's expertise and judgement, but it would stretch anyone. Josh was proud that his father had chosen so well.

'David's given me all the notes for the recipient, but I'd like to hear your thoughts.'

Josh nodded. 'She's a seven-year-old girl, who developed cholestasis as a baby due to an infection. There was a delay in getting medical help for her, as her birth mother was a drug addict who wasn't capable of looking after her daughter and subsequently gave her up for adoption. She was very seriously ill for some time and it took a lot of hard work to keep her liver from failing. It was permanently damaged though and she's now at a stage where she needs a transplant.'

'And there was no blood type match from her adoptive parents?'

'Nope. Or any of her adoptive family. Dad told me that he told her parents that anyone in the family who'd like to consider donation could come to his office for immediate testing and fourteen people turned up the following morning. But Amy's O Negative and none of them were a match, so her only chance is an unrelated donor.' Josh shrugged. All that mattered was in the notes, but there was more. 'And she's a good kid.'

Emma smiled suddenly. 'I can't wait to meet her. You'll be doing her surgery, and—' she consulted her notes '—Mr Sargent will be responsible for the donor's surgery?'

'That's right. Alex Sargent's one of the best surgeons I've ever met, and we've done a lot of these types of cases before. If I have time I usually pop in to the viewing gallery for the donor's surgery, just so that I can see if there are any issues I should be aware of.' He risked a smile. 'Will you be joining me?'

'Yes, I'd like to. Thank you.' Emma had a long list in front of her, the text too small to read at this distance and upside down, but her pencil hovered over one of the entries. Josh congratulated himself on answering the question before it was asked.

There were, however, plenty of other items on her list, and Emma had many other questions. Some of them were obviously at David's instigation, but others had a flair and thoroughness that were entirely Emma. She'd taken David's advice, but it was obvious that Emma was doing this her way too.

After half an hour, she ran out of questions, which was just as well because Josh had run out of answers. Emma drained what was left in her coffee cup and flipped her file closed.

'That's it, then.' Her expression told him that it wasn't it at all. There was one more pressing challenge that they both had to face.

'Josh, I... I know that things haven't worked out quite the way that we intended. I hope you're okay with that.'

He'd better stick with what they'd originally intended, because Josh was still struggling with what had actually happened. The way he'd given himself to her, and how over the last couple of days he hadn't been able to take anything back.

'We intended to draw a line under what happened between us, so that we could move forward. This feels like moving forward to me.'

'And to me. Thank you.' She gave him a gorgeous smile. The one he loved and would tell any number of lies for. He could pretend that he didn't want her every time he saw her if this was his reward.

'I have to go. I have a surgery this morning.' A thought occurred to him. 'Have they given you somewhere to work? You can take my office if you like. I won't be needing it for the rest of the day.'

Emma hesitated. 'They said they'd find me a desk in the main office...'

Right. No one here would have dared suggest that David take a desk in the main office. Emma may not be as senior as him, but part of her role here was to act as his representative. And in the complex politics of any large institution, nothing screamed *important* quite as much as someone's work space.

'I insist.' He rounded the desk, risking the contact required to propel her towards his chair. Emma gave a small yelp of alarm, but when she sat down she seemed more comfortable with the arrangement.

'Make yourself at home. I'll be back later.' Josh turned on his heel, ignoring her thanks, and walked out of the room.

Emma had spent the day familiarising herself with the hospital and speaking to everyone on the two medical teams. It was a wide range of people, nurses and medical doctors, surgical teams, physiotherapists and counsellors. But she was beginning to get the measure of everyone, and David had told her that this was the first thing she needed to do. Learn the process and learn the people.

At six o'clock, Josh popped his head around the door. 'Just getting my coat...'

'Come in. This is actually *your* office.'

'Hmm.' He looked around. 'Like what you've done with the place.'

She'd touched nothing. There was only a small tube of hand cream on the desk, from when she'd last washed her hands. Emma snatched it up and dropped it into her bag. But Josh seemed relaxed and cheerful and a day of activity had left her feeling less nervous and embarrassed too.

'Are you wondering how my day went?'

'Thought you'd never ask.' He grinned, lowering himself into one of the visitors' chairs. 'How did your day go?'

'Good. I managed to talk with everyone. I think everything's under control.'

In control. The words had just slipped out and she'd seen the warmth bloom in Josh's eyes. He'd told her how much he liked that, and she'd seen what had happened when he'd lost control. It had been earth-shattering.

And it had been a goodbye. Something that moved them on to a new stage in their relationship, and which couldn't be done again, however much Emma wanted it. Ached for it, every time she saw Josh.

'So, do you fancy a coffee? You can pay.'

Emma chuckled. Josh's easy-going humour had a way of cutting through awkward moments.

'I could murder a coffee. I've been talking all day.'

CHAPTER TEN

EMMA HAD WONDERED whether Josh might suggest that they meet up at the weekend and wondered what her answer would be. But he'd saved her the trouble of having to grapple with that particular problem, by acting like a friend instead of a lover, and saying he'd see her on Monday morning.

She spent another night in an uncomfortable bed, listening to the loud hum of traffic outside her window. There had been so much to do that she'd booked the first hotel on the list of places to stay, and breakfast had confirmed her opinion that she really ought to try and move somewhere a little more comfortable. Emma headed into the hospital, deciding that it was the only place where she'd get some peace and quiet to find somewhere else and also get some work done.

She found Josh's office unlocked, and when she opened the door he was sitting at his desk.

'Oh… Sorry, I didn't know you'd be here today.'

'That's all right.' He jumped to his feet. 'I just popped in. I'll get out of your way. You're working today?'

'I just popped in too. I'll be here tomorrow as well, to make sure that the donor gets settled and that there are no issues.'

Josh nodded. 'Yeah, good thought. I'll…um…'

He fell silent. One of those silences that spoke volumes. He looked tired and his brow was creased with worry.

'What's up? One of your patients?'

He shook his head.

'What, then?' Josh didn't answer, and Emma decided to take another tack. 'Have you had breakfast?'

'Uh? No.'

'Well, I hear there's a place around the corner that does a great breakfast. I could do with something more than a piece of limp toast and a cup of weak tea, so you'll be doing me a favour. I'm hoping for almond croissants, preferably still warm, although I think I'll take almost anything.'

Josh smiled suddenly. 'You mean Riley's? Yeah, everyone goes there. I think they do almond croissants...'

'You're getting my hopes up now.' She chivvied him to his feet. 'Come on...'

Riley's did indeed do almond croissants. And hot chocolate. Emma ordered two of everything, and Josh carried their plates to a table in the corner.

'Is this the Dr Owen care package?' He sat down, stretching his shoulders as if they ached.

'That's far too organised for me. Call it a friendly ultimatum. If you don't tell me what's up by the time I've finished this croissant, then I'm just going to keep ordering until you do.'

He gave her a long look. 'You're in not-at-work mode, aren't you?'

'I wasn't aware of transforming suddenly as I left the building.' Emma considered the idea. 'I guess I've been trying pretty hard to get everything right.'

Trying to be friendly but not too friendly. Walking that thin line, when all of her instincts were trying to push her off balance and back to a place where she was falling in love with him all over again. But Josh looked as if he needed a friend right now.

'It wasn't intended as a criticism. I like both your different personas.'

Emma leaned across the table, towards him. 'Then you should know that both of them are asking the same question. What's up?'

Josh took a deep breath. 'You know I told you that I had no contact with my biological family? Well, I got an email last night.'

'From who?'

'My biological father got married again after he and Mum divorced. The email was from one of his sons.'

'You mean your half-brother?'

'Yeah. Suppose so.' Josh seemed to be turning the idea over in his head. 'Seems a bit weird having a brother, even if he is only half a brother.'

He didn't seem overjoyed about it all. Emma could see that he must have conflicting feelings. 'And how do you feel about that?'

'I feel...pleased. He said he'd like to meet me and I'd like to meet him.'

'That's a good start, then, isn't it?'

Josh shook his head. 'I don't know. I keep wondering how Dad's going to feel about it all.'

Emma thought for a moment. 'I guess that David must always have known this was a possibility. He must have thought about it. Has he ever mentioned you getting in touch with your biological family before?'

'Once or twice. I always told him I didn't need to. But now...' Josh shook his head. 'His name's Jamie. Knowing that I have a half-brother, and that he has a name, makes it all seem a bit more real. As if my biological family isn't just an idea that I can dismiss.'

'You want to hear what I really think?' This was so personal that Emma hardly dared give an opinion.

'Nah. If you could just fob me off with a few platitudes, then I'm sure I'll feel a great deal better about things.' Josh grinned suddenly. 'Of course I want to hear what you think; it's why I caved in to the intolerable pressure you were applying.'

He was joking. But Emma had come to understand that Josh's jokes were capable of covering a whole world of hurt.

'I think you need to talk to David. Tell him what's happened and ask him how he feels.'

'I don't know whether I can. Maybe I should just say nothing.'

'And how do you think he'll feel if you do that? Josh, I think this is the first time I've ever heard you say that you can't talk to your father about anything.'

'It's the first time I've ever felt it. Apart from when I was a kid, and deciding to run away from home, but that's a long time ago, now.'

'You ran away because you were afraid David didn't want you?'

Josh nodded.

'I know you're really happy for him and Val, but...be honest. Has it occurred to you that his getting married or you getting back in touch with your biological family are things that might make him want you a little less?'

'No, I...' Josh answered quickly and then stopped to think for a moment. 'Maybe. Not in so many words, but it really touched a nerve when you said it. I can't discount the idea.'

'Should I just leave that with you?' Emma didn't want to press him too hard.

'Yeah.' He grabbed his hot chocolate, taking a sip. 'So what are you up to today? You have work to do?'

'Not really. To be honest, the hotel's a bit bleak and I reckoned I might as well come into the hospital.'

'Nothing else to do? What's got into you?'

Emma laughed. 'It's not serious. Just a twenty-four-hour thing, I'll be better in the morning.'

'Fancy a day out? Bettering ourselves?'

It was an old joke. They'd take the train into the centre of London and wander around museums and galleries. No plan, no direction, just taking everything as it came and appreciating whatever was in front of them.

'Why not? I haven't done that in a while.'

They found their way to the Victoria and Albert Museum. It was one of the places that Emma liked getting lost in the most, a celebration of the eclectic where it was never possible to be quite sure what was around the next corner. They'd wandered for hours, and then Josh had taken his phone from his pocket.

'I have a call to make. Do you mind?'

Emma knew who he'd be calling. 'Go. I'll meet you by the Exhibition Road entrance in…half an hour?'

'It shouldn't take that long.'

'Yes, it should. Three-quarters of an hour for good measure.'

Josh grinned. 'I'll go now before you make it an hour.'

Wandering wasn't quite so relaxing when you were looking at your watch every two minutes, but Emma stuck to her word. Forty-five minutes later, she walked back through the galleries, and out into the traffic-free zone outside the museum. Josh was sitting alone on a bench.

He seemed *very* alone, staring at his phone, obviously deep in thought. Emma walked over to him, sitting down next to him. Putting her hand on his shoulder seemed the obvious thing to do, and he looked up at her.

'So?'

'Dad's good with it all. He says that it's entirely up to me, but he'll back me all the way if I want to meet up with Jamie.'

So it was *Jamie* now. David had obviously put Josh's mind at rest.

'Did he know about your biological father's family?'

'He said that Mum tried to get in touch with him. She didn't much want to but she felt it would be good to at least know where he was in case I ever wanted to meet him. She sent a couple of letters but they went unanswered.'

'So...that means they at least thought about the possibility.'

'Dad says he's sending me something.' His phone beeped and Josh glanced down at it. 'Here it is.'

Maybe this was for Josh alone to see. Emma drew back, turning her head up towards the people strolling past them, then felt Josh nudge her.

'Here. You know the picture I have of the river, in my study?'

'Yes? I've always liked it.'

Josh grinned. 'That was the last birthday card my mum gave me. It's her own work.'

'She was very talented.' The watercolour of the Thames was brimming with life and colour.

'Dad keeps a scan of what she wrote inside, framed in his study. He says it's a reminder for him.' Josh handed the phone to her, and she saw three neatly written lines.

'Green ink. I like her style.' Emma smiled.

'Yeah, that's Mum all over. She used to write letters of complaint in red ink.'

'Even better.' Emma turned the phone, enlarging the image as much as the small screen would allow, and held it between them.

So close. A little too close for comfort but...comfort

was just what Josh needed at the moment. Emma read the inscription carefully.

Remember always that you can take whatever you want from life, Josh. And that, however far you travel, David and I will always be here for you.

'That's nice.' Unbearably sad too, because Josh's mother hadn't lived to see him leave the nest.

'Yeah. Dad kept her promise for her.' Josh looked up at Emma, and she brushed the tear away from her cheek.

'So are you any closer to deciding what you want to do?'

'I'm going to write to Jamie and tell him I'd like to meet up with him. Dad's all for the idea.'

'That's good. David's reassured you, then?'

'He tells me that I'm welcome to run away again, any time I like, because he's got a little project in mind to surprise Val with and he could do with the extra pair of hands. He's making her a vegetable garden at the house in Oxford.'

'She'll like that.' Josh had taken Emma to David's house in Oxford when they'd first met. It felt about a million years ago, now. It was large and beautiful, with plenty of land at the back to grow whatever food supplies Val set her heart on.

'Will she? I told Dad that a rose garden might be a little bit more appropriate.'

'Not for Val. She likes growing things you can eat.'

'In that case I may have to dispense with the running away part and go down there anyway to help him with the digging.' Josh stretched his arms out, as if readying them for the task. But it seemed a weight had been lifted from his shoulders.

'This hotel of yours. Is it really that bad?' he asked.

'It's really noisy. I'm not getting any sleep, so I think

I'll have to find somewhere else. I was in a rush when I booked it and I just took the first place on the list.'

Josh nodded. 'I don't suppose you'd consider staying at mine for a few nights? Solely in the interests of a productive working day. Take the spare room, or the sofa... or you could even go down to the garage and sleep in the car if you're reckoning on a quick getaway.'

'In case David phones, you mean?'

He nodded. 'Yeah. If he does that again, I think we should at least take the time to have breakfast.'

'Breakfast would be great. And I could do with an undisturbed night's sleep as well.'

'I'm your man, then. We can go back to mine to pick up the car, and then drive down to Battersea to get your luggage. We'll get something for dinner on the way back; my fridge is startlingly empty at the moment.'

Josh was planning again. Those plans didn't seem quite so restrictive now, just a way of fitting everything into the day. 'Okay. Thanks, that sounds really good.'

Josh felt...complete. Not just because of Jamie's email, or his father's reaction to it. Because Emma had been there, and she seemed happy to be doing all the things they'd done once upon a time, when he'd thought that he could map their future out together.

There were no maps, now. No navigation along a well-charted route. But that was okay, because worrying about tomorrow was how he'd lost Emma. She was here now, and he had to get used to the fact that she'd be finding another place to stay soon, and that she'd be gone.

Emma had insisted on cooking, and Josh had sat down to write his email to Jamie. He'd written a few versions, some of which were exactly the same apart from the location of the commas, before Emma made him put his deliberations to one side and come and eat.

When they'd finished, he put on some music and asked her to look at the latest incarnation of his email, and they sat on the sofa together while Emma read it carefully. She suggested that *I'd like to meet* might be injected with a little more enthusiasm, and that *I'd love to meet* might be better. Josh found that a little too gushy, and they compromised at *I'd very much like to meet*.

He pressed 'send' and they both stared at the screen. Just assuming that the email had left the building, in the same way that he usually did, didn't seem quite enough.

'Has it gone? I didn't hear anything.' Emma was clearly thinking the same.

Josh opened his 'sent' folder. 'Yes. It's gone.'

'Good.' She reached over, closing his laptop. 'It might be a while before he gets back to you. He must be getting used to all of this becoming a reality as well.'

'Yeah. He's only twenty and...' Josh thought for a moment. 'I'm not entirely sure what big brothers are supposed to do.'

'What you're doing now. Be a bit protective, but give him plenty of space. Listen to what he wants and tell him how you feel.'

'In other words, juggle.' Perhaps Emma could advise on that, because she seemed to do it a lot better than he could. 'Anything else?'

She rolled her eyes. 'How am I supposed to know? I don't have any brothers. Just be yourself, Josh. That's what he wants out of this. He said it in his email; he just wants to get to know you.'

'Fair enough.' He could think about the ramifications of that later. When his whole consciousness wasn't bound up with having Emma close. 'You fancy a film?'

'That sounds good. What have you got?'

'Whatever you want.' Josh handed her the remote for the TV and went to inspect the contents of the freezer for dessert. 'Vanilla or raspberry? Or... I think this is straw-berry.' He inspected the canister of home-made ice cream.

'You've been making your own ice cream?' Emma was flipping through the list of films on the TV screen.

'Gran bought me an ice cream maker for Christmas.'

'Really?' Emma's eyebrows shot up in surprise.

'Yeah, she's got a bit of a scatter-gun approach to present buying sometimes.' Josh decided not to mention that Gran had included a note, which said that one of the best ways to any woman's heart was to feed her home-made ice cream, and that she hoped her gift might rectify the notice-able lull in his love life over the past few years.

'Let's not disappoint her, then. I'll have the strawberry. Is it pink?'

'Very...' The ice cream looked slightly too pink, but when Josh took a taste of it, it wasn't too bad. 'Definitely strawberry, I think I may have added a few too many.'

'You can *never* have too many strawberries, Josh.' She dropped the remote on the sofa and jumped to her feet. 'Let me have a taste.'

Josh fetched another spoon from the drawer, and she leaned across the counter that divided the kitchen from the living space, taking a sample from the tub.

'Mmm...' Emma grimaced. 'I hate to say it, because I so wanted to like your gran's pink ice cream. But this is too sweet. You put sugar in as well?'

'Yeah. It's not so bad, is it?'

'You always did have a sweeter tooth than me.'

'So you'll have—?' *Raspberry.* He was going to say raspberry, but Emma had leaned over a little further and kissed him. And now he was caught in her spell, unable to think of anything else.

'Emma...' She'd kissed him, so it was only fair to kiss her back. Quid pro quo.

But that was a slippery slope and he was skidding down

it now. A caress of her fingertips... Another kiss that was all the sweeter because he couldn't pull her close and the sensation on his lips seemed so much more in focus...

'Em, I didn't intend on this happening.'

'Neither did I.'

And yet it had. She slid up onto the counter, swinging her legs over in one smooth move. Josh hooked his hands behind her knees, pulling her forward until their bodies touched and he heard her catch her breath.

One more heartbeat, and he would be completely lost. But he had to know.

'Are you sure, Em?'

'Unfair question.' She kissed him again, her eyes dark with desire. For all he knew her judgement was just as clouded as his was at the moment.

It took a supreme effort of will to back away from her. 'I really need you to be sure, Emma.'

The moment was slipping away, but it would take one look, just one kiss, to get it back. And just one word from Emma to make them friends again, ones who stayed the night in separate bedrooms.

'We're a good team. Great in bed...' She gave him a wicked smile.

'I'd say a lot better than great.' Josh grinned back, wondering where this was going.

'We just want different things, and we're afraid of what that means. So why don't we just stick to what we're good at, no promises, no looking forward? Just putting the past to rest.'

'Write our own rules?'

'Why not, Josh? Life's going to happen whatever we do, so we may as well do what we both want to.'

He walked towards her, planting his hands on the countertop on either side of her hips. 'Rule one. You should kiss me, now.'

Emma smiled and the moment was back. Better because his head was clear now, and he knew hers was too. She kissed him and the next moment seemed to rush in on them, impatiently.

'Rule two.' Her hand tugged at his shirt. 'Take it off...'

CHAPTER ELEVEN

EMMA HAD LOST COUNT. Numbers didn't matter in Josh's arms and neither did rules, because there *were* no rules to his brand of seduction. Just a slow, delicious appreciation of every moment. Half their clothes were scattered downstairs, and the other half tangled together beside the bed.

He lay her down, his steady rhythm propelling her on, like an unstoppable tide. She came almost straight away, feeling him harden inside her in response.

Maybe it was these new rules that were making her feel this way. Free to be loved by him, and free to love him back. Josh seemed different too, more ragged and unpredictable. He'd always been a tender man—he couldn't change that if he tried—but there was an edge of the exciting unknown in his lovemaking tonight.

'You adore this as much as I do?'

He smiled down at her. One arm was wrapped around her shoulders, and she felt his other hand on her leg, pulling it up a little so they could feel just that bit more of each other.

'Maybe *more* than you do...' He moved again, sending bright showers of feeling through her body.

'Not possible, Josh.' She clung to him, his pleasure feeding hers.

He bent, whispering in her ear. 'You're making a competition of this?'

'Yes, I'm making a competition of it.' Josh always had been able to inflame her imagination and now the effect was head spinning.

Her fingers found the pulse on his neck, and the quickening beat of his heart lent yet another strand of pleasure. The rhythm of their lovemaking stepped up a notch, and there were no words now. Just that sweet, sweet feeling that something was waiting for them, and that when it came there would be no stopping it.

When it *did* come, there was a kind of madness to it. A rippling, insistent rapture that spread right to her fingertips. It was only then that he too lost control, crying out in agonised pleasure.

They held each other tight for a long time, their bodies still sensitive and vulnerable. And Josh was still perfect. In the quiet end to a day that had changed so much, Emma felt his body curl around hers, as she drifted off to sleep.

Emma was standing in front of the mirror, at the top of the stairs that led down to the front door, plaiting her red hair. Josh was supposed to be making coffee, but in truth he was watching her.

He'd found that place she went to, when she lost all control and just let the storm take her. It was a little frightening in its intensity, but the more he went there, the more he wanted to go back. When he'd woken in the night, and heard her whisper, 'Are you awake?' he'd gone from zero to a hundred and ten per cent in less time that it took him to reply.

Maybe it was because the rules had changed. Emma had laughingly referred to them this morning and he guessed that they both thought that had something to do with it.

'I've got to go into work today too.' Now that she'd worked her way down to the end of the plait and fastened it, Josh could pour the coffee without spilling all over the countertop.

'You do? What are you up to?'

'Amy wants to see the operating theatre, and her parents asked me if that would be possible. I had a few concerns, largely on the basis that it might frighten her. But I've been thinking about it and Amy's been around hospitals all her life and she has a different attitude than most kids might. She wants to know.'

Emma nodded. Josh pushed her coffee across the countertop towards her and waited for her reply. But she just took a sip of her coffee, her brow creasing slightly.

'I'm going to see her mother today and I thought I'd tell her that I'll take Amy up to the viewing gallery. What are your thoughts?' Josh would be very surprised if Emma didn't have any.

'Um… Yes.'

'Just *yes*?'

'I… It's difficult, Josh. You want me to disagree with you over this, when we spent last night doing…what we did.'

Maybe growing up with David had made Josh a bit more comfortable with breakfast conversations about surgery. But he suspected that Emma's reservations were a bit more complicated than that.

'Do you regret last night?' Guilt stabbed at him. Maybe he should have emphasised the need for them both to be very sure about this a bit more, but he thought he'd made it clear.

She seemed to be reading his mind. Emma reached across the counter, laying her hand on the side of his face. 'No regrets, Josh. I was sure then, and I'm even more sure now. Have you got that?'

'Got it. So what's the problem? Boundaries?' It was something that most people seemed to negotiate successfully. The nature of the work meant that there were plenty of couples amongst the staff at the hospital. Emma had never had any difficulties about drawing a line between working with David and starting up a relationship with Josh when they'd first met.

'It's… I want to make my mark, but I don't want to step on anyone's toes. And yes, boundaries are something I'm aware of, because I'm new at the hospital and I'm still finding my feet.'

'Okay, I appreciate that. So…perhaps we have a dress code. When your hair's tied back we're work colleagues. When it's not, then we can be friends. And…'

'When I take off my clothes…?' Emma grinned wickedly.

'Yeah, that's it. That includes when I take your clothes off for you as well.'

'Of course. Goes without saying.'

Josh wrenched his thoughts back on to the problem in hand. 'And whatever our state of dress, I'd appreciate it if you'd tell me what's on your mind. Because if you hold back on giving me your opinion on anything, then I'm going to have to sit you down and ask who you are, and what you've done with the Emma that I know.'

She grinned, reaching across the counter, with the obvious intention of kissing him. Josh ducked out of the way, backing off.

'Uh-uh. That's not in the agreement.' He teased her. 'Hair…'

'All right, then. About Amy…' Emma considered the matter for a moment. 'I think that if it's what she wants, then you should listen to her. One of her parents will be there, I assume.'

'Of course. Her mother probably.'

'Then she'll have plenty of support. And she's probably got some idea of what an operating theatre looks like anyway, as she may well have seen one on television. The real thing might come as a bit of a disappointment.'

Josh nodded. 'That's true. I hope she doesn't think I'm going to whip out a scalpel and do a demonstration.'

Emma laughed. 'I think the thing you really need to worry about is if she decides she wants to try some surgery out for herself. Little girls aren't all sugar and spice, you know. What time do you have to be there to see her mum?'

'Not until this afternoon. But I'll come in with you this morning. I can always find something useful to occupy my time.'

'The donor is going to be checking in this morning, and I said I'd come and see how he was settling in this afternoon.'

'Okay. Well, we could stay here until lunchtime, and review anything that's outstanding.'

'I've nothing outstanding. You?'

He wished that Emma wouldn't smile at him that way when she was dressed for work. 'Nope.'

'So what's the rule for having my hair up and no clothes?' Emma started to unbutton her blouse.

Josh smiled, leaning back against the kitchen counter. Maybe she was going to let him watch her undress; he'd like that a lot. 'No idea. You tell me.'

Josh was as good as his word. When they walked into the hospital together, he was smiling but professional and it was easy to be the same with him.

'Would you like to come along and meet Amy? I'm going to take her mum for coffee first, so we can wait for you while you see the donor.'

'Yes, thanks. I'll text you?'

Josh nodded. 'Perfect. See you later.' He walked away without looking back, and even though her hair was fixed neatly again at the back of her head, Emma allowed herself to watch.

The wards in the Transplant Unit were all split into single rooms, and Emma found Iain Warner sitting on the bed, reading a book.

'Hey, Emma.'

'Hi. What's the book for today?' Iain usually turned up to the hospital with a book under his arm, and joked that he'd read his way through the process of preparing for a liver donation.

'This is on the syllabus for my students, next term.' He turned the corners of his mouth down. 'I thought I'd have a chance to get my teeth into it, but it's not really happening.'

Emma picked up the book, looking at the blurb on the back cover. 'It looks pretty scholarly.'

'I thought that having something to concentrate on might be good.' Iain shrugged. 'Hospitals aren't really the place to concentrate, are they?'

'Not if you're a patient. Leave the concentration part to me.'

'And the surgeon.'

'Yes, definitely. I met Mr Sargent the other day. I'm told he's the very best.'

'I heard that too. Not much of a sense of humour though...' Iain paused, grinning.

'All right, I'll bite. What makes you say that?'

'When I came down to London for a consultation with him last week, he told me that the nature of this particular procedure meant I wouldn't have much of a scar. I said I'd rather there was, so I could impress my other half and that I had my eye on a scimitar-shaped one.'

Emma snorted with laughter. 'Don't. Where is Peter?'

'Gone to pick up my parents; he'll be back shortly. Can I ask you a favour?'

'Of course.'

'When I have the op...if anything goes wrong...'

'There's a very small chance of anything going wrong. But okay, if something does go wrong...'

'Will you talk to Peter, and tell him what's happening? Mr Sargent—he seems a good guy and he's obviously great at his job but Peter has a habit of asking for facts and fig-ures when what he really needs is a kind but honest assess-ment. Which is what I reckon he'll get from you.'

It was a nice compliment. 'Thank you. I'll know how everything's gone as soon as your op is finished, so I can meet up with him while you're still in the recovery room. Give me his phone number.'

'Thanks. I appreciate it.' Iain reached over to the cabi-net at the side of the bed for his phone. 'Coming atcha...'

The message popped up on Emma's screen and she saved the number. 'Got it. Tell him to expect my call.'

'I will do. Thanks.'

'Is there anything else I can do for you? I can go and see if the hospital shop has anything to read that's a bit lighter than that.' Emma pointed to the book on the bed.

'No, that's okay, thanks. I've saved some films on my tablet. I might give one of them a watch.' Iain thought for a moment, and Emma didn't move. Sometimes you had to wait a bit to hear the things people really wanted.

'You know there was a meeting, up in Liverpool? Me and the little girl's parents.'

'Yes, that's standard. We have to assess whether there have been any inducements or pressure on you to donate.'

'Yeah, I get that. But the one thing that struck me... The mother... I could see the pain in her eyes. But all the same, just as we were finishing up, she turned to me and told me that I had to be sure that this was what I really wanted to do.'

'She was right—you do have to be sure.'

Iain nodded. 'I get that too. But for her to say it, when

she was obviously hoping against hope that I could help her little girl. It was generous, don't you think?'

'It takes one to know one, Iain. What you're doing is incredibly generous too.'

'I know it's against the rules and everything, but… I'd like her to know that I'm still sure.'

Emma took a moment to think. 'There isn't anything laid down in the regulations about donor recipient contact. We manage that on a case by case basis, and it's subject to everyone's wishes. What I can do is let the team dealing with your recipient know that there's a message and they'll do what they think is best for the family.'

'Yeah, that sounds good. Thanks.' Iain nodded his approval.

'On one condition.' Emma held her finger up to emphasise the point. 'You're to stop worrying about everyone else. That's my job. You concentrate on yourself and your recovery, all right?'

'Yes, Doctor.'

Emma had waited with Iain until Peter returned with his parents, then texted Josh. He'd asked her to meet him outside the viewing gallery for Theatre Four, and after getting a complex set of directions from one of the nurses in the Transplant Unit, and making a couple of wrong turns, she finally found it.

Josh was standing with a woman and a little girl in a wheelchair. The yellow tone of her skin and sclera said that this must be Amy. Josh had clearly gone all out to make this experience as authentic as possible for Amy, and had changed into a pair of dark blue scrubs. They suited him far better than Emma could allow herself to contemplate while she was working, and she felt her heart thump as he turned his bright blue gaze on her.

'Ah, here she is.' Josh turned to the woman. 'This is

Dr Emma Owen. She's taken over from David Kennedy. Emma, this is Julie Thompson, Amy's mum.'

'Hello. I'm sorry my husband isn't here to meet you. He's gone home to get some sleep.' Julie held out her hand to Emma. She was neatly dressed, her fair hair tied back in a curly ponytail, but the dark rings under her eyes showed the stress that she was under.

'I'm glad to have this opportunity to meet you and Amy.' Emma shook Julie's hand, then bent down towards Amy. 'Hi, Amy. I'm Emma.'

Amy looked at her steadily, clearly wondering who she was and why she was here.

'Dr Emma works with Dr David. She's got everything under control,' Josh volunteered, and Amy nodded, clearly impressed.

'Can we go inside, now?' She looked up at Josh.

'Yes, we can. We can't go into the operating theatre itself, but we can see everything from the gallery.'

'That's where people watch.' Amy turned to her mother to impart the extra information and then looked back up at Josh. 'Is someone going to watch *my* operation?'

'Not if you don't want them to,' Josh replied.

'I don't mind. I've seen it on TV—they watch and learn how to do it. You could show them, couldn't you?'

'No, I'm there just for you, no one else.' Josh had clearly seen Julie's alarmed expression.

'What about Mum and Dad? They could watch.'

A tear rolled down Julie's cheek at the thought, and Josh squatted down in front of Amy. 'I've asked your mum and dad to wait outside, so that I can concentrate on doing my very best for you. But they'll be right here for you and they'll be the first people you see when you open your eyes.'

'Okay.' Amy leaned forward in her chair, putting her hand on Josh's knee. 'I trust you, Dr Josh.'

'Thank you, Amy.' Josh stood up suddenly, and Emma thought she saw him blink rapidly as he did so. 'So we'll go in now, shall we?'

Like so many seriously ill kids, Amy was older than her years. If everything went well tomorrow, then Josh would be restoring not just her health, but her childhood. All of her parents' hopes and fears rested on Josh's shoulders too, and Emma knew it was likely a heavy burden to carry.

But he did so lightly. Amy's wheelchair was placed at the centre of the curved viewing gallery, and her mother sat on one side, with Josh on the other. He explained everything and answered questions, and Emma saw that Julie was becoming more relaxed as he talked too.

'There's one more very important decision we need to make, Amy.' He reached for the bag he'd put on the empty seat next to him and drew out two scrub caps. 'Stars or stripes?'

Amy considered the question and Julie smiled suddenly. 'What do you reckon, Amy? The stripes are colourful.'

'Ah. Your mum wants me to stick out in the crowd.' Josh chuckled.

'I like…stars.' Amy pointed at the dark blue cap with shooting stars on it. She was right, it would bring out the colour in Josh's eyes…

'Shooting stars it is, then, just for you. Now what do you say that you and your mum go and get a good night's sleep and I'll see you in the morning, eh?'

'Okay…' Amy seemed reluctant to go, and Emma caught Josh's eye, beckoning to him.

'All right, you can stay and look for just a few minutes, while I go and check something with Dr Emma.' He got to his feet, leaving Amy leaning forward to stare down into the operating theatre.

Emma quickly relayed Iain's message to him, and he nodded. 'What do you think?'

'You know Julie better than I do, and you're a senior member of Amy's team. It's your decision.'

'Okay. Will you sit with Amy while I take a couple of minutes to talk to Julie?'

'Sure. Thanks.'

Amy was tiring now, and she'd run out of questions to ask. Emma checked the drip that hung at the back of her wheelchair, smoothing the blanket that was tucked around her legs. Josh was standing with Julie at the back of the gallery, speaking quietly to her.

She saw Julie's hand fly to her mouth and she looked for a moment as if she was about to fall over. Josh put out his arm to steady her and she buried her face in his chest, her shoulders heaving with silent sobs. He produced a paper towel from his pocket, giving it to Julie, and she quietly dried her tears and blew her nose, listening to something that Josh was saying and nodding. It was a mime show of emotion, just one of the many that Julie must have had to keep from her daughter, and Emma's heart ached for her.

But Josh *had* made the right decision, because Julie was walking back down towards them, smiling broadly now. She sat down next to Amy, stroking her hair tenderly.

'Are you ready to go now, button?'

Amy nodded sleepily. Emma carefully manoeuvred the wheelchair past the line of seats, and out of the viewing gallery, and Julie walked beside her back to the paediatric transplant ward. Josh lifted Amy out of the wheelchair and into her bed, while Emma hooked the fluid bag back above her head, checking the drip chamber again to make sure that it was half full and properly regulating the fluids going into Amy's arm. Then a nurse came to shoo them away.

'See you tomorrow, Dr Josh,' Amy's voice sounded from the bed, and Josh turned quickly.

'See you tomorrow, Amy.'

Julie followed them out of the ward. 'Thank you, Josh. I

really appreciate the time you've taken today. She'll sleep for an hour and then she'll be telling all the nurses about her visit to the operating theatre.'

'My pleasure. I hope it's helped her.'

'Yes, I think it has.' Julie turned to Emma. 'And thank you for the message. I don't know what to say in reply, there are so many things...'

'I think that just the fact it's been delivered will be enough. May I say that?'

'Yes, yes. And please...my heartfelt thanks as well.'

CHAPTER TWELVE

EMMA KNEW THE SIGNS. They'd gone to bed early, and Josh had slept soundly. He was up early, and when she got downstairs he'd made breakfast. A good night's sleep and a good breakfast was always the way when he had a long surgery scheduled.

But this time, she understood a little better. She'd always known that her job was a matter of meticulous care, over weeks and months, while his was an all-or-nothing turning point in his patients' lives. But she'd reckoned that Josh somehow distanced himself from his patients, as a way of coping with that. Seeing him with Amy had quashed that assumption completely.

How little they'd talked in those few months, caught up in a whirlwind romance that had never really found any solid ground before they'd argued so bitterly. There had been no professional contact, no real friendship, just an instinctive connection. So fragile that it was always destined to break, and when it had it had wounded them both, far more than Emma had ever anticipated.

'You're going up to see your donor?' he asked as they walked through the hospital reception together. Josh never mentioned Iain by name, and Emma knew this was his way of maintaining the separation between donor and recipient teams.

'Yes. You?'

'I'll be checking on Amy and then I'll sit in for a while in Theatre.'

'I'll probably see you there, then.'

He nodded, and they went their separate ways.

She found Iain sitting in a wheelchair, a little nervous but still determined. Peter was holding his hand tightly, smiling reassuringly.

'Emma. Could you get this guy off me? He's cutting off the circulation to my fingers.' Iain's bravado wasn't fooling anyone but himself.

'I think that they're about ready to go now anyway.' One of the nurses had just appeared in the doorway behind Emma.

Iain nodded. 'Right, then. Let's get this done, shall we?'

She'd walked down to the anaesthetic room, taking Peter's arm and leading him away when it was time to go. 'I'll wait here.' Peter pointed to a row of seats in the corridor outside.

'No, you won't. He isn't going to be coming out of that door, and you'll only be in the way.' And Peter would be seeing a procession of one patient after another going into the theatre suite. That was enough to unsettle anyone.

'Okay...um...four hours, isn't it?'

'At least. It may be a little longer, but that's no indication of how things have gone.' That wasn't strictly true, and Emma hoped that it would be four hours at most. 'Would you like to go for a coffee?'

'No, probably not. I don't think so.'

'Okay, well, you know where the cafeteria is if you change your mind. What about some fresh air and stretching your legs for a while?'

'Yeah. That sounds good. You have my number, don't you?'

'I have it, and I'm going to be keeping tabs on exactly

what's happening. I'll call you as soon as there's any news. Have you got my number?'

Peter took his phone from his pocket. 'No, I don't.'

His hand was shaking and Emma took the phone from him, putting her number into the memory. 'Call me any time you want. If I'm busy and can't answer I want you to leave a message, so that I can get straight back to you.'

'Thanks.' Peter let out a sigh. 'Iain and I have been together five years now and he's the bravest person I know. He's got this chance of changing some little kid's life and it's not something he's prepared to let go of.'

'What he's doing is amazing. What you're doing in supporting him is hard too, Peter. Hang on in there, because he's relying on you.'

Peter straightened suddenly. 'Thanks. I'll see you in four hours.'

The process was well choreographed. The right lobe of Iain's liver would be extracted, meanwhile Amy would be prepped for surgery. There would be a careful examination, to make sure that the liver section was viable, and it would be taken through to the adjoining operating theatre, where Josh would be waiting to make his first incision. While that was happening Alex Sargent would be finishing up, closing Iain's wound.

Emma found Josh sitting in the operating theatre viewing gallery watching as Alex operated. He was leaning forward, obviously deep in thought, and Emma sat down quietly beside him.

'Everything okay?' He didn't look around.

'Yes, fine.' Going into details would only break his concentration.

His terse comments were useful though. He clearly held Alex in high esteem as a surgeon, and he was nodding his head in approval of the way things were going. He didn't need to explain anything to her, but the finer points of the keyhole incision were interesting, along with the way he read what was going on. When Alex turned, holding up his hand to the gallery windows, he stood up.

'That's my invitation to leave.'

Emma nodded. They both had their parts to play; Josh knew she'd be keeping both Iain's and Amy's families informed and trying to make their wait less harrowing. And she knew that he'd be giving all he had to make Amy's transplant operation a success.

But there was one moment for each other. One moment when she looked up into his eyes and saw the weight of responsibility. Saw the smile that told her he knew she was feeling it too. This wasn't just comfort for each other, it was the pathway that David had told her was so important. Creating joined-up care for patients and their families, helping them understand and see the right way forward.

Emma watched him go. Her appreciation of the way that Josh moved wasn't anywhere on David's list of things to do, but he'd told her that she would find her own ways of getting through the day. Whatever worked, worked.

A long day. A good day. Emma had taken advantage of a coffee break to slip into the viewing gallery to watch Josh operate. Amy's small form was all but obscured, but she easily picked Josh out from the shrouded figures around her, by the shooting stars cap. She smiled. He'd kept his promise to the little girl, even if she didn't have any way of knowing he had.

He'd been standing for three hours at that point, and would be doing so for at least another three, but he showed no sign of it. Josh was locked in deep concentration, seeming relaxed but totally focused. His back wouldn't ache, and he'd feel no hunger or fatigue until the operation was finished. Then it would all hit him.

She'd seen enough procedures to know that Josh ran his theatre well. He didn't have to look up to make sure that anyone was doing as he asked—Josh was in sole charge. As always, he had everything under control, right down to the last detail.

Ironic. That might be one of his worst failings when it came to a relationship, but it was a major asset in doing his job. Emma was too busy to address that thought at the moment...

But there was time later.

Once Josh had finished the operation, they had reported the good news on Amy's condition to her parents and left them with her in the recovery room. Josh looked tired now, the weariness of six hours' intense concentration finally catching up on him.

'You should go home.' She smiled up at him.

'You're not coming?' Weary as he was, the implications of her words didn't quite elude him.

'I want to speak with the donor and his family. And I've got a few other things to do, before I report back to David and tell him how it all went.'

And Emma wanted to take some time out to think. She'd been so wrapped up in her work today that the constant doubts about her relationship with Josh hadn't had time to surface. Now that they had, it was possible to look at them with fresh eyes, and that new perspective was making her wonder what on earth she thought she was doing. Sleeping with Josh, getting involved again, when there was no way forward with him.

'I'll leave the car if you're going to be coming home late.'

No. She didn't want that. She wanted to be cut adrift from Josh for a while, because being with him didn't allow her to think straight.

'Take it. I'll get a taxi if it's late.'

He nodded, shooting her that delicious smile that made all of her doubts disappear. Right now, Emma didn't want them to go anywhere because they were the one thing that were holding her down, grounding her. Without them she was rudderless, and liable to make mistakes.

'Okay. Shall I save you something to eat?'

'No thanks. I don't know how long I'll be and... Don't wait up for me. I may catch a few hours' sleep here.'

The flicker at one side of his eye told her that he could feel her drawing away from him. Or maybe he was too tired to feel anything at the moment. Josh lifted his hand, brushing his fingers against her sleeve.

'I'll see you when I see you, then.'

Josh's back ached and he was hungry. He eased the knots from his shoulders as he waited in line at the cafeteria for coffee and a sandwich, and then walked to his car.

A good night's sleep in one of the on-call rooms generally required a greater level of fatigue than Emma was carrying around at the moment. He couldn't shrug off the nagging feeling that something wasn't right, but Emma didn't have to explain her decisions to him. Maybe he was just becoming hyper-sensitive, and that wouldn't do because he'd promised her a relationship without any strings.

Sleep wasn't difficult when he arrived home, and he woke up at three in the morning, still on the sofa. For a moment he felt the thrill of wondering whether he'd woken because Emma had arrived home, and then in the still darkness he realised she hadn't. When he went upstairs, hoping she might have gone to bed without waking him, the bedroom was dark and empty.

Josh flung himself down on the bed, staring up at the ceiling. He'd known that this would happen and he felt... just the familiar numbness of having to move on, because he'd done it too many times before and feeling loss would be too overwhelming. He should just accept it, because it went with the territory where Emma was concerned.

But he was wide awake, now. And without even thinking about it, he'd gone into the bathroom and splashed water on his face, dropped his clothes into the washing basket and pulled out a pair of old jeans and a sweater. He then spent ten minutes looking for his car keys, before going downstairs to the garage.

Josh had expected to have to hunt for Emma, but he saw her as he drove into the hospital, standing outside the main entrance with a man. He kept her in his rear-view mirrors as he drove along the slip road into the car park, and saw a taxi draw up in front of her. Maybe she *was* on her way home to him. But the thrill of the thought turned into dashed hopes as he saw the man get into the taxi, and it drew away, leaving Emma standing alone.

Now wasn't the time for dashed hopes. It wasn't the time for feeling nothing either. He got out of the car and walked across to the bench where she was sitting, the lights from the reception area glinting in her hair.

He sat down. Neither of them said a word for what seemed like an age.

'That was the donor's partner. I've only just managed to persuade him that sitting in the waiting room all night isn't going to help anyone.'

So she really did have something to do here tonight. Josh nodded, silently wondering if she'd reckoned on this when she'd told him that she wasn't coming home. That was probably an unfair question.

'What are you doing here, Josh?' Emma was staring straight ahead of her. 'We said—'

'Yeah, we did, didn't we? No strings. I get that, and I'm already forgetting what your face looks like.'

He could tell that had hurt her. Had he gone out to hurt

her, just to see what it looked like and maybe to feel a little bit of it? Emma had turned away from him, now.

'How many friends do you have from before medical school? And when you were at medical school?'

Josh saw anger in her slight shrug. That was okay, not knowing how many meant there were some, and that was answer enough.

'Loads, I imagine. I'll bet you keep in touch and meet up from time to time. I don't have a single one. That was what I learned during my first ten years. That having to move on hurts. And I didn't want to feel that hurt. So I tried to switch it off. When my mother died, I just packed my rucksack and walked away, and I hated David for bringing me back and making me feel the loss.'

Emma turned, suddenly. 'What's this all about, Josh?'

'I'm guessing that you've been having your reservations about sleeping with me. Maybe today put everything into perspective.' He felt a lump rise in his throat. But this was what it was all about, wasn't it? Making yourself address the hard issues so that you didn't lose someone completely.

She heaved a sigh, and then her lips formed a reluctant smile. 'All right. Since you're going to be an adult about this, I'm not going to let you outdo me. Yes, today put things in perspective. And I am wondering what we think we're doing.'

'Me too. I know I'm losing you and…' Josh shrugged. This next part was the hardest thing to say. 'Forget the sex for a moment; what I really care about is keeping our friendship. Whatever you do and whatever you say, I'm not going to just let you drift away without putting up a fight. I'm not going to accept it and walk away.'

Emma raised her eyebrows. 'You want to forget the sex?'

'Okay. So it's unforgettable. But I have to, just for the

moment, if I'm going to feel what losing your friendship is like. And learn to fight for it.'

'That's—' she gave him a sudden smile '—one of the nicest things anyone's ever said to me.'

'That they want to be your friend?' Josh reckoned that many, many people had said that to Emma in the course of her life, and that she'd had little difficulty in keeping her side of the bargain.

'That you'll fight for me.' She reached out and took his hand. 'I'll fight for you too.'

He nodded, wondering if Emma knew how much this meant to him. Whether she understood that what came so naturally to her was something he had to struggle with. Then he felt her fingers tightening hard around his.

'I'd really like to be your first, Josh.'

'My first?' At the moment he was feeling too much to fathom quite what she meant.

'The first friend that you don't let go of.'

'Ah. Yeah, I'd like that too.'

She leaned towards him, and he felt her shiver. Taking off his jacket, Josh wrapped it around her shoulders, holding it in place with a hug.

'What about the sex?'

Josh swallowed hard. Looked up at the sky that was beginning to show the first traces of light. 'I… It's not as important as… I don't want this to be all or nothing, Em.'

'I get that. Now that we've agreed that it's not going to be *nothing*… Do you have any difficulties with *all*?'

He felt her move against him and knew that she was looking up at him. Josh couldn't quite meet her gaze at the moment.

'If…um… I was thinking maybe you did, since you stayed here tonight.'

Emma moved again, whispering in his ear. She had the *all* part of their relationship down to a very fine art and

Josh tried to calm the shivers that were running through him. Closing his eyes didn't help in the slightest.

'We both have to be back here again in five hours. And you haven't had any sleep.' He dared to look down at her, and her smile aroused him even more than her words.

'I had a nap in your office for a couple of hours. If you drag those two easy chairs together, they're actually very comfortable.' Emma stretched up to kiss his cheek. 'We could try rushing?'

There was nothing more to be said. Josh got to his feet and caught her hand, hurrying over towards his car.

CHAPTER THIRTEEN

THIS WAS MADNESS. Josh had been hurt enough already. She'd been hurt too, and Emma needed to find a place in her life that allowed her to move forward. She doubted very much if she could do that while she was with Josh. But that one word—doubt—held the key to everything. While there was still one chance that they might work things out, Emma couldn't leave him.

And it was working now. She'd taken fright and Josh had dismissed her fears and come to fetch her. He'd fought for her and that meant a lot.

Amy was making a good recovery, and left the Paediatric Intensive Care Unit on the third day after her operation. Iain too was recovering well. He was still in pain, but if anything, he felt more positive about his experience than he had before, saying that his gift was no longer just something he felt was right, but was now a part of who he was. Emma had suggested that he make a video diary, and had been in his room recording the first entry.

He'd finally said all that he wanted to say for today and started to doze. Emma walked back to Josh's office.

'Hey. How did it go?'

'Good. Donating part of his liver has been a life-changing experience, and however positive he feels about it, it's still good to talk and make sense of it.'

Josh nodded. 'It sounds like a worthwhile project.

Something that the foundation might be interested in taking forward.'

'They do that kind of thing already, don't they?' Emma sat down in one of the visitors' chairs.

'They record interviews with donors and recipients, for the website. This isn't quite the same thing though; it's more a matter of a personal journey. Why don't you ask Dad?'

Emma nodded. 'I did mention that I was doing it. He said he'd be interested in hearing how it went.'

Josh chuckled. 'Sounds to me as if he's hooked, and he's just waiting to see what you come up with. He does that kind of thing. We could brainstorm, if you like?'

'Brainstorm. Josh, have you not got anything better to do? Something like surgery?'

'Actually, no. I had a surgery cancelled this afternoon. If you don't want to brainstorm, you could always let your hair down…'

'Don't tempt me, Josh. And might I just mention that most people who have worked late every night for the last week would be thanking their lucky stars for a couple of free hours and the prospect of going home on time.' It was just as well that Josh thrived on being busy, because he usually was.

He didn't get the chance to answer, because Emma's phone started to buzz and she took it out of her pocket, scanning the message that had popped up. 'I've got to go now, I'm wanted in A & E. So you'll have to find something else to keep you amused.'

'Someone's talked you into covering? Why didn't they ask me?'

'I offered. Whoever's on the rota for today is off sick.' Emma fiddled with the app. 'Is there some way I can confirm, and say I'm on my way?'

'Just hit "accept."' Josh was on his feet now too, and making for the door. 'This way. It's quicker.'

He led her down a deserted back staircase and into a service lift, then along a couple of corridors and across a small quadrangle, ending up at one of the side entrances to the hospital's A & E department, in about a quarter of the time that it would have taken Emma to get down to the main reception and then along to A & E. Josh made a beeline for a young doctor who seemed to be doing three things at once, and she shot him a smile.

'To what do we owe this honour, Mr Kennedy? Or have you just lost your way?'

Josh chuckled. 'I was actually making sure the doctor you requested made it down here without getting lost.' He made a quick introduction. 'Emma Owen… Demi Ange-lou.'

'Thanks for coming so quickly.' Demi turned to Emma, handing her a folder with a patient assessment form clipped to the front. 'I've got a forty-five-year-old male, with symptoms of moderate liver failure. I can get him an early appointment with a consultant, but I'd prefer someone took a look at him now.'

That was wise. Patients with liver failure often didn't experience drastic symptoms until the damage was too great to correct easily, but finding out exactly what was wrong took time and Emma could see that the A & E department were busy.

'Leave it with me. Have you asked for an ultrasound?'

'Yep, the nurse has already given him plenty of water to drink and they're sending a technician down. Might be a while though.'

Emma looked up at Josh, who was clearly trying to read the notes over her shoulder without being too obtrusive about it.

'Care to do the honours?' She smiled up at him.

'Yeah. Thanks.'

Demi snorted with laughter. 'I'm just going to pretend that we don't have a hotshot surgeon down here offering to do ultrasound scans. It might go to my head.' She looked up as someone beckoned to her. 'Unfortunately I can't hang around to watch. Cubicle Four...'

Terry Adams looked older than his forty-five years and was ashen and clearly in pain. Emma introduced herself and Josh, and the woman sitting by his bedside brightened immediately.

'Thank goodness. I don't think that young girl knew very much at all.'

'She's young but extremely talented.' Josh issued the reproach so pleasantly that it clearly didn't register as one, but the woman stopped complaining.

Emma sat down and started to go through Terry's medical history with him, referring to Demi's notes as she went. Terry's responses were limited mostly to nods, and it was his wife, Janet, who answered most of the questions.

She moved on to her examination, probing his stomach. 'Does that hurt?'

'He said it hurt a little further down,' Janet answered.

Emma ignored her, turning to Terry. 'I need you to tell me, Terry.'

'A bit...' Terry nodded.

'Right, then, it looks as if Mr Kennedy's ready with the ultrasound...' She glanced at Josh and he nodded. 'It won't hurt at all, but there's a cold sensation on your skin from the gel.'

Josh smiled at Terry, and started the examination, with just the same care and concentration that he took when he was in the operating theatre. Janet was watching him, leaning round to see the display, and that gave Emma the chance to talk to Terry.

'How many units of alcohol do you drink a week, Terry?'

'None. I don't drink.'

'Okay, that's good news when you have the kind of pain you're experiencing. And have you been taking any medications? Either prescribed by your doctor, or off the shelf?'

'I get headaches—'

Janet turned, interrupting him. 'Migraines. He's been getting a lot of them recently and he has to have something for them.'

'What do you take?' Emma doggedly continued to question Terry, and he gave her the name of the tablets he took. 'And you take them according to the instructions on the packet?'

'Of course he does.' Emma ignored Janet's reply and waited for Terry's.

'Sometimes I take a few more. It doesn't do any harm and when the headaches are bad...'

'All right. Well, as a general piece of advice, you mustn't ever take more than the recommended dose. I know it's sometimes tempting when you have a bad headache, but these are quite strong and it's easy to take too much when you're not feeling well.' Emma waited for Terry's nod before she continued. 'Anything else?'

'Just Janet's herbal pick-me-ups. I'd like to lose a bit of weight.'

'They won't do him any harm. It's just herbs.' As expected, Janet had something to say about it. Emma wondered whether she should mention foxgloves and digitalis to her, and decided against it. This was a stressful situation for her too, and it was probably just the way she was coping with it, however annoying it seemed.

'What's the name of the supplement you're using?'

Josh had obviously seen the direction that Emma was going in, and interjected with a few questions that she'd already asked. That diverted Janet's attention for long enough to allow Emma to pull out her phone and look up the herbal supplements to see what they contained.

He finished the ultrasound, replying to Janet's questions with a lot more patience than Emma could have mustered. She got to her feet, telling Terry that she'd be back in a moment, and holding the door open while Josh manoeuvred the ultrasound trolley outside.

'Did you find anything?' she asked after closing the door behind them.

'There's a slightly increased echogenicity, indicating steatosis, but it doesn't account for the symptoms.' Josh frowned. 'How about you?'

'Terry doesn't drink, but he does take painkillers for migraine pretty regularly. He admitted that on a couple of occasions he's taken a little more than the recommended dosage.'

Josh nodded. 'If he's owned up to it, then he might well be doing it on a regular basis. Did you find out what were in those herbal supplements?'

'Yes, and a couple of the ingredients are contraindicated for liver damage. I think we need to keep him in for a couple of days to do some more tests, but at the moment it looks as if we have a case of DILI on our hands.'

'I agree. You want me to go upstairs and arrange for a bed for Terry?'

'Don't pretend that you don't want to see things through. Just make the call up to the unit, the way you usually would. You can come and break the news with me.' Telling a patient that they may have a drug-induced liver injury, which they'd inadvertently caused themselves, always required a degree of tact.

'Right. Didn't want to crowd you.' Josh gave her a smouldering look, which Emma did her best to ignore.

He was positive and kind, telling Terry and Janet that he'd seen no signs of serious liver disease, although the slightly brighter patches on the ultrasound image did indicate that there were some fatty deposits in the liver.

'This kind of thing is typically picked up in just these circumstances, where we do some tests for another reason. It can often be improved significantly by diet and losing a little weight, so this is a good opportunity to do something about it before it becomes problematic.'

'So this isn't what's making me feel so rough.' Terry understood immediately and Josh nodded, glancing at Emma in an indication that this next part was for her to explain.

'My initial thoughts, Terry, are that the pain and nausea you're feeling right now is due to the medications you've been using. We'd like to admit you for a couple of days so that we can do some tests to confirm that.'

'What? But...' The expected objection came from Janet, but her combative tone had disappeared. She was as white as a sheet, tears forming in her eyes.

Terry reached out and took her hand. 'Let's just listen to what the doctor has to say, eh, love?'

Janet looked as if she was about to faint, and Josh reached for a tissue, giving her an encouraging smile.

'This isn't uncommon.' It wasn't particularly common either, but Emma decided to emphasise the positive. 'And the good news is that the liver is amazing. It's a kind of detox centre for the rest of the body, and that means it's capable of filtering out waste products and even regenerating itself if necessary. We just have to allow it to do so, by finding out exactly what's causing the damage.'

'And you think...my migraine tablets?' Terry frowned.

'Most over-the-counter painkillers are very safe drugs to take, but it's really important that you don't exceed the recommended dose because taking too many of them can cause liver damage. I've taken a look at the herbal preparation you've been using, and that does contain a very high concentration of products that have been found to compromise liver function in some circumstances as well. As I said, we'll be doing some other tests to make sure that everything else is in good shape, but it's likely that all you need to do is discontinue the medication you've been taking, and give your liver a chance to recover.'

'But…the headaches.' Terry's brow creased. 'They get really bad sometimes.'

'Have you spoken with your own doctor about them?'

'No, I just… We got some tablets from the chemist and they seemed to be working.'

'Well, I think we might be able to make things better for you there as well. We can discuss some of the things that may be triggering your migraines and suggest some alternative medicines to control it.'

Janet's shoulders were drooping and she covered her face with her hands. 'It's all my fault.'

'That's not true, Mrs Adams,' Josh replied quickly. 'The very best thing you could have done was to bring your husband here to see Dr Owen today.'

'But the herbal remedies…' Janet wasn't about to let herself off the hook so easily.

'Were an honest mistake. Let's fix it now, shall we?' Emma added.

'Yes. Yes, we'll fix it, Terry.' Janet took her husband's hand.

It was seven o' clock before they got home. Josh had spent over an hour with Janet, reassuring her and talking to her about how the liver functioned and ways in which diet could improve the mild steatosis he'd seen, and Emma had been concentrating on Terry, and putting some of the tests she wanted into motion. By the time they left, Janet and Terry seemed like different people, relaxed and chatting to the nurses, and Janet was thanking them for all that they were doing.

'Dad calls it hospitalitis.' Josh grinned at her as he opened the front door of the mews house. 'People feel there's something wrong and they just hope it'll get better on its own. By the time they get to the hospital they're so stressed about everything that they actually don't hear a word that anyone's saying to them.'

'I'm glad that Terry didn't wait any longer. DILI is a very slippery slope.'

'Yeah. You probably saved him an encounter with me in the operating theatre.'

Emma laughed, rolling her eyes. 'That's the general plan, Josh. I'd be more than happy if I could halve your workload by educating people about how to look after themselves.'

'I'd spend the extra time listening to you talk about the liver. Did you know your eyes light up when you talk about how it regenerates?'

'Don't you think it's amazing?' Emma threw herself onto the sofa, tugging at her hair. Friend time, although the lines were becoming increasingly blurred between their various personas.

'Yeah, I do. Even more so when I hear you talk about it. Glass of wine?'

'Thanks. Just a half-glass.'

He poured two half-glasses of wine, picking up his tablet. Josh always checked his personal email as soon as he got home. Once a day was enough, and it usually took him a few minutes to tap out his replies, and then he put the tablet aside and left it alone.

But this time he was reading something carefully, hands planted on the countertop, head bowed in concentration. He reached for his glass, almost knocking over the other one, but didn't seem to notice. Maybe this was Jamie. Josh hadn't said a word about it, but Emma knew that he was hoping for an email from him.

Or maybe David had taken it into his head to write one of his long, bullet-pointed emails, and Josh would be tapping out a brief *yes, okay* in reply any minute now. Emma sat for a few minutes, while he finished reading, and then decided that the wait would be better with a glass in her hand.

When she walked across to the kitchen, picking up her wine, he didn't seem to even notice her. But as she turned to leave him he pushed the tablet towards her, his face impassive.

Jamie. Emma saw the name at the top. She picked up the tablet, walking slowly back to the sofa as she read, hoping that Josh might snap out of his reverie and follow her. She read carefully, and began to see why he hadn't.

The tone of Jamie's email was different from the first, with none of the excitement and warmth he'd displayed. This was in turns apologetic and formal, as Jamie explained that he'd told his father about his contact with Josh and he hadn't reacted well. If Jamie had anything to do with Josh he was on his own. There would be no more family, no funding for uni; he'd be cut off completely. Jamie had ended with a half-hearted suggestion that they might meet in secret, but it was clear that he didn't think that was a good idea.

'Josh, I'm so sorry.'

'It's okay.' He shrugged, emptying his glass in one gulp. 'I took a risk. There was always that possibility.'

He opened the fridge, refilling his glass again. It wasn't like Josh to drink a second glass of wine, but at least he put the bottle back again. In his shoes, Emma would probably have kept hold of it to save herself another journey.

'Do you have any idea what you're going to say to him?'

'Yeah.' He joined her on the sofa, his long legs sprawling out in front of him. 'I'd already thought about it and

I'm going to write back and tell him it's okay. And that I'll always be here, and he can contact me whenever he wants.'

'That's generous of you.'

'What am I going to do, Em? He's twenty years old and the father he's known all his life is threatening to cut him off.'

'It might be just an empty threat.'

'You'd take that chance? He's done it before.'

Josh was right. This must be cutting him into little pieces, but he'd said nothing about what he wanted or needed, just tried to do the right thing by a brother he hadn't even met.

'You're right. I hope I'd be brave enough to do what you're doing and make sure that Jamie's okay.'

He put his glass down. 'Will you just...come here?'

It was easy to slide across and hug him, and Josh held her tight. Less easy to wonder whether she wasn't doing just the same as Jamie had just done. Offering Josh something, in the knowledge that she'd be leaving soon. Saying that they'd promised each other nothing was a cop-out, because their unspoken promises had been made every night, in his bed.

'What I really want to do is make a visit to my biological father. Maybe punch him around a bit and tell him that he has no right to tell me what I can and can't do. Or Jamie, for that matter; he's an adult. And that if he doesn't step up to his responsibilities towards him, then he'll be hearing from me again.'

Emma squeezed him tight. 'And you're a surgeon. You know just where to punch.'

'Yes, I do.'

Now wasn't the time to talk about her own doubts, or her growing guilt. Josh needed her tonight. 'What do you say we go out for dinner? I know a great place in South

Kensington; it's my treat. We'll walk there to clear out the cobwebs.'

'I'm getting dinner, am I? I'll have to make you feel sorry for me a little more often.'

'I don't feel sorry for you, Josh. I'm proud of you.'

'That's a bit harder to earn. In that case, I'll accept your offer.'

She'd never known Josh to ask for any sympathy over anything. He didn't waver, whatever happened, and that was one of the things that made him a good surgeon. Decisive, cool and in control. However much he was hurting.

'I'm going to go and get changed, then. Are you coming?'

'In a minute. I'm going to write back to Jamie.'

'Now?' Maybe that was overdoing the decisiveness.

'That must have been a difficult email for him to write—he could have just not written back. I want him to know that I appreciate his honesty and that keeping his family is the right thing to do. And I want to be a friend to him, even though he can't be a friend back.'

Emma kissed him. 'You're not going to let him go?' Every time she started to wonder what she was doing with Josh, he did something that gave her hope.

'No. I want him to know that whatever he does, I'll be there for him. I've learned that from some important people in my life.'

David. His mother. Maybe a little part of it from her, but Emma wasn't sure that she deserved any credit for it. She was just holding on, closing her eyes and hoping that somehow this would all work out.

'Write your email.' She wriggled out of his embrace and stood up. 'I'm going to find something really nice to wear tonight.' Josh always took notice of what she wore and Emma liked his appreciative glances.

'Do *not* tempt me to come up there with you and devise a strategy on getting you back out of the really nice thing as soon as you've got into it.'

'I expressly forbid it, Josh. I prefer your talent for spontaneity when you're engaged in getting me out of my clothes.'

She heard him chuckle behind her as she climbed the stairs.

It was one of the hardest emails he'd ever had to write, and if he allowed himself to think about it too much he'd lose his nerve. But Emma made it easier, walking back downstairs in a wraparound top that hugged her figure and looked as if it might take a little strategising before he could work out exactly how it was fastened. Casual trousers and flat shoes showed that she was serious when she'd said they'd walk.

She sat down, reading the email he'd written carefully. Finally she nodded. 'That's perfect, Josh. It doesn't leave any room for doubt, but you've also made it clear that you'll welcome any contact from him in the future if things change.'

'Right.' His courage failed him. 'Will you send it, then?'

'You're sure?'

'I'm sure. Send it.'

He heard the tone as the email was sent. Then Emma powered the tablet down, and clipped the cover in place, tucking it away in the bookcase. 'Go and get changed. Hurry up, I'm already hungry.'

She was always a delight, but tonight Josh was realising the full meaning of that. It wasn't something fragile, which might fail at any time; her charm had muscle behind it. He needed to walk tonight, to laugh and feel the evening breeze on his face. He needed Emma, and she didn't fail him.

* * *

He'd been doubtful that he'd be able to eat too much, but by the time they reached the restaurant he was hungry. Emma had chosen a place that served simple food that was fresh and flavourful, and although she thought the chocolate pudding a little too sweet when she leant over to taste his, Josh reckoned it was just right.

His phone buzzed and he automatically picked it up, without thinking that he'd decided not to look at his email again tonight. When he saw the notification, he couldn't put it back down again.

'It's an email. From Jamie.'

Emma's expression became suddenly thoughtful. 'I guess… You know it's there now, Josh. You're only going to be wondering what it says, all the way home.'

The email was just one line and Josh handed Emma the phone so that she could read it too.

'That's nice. Do you suppose he knows that *au revoir* really means *I'll see you later*?'

'I don't know.' But Jamie had thanked him and called him brother. That on its own meant a lot.

She closed the email, laying the phone back down on the table. 'This tells me that he understands, Josh. Whatever happens next, I hope you'll always feel that you handled this compassionately and thoughtfully. Because that's what I see.'

'It hurts.' Two little words that were so difficult to say.

'I see that too. Would you like to go?'

Josh shook his head. He'd lost Jamie, at least for a while. But Emma was still here and she'd given him the strength to go through with what he felt was right.

'Shall we have coffee?' He pushed the rest of the chocolate pudding aside.

They lingered over coffee, Emma clearly making an effort to lift his mood. And then suddenly he stopped noticing that, because the constriction in his chest had eased and he felt able to smile again.

Josh insisted that he hail a taxi for the journey home, reckoning that she'd walked far enough already and she must be tired. But Emma leaned forward, stopping the taxi and getting out when they were half a mile from home. The cool, evening air cleared his head and he followed Emma up the stairs, pulling her close to kiss her. He wanted her more than ever.

'I think I've worked out my strategy on your top.'

Her eyes were bright and clear tonight, seeming to see right into him. 'You may find that my ingenuity slows you down a bit.'

'My strategy will trounce your ingenuity.'

'You reckon so?'

She broke away from him, running up the second flight of stairs. Josh caught her at the top, kissing her again, turning her towards the bedroom door in a slow dance. One day he might hear from Jamie again. But in the meantime, his family were the people he chose, and the woman he chose was in his arms.

CHAPTER FOURTEEN

JOSH SEEMED A little thoughtful as they walked to the hospital the next morning, but his ready smile seemed to indicate that the thoughts weren't bad ones. Maybe he'd been expecting something like this, and his biological father's second rejection came as no great surprise. Or maybe he was in denial; it was sometimes difficult to tell.

He was in the operating theatre this morning, which always seemed to subsume any of his other emotions for a while. Emma had a long list of things to do, as well as liaising with David over another patient whose transplant he'd been supervising, so she'd been busy as well.

At lunchtime she ended the video call with David, whose infectious smile stayed with her all the way to Amy's bedside. The little girl was yet another reason to smile. The yellowish tint of her skin and sclera was much less pronounced, and there were no signs that her body was rejecting the new liver. Careful pain management meant that she was comfortable and responsive, and Julie seemed less exhausted as well. Emma spent some time with them, answering Julie's questions and listening to Amy's plans for what she was going to do when she was well.

Then she saw Iain.

He seemed rather more subdued today, maybe as a result of his pain meds having been reduced, and when Emma asked how he was feeling Peter answered.

'He hasn't eaten any lunch.'

In Emma's experience visitors and family could often provide valuable information. They saw the small changes in someone that were often missed by busy medical staff.

'Okay. Iain, are you in pain?'

'It's not so bad. I've just had half my liver removed, remember.' Iain gave her a wan smile.

And sometimes patients were the last people you should ask. Iain was clearly in pain, and when Emma pulled on a pair of gloves and checked his stomach, it was a little bloated. His blood pressure and pulse were normal, but his temperature was a little high.

'How long have you been feeling like this, Iain?'

'My stomach's not been so good since I woke up this morning. It's probably from too much time in bed. Although…uh… I feel sick.'

Emma managed to catch up one of the disposable vomit bowls from beside the bed, as Iain began to retch. She signalled to Peter to press the call button to summon a nurse, and Iain sank back onto the pillows. He was clutching his stomach now, clearly in a lot of discomfort.

A nurse arrived, and Emma slipped out of the room for a moment. Both Iain and Peter had read every piece of available information on liver transplants and she didn't want them jumping to any conclusions until she'd discussed her provisional diagnosis. She dialled the number for the Transplant Unit's reception.

'It's Emma Owen—is Alex Sargent available, please?'

'No, he's in surgery. Can anyone else help?'

This couldn't wait. 'Josh Kennedy, then.'

'Yes, he's here. Putting you through.'

The sound of retching came from Iain's room again and Emma turned to look through the open door. The nurse was dealing with it, but it was looking increasingly likely that Iain was going to need at least a diagnostic procedure.

'Emma?' Josh asked, sounding concerned.

'Josh, are you available to come and see Iain Warner, Amy's donor? Alex is in surgery and I suspect a biliary leak. We're in Room 407.' Emma wasn't going wait for Alex to be available just because Josh had been Amy's surgeon. There was no question of any conflict of interest now, in getting Iain the best treatment as soon as she possibly could.

'Sure. I'll be right up.' Josh ended the call abruptly.

By the time he arrived, Iain was lying back down again. The nurse had a fresh vomit bowl ready, in case it should be needed, and Peter was sitting by the bed holding Iain's hand. Every head in the room swivelled towards Josh, as he picked up the notes at the end of the bed.

'Hi, Iain, I'm Josh Kennedy and I'm a consultant transplant surgeon.'

'You're not the right guy.'

Josh looked up from the notes and chuckled. 'Yeah, story of my life. Mr Sargent's not available at the moment and so I'm going to take a look at you if I may.'

'Yes…' Iain winced again, from another wave of pain.

'First things first. Let me take a look at your incision.'

'Sure. If you can find it. I'm personally rather disappointed…' Iain attempted a joke.

'I wouldn't get your hopes up, Iain. Mr Kennedy doesn't give his patients scimitar-shaped scars just for show either.' Emma grinned back at Iain, and Peter suddenly snorted with laughter. The tension in the room broke, and Peter allowed Emma to lead him away from Iain's bedside and guide him firmly towards the doorway.

'I need you to wait outside for a moment, Peter. We'll call you when we're finished.'

Peter had stopped laughing now. 'What's the matter with him, Emma?'

'That's what we're trying to find out. Let us take care of him.'

'Okay.' Peter turned suddenly, leaving the room.

Josh's examination was quick, but his jokes and relaxed style were enough to put Iain at ease. Every patient was different, and a doctor didn't always have the time to assess which atmosphere would put them most at ease. But the trust that had grown between Emma and Josh allowed her to shortcut the process for him. It also allowed Josh to assess Iain's responsiveness and his level of pain better. Emma watched as he discounted each possibility in turn, leaving only one conclusion.

'I think you're right.' He murmured the words to her, as he turned to fetch Peter back to sit with Iain.

'Iain, your symptoms suggest that you have a biliary leak. It's not uncommon after liver surgery, and as this has been caught early we can rectify it very easily.'

'He could have said something sooner.' Peter gave Iain a reproachful look, which Iain ignored completely.

'Now is soon enough.' Josh gave Peter a reassuring smile and turned back to speak to Iain. 'I'd like to do an ERCP, which involves passing a very small tube from your mouth to your stomach, so we can see what's going on. I'll have the anaesthetist come and see you to discuss the options, but usually this procedure is done under sedation. Depending on the exact nature of the problem I may also be able to rectify it without the need for surgery.'

Iain glanced at Peter and then nodded. 'Yeah. That sounds good, thanks.'

'I'll prescribe something for the pain in the meantime, and get someone to sort out the consent forms, while I check on theatre availability. Have you had lunch?'

'Couldn't face it.'

'When was the last time you ate or drank anything?'

'Breakfast. I've had some sips of water since.'

'Okay, don't have anything to eat or drink for the time being.' He glanced at the nurse, who nodded.

'Thank you, Doctor.' Peter spoke up. 'What does ERCP stand for?'

Josh grinned. 'Endoscopic retrograde cholangiopancre-atography.' He could see where the question was going as well as Emma could, and clearly Peter was going to have difficulty typing that into a search engine. 'I think Dr Owen's probably your best bet if you have any questions.'

It was two hours before Josh could secure a slot in the endoscopy department for Iain, which wasn't a bad thing because it meant that Iain would have been fasting for eight hours, and there was no need to take the precaution of a general anaesthetic with rapid sequence induction. At St Agnes, Emma's home hospital in Liverpool, ERCPs were usually done by gastroenterologists, but Josh was qualified to perform the procedure. His ongoing care of his transplant patients made this a valuable addition to his skills.

His professional demeanour when he asked Emma if she'd be joining him pleased her, but she reminded herself she'd be involved with Iain's care when he returned to Liverpool, so it was a matter of continuity, rather than any personal consideration.

Emma gave Iain a little wave as he was wheeled into the theatre, just so that he'd know it was her behind the mask. Josh's headspace was already in surgical mode, watchful and concentrated. The nurse helped Iain up onto the couch, getting him to lie on his side, and he smiled nervously at Emma.

'When do I get the happy stuff?'

'You're getting it now.' The anaesthetist was already administering the sedative via a catheter that had been attached to the back of Iain's hand. It was fast-acting, and Iain would be starting to doze soon.

'You're gonna need all this?' Iain's speech was already beginning to slur slightly and he was looking around at the screens and other technology that surrounded him.

'Only the best for our donors.' Josh's voice sounded behind her. 'X-ray equipment here, and there's the display for that. This screen's for the camera, mounted on the probe...'

Iain had been trying to follow what Josh was saying, but his eyelids were drooping. When they closed, Josh glanced at the anaesthetist, who nodded back at him. They were ready to start.

Josh fitted a mouth guard and then began to pass the endoscope into Iain's mouth and down into his stomach. It was careful, concentrated work, watching the screen, which relayed the images from the camera, to make sure that he did no damage. When the camera reached the bile duct, a fine tube was passed down the endoscope and dye injected. The radiographer operated the X-ray equipment, and an image flashed onto the screen that was adjusted to Josh's eye level.

'Ah. There see, there's a leak in one of the ducts on the cut surface of the liver.' Josh indicated the area on the screen, and Emma heard the click of the camera as he saved an image. He'd been documenting the whole process carefully and that would form part of the notes she took back to Liverpool with her.

He inspected the cut surface of the liver carefully along with the surgical sutures. It was a painstaking process, but Emma knew that this must be done well to avoid the need for further procedures. Her back began to ache from standing in the same position, and the heavy protective apron she wore to shield her from the X-rays was becoming more burdensome by the minute, but Josh showed no signs of discomfort, completely focused on what he was doing.

Finally, he carefully withdrew the endoscope and Iain

was readied to leave. He'd be taken to the recovery room first and then back to his room on the ward.

Josh stripped off his gloves and held the door open for her, the momentary twitch of his lips saying that he was allowing himself just one moment of chivalry, now that the serious business of the evening was done.

'I'll go and see Peter.' He pulled his apron off, finally allowing himself to stretch his shoulders. 'Just to let him know that Iain's okay and he should continue to make a good recovery.'

'I'll walk with you.' Emma smiled up at him, falling into step as he made his way to the relatives' waiting room.

Respect and friendship. It allowed them to work together well and that brought a depth and breadth to their relationship that they hadn't experienced the first time. They'd be going home soon, and when they got there he'd pull the fastenings from her hair. Then it would turn into something delicious.

Happy. That was a good word. So were laughter and caring. Loved and in love—those words had always been a little more problematic for Josh, but he was getting his head around them. He was sure that he'd said something of the sort to Emma last night.

There was only one problem. Iain was getting better by the day, and soon he'd be out of hospital and convalescing for a few days with his parents before going back up to Liverpool with Peter. Amy would be staying in hospital a little longer, but she'd improved so much that it was hardly possible to recognise the little girl he'd got to know. He'd given her the shooting stars cap, and she'd taken to wearing it whenever the doctors visited her bedside. That was all good, but the difficulty lay in the fact that Emma would be leaving too.

He had a plan though. Josh had been turning it over

in his mind for days and it all fitted together perfectly. It had to be today, because Emma would be taking the train back to Liverpool first thing tomorrow, and it started with apricot jam and cappuccino because that was Emma's favourite Saturday morning breakfast in bed.

'You are too perfect.' She kissed him before getting out of bed. 'I think you might be a figment of my imagination.'

'How do I function when you're not around, then?'

She grinned. 'How do I know that you do? I might just have made up a whole load of things that you did when I wasn't around, like you do in dreams. Or perhaps it's all momentum. Like a stone rolling down a hill.'

Emma was teasing, but she might have inadvertently hit on something there. Josh was beginning to feel that whatever he did when she wasn't around *was* just a matter of momentum, carrying him forward to the time he'd see her again.

'I could ask you the same question.' He could, but Josh didn't reckon he had the imagination to conjure Emma up all by himself. She was too vivid, far too complex and entrancing.

'You've got a point.' She was heading for the shower, and Josh collected the plates together to take them downstairs. 'I'll have to do something really unexpected, that you couldn't possibly have dreamed up, and then you'll know you didn't make me up.'

She did those things all the time. And Josh was about to break all the rules too and do something unexpected... something that had a future. Something real.

It was a sunny day, and they strolled down to Portobello Market together. They considered the pros and cons of things they knew they weren't going to buy, had coffee and then did some more window-shopping.

'I've been meaning to ask you...' He'd been working

his way around to this since they started to walk home, and seeming to get no closer to it. It was time to just say it.

'Yes?'

Josh took a breath. 'Would it be okay if I came up to Liverpool sometime, to see you?'

She thought for a moment. More than one moment—the pounding of his heart told him that.

'Yes. I'd really like that, Josh.' She smiled up at him. 'What we have...'

'I don't want to let it go either.' He could breathe again, and the other things he wanted to ask seemed so much easier. 'Next weekend?'

'Maybe the weekend after. I'll be busy when I get back and it'll give me two whole weeks to look forward to it.' She put her arm around his waist, pulling him closer as they walked.

Her agreement buoyed him and he could see his goal now, so he took his shot. 'We've needed another hepatologist on the unit for a while now. I made enquiries and they're looking to recruit someone but people with the right experience are hard to find. I'm sure Dad would give you a glowing reference and there'd be no problem over getting somewhere to live. I might have to get a smaller car, so that your Mini would fit into the garage...'

Suddenly the world turned again and everything he thought he'd gained was snatched away. Because Emma was staring up at him, a look of horror on her face.

Emma was glad that Josh had asked about visiting, because she'd been wondering how she might ask him up to Liverpool for the weekend. It seemed that they were both of the same mind, that their relationship was worth throwing the rulebook out of the window and just seeing where that went.

And then... Strip away the veneer of change and he was still the same Josh. Still aching for security and needing commitment. And she was still the Emma who needed to move on with her life, after her father's death. Keeping her wheels turning wasn't just about moving from place to place, it was about healing.

Maybe she could still do this. But *maybe* wasn't enough, and she shouldn't make promises that she didn't know she could keep.

'You mean...' She cleared her throat, trying to think straight. 'You think that I should move. Give up my job...?'

'Or I could move to Liverpool.'

Right. Now he was just clutching at straws. Josh was needed here, and that didn't make any sense at all.

'Josh, I'm sorry, but... I don't think that's a good idea. Not just yet.'

He fished his keys out of his pocket, opening his front door. Maybe that was an end to it, but his face was grave and the bright, sunshiny prospect of seeing him again in two weeks had suddenly tarnished as well.

She walked up the stairs, looking around the living area desolately. Suddenly, sitting down on Josh's sofa, or going to Josh's fridge to get some juice, was the kind of thing it was necessary to think about—not something you'd do naturally because you felt at home in his home.

'Em, don't you see it?' Clearly he wasn't going to let this go. 'Don't you feel that we should be together?'

'What I feel is that we've spent three weeks together. It's been great—better than great—it's been wonderful. What we decided...that we'd just kiss goodbye and then let fate decide whether we bump into each other again...that's not what either of us wants now. But don't you think it's a bit early to start making the kind of commitment that means I give up my job and move down to London?'

He frowned. 'I'm not asking you to do all of the leg-work, Emma. I said that I'd move...'

'No. That's not my point, Josh. My point is that *neither* of us should be moving, because...' They were both too fragile. Still looking for different things.

'Because what?' His face was stony. 'The least you could do is give me a reason.'

One that didn't make him feel that she was flinging everything he'd told her back in his face. Which was hard, because everything he'd told her had only brought her to the conclusion that they couldn't be together.

'We're very different people, Josh. You want commitment, and I... I can't give you that right now. I need to find a way of moving forward that means something to me, because...because I lost that when we were together the last time. And I can't lose it again, not now.'

Too much truth. Too much *painful* truth, which had sounded through her words. His face darkened suddenly.

'You're saying that *I* took that away from you?'

'I'm saying that I lost it. Because I loved you and I shouldn't have.'

'No, Em. You should have loved me because I loved you. Because if we do love each other, then we can compromise.'

'I should go.' Emma couldn't risk their hearts breaking the way they had before. Maybe that was what love and honesty were. She'd always felt that Josh was the one who was risk-averse, but maybe it had been her all along. Loving him had shown her that she was afraid too, when she'd thought herself fearless.

He turned suddenly, an expression of rage on his face. 'No, Emma, I'm not going to watch you go. Not again.'

'What, you're going to lock me in?' She regretted the words as soon as they were said. Josh could no more do that than fly. 'Let's not do this, Josh. I refuse to say all the things I said before.'

Too late. They might remain unsaid but they both knew what she'd said and what he'd said. The words were still stuck in their heads.

'I said I wouldn't watch you go.' His tone was as cold as ice. 'I'm not trying to tell you what to do, I'm just saying what *I* can and can't do.'

He turned, walking back down the stairs, his footsteps loud in the sudden silence. Emma called after him, but he didn't turn. She heard the sound of the garage doors, and when she ran to the kitchen window he'd backed the car out and was slamming the doors shut.

'Don't drive, Josh...' She leaned across the sink, reaching for the catch on the kitchen window. But he was already back in the car, driving slowly and carefully across the smooth cobblestones.

That was Josh all over. She would have slammed the Mini into first gear, stalled the engine a couple of times and then roared up the mews, preferably leaving a trail of exhaust fumes behind her. Josh wasn't like that. She'd seen it in the operating theatre with her own eyes. Stress just made him even more focused on the task in hand.

And there was no going back now. They'd taken a risk, knowing that things hadn't worked out between them the last time, thinking that they could shorten the odds with a few rules. Now it seemed an insane thing to do, but Emma was hurting enough already to know why they'd done it.

She couldn't think about that now. It was done and the past couldn't be changed. The future could, and hers lay in leaving before Josh came back and they argued again, maybe even more hurtfully, although it was difficult to see how anything could hurt much more than this.

She needed to go back to Liverpool and let him get on with his life. Maybe meet someone else…

Okay. Turned out there was something that could hurt more: the thought of Josh giving everything he'd given her to someone else. Emma walked upstairs and began to pack her bags.

CHAPTER FIFTEEN

JOSH HAD DRIVEN a long way. He'd crossed from Bucking-hamshire into Oxfordshire before he realised which way he was going and turned back again. He knew that David would welcome him, and that whenever he wanted to talk he'd be there. Josh didn't want to talk right now though.

It was dark by the time he got back home. The faint hope that the lights would be on in his apartment hadn't been worth his time. When he walked upstairs, the living space was neat and quiet. Emma had done just as he'd asked her to, and hadn't made him watch her go.

He flopped down onto the sofa, staring at the ceiling. It would be two nights and a day before he got any relief from this feeling. The operating theatre was the one place in the world that blotted everything else out, because of Josh's intense concentration on the life that he held in his hands.

As to the rest of it... He loved Emma more than he'd thought he could ever love anyone. But he'd ruined her life as well, because she couldn't see a way forward with him. So she'd kept her wheels turning, because that was how she dealt with things. She was gone and somehow he had to find a way to make his life mean something again.

Emma had tried. She'd *really* tried. For the last two weeks, she'd spent twelve hours a day at work, and then gone home and spent her time cleaning. Last weekend she'd got to the point where her patients were clearly wondering when she'd leave them in peace, and her house couldn't take any more disinfectant. So she'd spent the whole weekend in bed.

None of it did a thing to lessen the pain or take her mind off things. This weekend she'd tried feeding ducks in the park, visiting an art gallery and going to the cinema. But however much she did, it all felt like spinning her wheels in cloying mud, leaving her stuck, motionless and unable to move forward. And no amount of listless misery and crying could get Josh out of her system.

If he hadn't cared, then that would have been some kind of closure. But Emma knew that he did. She knew that she'd hurt him but that he would forgive her in the blink of an eye. That was the problem—she'd go back to him and then hurt him again.

There were two solutions. She could tell herself that this would pass and keep on going. Past experience told her that it wasn't so easy to forget Josh, and this time there was so much more to forget. Or she could do something about it. But what? She couldn't go back but she couldn't go forward without Josh either.

It was time to make a gesture, one that forced them both to change. Something that could tap into the trust they'd built, as friends and colleagues, and allow them to work through their emotional differences. And in a sudden flash of inspiration, Emma knew just the thing…

Josh had been working every shift that came available. It was tiring, but it meant he slept at night, and didn't spend his days thinking too much about Emma.

He'd turned down an invitation from David and Val to spend this weekend with them in Oxfordshire. He'd go next weekend instead, and hope that Val didn't talk too much about Emma, because even if she missed his reaction to the mention of her name, he doubted that his father would. He heard the letterbox open and then snap shut again downstairs. Perhaps whatever the postman had for him this morning would take up a few minutes of his time, in a weekend that already seemed interminably long.

He walked downstairs and gathered the mail, sorting through the letters. Bills, an invitation to a barbecue, a couple of medical journals... And a postcard. He flipped it over, wondering what on earth Gran was doing in Liverpool.

Emma. Just her name, nothing else. He shook his head. Didn't she know that postcards weren't just postcards? That they had a value far beyond a piece of card with a stamp on it? He flung the bundle of post back down onto the floor, and walked back upstairs, fuming.

Then it hit him. Emma knew exactly what a postcard meant to him: it was his gran's way of telling him that she'd never let him go. It was the message he'd wanted to send to her, and the one he'd yearned to receive from her. It was audacious, and full of Emma's ability to make the best of things.

He almost fell down the stairs in his haste. Sitting down at the foot of the stair, he picked up the postcard and studied it carefully. Nothing but her name, no clues that he could see in the picture. No kisses. He would have liked kisses—Emma had a thing or two to learn from Gran about postcard writing—but this was the most precious thing...

He knew now what Emma was saying to him. They might have nothing more to say to each other, they might have a sum total of nothing. But she wouldn't give him up. She couldn't stop loving him.

He should phone her. Tell her that he'd find a way... Josh ran back up the stairs and grabbed his phone. But before he dialled, the elegance of Emma's gesture stopped him. They didn't have to rush to find answers, or agonise day and night about them. Emma was standing her ground, and she'd be waiting for him.

He picked up his jacket and keys, walking out of the mews apartment with a spring in his step for the first time in weeks. Josh had a postcard to buy, and he wanted to get a really nice one.

The weekend had been torture. Would Josh understand? Would he hear what she had to say to him, and would he even want it? When Emma arrived home on Monday evening, a postcard was lying behind the front door. She dropped her bags, picking it up.

The Tower of London. It was a nice picture. She hardly dared turn the postcard over, but she couldn't just stand here all night, looking at the image. She took a deep breath...

I'll wait for you, Emma.
Knowing you're there is everything. Always, Josh

Emma sank to her knees, shaking with emotion. It was just one step, and there would have to be a second and then so many more. But they'd made it.

She went out at lunchtime the next day, bought another postcard and sent it. When she got home there was one from Josh, waiting for her. Each day she sent a postcard and each day there was one in return. She was beginning to dread Sunday, when there would be no post. A whole two days without the one thing that gave her hope, and something to look forward to. On Saturday, there was a postcard from the London Eye and she smiled as she bent to pick it up. Josh was clearly doing the same as she was, going further afield each day to find postcards to send.

I didn't get anything from you today.
But I'll always love you and trust that you're there.
Josh

Dammit! She'd sent one and it had probably been delayed in the post. But Josh had trusted her enough to know that. The trust they'd built as colleagues and as friends was finally, finally seeping through into their emotional lives. And that was the sweetest thing imaginable.

Fourteen postcards. They were carefully tacked up on the wall, in order, so that Josh could read Emma's side of their daily conversation. It had started with just one word, and it was the word he loved the most in this world. Emma. Now the postcards were loving messages, which turned his whole world upside down. They were constant reminders that Emma was there for him, and if a postcard didn't arrive one day, he just looked forward to two the next morning.

If anyone had asked him, he would have said that this would be torture, a kind of punishment for them both for having dared to love each other. But it wasn't. They were learning to trust each other, to be together without the pressures that life had put on them both. It was a slow process, but it felt to Josh that it was going at just the right speed.

He spent Saturday morning at the hospital, going through patient notes and planning his schedule for the next week. It was no longer necessary to stay until fatigue forced him home again, and he walked back to Notting

Hill after lunch, stopping to buy a window box and some plants. Many of the apartments in the mews had bright window boxes, and he'd never had the time to add to the display. But time was on *his* side, now.

He turned into the mews, and saw a car parked across the doors of his garage. And then he dropped his purchases and ran, because the car was a red Mini, and Emma was leaning up against its front wing, looking as if she'd just driven here straight from the sixties, in a pair of flared jeans, a rainbow-coloured top and the baker boy cap that suited her so well.

'You came.' Now that he could hold her, he could stop shaking.

'I couldn't help myself.' She reached up, laying her hand on his cheek. 'Are you ready for this, Josh?'

'I'm not sure I'll ever be truly ready for you, Em, that's one of the reasons I love you so much. But I do know one thing. I'll never give up on you. If I want to trust you, then I have to trust myself, and I've made that step now.'

He kissed her and she melted into his arms. 'I love you so much, Josh. I have all the future I need, right here with you. And I'm never giving up on you either.'

'I know. I knew it right from the first postcard. How long have you been waiting?'

'I've waited all my life to come home to you, Josh.'

He chuckled. 'You *are* my home. But I meant how long have you been waiting out here for me?'

'Half an hour. I was going to phone you, but I'm glad I didn't. The look on your face when you saw me and dropped your shopping...' She grinned at him. 'What on earth is it anyway?'

'Nothing... Window boxes.' Josh kissed her again, feeling the warm excitement of her response. *This* was love. He knew it as surely as he knew himself.

'Window boxes? So pretty...' She kissed him back and suddenly window boxes became an object of intense interest to Josh.

'I'll go and fetch them.'

'One more kiss before you do. I love you, Josh.'

EPILOGUE

One year later

IT WAS THE kind of summer's day that was perfect for driving. They'd followed the 'Routes Bis,' taking their time in working their way across France via shady country roads and small villages, in a silver Lotus Elan. Tomorrow they'd arrive in the Côte d'Azur, where they could enjoy a luxurious week in Cerise's apartment, while she was on tour in Germany.

'Josh! Stop the car...'

He slowed, stopping in a lay-by. 'We've gone the wrong way again?'

The map slipped off her lap and into the footwell. 'No, I don't think so. I just really wanted to kiss you.'

'So it's a *real* emergency, then.'

He leaned over, taking her in his arms and kissing her. As urgently as anyone could wish.

'Six days... This marriage is going really well so far.'

Josh laughed. 'I can't see any way it could have been better.'

They'd been married in the tiny village church, close to where David and Val lived in Oxfordshire, and the reception had been held on the vast lawns of the manor house. The day had been perfect, full of sunshine and laughter and a lot of love.

Love had made everything fall into place. The weekends together, in Liverpool and London, when they'd talked all day and made love all night. The job offer that had allowed Emma the freedom to come home to Josh and London full-time. David had slowed down, cutting his frenetic work schedule in half to spend time with Val, and had offered Emma the job of her dreams, working at different hospitals around London with the GDK Foundation. The engagement ring that Josh had gone down on one knee to offer her, knowing that she'd accept. Two diamonds, separate but bound together in a tracery of gold.

It hadn't always been easy, but they'd held each other close, talking a lot and listening a lot. Slowly their life together had turned into something more beautiful than Emma could ever have imagined.

'You're my one, true home, Emma Kennedy.' Josh echoed the wedding vows they'd made to each other.

'And you're mine.' Emma leaned over so she could whisper in his ear. 'I've got a secret…'

'Already? You're keeping secrets from me?'

'Only for three hours. I was going to tell you tonight, but I can't wait.'

Josh laughed. 'Not being able to keep a secret is one of the things I love about you. So… Three hours ago we were still at the boarding house. We had breakfast…'

'Before breakfast.' Emma was almost dancing in her seat and Josh was looking increasingly mystified.

'Before that…you were in the bathroom. You screamed, I nearly jumped out of my skin and you shouted through the door that you'd just found the biggest spider you'd ever seen.'

'Josh! Since when have I been afraid of spiders? I was rather hoping you'd see through that excuse and barge in and demand to know what was going on.'

He stared at her. She could see the light beginning to

dawn in his blue eyes. Emma reached down to her hand-bag and took out the pregnancy test, handing it to him.

'This…this is positive, right?'

'Yes, those lines mean positive. And I did three of them so—'

Josh let out a whoop that echoed across the cornfields and sent birds flapping upwards from the trees by the side of the road.

'Three's a definite.' He was hugging her so tight now that she could hardly breathe. 'Are you all right? What made you do the test?'

'I'm fine. I was a bit late, but I thought that was because of the running around for the wedding. But then I just… I don't know how I knew but I did. I didn't tell you because I didn't want to disappoint you if it was just my imagination, but I bought the tests while I was in the pharmacy yesterday.'

'Emma.' He drew back, his hands on her shoulders. 'I'm not going to mollycoddle you. I'll send you out to the corner shop in the rain, and make you repair the car…'

'Really? I was hoping for breakfast in bed and back rubs.'

He grinned. 'You were?'

'Yes, because you do both of those very well and it would be a shame if I had to miss out. I've got a husband who'll love and protect me always. Our baby's going to need that as much as I do.'

He lay his hand on her stomach, tears in his eyes. 'I promise, little one. Always.'

This was real now. Emma flung herself towards him, wrapping her arms around his neck, joy bursting from her.

She felt Josh tapping urgently on her shoulder.

'Em… Em, loosen up a bit. You're strangling me.'

'Oh! Sorry.'

'That's okay. You want to go for a walk? I don't think I can sit still enough to drive at the moment.'

'Me neither.'

They climbed over a stile, a long path ahead of them that meandered through the fields. The warm breeze shimmered across the corn, and when she put her arm around his waist, Josh swept her into a long slow dance.

* * * * *

COMING SOON!

We really hope you enjoyed reading this book.
If you're looking for more romance, be sure to
head to the shops when new books are
available on

Thursday 17th February

To see which titles are coming soon, please visit
millsandboon.co.uk/nextmonth

MILLS & BOON

MILLS & BOON

Coming next month

THE VET'S UNEXPECTED FAMILY
Alison Roberts

Finn's smile faded. He was standing very close to Hazel and she was still smiling at him. Without thinking he reached up and touched her cheek with the back of his forefinger.

'It's a good thing that Michael is long gone,' he said. 'The guy was a complete jerk.'

There was something in Hazel's gaze that he'd never seen before despite it looking like something that could have been there forever. Something... lost? It made him want to take her into his arms and hug her. Instead, he just held her gaze.

'Don't let anyone think you're not beautiful just the way you are,' he added softly. 'Because it's not true.'

It felt like time had stopped. Or maybe Hazel had just frozen, shocked by what he was saying. She didn't believe him, did she? But what else could he say that might convince her?

Maybe he didn't need to say anything. The idea of showing her was a lightbulb moment, like tempting her to stay here by offering a place for Ben to recuperate. Only this flash of inspiration wasn't purely intellectual. It was more of a physical thing.

Because... because Hazel really was beautiful and... and he really did want to kiss her.

Just gently. Good grief, he wasn't trying to seduce her or anything. He just wanted her to know that he meant what he'd said. And that she deserved something a hell of lot better than someone who didn't think she was perfect just the way she was.

And... maybe it was his imagination but it looked as though Hazel wanted him to kiss her. She certainly wasn't ducking for cover as his mouth drifted slowly closer to her own. And then his lips brushed hers and it was Finn who felt like he needed to duck for cover because there was a strange sensation that came with that barely-there kiss. A tingle that felt like static electricity or something. A strangeness that was disturbing, anyway.

So Finn backed away fast. He put on his most charming smile, as if that kiss was nothing out of the ordinary for two friends and turned away to pick up the tray on the table.

'Call me,' he said. 'If you need any help in the night. With Beanie or Ben.'

Continue reading
THE VET'S UNEXPECTED FAMILY
Alison Roberts

Available next month
www.millsandboon.co.uk

Copyright © 2022 Alison Roberts

MILLS & BOON

THE HEART OF ROMANCE

A ROMANCE FOR EVERY READER

MODERN

Prepare to be swept off your feet by sophisticated, sexy and seductive heroes, in some of the world's most glamourous and romantic locations, where power and passion collide.

HISTORICAL

Escape with historical heroes from time gone by. Whether your passion is for wicked Regency Rakes, muscled Vikings or rugged Highlanders, awake the romance of the past.

MEDICAL

Set your pulse racing with dedicated, delectable doctors in the high-pressure world of medicine, where emotions run high and passion, comfort and love are the best medicine.

True Love

Celebrate true love with tender stories of heartfelt romance, from the rush of falling in love to the joy a new baby can bring, and a focus on the emotional heart of a relationship.

Desire

Indulge in secrets and scandal, intense drama and plenty of sizzling hot action with powerful and passionate heroes who have it all: wealth, status, good looks…everything but the right woman.

HEROES

Experience all the excitement of a gripping thriller, with an intense romance at its heart. Resourceful, true-to-life women and strong, fearless men face danger and desire - a killer combination!

To see which titles are coming soon, please visit

millsandboon.co.uk/nextmonth

JOIN US ON SOCIAL MEDIA!

Stay up to date with our latest releases, author
news and gossip, special offers and discounts, and
all the behind-the-scenes action
from Mills & Boon...

 millsandboon

 millsandboonuk

 millsandboon

It might just be true love...

JOIN THE
MILLS & BOON
BOOKCLUB

* **FREE** delivery direct to your door

* **EXCLUSIVE** offers every month

* **EXCITING** rewards programme

50% OFF
YOUR FIRST
PARCEL

Join today at
millsandboon.co.uk/subscribe

WANT EVEN MORE

ROMANCE?

SUBSCRIBE AND SAVE TODAY!

'Mills & Boon books, the perfect way to escape for an hour or so.'

MISS W. DYER

'Excellent service, promptly delivered and very good subscription choices.'

MISS A. PEARSON

'You get fantastic special offers and the chance to get books before they hit the shops.'

MRS V. HALL

Visit millsandboon.co.uk/Subscribe and save on brand new books.

MILLS & BOON
True Love

Romance from the Heart

Celebrate true love with tender stories of heartfelt romance, from the rush of falling in love to the joy a new baby can bring, and a focus on the emotional heart of a relationship.

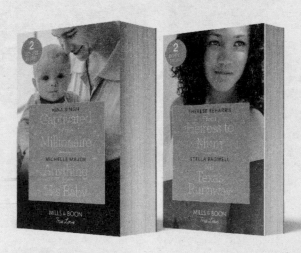

Four True Love stories published every month, find them all at:

millsandboon.co.uk/TrueLove